BODIES
FROM THE LIBRARY
4

BODIES FROM THE LIBRARY
4

Forgotten stories of mystery and suspense
by the Queens of Crime
and other Masters of the Golden Age

Selected and introduced by

TONY MEDAWAR

COLLINS
CRIME
CLUB

COLLINS CRIME CLUB
An imprint of HarperCollins*Publishers*
1 London Bridge Street
London SE1 9GF
www.harpercollins.co.uk

HarperCollins*Publishers*
1st Floor, Watermarque Building, Ringsend Road
Dublin 4, Ireland

This edition 2021

1

Selection, introduction and notes © Tony Medawar 2021
For copyright acknowledgments, see page 407.

These stories were mostly written in the first half of the twentieth century and characters sometimes use offensive language or otherwise are described or behave in ways that reflect the prejudices and insensitivities of the period.

A catalogue record for this book
is available from the British Library

ISBN 978-0-00-838097-7

Typeset in Minion Pro 11/15 pt by
Palimpsest Book Production Ltd, Falkirk, Stirlingshire

Printed and bound in the UK using 100% Renewable Electricity
at CPI Group (UK)

MIX
Paper from
responsible sources

FSC™ C007454

www.fsc.org

This book is produced from independently certified FSC™ paper
to ensure responsible forest management.

For more information visit: www.harpercollins.co.uk/green

CONTENTS

INTRODUCTION

'Why do we read crime stories? Short answer: for fun.'

H. R. F. Keating

Welcome to the fourth volume in the series *Bodies from the Library*, in which once again we bring into the daylight the forgotten, the lost and the unknown.

Among the stories that appear in this volume for the first time are unpublished mysteries by Edmund Crispin, Ngaio Marsh and Leo Bruce, previously unseen pieces written for radio by Gladys Mitchell and H. C. Bailey (featuring Reggie Fortune), and a complete short novel by Christianna Brand.

Mysteries have been around for centuries—one can even be found in the biblical Book of Daniel—but they exploded in popularity in the late nineteenth century with the emergence of the 'great detective'. Foremost among these are of course the omniscient Sherlock Holmes and Hercule Poirot, the self-styled 'greatest detective in the world', but detectives come in all shapes and sizes. As also do crime stories.

There are whodunits, whydunits and howdunits, including locked-room puzzles in which a crime is committed in circumstances that suggest it could not have happened—but it did. There are detective stories without detectives and crimes without arrestable criminals; and there are cases where, as in a closed-circle crime, there is a strictly limited choice of suspects. Fictional crimes and criminals can be found anywhere—from an isolated mountain village to a Caribbean island, from just about anywhere on earth to the moon and beyond.

Countless volumes of such stories have been published, some collected by author, others with a (sometimes tenuous) theme. But there remain stories and plays that for one reason or another have never been collected. Stories that may have appeared in a newspaper or magazine and been forgotten. Or been collected in an anthology that has long been out of print. Or that were absorbed, unpublished, into an author's archive when they died. Or ephemeral works—plays not aired, staged or screened for decades . . .

Which is where *Bodies from the Library* comes in.

Tony Medawar
April 2021

CHILD'S PLAY

Edmund Crispin

'And of course,' said Mrs Snyder, 'you'll have to make allowances for Pamela at first. It's only a month, you see, since her parents were killed, and naturally the poor child is still very distressed. We must do all we can to make her happy here.'

Judith Carnegie nodded and said appropriate things. Inwardly she was striving to analyse the slight distaste which Mrs Snyder inspired in her. The small, hard eyes suggested a vein of rapacity; and the mouth, though large, was not generous. But to judge people physiognomically, Judith told herself, was a folly from which she ought to be exempt. It would be nearer the truth, perhaps, to say that she mistrusted the curious undertone of *triumph* in Mrs Snyder's voice. The mere getting of a governess, even in these awkward times, was surely not sufficient to account for that . . .

'Eve and Tony and Camilla are our own children, you understand,' Mrs Snyder was saying. 'They're scarcely saints—I'm not one of those mothers who imagine their children can do no wrong—but I think you'll like them.'

'I'm sure—'

'And I think *they'll* like *you*.' The large mouth smiled, but without warmth or humour. 'Oh, there's just one other thing.'

'Yes, Mrs Snyder?'

'You must deal with them in your own my—I shan't interfere—

but I'd rather there were no corporal punishment. Some children it doesn't harm—I doubt if it would harm little Pamela, for instance—but my own three loves are very sensitive, even Camilla, and I think that striking a sensitive child may do a lot of damage; psychologically, I mean. I'm sure you won't mind my mentioning it.'

Judith assented readily enough. She had a real affection for children, and detested the thought of their being hurt. At the same time, she noted the invitation to discriminate between Pamela and the others, and made a firm inward vow to ignore it—even, if it came to that, to fight against it.

'Very well, then.' Mrs Snyder pressed a bell beside her chair. 'It's getting late, and I expect you'd like to see your room and settle in. I hope you'll be comfortable. You must let me know if there's anything you want, or any way in which I can help you . . . Goodnight, Miss Carnegie. I have every confidence in you.'

Which was very gratifying, Judith reflected as soon as the maid had shown her to her bedroom and left her alone there: but unluckily the feeling was not mutual. Unpacking, she tried to reason away her dangerous initial prejudice. Mrs Snyder had been very courteous and considerate, after all, and Judith was aware that even at twenty-nine she was still prone to the over-ready intolerance of youth . . . Still, a faint aversion remained, and Judith could only hope that time would erase it. In the meantime, it didn't matter. The children were what mattered.

At the end of the following day she was able to sum up her first impressions of them.

Pamela Catesby she had liked at once. This thin, black-clad, fair-haired child, small for her ten years, was going to need all the sympathy and understanding of which Judith was capable. She was timid, quiet and cruelly racked with homesickness. Judith's heart went out to her, but she was shrewd enough not to be too demonstrative too quickly. There would be plenty of time for that; for the present, it was better to treat her in a kindly but still business-like way, making no overt distinction between her and the others.

And then, the Snyder children . . .

Camilla, the oldest, was fifteen—a boisterous, tomboyish creature with an untidy mop of mouse-coloured hair; talkative and unquenchably energetic, but not over-endowed intellectually.

'Miss Carnegie, *why* does everyone have to spell everything the same way? After all, you said yourself that Shakespeare—'

'If you don't spell properly, my dear girl, people will think you're either ill-educated or a crank. And they'll treat you accordingly, which won't be pleasant. Now, once again, how many ells in "always"?'

'Two, Miss Carnegie—oh, no, one, I mean.'

If Camilla had the energy, Tony certainly had the looks. He was an extraordinarily handsome boy of thirteen, with that bold, sharply chiselled beauty of lip and eye which hints at insolence. Clever too—precociously so—though only in flashes. Judith saw at once that his besetting vice was idleness. And unlike Camilla he was taciturn, sometimes almost to the point of rudeness. Tony would require patient and careful handling.

And lastly, Eve . . .

Judith realized with something of a shock that she disliked Eve. At twelve, Eve was lean, dark, plain, and a practised hypocrite.

'Oh, yes, Miss Carnegie, I quite understand now. You make it all so clear.'

But premeditated sycophancy, though displeasing, was by no means the chief count in Judith's reluctant indictment of Eve. Judith was remembering what she had seen in the play-room that morning.

Eve had been alone in there. It chanced that Judith was wearing rubber-soled brogues, and so Eve did not hear her when she entered in search of a book she had left there.

On the window-sill lay a small green caterpillar, and Eve was holding a lighted match to it. It curled and rolled and twisted in a mute frenzy of pain; and Eve was watching it with a little bubble of saliva at the corner of her mouth.

In three strides Judith was across the room. She struck the match from Eve's hand, brushed the caterpillar on to the floor, and trod on it.

'Eve!' she exclaimed. 'How could you?'

The girl's face was flushed; she licked her lips. 'Oh . . . Miss Carnegie, I'm *so* sorry . . . You see, someone told me they didn't feel fire, so I was just trying. I'm *so* sorry, Miss Carnegie.'

'You were being abominably cruel, Eve. *Never* do anything like that again.'

And so later, alone in her bedroom, Judith found herself half involuntarily re-enacting the whole repulsive little scene. Of course, she was probably over-estimating its importance. Curiosity, in children, tends to engulf consideration. Children are often cruel. They don't realize they're being cruel, and they don't mean to be . . .

But Eve had meant to be cruel. And she had been enjoying it.

The Snyders' house was comparatively isolated in a fold of the Downs. A quarter of a mile away there was a larger place, its chimneys just discernible through rifts in the trees of a park, and a mile further on lay Silchurch, an undistinguished country town where the shopping was done and where Mr Snyder practised as a solicitor. These were the nearest neighbours. But Judith, bred in a country rectory, had no sense of loneliness. She loved the small coppices and shaven slopes of the Downs, and although her afternoon's freedom each week enabled her to get comfortably to London and back, she felt no particular desire to make use of the opportunity. In the first weeks, too, the children preoccupied her almost exclusively.

In general, she found that her first impressions of them had been just; and she worked, as hard and as tactfully as she knew how, to encourage what was good in them and to root out what was bad. Rather to her surprise, Mrs Snyder's promise held: she did not interfere. And as to her husband, he was seldom seen. At his first meeting with Judith he had mumbled something conventional and evasive, and had seemed glad to get away. Judith judged that he disliked responsibility, and that in consequence his wife dominated him.

The parents, then, kept themselves to themselves; and Judith's chief confidant was the cook-housekeeper, Mrs Fley—a plump, comfortable, untidy woman of middle age, much of whose time was occupied in disentangling the muddles created by Mrs Snyder's managerial incompetence. She was able to enlighten Judith on the subject of Pamela's status in the household.

'Why, Miss, the Catesbys were killed in one of them airplane crashes. And Mrs Snyder was a cousin of *his*, so they'd left orders Pamela was to come here if anything was to happen to them.'

'And were Mr and Mrs Snyder glad to have her?' The question crystallized a doubt which had haunted Judith's mind ever since her arrival.

'Glad, Miss?' Mrs Fley sniffed. 'That's putting it mildly. The Catesbys were well-to-do folk, and I've heard tell they left the master a thousand pound a year for looking after the poor mite. And—well!—it's not likely they'll be spending all that money on the *child*.'

'Oh, but surely, Mrs Fley—'

'I know just what you're going to say, Miss, and I'm sure it's a credit to you to be always thinking the best of others.' Mrs Fley nodded her approbation of this judgment while Judith reflected rather morosely on its falsity. 'But I stick to my point: that money came only just in the nick of time.'

'What do you mean?'

'*Ah*,' said Mrs Fley cryptically. 'Well, Miss, perhaps I ought to be keeping what I know *to* myself—but it's like this: things

weren't going too well with the master before Pamela came here.'
She gestured broadly. 'Why, surely you'll have noticed all the
repairs and such? And the new furnishings and fittings? There
wouldn't have been any of *them*, Miss, not without that airplane
crash. Nor you wouldn't be here, either.'

So that explains it, Judith thought: that explains why I sensed
an undertone of triumph when I came here. Well, Pamela might
have had a worse home; she was not stinted in anything, nor—
in spite of the vague implicit threat which had troubled Judith
at her first interview with Mrs Snyder—was she treated differ-
ently from the others. Judith was about to say as much when a
new thought occurred to her.

'That house in the park, Mrs Fley—the one nearest to here—'

'Holygate Manor, Miss? My, that's where the Catesbys used
to live.'

Judith nodded. 'I see. Yes, that accounts for it. You know I
always leave the children entirely to their own devices after tea
each day? Well, I've several times seen Pamela walking over in
that direction, and I've wondered if it was the house she we
going to.'

'And isn't it natural, Miss Carnegie?' said Mrs Fley. 'Of course,
the Manor's shut up now, and up for sale (though there's precious
few could afford to live there these days); but I dare say the poor
young thing likes to walk a bit in the grounds and the gardens—
and who's to blame her?'

'Yes, of course. But still, Mrs Fley, I'm rather sorry the place
is so close. I can't in charity stop Pamela going there, but it isn't
good for her to brood. It'd be far better if she could make a
complete break with the past.'

'Ah, you're right there, Miss,' said Mrs Fley. 'Poor mite! It's
like as if she was stunned, isn't it? And she still seems as put
about as when she first came here.'

And that, Judith realized as she left the kitchen, was one of
the things which had been subconsciously worrying her. Of

course, Pamela had been an only child, and the shock of suddenly losing both parents must have been very great; moreover, her visits to Holygate Manor were obviously keeping the wound raw and painful. But children are resilient creatures, and it seemed to Judith ominous that she had never once seen Pamela smile.

That afternoon—it was a day of wind and warmth—Judith borrowed Mrs Fley's bicycle to go shopping in Silchurch. Autumn (which seemed to come early that year) was already gilding and stripping the trees; shaggy chrysanthemums reigned unchallenged in the gardens; cloud scurried in curling white shreds across the sky. And Judith, returning, met Pamela walking away from the Snyder house, small and alone against the vacant and restless landscape, like a painter's allegory of solitude. On an impulse Judith dismounted.

'Hello,' she said, smiling. 'Are you on the way to Holygate Manor?'

Pamela looked away at the hedge, but not before Judith had glimpsed the defensive glaze which came into her eyes. 'Yes, Miss Carnegie.'

'That's where you used to live, isn't it?'

'Yes, Miss Carnegie.'

'I've often wanted to look at it properly. May I come with you?'

'I—I suppose so.'

It was a deliberately grudging permission, but Judith chose to ignore the hint. She chattered lightly about the Silchurch shops as they walked together, and presently, along a side road whose hedges were sprinkled with snowberries, they came to wrought-iron gates standing sentinel to a short, straight avenue of limes. Judith halted and drew a deep breath.

'But it's beautiful!' she exclaimed.

Her admiration was spontaneous and deeply felt. The house at the end of the avenue, sheltered by trees, framed by flower-beds

and lawns, had all the grace and nobility of eighteenth-century
architecture at its best. But she could see the beginnings of
neglect: the hedges needed trimming; a hinge had come off one
of the shutters and had not been replaced; the paths were
unswept. There was no sign, as yet, of actual decay, but there
was evidence here, none the less, of a counterpoint to the renewal
of the Snyder house. To Pamela, who would certainly notice the
little things, the condition of her former home, watched and
studied day after day, must seem like the progressive and mortal
emaciation, on a sick-bed, of someone deeply loved.

Judith walked forward, wheeling her bicycle, into the drive;
and it was some seconds before she realized that Pamela was
not following her. She stopped and turned.

'Aren't you going in, Pamela?'

The child moved uncertainly, a small and grubby handkerchief
crumpled in her hand; then seemed to make up her mind. 'No,
Miss Carnegie,' she said.

'But you usually do, don't you?'

'Y-yes, but I—'

'But you don't want me with you.' Judith spoke more bitterly
than she had intended, and Pamela shrank back a little. 'I mean'—
Judith caught herself up and smiled—'I mean, I can quite
understand your not wanting me—or anyone, for that matter.'

Pamela, twisting the handkerchief nervously and staring at
her shoes, did not reply; and Judith was momentarily at a loss.
She had hoped that at Pamela's old home, if she were empathetic
and understanding, it might be possible to establish a real bond
of affection and trust between them; but at present the auguries
were not good. She said:

'You loved you parents very much, didn't you?'

'Yes.' The word was spoken curtly—a rebuke, pathetic in its
pride, to Judith's prying. Judith said gently:

'Listen, my dear, and be honest with me, because I want to
help you; are you happy living with Tony and Camilla and Eve?

I know you can't be as happy as you used to be, but—well, are they nice to you? Do you think you'll get to like it there?'

For a moment there was silence. Darkness was coming across the Downs, and with it the stillness of twilight, so that you could hear the dry leaves, wind-driven, scratching on the surface of the road. Pamela's knuckles grew white; the handkerchief tore in her hands.

'I hate it,' she gasped, and suddenly her voice grew shrill. '*I hate it, I hate it!*' She stumbled back along the road, convulsed by sobs.

Somehow Judith managed to soothe the child by the time they reached the house. But the incident left her seriously disturbed. The misery of loss, for Pamela, was clearly aggravated by the misery of a hostile environment. But no—'hostile' was far too strong a word. No doubt that was how Pamela felt it, but she we certainly exaggerating, for Judith had seen no evidence of hostility in the other children when she was present. Inevitably they would regard Pamela as something of an interloper; but real enmity . . .

She talked to them about Pamela that same evening, and received the impression that they understood, and would do their best to be considerate and kind.

A week later that illusion was felled in ruins.

Judith came on the four of them playing with a tennis-ball on one of the lawns. Eve, Tony and Camilla were standing in a triangle, throwing the ball to one another; and Pamela was in the centre, trying to intercept it. When she did so, the person who had thrown it would take her place.

That, at least, was the theory of the game. What was actually happening was that the Snyder children were throwing the ball *at* Pamela, hard and malevolently and with visible enjoyment.

Judith felt the beginnings of physical nausea as, unseen by them, she looked on. She had returned from an outing sooner than she had expected—and sooner, evidently, than they had expected. Bracing herself, she stepped out on to the lawn.

Eve saw her and muttered something. Tony, his arm raised to fling the ball, threw it into the air instead, and caught it again. Camilla lounged away to examine a flower-bed. And Pamela, bursting into tears, took to her heels and vanished round the side of the house.

There ensued a stormy scene in the play-room.

'Oh, well, Miss Carnegie,' said Camilla sulkily, 'she's such a little *beast*.'

Judith quelled her anger with an effort. 'How is she a "beast", Camilla?'

'We don't want her here,' Tony interposed truculently. 'We were all right before *she* came. Why do we have to have her, anyway? Can't she find somewhere else to live?'

'Let's get this straight, Tony: what is it you don't like about her?'

'Oh, everything.' He kicked testily at the fender with the side of his shoe.

'Answer sensibly,' said Judith. But he was silent.

'Well, *I* think we ought to tell her we're sorry.' Eve spoke with her accustomed impregnable glibness. 'We *were* doing wrong.'

'I'm glad you appreciate that,' said Judith coldly; the words *right* and *wrong* were disagreeably frequent on Eve's lips. 'Pamela has suffered a great deal, and it's up to you all to make things as easy as possible for her. I shall certainly not tolerate any bullying.'

After a moment's pause: 'Yes,' said Camilla reflectively, 'I s'pose we were being rather rotten, Miss Carnegie. But you know how it is: you get excited and do things you don't really mean to. Well'—she glanced at the others, and Judith seemed to glimpse a warning in her eyes—'well, I'm sorry, anyway.'

'Poor Pamela,' Eve murmured.

But Tony's cheeks were pink with anger. 'I'm not going to apologize,' he said brusquely.

'In that case, Tony, you'd better go at once to your room.'

'I shall not,' he muttered.

Judith said: 'Be careful, Tony.'

'I'll do what I please,' he answered, turning away. 'I'm not taking any orders from you.'

That was when Judith boxed his ears.

Even later, when she was calm again, she did not regret it. But she expected repercussions, and they came promptly enough. During the evening Mrs Snyder summoned her to the drawing-room. And Judith found, as she strode across the hall to this interview, that a sense of moral rectitude is no certain defence against inward trepidation.

Her employer greeted her bleakly and came at once to the point.

'Tony has told me, Miss Carnegie, that you struck him this afternoon. Is that true?'

'Yes, Mrs Snyder, I'm afraid he deserved it.'

The older woman threw her cigarette-end into the fire. 'That's scarcely the point, is it? I was under the impression we'd agreed that such treatment was undesirable.'

'Yes, in general. Only—'

'Only you happened to lose your temper.' Mrs Snyder lit a fresh cigarette and blew smoke from her prominent nostrils. 'Well, I agree that children are often trying. But surely it's our business—and in particular, I should have thought, *your* business—to control ourselves for their good . . . Oh, and there's one other thing.'

'Yes, Mrs Snyder?'

'It's clear to me, from what Tony said, that you misinterpreted some—some incident or other which happened earlier on. I didn't see it, of course, but it's preposterous to imagine, as you apparently do, that my three children are deliberately persecuting Pamela.'

'I'm sorry, but I didn't misinterpret anything,' said Judith doggedly. 'They may have just got over-excited, but they *were* bullying.'

'Tony denies that, Miss Carnegie. I'm sure he wouldn't lie to his mother. If Pamela was hurt, it was entirely an accident. I think we'd better regard the whole unpleasant incident as closed.'

With a gesture of dismissal, Mrs Snyder turned away. 'Good night, Miss Carnegie,' she said.

For an instant Judith stood helpless with anger, her cheeks burning; then, rather noisily, she left the room. There was some consolation, she reflected wryly as she returned upstairs, in the fact that she had somehow controlled an almost overmastering impulse to give in her notice there and then; for it was clear by now that Pamela was going to need active protection, and Judith was prepared to suffer almost any humiliation rather than throw up her job and abandon the child to persecution and misery.

She slept little that night; there were too many plans to be made and rejected, too many possibilities to be considered and guarded against. It was four o'clock, and a gentle insistent rain was falling in the darkness beyond her windows, before she fell into a troubled, unrefreshing slumber.

But she might have spared herself the anxiety, for on the following afternoon Pamela Catesby was murdered.

It had grown suddenly cold, and the Downs were veiled in mist. The night's rain had made little impression on the earth, which was hard from many weeks of drought, but it had clotted the drifts of fallen leaves round the gateposts and washed the dry air. Fires became inevitable and colds an impending certainty. After tea, Judith sorted the children's winter clothes in her tiny sitting-room.

In retrospect, she found the events of the preceding day less alarming than they had seemed at the time, and was inclined to scold herself for over-dramatizing them. The Snyder children, that morning, had shown signs of active repentance. From Eve, of course, it was to be expected, but Tony's seigneurial courtesies towards Pamela, and Camilla's conscientious helpfulness, were something of a novelty. Pamela herself had remained timid—had, indeed, seemed so pale and nervous that Judith had excused her the afternoon's work and sent her out to get some exercise. Fairly soon—Judith glanced at her watch—she ought to be back. But the others had had their tea early, and in Pamela's continued absence there seemed, as yet, no special cause for anxiety.

Brooding over the ravages of clothes-moths, Judith was scarcely aware of the knock at the front door; but she looked up at the murmur of voices which followed its opening, and presently there were footsteps on the stairs and her own door opened and the maid said:

'Excuse me, Miss Carnegie, but there's a gentleman asking to see you. He really wanted Mrs Snyder, only she's out, so he asked if there was anyone else and I said you. It's the police, Miss.'

'The police!' Startled, Judith got to her feet. 'All right, Anne, I'll come.'

'No need for you to move, Miss,' said a new voice. A pale, tired-looking man in the uniform of an Inspector followed the maid into the room. His voice held a hint of the Kentish accent, and he carried a brown-paper parcel under his arm. 'You'll forgive me for intruding,' he added, 'But it's rather urgent.'

'Y-yes, of course,' Judith stammered. 'Won't you sit down?—That will be all, Anne.'

Radiating inquisitiveness from every pore, the maid reluctantly departed. And the visitor, without accepting Judith's invitation, said:

'My name's Williams, Miss. Silchurch Constabulary. You're the children's governess, I believe.'

'That's so.' Judith was having difficulty in keeping her voice steady. 'What's happened, please? Has there been a—an accident?'

For a moment the Inspector did not reply. Instead, he took the parcel over to a table and unwrapped it. Inside it was a child's blue frock.

Judith's head swam. She sat down heavily and covered her face with her hands.

'You recognize that, Miss?' The Inspector's voice was grave without being maudlin, and Judith felt a queer, irrelevant flash of gratitude.

'Yes,' she whispered. 'It belongs to—to Pamela. Pamela Catesby.'

'She was wearing her identity disc, of course,' said the Inspector. 'But we needed confirmation.'

Judith said, with hysterical quietness: 'Is she dead?'

The Inspector nodded. 'I'm afraid so. She's been deliberately murdered.'

Judith's control snapped. She opened her mouth to scream, and in that moment the Inspector struck her hard and viciously across the cheek with the flat of his hand. The scream died unuttered in her throat. She raised her fingers shakily to her face.

'Far better not to give way, Miss,' the Inspector said with a little smile. 'I've known cases where people gave way and—well, never got over it.'

Almost inaudibly, Judith said: 'Th-thank you. I—I think I shall be all right now. But *murder*—a child—'

'It's very horrible. But we shall find whoever did it, and he'll hang.' The Inspector looked at her kindly, and put a hand on her shoulder. 'You'll help us, I know.'

'But how—where—?'

'In the grounds of Holygate Manor, Miss. She was'—he hesitated fractionally, watching Judith's eyes—'she was strangled. And then when that didn't work, her head was beaten against a wall.'

Judith shuddered convulsively. 'Oh, God,' she said, and began quietly to cry. 'Oh, God.'

For a while the Inspector said nothing; but presently:

'I shan't trouble you much just now,' he told her. 'We must

have a proper talk later on. But in the meantime, there are just two questions I'd like to ask.'

Judith controlled herself, slowly and painfully. She was horribly and acutely conscious of her surroundings: of the heat of the gas fire; of Camilla talking to Mrs Fley in the hall below; of Eve and Tony arguing distantly in the play-room. She breathed deeply and her head cleared a little.

'Yes?' she said.

'This dress, now.' The Inspector took her by the hand and led her to the table on which it lay. 'This is what she was wearing when she was killed.' He unfolded it and spread it out with the front uppermost. 'You'll see it's torn at the neck, where it buttoned up. Now, was it like that when you saw her last?'

'No. No, of course not.'

The Inspector nodded. 'Then we can assume there was a struggle.' He turned the frock over and flattened it out. 'And on the back here, at the waist, there's a little spot of something purple. What about that?'

'Oh, it's only paint,' said Judith. 'It's been there a long while. I've been meaning to get it off, only somehow—'

They were interrupted. As she spoke, Judith was conscious of footsteps racing up the stairs. And before either she or the Inspector could make a movement the door had burst open and Camilla was in the room.

'Oh, Miss Carnegie,' she began; and then stopped short, her eyes on the Inspector, on Judith's tear-stained face, on the frock on the table.

'Oh,' she said, 'oh, I'm so sorry. I didn't realize—'

Judith said: 'Is it important, Camilla?'

'No, Miss Carnegie. No, not a bit. I *am* sorry. ' And with one more startled glance round the room, Camilla fled.

The Inspector tuned to replace the dress in its brown paper, and as he did so, they heard the front door open, and Camilla's careless shout of: 'Hello, Daddy! Hello, Mummy!'

'Well, now,' said the Inspector, 'it seems that Mr and Mrs Snyder are back, so I'd better go and talk to them at once. I'll be seeing you again later, Miss.' In the doorway he paused and looked at her steadily. 'I've got kids of my own,' he added, 'and no one's going to get away with this sort of thing if I can help it.'

Then he was gone.

How Judith got through the next few hours without breaking down she was never afterwards able to remember. For in the welter of disorganized thoughts seething through her mind, there was one that was strident and unceasing, like a tattoo of drums.

'It's my fault she was killed. My fault. My fault . . .

'I ought to have watched her, every hour of every day. I ought to have had her sleeping in my room at nights. I ought never to have allowed her to go out alone.

'Failure. Failure. Failure . . .'

While she was occupied with the other children she could keep it a little at bay. But when at last they were in bed (their curiosity hardly sated by vague talk of an 'accident'), then the floodgates were open.

'Dead, and I to blame. Dead, and I to blame. Dead, and I . . .'

She took too many aspirin, and was numbed. But when at last, at ten-thirty that evening, the Inspector came again to her sitting-room, the first shock had a little receded, leaving only a dull ache at the heart. He sat down opposite her, looking very pale and tired.

'Well,' he said, 'we've collected about as much evidence as we shall collect. And that's precious little, I'm sorry to say. No footprints. No fingerprints. No witnesses. No material clues. And very little blood, so that it's doubtful if the murderer was splashed at all.'

Judith said: 'How—who found her?'

'Some people who came with the agent to look over the house. That was at about four-thirty. The doctor says she was killed some time between two and four, but unfortunately he can't, or won't, be more definite than that.'

'You've—you've seen Mr and Mrs Snyder?'

The Inspector glanced at her shrewdly. 'Yes. Why do you ask?'

'Well, I haven't, you see. They haven't spoken a word to me, or to the children, since you brought the news.' Judith fingered the arm of her chair, restlessly. 'And I'm dreading what they'll say. I ought never to have let Pamela go out alone.'

'Nonsense,' said the Inspector incisively. 'You're not in the least to blame, so you may as well stop worrying at once.'

'I suppose'—Judith hesitated fractionally—'I suppose Mr and Mrs Snyder are very upset?'

'Yes, they are. Apart from anything else, they'll lose—' The Inspector checked himself. 'Yes, of course, they're greatly distressed. And now, Miss Carnegie, there are one or two more questions I want to ask. In the first place, when did you last see Pamela?'

Judith felt tears coming, and blew her nose angrily; through her handkerchief she said: 'It was after lunch. About a quarter to two. She wasn't looking very well, so I sent her out for a walk.'

'Did you see what direction she went?'

'No. But she always went to Holygate Manor whenever she had the chance. It was her old home, you see.'

'Ah.' The Inspector stroked his chin, and Judith realized suddenly that in spite of his grey hair he was no more than middle-aged. 'Well, unless we're dealing with a casual maniac, the murderer must have known that.'

'Surely,' Judith faltered, 'that's the only possible explanation?'

'A maniac? Not necessarily. There's robbery, for instance. Would she have had anything valuable on her? Family jewels, or something of that sort?'

Judith shook her head. 'No. Nothing.'

'Then that's out. It might have been some kind of vengeance, but there's no evidence for that. And there's no evidence, so far, that she knew anything which would make her a danger to any person. That leaves the usual motive—money. Pamela was due to inherit a good deal when she came of age.'

Judith sat erect in her chair; a disagreeable suspicion, hitherto stilled by shock and grief, was beginning to burgeon in her mind.

'I've telephoned the solicitor in London,' the Inspector went on in the same level tone, 'and the fact is this, that now Pamela's dead, the fortune is to be divided between the three Snyder children, as soon as they're twenty-one.'

For a moment Judith simply failed to grasp the implications of this; but when she did, she almost laughed outright. 'You can't mean—you can't conceivably imagine—'

But then a new possibility occurred to her. 'Mr and Mrs Snyder—you mean—for their children's sake—'

'No.' There was an edge now to the Inspector's voice. 'They've been in Silchurch all day, and they've got a waterproof alibi. I've had time to check it.'

'But the other . . .' Judith leaned forward earnestly. 'It's impossible—fantastic!'

'I hope so. I hope so. But I've got to look into every possibility. Would these Snyder children have known about the terms of the will?'

'But you must be wrong!' Judith exclaimed. 'It's unbelievable that any child—'

'*Would they have known?*' he repeated with sudden vehemence.

Judith shrank back. 'They might have known,' she whispered. 'It isn't the sort of thing I'd tell my children, but—'

'I shall find out,' the Inspector said roughly. His nerves were raw. 'And now you must tell me, please, what you know of their movements during the afternoon.'

Judith was so stunned that she no longer had the power to protest. She heard her own voice, expressionlessly elucidating, as though it came from miles away. On two afternoons a week, of which this had been one, there were additional lessons, to bring the laggards in certain specific subjects up to standard. The lessons had been between two and four. Eve and Camilla had been at geography, but not Tony; Eve and Tony had been at geometry, but not Camilla; Camilla and Tony had been at English, but not Eve.

'And you don't know,' said the Inspector, 'where any of them went, or what any of them did, when they weren't actually with you?'

Judith said: 'No, I don't know.'

'Ten minutes to Holygate Manor,' the Inspector muttered. 'Time enough. But if none of them has any sort of alibi . . .'

Judith stared at him dully; her senses were as though anaesthetized. 'You don't believe that,' she said. 'Please tell me you don't believe that.'

He stood up. 'Not necessarily, Miss Carnegie. A maniac remains possible. But I shall have to talk to those children tomorrow, and see what account they can give of themselves.' He hesitated. 'It's the safest age to commit a murder, isn't it? The penalty'—he shivered a little—'the penalty if you're found out—well, it's trivial in comparison.' He went to the door, opened it, looked back at her. 'Good night, Miss Carnegie.'

For ten minutes after he had gone Judith sat motionless. Then she dragged herself to her feet, automatically tidied the room, and went out on to the landing. From the drawing-room below came a murmur of voices, Mrs Snyder's sharp and protesting, her husband's muffled and dull. In Eve's bedroom, too, there were voices, rapid and conspiratorial. Judith halted and threw open the door. Camilla was there in her pyjamas.

Judith said: 'Get back to your room, Camilla. Eve, put out your light.'

Chastened and subdued, the older girl followed Judith out on to the landing. But presently, as they approached her door, she said:

'Miss Carnegie, is it true that Pamela was murdered?'

'I'm not prepared to discuss it now, Camilla.'

'You see, I couldn't help seeing her frock was torn. Does that mean—'

Judith said: 'Go to bed, Camilla.' And after one look at her face the girl silently obeyed.

Judith herself was soon in bed, and oblivion came with merciful quickness—though it was an oblivion fitfully illuminated with nightmares. Then, quite suddenly, she found that she was awake and sitting up in bed and searching for some fact or scene or face which lingered maddeningly just over the edge of consciousness. Was it something she had dreamed? Was she still dreaming? But it was important, she knew that. And she groped back along the twilit tunnel of sleep until, infinitely distant, she saw figures and movements etched with sharp clarity as if on a cinema screen. It was enough. In a spasm of sickness she bit at the pillow.

The nausea passed and she switched on her light. Two o'clock. Like one moving in a trance, she got out of bed, put on dressing-gown and slippers, and left the room. The house was very still, and the ticking of the grandfather clock in the hall sounded preternaturally loud. In the light reflected through the open door from her bedside lamp Judith could just make out, at the other end of the corridor, the doors of the children's rooms.

Tony. Camilla. Eve.

It was to Camilla's room that she went.

Camilla, when Judith turned on the light, was sleeping restlessly, the sheets disordered; her face was flushed and there were little beads of sweat on her forehead. For a few seconds Judith studied her, with a kind of dispassionate curiosity; then, quite softly, spoke her name.

Camilla stirred. Her eyes opened and she stared at Judith unseeing for a moment. At last, and very quickly, she sat up in bed.

'M-Miss Carnegie!' she stammered. 'What—?'

Judith sat down on the edge of the bed. She said: 'I want to talk to you, Camilla.'

There was something like fear in Camilla's eyes. For the first time Judith noticed how small they were, and how like her mother's. Camilla said: 'Wh-what's the time?'

'It's two o'clock.'

'Oh, but Miss Carnegie—'

'It won't take long to say what I have to say.' Now that the crisis had come, Judith was in complete command of herself. 'You killed Pamela, didn't you?'

Camilla edged away from her. The flush had passed, leaving her cheeks pale, and one hand was pressed hard against her small breasts. Judith went on, levelly:

'You gave yourself away, Camilla, by saying that you'd seen Pamela's frock was torn. The frock was lying front downwards when you came into my sitting-room, so you couldn't have seen anything of the sort. There can only be one explanation of how you knew.'

A silence followed, which prolonged itself almost unendurably. Camilla was moving her mouth unnaturally, as though it gave her pain. And Judith's voice trembled a little as she said:

'I shall have to tell the Inspector, of course.' She leaned forward, trying vainly to smile. 'You're sick, Camilla—ill. You must be ill, to have done a horrible thing like that. They—they won't hurt you, you know. They'll take you to a—to hospital, and the doctors will see to it that you get better.'

Again there was silence. But Camilla's mouth had stopped moving, and there was something in her eyes which Judith could not interpret.

'Well?' Judith prompted.

'You're quite wrong, Miss Carnegie,' Camilla said.

Judith stared at her. 'Wrong?'

'Oh, yes, Miss Carnegie.' Camilla's voice was high and clear. 'I never said anything about Pamela's frock being torn.'

Instantly Judith's flesh grew cold. 'But you did, Camilla. Of course you did.'

Camilla took her hand away from her breast and smiled. 'I'm sure you're mistaken, Miss Carnegie. You must have imagined it.'

Judith understood. 'Listen, Camilla,' she said desperately, 'you'll be miserable if you try to escape the consequences. For the whole of the rest of your life the memory of what you've done will torture you. Don't you see that, child?'

'But, Miss Carnegie,' said Camilla sweetly, 'I haven't done anything. And I'm terribly, terribly sad about poor Pamela.'

Judith fought against an overwhelming wave of revulsion. 'But you knew about the will? You knew that you and Eve and Tony would get the money if Pamela died?'

'Oh, yes, I knew about *that.*' Camilla began smoothing the sheets. 'I overheard Mummy and Daddy talking about it . . . Of course, I oughtn't to be thinking about such things'—her eyes never wavered from Judith's face—'only it will be nice—won't it?—to be able to have anything I want when I'm grown up—clothes and cars and a big house . . .'

Judith stood up abruptly. Sheer helpless anger was almost blinding her. Camilla would be found to have no alibi; but if, as the Inspector had said, there were no clues, then Camilla was safe. She might make a second mistake; but that wasn't very likely . . . Judith understood a great many things now; understood, above all, that the Snyder children's hatred of little Pamela had been rooted in black envy. She said:

'For the last time, Camilla: are you going to confess?'

'But I've got nothing *to* confess, Miss Carnegie,' Camilla said; then her mood changed abruptly, and she scrambled out of bed on the other side and shrank against the wall. 'You're mad, do you hear me? Mad! Daddy's a lawyer, and he'll deal with you if you try to accuse me of anything.'

A red mist swam in front of Judith's eyes. She was hardly conscious that she had picked up the heavy bedside lamp and was moving slowly round the bed.

Camilla screamed.

Almost at once, it seemed, the house was awake. There were footsteps, doors banging, anxious voices. And sanity returned to Judith in a dreary engulfing flood. She stood motionless, staring at the figure crouched against the wall. When she spoke, her voice was dull and hopeless.

'You did tell me that you'd seen Pamela's frock was torn.'

Then, with the confused and urgent footsteps very close, Camilla suddenly sniggered; and the sound was so deadly that Judith had to turn her face away.

'Honestly, Miss Carnegie,' Camilla said, 'I don't know what you're talking about.'

EDMUND CRISPIN

Bruce Montgomery was born in Buckinghamshire in 1921. Somewhat of an outsider most of his early life, he came into his own at Oxford, where he met lifelong friends and discovered detective stories, in particular the Dr Fell mysteries of the American writer, John Dickson Carr. Adopting the pen-name of 'Edmund Crispin'— an amalgam of the names of characters in *King Lear* and *Hamlet, Revenge!* by Michael Innes (1937)— Montgomery's first detective mystery was *The Case of the Gilded Fly* (1944, also published in the US as *Obsequies at Oxford*). The novel featured an English language professor called Gervase Fen.

As well as producing a relatively small number of hugely enjoyable, sublimely clever and extremely funny mysteries (all featuring Fen), Montgomery was a respected composer, scoring over forty films. He spent most of his life in Devon, from where he would travel up to London with his near-neighbour Agatha Christie for meetings of the Detection Club. He was active in a range of local community groups, balancing his twin careers as writer and composer until it became clear that, while the former gave him greater pleasure, the latter was considerably more profitable.

After 1950, Montgomery wrote little fiction but he reviewed books as 'Edmund Crispin' and also became something of a radio personality. In 1977, after a gap of more than twenty-five years, he published a ninth and final novel, *The Glimpses of the Moon*, but Gervase Fen's resurrection was to be short-lived. Bruce Montgomery died the following year, aged just fifty-six.

'Child's Play' has not previously been published.

THIEVES FALL IN

Anthony Gilbert

Elsie had an eye on the couple from the moment she joined the queue for the London-bound coach.

The woman, Ada, was unremarkable, thirty-fiveish, laden with a big black handbag, an open-mouthed shopper and two bunches of daffs she had bought while waiting.

The young man, who had stationed himself just behind her, was ten years younger, a regular smartie with shoes so pointed they added an inch to the length of his feet.

In the bus Elsie contrived to sit behind Ada and the young man, who took the last vacant place at her side. Closer than a brother, Elsie thought.

He put the shopper and flowers on the rack, slumped down and buried himself in an evening paper.

It happened, what she had anticipated, when the conductor came round collecting fares and Ada, poor thing, found her purse had gone.

She had had it when she bought the daffs, she insisted, maybe she had slipped it into the shopper.

But if she had it wasn't there now, wasn't in her pocket, not on the floor, not anywhere it seemed. Only I could guess, thought Elsie.

'Didn't see it when you put my stuff up there, I suppose?' Ada inquired of the young man, and he blew up like a geyser.

'No, I did not. What are you getting at? Probably left it on the flower-stall.'

These women, his attitude said.

'It's a combined purse-and-note case,' Ada explained. 'Everything I had . . .' She sounded distracted.

The other passengers were enthralled: made a nice break in a dull ride.

Eventually Elsie coped—coping was her strong suit—by offering to lend Ada the fare (and the change from a ten-bob note to cover bus-fare when they reached Victoria), loan to be repaid by postal order, prompt.

Ada, cynosure of every eye, dropped her head, said it was ever so kind, and muttered it was queer all the same.

Elsie found a pencil and a bit of paper and said: 'My address, and you give me yours.'

And there was a bit of fuss over that, and as soon as there was another seat free the young fellow shifted.

At Victoria he was first off the bus, turning sharply to the left making for a tavern.

Elsie said sharply to Ada, 'Then I'll be hearing from you?' and crossed towards Victoria Station where the big red buses waited in the station yard.

Ada, loaded with parcels, watched her go.

Then she hurried along to the pub where Lennie was waiting for her.

Lennie was in a bad mood. 'You're losing your touch,' he scolded as she came up and dumped her parcels on a convenient chair. 'Giving the whole coachload a chance to know me again.'

'Have to dye your hair,' said Ada, flippantly.

'Have to lay off the buses for a bit. Don't want some Nosey Parker next time an old girl misses her housekeeping, saying, "I remember that chap, he was on the bus when that woman started creating . . ." You keep away from me for the future, Ada. You're about as healthy as a glass of poison.'

'What was the sense taking my purse anyway?' Ada inquired. 'Made me look a proper Charley.'

'See what I mean? You didn't even tumble. If a lady says she's lost her purse, ten to one some Lady High and Mighty is going to offer the fare, and while she's fumbling in her bag that's the chance for a chap with his head screwed on right . . .'

'Lennie! You never!' She stared at the elegant green leather wallet he casually dropped on the table. 'That's hers!'

'That's what she thinks.'

'I wouldn't have had the nerve,' Ada confessed.

'That's what I mean. Time you turned it in, old girl. It comes to all of us.'

'That'll be the day.' Ada peeled off her gloves. She had beautiful hands, supple as anything, and that was the way she meant to keep them. No charring at five bob an hour for her.

'Here, take this.' A red purse and note case combined lay in her lap. 'Who steals my purse steals trash? What were you doing all the afternoon? Playing buttercups and daisies? A measly five pounds . . .'

'That's the way it goes. Swings and roundabouts. My lot all seemed to have padlocks on their purses today. Still, you didn't do too bad. Must be all of twenty quid there.'

'And another fifty-plus here.' He tapped his breast-pocket, and opened his coat an inch or so to let her see a flat black pocket-book.'

'You're a wonder,' she assured him. 'Lucky me, having a partner like you.'

'Less of the partner,' said Lennie coldly. 'You can't have been listening. We're through, Ada. You work the buses again, you work 'em on your own.'

Ada stiffened. 'Oh, no, Lennie,' she said softly. 'You don't do this to me. Fifty-fifty's what we agreed and what it's always been. Everyone has a thin afternoon sometimes.'

'You must be going on a diet,' jeered Lennie. 'And don't chuck that drink in my face. Waste of good stuff.'

'Don't think you're going to get away with this, Lennie.'

'How you going to stop me? Send for the police?'

'No need for that,' said a new voice, and they turned like a pair of puppets.

'You!' Ada gasped. It was Elsie.

'Sergeant in the Women's Police. I've had my eye on your little lot for some time. Now, drink up, madam, and we'll all go for a little walk up the road.'

'How do we know she's anything of the kind?' Lennie muttered.

'They'll tell you at the station. We don't sleep in our uniforms, you know.'

Lennie moved with the speed of light; shoving against Elsie so he nearly threw her down, snatching at Ada's restraining arm, he was away in a flash.

'Not to worry,' said Elsie grimly. 'He'll be taken care of. Now, do as I say, madam, and we'll go along to you-know-where. Don't want a scene, do we? Bad for trade and you have to think of others.'

Lennie whirled out of the pub and picked up a cruising cab at the top of the road. For £3 he bribed the driver to take him to Coultham where he had a pal who, for a consideration, would swear he had been sitting in at a bingo session all afternoon.

He knew his onions, did Lennie, never gave Ada his real address (or his real name, come to that), and a crew cut, a moustache, specs, perhaps, and his own mother wouldn't know him.

He had a contact in Brighton, a girl in the same line as himself, no more Ada for him, thank you very much. Too bad about the green wallet, but he still had the fifty-plus and that 'ud do to be going on with.

Or so he thought then.

About the time the taxi reached Coultham, Ada and her friend
Elsie were sitting in the cosy bar of the Sleeping Cat, sipping
rum fizzes.

'Nothing like rum for keeping out the cold,' said Elsie.

'Honestly, Elsie, you slay me,' Ada confessed. 'The way you
walked in—Sergeant in the Women's Police, and if you don't
believe me come along to the station!'

'And he bought it,' marvelled Elsie. 'As if any policewoman
would come into a bar, in mufti, mark you, without a uniformed
man at her back.

'You're well quit of young Lennie, my girl. Chap who can lose
his head in an emergency is bound to lose his liberty sooner or
later. If he had stopped to think . . .

'Lucky, really, you fell in with me. Where will he be?'

'Got a pal Coultham way. Thinks I don't know. The cheek of
it!' Ada said. 'Thinking he could shake me! Never even guessed
I knew he had been holding out on me for weeks past. And I'll
tell you something else. There was a lot more than five pounds
in that wallet when he sneaked it.'

'He's not even smart. The time I had to fumble with that
message to let him take my wallet. Easier to have put it in his
pocket myself. Still, didn't I hear him say he had done nicely on
his own account . . . Ada, what's that you've got in your hand?'

Modestly Ada showed a fat black note-case. 'It was when he
pushed me down,' she explained. 'Got to learn manners somehow.
Mind you, when he finds he's got nothing to pay his taxi with
he'll be out for my blood.'

'Will he be looking for it at Bournemouth? I thought we'd go
down first thing in the morning.'

'I like Bournemouth,' Ada agreed. 'It's got class.'

'And holiday-makers. Heaven's gift to the working girl. Think
of it, Ada—leaving their stuff all over the beach while they go
for a paddle, putting their purses on counters while they choose
picture postcards. Seems a shame to take the money.'

Ada, calling for one for the road, asked casually, 'Lunch on the train, do you think?'

And Elsie thought why not? Never any harm beginning as you mean to go on.

ANTHONY GILBERT

'Anthony Gilbert' was the pen name of Lucy Beatrice Malleson (1899–1973). Named after her paternal grandmother, Lucy Malleson wanted to be a writer from the age of fourteen. In addition to over sixty full-length detective mysteries, many short stories and several radio plays as 'Anthony Gilbert', she also wrote verse and fiction under her own name and various other pseudonyms. The best known of these is 'Anne Meredith', under which name—curiously—Malleson published an autobiographical memoir, *Three A Penny* (1940). As 'Meredith' she also wrote several novels, but as there were *two* writers called Anne Meredith active in the 1940s and '50s, titles attributed to Malleson are sometimes the work of the other author, who died in 1960.

Lucy Malleson was born in the London suburb of Upper Norwood and she attended St Paul's Girls School. After leaving school and while holding down a job as a short-hand typist, she began to sell verse. Her earliest published work is a poem, 'Good Night', published under her own name in *Poetry of Today* in 1919. Malleson's jaunty and evocative poems were well regarded; they include 'The Gossip', which appeared in *Punch* in 1925 and, in the same year, 'The Town Wind', which won a poetry competition in *The Bookman*. The latter had been submitted under the name of 'J. Kilmeny Keith', a pseudonym that Malleson also used for her first book. She would later recount how her career as a crime writer had been inspired by John Willard's celebrated 'old dark house mystery' *The Cat and the Canary* (1922), whose influence can certainly be detected in *The Man Who Was London* (1925). In this melodramatic thriller a financier is found stabbed to death in his library, the only clue being a business card bearing the inscription 'Nemesis-London'. The novel received mixed reviews with several criticizing the author for involving too many characters who were difficult to distinguish; one reviewer suggested that, with its anti-big business theme, the novel would appeal to terrorists. Her second novel was a melodramatic affair entitled *The Sword of Harlequin* (1927), which told the story of two sisters, Rhoda and Judith Kennedy, and their selfish mother. This marked the final appearance of 'J. Kilmeny Keith' and Malleson next disguised herself as 'Anthony Gilbert', which would become her main pen-name.

As 'Gilbert' she published several lightly criminous serials, including 'A Seeker after Romance' for *The Sketch* in 1927, and 'The Cavalier of Fleet Street' for *Twenty Story Magazine* the following year. She also wrote several short detective stories for a range of publications including *The Graphic* and *Eve,* and in 1927 her first Gilbert novel *The Tragedy at Freyne* was serialized under the title *The Woman in Black.* It featured Scott Egerton, amateur detective and politician who would go on to appear in ten novels, including *The Body on the Beam* (1932) in which he bests Inspector Field, a police detective about whom Malleson wrote a series of entertaining short stories.

Malleson had adopted a male nom de plume in the expectation that this would help sales. However, when *The Tragedy at Freyne* did indeed meet with success, her publisher received requests for photographs of the author. Malleson obliged. She cut her hair, donned a false beard and was photographed in men's clothes. Perhaps unsurprisingly, the disguise was not convincing and 'Anthony Gilbert' was openly identified as Malleson in the press by the early 1930s. Nevertheless, her heroic failure might have inspired one element of the plot of *Speedy Death* (1929), the first crime novel by Gladys Mitchell who, like Malleson, would become a member of the illustrious Detection Club.

Although her crime fiction sold well, Malleson ached to be recognized as a non-genre novelist and she therefore adopted more pseudonyms. She wrote four melodramas as 'Sybil Denys Hooke', and two as 'Lucy Egerton': the light-hearted thriller *Lady at Large* (1936) and, closer to home, *Courage in Gold* (1938), which centres on a woman with a fanatical devotion to the theatre and a thwarted love—Malleson never married, spending much of her young life caring for her father, with her 'best friend' an Aberdeen terrier called Sam. The most successful of her pseudonymous novels is *Portrait of a Murderer* (1931), published as by 'Anne Meredith'. Because the guilty party is identified after only 75 pages, the novel is sometimes described as an inverted detective story and, as with the novels of 'Francis Iles' (Anthony Berkeley Cox)—the first of which first came out in the same year—the focus is psychological rather than detection.

As none of her straight novels landed particularly strongly with the public or critics, Malleson decided to concentrate on crime fiction. In a forty-year career, she built a reputation for witty, sometimes sordid metropolitan mysteries, several of which were filmed, including *My Name Is Julia Ross* (1945), a classic of gothic suspense. Though the character was omitted from the film, the novel on which it was based—*The Woman in Red* (1941)—featured Malleson's best-known detective, the bumptious, beer-swilling solicitor Arthur Crook whom she claimed to have created 'as a sort of protest against the erudition and culture of the Lord Peter Wimseys' of Dorothy L. Sayers and other writers. Described by one contemporary critic as 'delightfully vulgar' and by another as a 'human bloodhound', Crook's specialty is demolishing an apparently watertight case to the irritation of the police and the delight of his clients. Crook appears in fifty books, the last of which appeared posthumously in 1974. They include the sinister domestic killings of *Is She Dead*

Too? (1955), *Knock, Knock, Who's There* (1964)—a story of blackmail largely set in a Thames-side public house—and *Death Knocks Three Times* (1949), in which Crook investigates the murder of an eccentric colonel, possibly by his nephew—ungrateful relatives, like strong female characters, blackmail and homicidal spouses, being something of a staple of Malleson's work.

'Thieves Fall In' was first published in the London *Evening News and Star* on 22 May 1962.

RIGOR MORTIS

Leo Bruce

'*Rigor mortis* and all that sort of thing may be all very well,' said Sergeant Beef contemptuously, 'and I daresay doctors can tell how long anyone has been dead. Give me human nature every time.'

He was holding forth in this pompous way to young Thackeray, who had once served under him as a constable and was now at the Yard.

'Now forget about the corpus for a minute,' he went on, 'and give me the facts. I want to know all about these people before I hear what time the old man was murdered.'

So Thackeray patiently began at the beginning. Old Herbertson, it appeared, was a village Lear with three daughters, all married to prosperous men in the district of Whipston, where he lived. He had also a young niece who kept house for him. He was a little man, not much more than five foot in height and very thin. He was not enormously rich but had enough money to provide a motive for murder. ("How much is that?' asked Beef. 'Men have been killed for a few shillings.')

On a Wednesday afternoon he had set out from his little house outside the village with the intention of calling on Stella, one of his daughters, married to Bert Gabriel, a butcher who was supposed to be well-to-do and lived in a large house called 'The Byres'. The old man was murdered that evening and Bert

Gabriel was now the chief suspect, so Thackeray paused to give some description of him.

'A big heavy chap in his thirties,' he said, 'red-faced and deep-voiced. Does not talk a lot but supposed to be a heavy drinker. Nothing against him before this. The sort of man who *could* have committed a murder but, if it were not for the circumstances which point to him, not the kind you would pick for it.'

His story was simple, so far as it went. He was at home when old Herbertson arrived as it was early closing day. He told his father-in-law that Stella was in London for the afternoon. He made a pot of tea and the old man drank two cups and asked him why the house was so cold. Bert explained that owing to the fuel shortage, the central heating was off but that he was expecting a supply of coke and anthracite that day. At five o'clock, according to Bert, old Herbertson left the house to walk the mile home. It was a dirty winter's night, but old Herbertson said he had a torch and would be all right. Bert Gabriel added that he hated to be fussed over, so he let him go.

At half-past five, Bert Gabriel says, John Griggs, a young man who delivered coke for the local coal merchant, arrived with half-a-ton each of coke and anthracite. Bert went out with him to unlock the boiler-room which adjoined the house. This room had a Yale lock, recently fitted because of coal thefts in the district. There were only two keys, of which Bert had one and his wife Stella had the other. He turned on the light and showed Griggs where to dump the fuel. Questioned afterwards, Griggs was positive that there was no fuel of any sort there before he started to deliver, the small room being completely bare. When the coke was all in and the boiler-room locked, Gabriel asked Griggs if he would mind following him down to his butcher's shop as his cheque-book was there and he wished to pay for the coke right away. Griggs agreed and Gabriel led the way in his saloon car while Griggs followed in the lorry. The cheque was paid and as Griggs prepared to drive away he heard the church clock strike six. From a few minutes after opening until he was summoned home just before ten, Gabriel remained at the Duke of Suffolk inn. He went once to his shop at about seven to get a pound of sausages for the innkeeper, but he was absent for only fifteen or eighteen minutes.

Old Herbertson was never seen alive again, though David Ercott, another son-in-law and a local farmer, thought he recognized his back as he, David, drove home soon after five. His headlights were weak, however, and he cannot be sure.

When seven o'clock came and the old man had not returned, his niece Agatha began to grow worried and telephoned to a number of relatives. At eight she was frantic and asked John Perris, the third son-in-law, to come down at once with his wife Freda, Herbertson's youngest daughter. Perris was a solicitor who practised in the nearby town but had an office in Whipston. When he arrived at old Herbertson's home and heard the circumstances from Agatha, he decided that the police should be informed.

Enquiries were soon made and possibilities exhausted. In a village like Whipston it is possible to get categorical information on such points. Old Herbertson had left neither by bus nor train and could not have gone far on foot. The only way he could have been taken away was in a private car. Thus the mystery stood for an hour.

Then Stella Gabriel, the eldest daughter, arrived from London at Whipston Station at 9.15 and walked the few hundred yards to her home. Finding the central heating still not on, she went out to the boiler-room to see whether the coke had been delivered. She found it locked (the lock had not been tampered with), and she opened it with her own key.

As she was examining the heap of coke she saw that a dark liquid had oozed out from under it and was horrified to find that it was blood. Bravely, for she felt quite alone, she raked away the coke enough to realize that a body was underneath it. Then she ran screaming from the house.

'The doctor made his examination,' said Thackeray, 'and it brings us to the point about *rigor mortis*, which you seem to think so unimportant. He believes that old Herbertson was murdered about five hours before he was called in, that is to say just when the old man was leaving Bert Gabriel's house to walk home. According to Gabriel, that is'

Beef grunted. 'What about motive?'

'So far as we know, it must have been money. The old boy's estate after death duties and everything is paid is worth about twenty thousand pounds. That means five to each to the three daughters and niece to whom it was left in equal shares.'

'Weapon?' asked Beef laconically.

'Something heavy and blunt. Lead pipe or very heavy cudgel. He was struck from behind and his skull broken.'

'Fingerprints? Bloodstains? Clothes sent to the cleaners?'

'Nothing at all.'

'It's a nice little mystery,' pondered Beef. 'It must have been Bert, you suggest, because no one else could have put him in the boiler-room. Yet it could not have been Bert, you go on, because the corpse was not there when the coke was delivered and Bert had no opportunity of moving him there afterwards.'

'Unless,' said Thackeray, 'he had got the poor old chap on ice somewhere and moved him into the boiler-room when he left the "Duke of Suffolk" to get those sausages. If so, he was pretty quick.'

'Very quick,' agreed Beef. 'And what about the blood meanwhile? If he murdered Herbertson it was, according to the doctor, around five o'clock. Wherever he put it, the corpse must have been bleeding from then till seven. Where? You've searched the premises?'

'Of course. Not a vestige.'

'I see. Well, I suppose I shall have to go down to Whipston.

I don't know where you'd be, young Thack, if you hadn't got me to work things out for you. *Rigor mortis* and doctor's timing! I use my loaf.'

Beef was back two days later and was annoyingly boastful to young Thackeray.

'Of course I know who was guilty,' he said. 'And not through timing it, either. You gave me my first idea when you said that Bert might have kept the corpse "on ice" for a couple of hours. Why, I asked, should he not have murdered the old man, put the corpse in the back of his car where it remained while he drove down to his shop with Griggs? Then, after Griggs had driven off, he could have hauled it into the shop. Nothing odd about bloodstains there, as he well knew. When he went for the sausages, I thought, he could have had time to drive to his home and put the corpse under the coke in the boiler-room before he went back to the "Duke of Suffolk".'

'Then?'

'Wait a minute,' commanded Beef. 'I've always been interested in bloodstains. I solved my first big mystery by examining them. I know that if this theory was right there would be some traces in the back of Bert's car, or else it would recently have been cleaned out. Bound to be. No other way for it. But there weren't, and it had not. Bert had not carried the corpse in his car.'

'So?'

'So I had to start all over again. I went for motive. Who could want the old boy out of the way? All three daughters and all three husbands. Yes, but what about the niece? She had just as much motive, but she had not got a husband. Or had she? An intended one, I mean. It was my enquiries on this point which really gave me the key, for I found that for a long time there had been an understanding, which they hoped was secret, between her and John Griggs.

'Yes, you've got it. Griggs was on his way to deliver his two ton of fuel to Gabriel when he sees in the headlights of his lorry the old man walking home. He stops, and running after Herbertson cracks him over the head from behind. Then, probably pulling the corpse through a hedge or somewhere out of sight of passing cars, he stuffs the little man's corpse into one of his sacks and drives on to Gabriel's. It was reasonable to suppose that Gabriel would not watch him carry in every one of his twenty sacks, and indeed as he has told me now, he did not wait in the wet night after unlocking the boiler-room.

'Even if he were watched carrying his sacks in, Griggs knew that one more would make no difference. He unloaded the corpse, covered it with coke and left it to be discovered. Gabriel, he knew, would be suspected long before he was. In that he was right.'

Beef considered for a moment.

'It was not such a stupid idea,' he said. 'It might even have come off. The trouble with these violent murders, though, is that however you father them on other people they leave plenty of traces. I leave those to you, Thack, but I don't think you'll have much trouble. Griggs' clothes, the lorry, the sack he used, the instrument, I don't think he can have removed all traces very well. Probably he has done something really silly which will give you a certain conviction. They nearly always do. You go and find it and get your promotion. I'm off for a pint of wallop at the local.'

LEO BRUCE

Leo Bruce was the pen name of the prolific writer Rupert Croft-Cooke (1903–1979). Raised in St Leonard's, a coastal town in south-east England, Croft-Cooke was something of an outsider within his own family. Aged only eighteen, he published his first work, a slim volume of poetry, and, after a brief spell as a tutor, he left home to travel the world.

On returning, Croft-Cooke's experiences in Europe and South America helped him to secure a job with 2LO, the organization that would become the BBC. At 2LO, in only his mid-twenties, he broadcast regularly, giving talks on subjects as diverse as life in Brazil, the flora and fauna of the Falkland Islands and—decades ahead of his time—the allure of Portugal and Spain as a holiday destination. He also hosted programmes on the music of Argentina and Czechoslovakia, and he wrote various radio plays, including *The Telegram* (1926), *In the Tunnel* (1927) and *Anniversary* (1928).

Croft-Cooke's approach to the acquisition of knowledge and experiences was omnivorous. He wrote on anything and everything that took his interest—from the joys of darts, pubs and circuses to Romany life. Somewhat implausibly given his sexuality, he even wrote an article advising how to pick up women from different European countries, a piece published—even more implausibly—by the *Daily Mirror*, a left-wing British newspaper. As well as poetry, journalism, reviews and short fiction, he produced an enormous number of carefully researched, readable books as well as biographies, including more than twenty volumes of autobiography, published over thirty years, and an as yet unpublished mystery for younger readers, *Where Was Withers?* There were also stage plays, including *Banquo's Chair*, based on Croft-Cooke's short story of the same title, and an all-female light thriller, *Tap Three Times*. However, he is best known today for his detective fiction, mostly published under the pen-name of Leo Bruce, in particular the novels and short stories featuring the lugubrious Sergeant Beef.

A lost Beef story, 'Rigor Mortis' is published here for what appears to be the first time. I am indebted to Curtis Evans, historian of the Golden Age of crime fiction and author of that essential volume, *Masters of the 'Humdrum' Mystery* (2012), for drawing it to my attention.

THE ONLY HUSBAND
H. C. Bailey

CHARACTERS

MR FORTUNE: Mellow, genial tenor.

LORD AVALON: Husky, jerky, short of breath.

LADY AVALON: Fruity contralto, 'refined' accent.

HON. CECIL RICHARDS: Precise, supercilious, thin tone.

NELL RICHARDS Staccato, girlish voice, but pleasant.

PETER WELLS: Sharp and snappy.

DR SOMER: Loud, important.

CAPTAIN BLACKWOOD: Deep and grave.

INSPECTOR COOCH: Brusque, broad vowels, consonants emphatic—countryfied speech.

BUTLER: Funereal.

PART I

LADY AVALON: Your coffee, Ben.

(Jingle of china)

LORD AVALON: What? Thanks.

(Tearing of paper. Crumpling of paper)

LADY AVALON: Isn't there anything in any of those letters?

LORD AVALON: Eh? No. Not this morning. Business and beggars.

LADY AVALON: You poor dear. *(Laughs sympathetically)* Have you seen Cecil and Nell this morning?

LORD AVALON: No, why should I?

LADY AVALON: She's always down before us.

LORD AVALON: Is she? I suppose she is.

LADY AVALON: Ben, you're not eating anything.

LORD AVALON: Don't be silly. You see I am. I'm eating toast. That's all I want.

LADY AVALON: My dear , don't you feel well?

LORD AVALON: Must you fuss? I'm all right.

(*Noise of opening and shutting door*)

CECIL RICHARDS: Good morning, my lady. (*Tone faintly sarcastic*) Good morning, father. (*More amiably*) You are early.

LORD AVALON: Nothing of the sort. Where's your wife?

LADY AVALON: What have you done with Nelly, Cecil? She's always first at breakfast.

CECIL RICHARDS: How dreary! Nell would be tired of that. But you're not fair to her. She isn't always anything.

LADY AVALON: Really, Cecil. (*Laughs*) You bad fellow! Only six months married and you take her character away!

CECIL RICHARDS: One doesn't ask for a character when one marries.

LORD AVALON: Where's the girl got to?

CECIL RICHARDS: I expect she's gone into the garden, sir. I'll see.

(*Sound of an opening and shutting French window and his footsteps. He calls*)

Nell!

NELL RICHARDS: Angel face.

(*More footsteps*)

CECIL RICHARDS: Why do you shun the family board?

NELL RICHARDS: I was waiting for you. I couldn't face the parents alone.

CECIL RICHARDS: I have felt that myself. It was the reason I married.

NELL RICHARDS: Brute. Have they been asking why you married me?

CECIL RICHARDS: I came here to show them. My father is not without intelligence though I am his son. He dares not confess it, but you have found favour with him.

NELL RICHARDS: They hate us being here.

CECIL RICHARDS: One must distinguish, my child. She does us the honour of wishing us at the devil. He is uncomfortable at our observing the felicity of his second marriage.

NELL RICHARDS: How long are we going to stay, Cecil?

CECIL RICHARDS: My dear child, the promised week of filial affection. An absurd feeling, but I suffer from it.

NELL RICHARDS: I know. But she thinks I married you for your father's money and we've come here to look after it. I'm sure she's told him so.

CECIL RICHARDS: Her ladyship has a mind of that sort and a tongue. (*Laughs*) She says—what says she?—let her say! He will not take her opinion on me. He was well assured I am a fool before she married the money he made out of Dick's Dainties—a fool who declined to go on making it because he preferred chemical research—an utter fool to the mind of Benjamin's Richards, first Lord Avalon, risen from a little pastry shot to roll in wealth. It hurts him to leave no son of his body, no second Dick purveying Dick's Dainties, only a limited company. I am a bitter disappointment to him. He'll never forgive me, but he is a just man, he does know I am not a gold digger.

NELL RICHARDS: It was fine of you, Cecil. I'm proud. P'r'aps you didn't know.

(*Sound of a kiss*)

CECIL RICHARDS: Darling. I am vain enough to think so when we are alone. Now come and be proud of me to the parents.

NELL RICHARDS: Oh, they'll believe I am. (*Laughs rather bitterly*)

CECIL RICHARDS: Don't be afraid of them.

(*Sound of footsteps*)

NELL RICHARDS: I'm not afraid of anyone.

(*Sound of opening and shutting French window*)

Good morning. Good morning, father. How are you?

LORD AVALON: Eh? Hmph! Morning.

LADY AVALON: Whatever have you been doing all this time, Nelly? You were down before any of us.

NELL RICHARDS: Where were you then?

(*Sound of moving chairs and clinking plates*)

LADY AVALON: I saw you come in here.

NELL RICHARDS: Oh no, you didn't. I haven't been in this room till now.

LADY AVALON: Really! (*Laughs unpleasantly*) I suppose I may believe my own eyes.

NELL RICHARDS: If they saw me, they saw me go straight out into the garden.

CECIL RICHARDS: I'm sure you did. You have an awkward taste for fresh air, Nell, and a painful habit of going straight.

LADY AVALON: What a testimonial! So Nelly had to meet you in the garden before she could come to breakfast with us.

NELL RICHARDS: Isn't that wonderful? But he happens to be the only husband I ever had.

(*Sound of a cup being knocked over*)

LORD AVALON: Ugh! Cursed mess!

(*Sound of mopping*)

CECIL RICHARDS: Let me get you some more coffee, sir.

LORD AVALON: What do you say?

LADY AVALON: Nelly was telling Cecil she hasn't been married before. I suppose he wasn't sure.

CECIL RICHARDS: Cecil knows his wife. That does give confidence, doesn't it, father?

LORD AVALON: What? What?

LADY AVALON: We are so glad to hear you are happy, Cecil. Your father—

(*Sound of a chair pushed back violently*)

Why, Ben, you haven't finished!

LORD AVALON: Coffee all over me, clean up the mess.

(*Sound of a door slammed. Another door shut. Tinkle of telephone bell*)

Damn the phone! Trunks. I said trunks. Give me Wimpole 303. Is that Wimpole 303? I want to speak to Mr Reginald Fortune. Lord Avalon calling. Lord Avalon, tell him.

(*Pause. Impatient drumming of fingers*)

Hullo! Hullo! Confound the people!

MR FORTUNE: Fortune here. (*Pathetically*) Well?

LORD AVALON: This is Lord Avalon. Mr Fortune, I—

MR FORTUNE: So they told me. Why?

LORD AVALON: I'm speaking from Rosford House, my place in Durshire. I—

MR FORTUNE: Early, aren't you? It's very early here. (*Plaintively*) Haven't had my breakfast.

LORD AVALON: (*gasping*) Oh, for God's sake! (*Coughs*)

MR FORTUNE: Yes, what?

LORD AVALON: (*Earnestly*) You remember me, Mr Fortune? I met you over that prisoners' help fund you're interested in. I did my little bit.

MR FORTUNE: My dear sir! Very generous. I have not forgotten. And now?

LORD AVALON: I want to consult you. It's very urgent. I want you to come down here at once.

MR FORTUNE: Who's your doctor?

LORD AVALON: I didn't mean a medical consultation. It isn't that, Mr Fortune.

MR FORTUNE: Oh. But you're not feelin' very fit, are you?

LORD AVALON: Not quite the thing. Never mind that. I should be well enough if I wasn't worried to death. It's a—(*breaks off*)

(*Sound of a door opening and closing and rustle of movement*)

MR FORTUNE: Hullo! Are you there?

LORD AVALON: Yes, yes. I thought somebody was coming. I was telling you—(*hoarse whisper*)—it's a personal affair, family affairs. I want your opinion, your advice. Can you come? Right away, I mean, start at once? (*In breathless haste*) You might get here this afternoon, the morning train's quite good if you could catch it, then we could go into the whole thing, it will take some time, would you mind staying the night? I—

MR FORTUNE: One moment. Have you been to a doctor lately?

LORD AVALON: Yes, I have, my regular man down here, Somer. He says my heart's not quite what it was. He talks about some little lesion. He's given me stuff for it.

MR FORTUNE: Has he? Got the prescription?

LORD AVALON: No, he makes up his own medicines, the old-fashioned country practitioner, you know, but he's quite a good man.

MR FORTUNE: His medicine done you any good?

LORD AVALON: I think it did. I hadn't been feeling my heart nearly as much till it came on again lately. It's racing . . . can't get my breath. It's the devilish worry. (*In a whisper*) Family trouble.

MR FORTUNE: When did the heart go wrong again?

LORD AVALON: A few days ago.

MR FORTUNE: And when did the family start troublin' you?

LORD AVALON: I can't tell you about it over the phone.

MR FORTUNE: Oh. As bad as that. However. Like to have some facts. The family is Lady Avalon—and a son, what? Son by first wife.

LORD AVALON: Yes, But if you'd only come down—

MR FORTUNE: Son's a chemist, isn't he?

LORD AVALON: Yes, that's right, but—

MR FORTUNE: Steady. Livin' with you?

LORD AVALON: Not regularly. (*Whispers fast*) He's here on a visit with his wife. I can't talk over this phone, Mr Fortune. There's nothing to be done like this. For God's sake come down! You could be here this afternoon. I know it's a lot to ask of you, but I don't care what I pay, name your own fee.

MR FORTUNE: (*Reproachfully*) My dear chap. Oh, my dear chap!

LORD AVALON: I beg your pardon. You will? It's not much over a hundred miles, the eleven o'clock from Paddington would get you down to Durchester soon after two. I'd have you met there. Can you manage that?

MR FORTUNE: I'll be at Rosford House by one. Take care of yourself.

LORD AVALON: Thank you, thank you, But how are you coming, then?

(*Tinkle of the bell*)

Lord, he's rung off.

(*Sound of door closing and his footsteps in the hall*)

Nell, is it? What are you doing?

NELL RICHARDS: Cecil wondered if you'd gone out.

LORD AVALON: Did he? Well you see I haven't.

NELL RICHARDS: Won't you come and have your coffee? Lady Avalon has had some more made.

LORD AVALON: Hmph. All waiting for me, are you?

(*Footsteps and door opening and closing*)

LADY AVALON: Oh, Nelly has found you, Ben. (*Laughs*) Now tell Cecil what you've been doing. He was in a fret to know.

LORD AVALON: Much obliged to him.

(*Clink of a cup*)

CECIL RICHARDS: Here's your coffee, sir.

LORD AVALON: Thanks for reminding me.

LADY AVALON: Poured out with his own fair hands.

CECIL RICHARDS: As your ladyship had left the family table.

LADY AVALON: Dear Cecil, how ungrateful. You were so curious about your father you made me feel I was cramping your style, I had better sit in a corner.

CECIL RICHARDS: And think beautiful thoughts.

LADY AVALON: But of course. How could I think anything else? You have always been so kind to your father, so helpful, so attentive. Too precious of you to come and show such an interest in him.

CECIL RICHARDS: I have valued the maternal welcome. It compels me to stay.

LADY AVALON: We are so glad, aren't we, Ben?

LORD AVALON: What? Stay as long as they like. I don't care.

LADY AVALON: No, we understand perfectly, Cecil.

CECIL RICHARDS: Perfection is finality. And finality is death.

LADY AVALON: Good gracious! Whatever do you mean? Do you hear, Ben? Cecil is talking of death, somebody's death.

LORD AVALON: I heard him. Whose death?

CECIL RICHARDS: Her ladyship is literal. What I quoted was an old saying. Perfection is—

LORD AVALON: I know.

(*Noise of his pushing back his chair*)

Damned pleasant conversation.

NELL RICHARDS: Don't be worried, father, Cecil was making fun. We always do if people are cross. You should. It's not a bit of good taking them seriously.

LADY AVALON: Dear Nelly! Isn't she affectionate, Ben?

LORD AVALON: That'll do, my girl.

(*Sound of walking across to the window and opening it*)

(*Hums to himself*)

'She was a miller's daughter,

She lived beside the mill—'

NELL RICHARDS: Is that a song?

LADY AVALON: Where are you going, Ben?

LORD AVALON: Might bring down a bird or two.

LADY AVALON: Good luck, dear. I would come but I have to go into Durchester to the dentist.

(*Sound of Lord Avalon walking away and she after him, shutting the room door*)

CECIL RICHARDS: At last alone! Cigarette, Nell?

(*Striking of match*)

More power to the dentist.

NELL RICHARDS: Ugh! Was that ghastly? We are having fun.

CECIL RICHARDS: Her ladyship has a winsome nature.

NELL RICHARDS: We can't go on like this. I can't stick it, Cecil.

CECIL RICHARDS: We don't run away from her ladyship. I have some affection for my father.

NELL RICHARDS: Oh, I know. But it's perfectly beastly for him.

CECIL RICHARDS: And if we retire defeated and abandon him to her tender mercies? That wouldn't be a pleasant future, darling.

NELL RICHARDS: You mean for us? (*Sharply*)

CECIL RICHARDS: I shouldn't enjoy it myself. But I meant for him.

NELL RICHARDS: Well, what's the use of staying? We only make him wretched.

CECIL RICHARDS: We? Perhaps we do, but only by contrast. He sees you and me. He sees her ladyship in the light of you. You've won upon him, darling, I knew you would.

NELL RICHARDS: You always said that. But it hasn't come off. He hates me. You saw him just now when I called him father and put my hand on his shoulder, he thought I was trying to vamp him. Ugh!

CECIL RICHARDS: Her good ladyship told him so. He didn't believe it. You shouldn't.

NELL RICHARDS: It's all very well, but he just shook me off and went to the window and what was that song he hummed?

'*She was a miller's daughter,*

She lived beside the mill—'
I never heard it before but I'm sure he was jeering.

CECIL RICHARDS: So am I. We wasn't jeering at you though.

NELL RICHARDS: Why, do you know the song?

CECIL RICHARDS: Yes, darling. It's a musical comedy jingle of the days before you were born.
'*She was a miller's daughter,*
She lived beside the mill.
Still and deep ran the water
But she was—deeper still.'

NELL RICHARDS: Well. (*Laughs bitterly*)

CECIL RICHARDS: Precisely. No man in his senses will ever think you deep, darling. But her ladyship—it is one of the right words for her. All goes well.

NELL RICHARDS: Does it? Then what did he mean by saying he 'might bring down a bird or two' when he went off?

CECIL RICHARDS: You know too much slang. My father seldom uses it. I am sure you were not the bird he hoped to bring down. I'm afraid it wasn't her ladyship. Only a pheasant or two. He always liked to walk round the woods of an autumn morning with his gun. I'm inclined to join him. He used to like that too. We'll try it again.

NELL RICHARDS: He didn't ask you.

CECIL RICHARDS: No, he was afraid of her ladyship. But I think he'll be pleased.

NELL RICHARDS: I'll go with you.

CECIL RICHARDS: Ah, that would be jolly. I'm not too sure he'd care for it, though.

NELL RICHARDS: Wouldn't he? (*Sharply*) You said I'd 'won upon him'.

CECIL RICHARDS: And you have. But he's old fashioned, he doesn't care for women shooting.

NELL RICHARDS: I wasn't going to shoot. I'll just walk down to the woods. Unless you don't want me.

CECIL RICHARDS: I always do. Charming of you. Put your things on while I get my gun.

(*Sounds of movement and shutting door. Fade up twitter of birds and voices of Nell and Cecil*)

NELL RICHARDS: It's much too lovely a day to go killing things, Cecil.

CECIL RICHARDS: (*Laughs*) Even a pigeon? Well, I never was a deadly shot. I dare say you won't see any killing.

NELL RICHARDS: I don't mean to.

CECIL RICHARDS: You shan't, darling. But you needn't go back now. We're not near the woods yet. Don't desert me.

NELL RICHARDS: I'll go a little way further and sit down.

(*Faint sound of a motor engine*)

Why, what's that?

CECIL RICHARDS: A car somewhere, wasn't it? On the road.

(*Sound dies away*)

NELL RICHARDS: I suppose so. Where do you think your father will be?

CECIL RICHARDS: Bear right. Avoid the combe, it is picturesque but laborious. Willows white, aspens quiver down by the laughing water, and it makes a great mess till you get down to the bridge by the sham antique temple. A useless mile. We'll cross the Rosset stream over the stepping stones at the combe head and then make for the corner of the woods. We shall see my father prowling there one way of the other.

NELL RICHARDS: How can you be sure?

CECIL RICHARDS: Isn't it wonderful? No, not the least. The leopard cannot change his spots, nor my father his habits. He never has since I knew him. Except when he made Miss Agnes Wallace Lady Avalon. Whenever he takes a morning gun he goes to this corner of High Rosset Wood.

NELL RICHARDS: And he always liked you with him?

CECIL RICHARDS: That also was a habit. He taught me to shoot there. When I was at home he counted on my company for these morning diversions.

NELL RICHARDS: I wonder if he does today.

CECIL RICHARDS: He hopes for it. He meant to invite me, saving her ladyship's presence.

NELL RICHARDS: You're very sure. I can't see him, Cecil.

CECIL RICHARDS: There he is.

NELL RICHARDS: Where?

(*Faint sound of an aeroplane engine*)

Whatever's that? Oh, it's an aeroplane.

CECIL RICHARDS: (*Laughs*) Yes. Not father shooting.

NELL RICHARDS: I don't see him at all.

CECIL RICHARDS: He's turned round the corner of the wood. I'll go ahead. You're not coming any further, are you?

(*Sound of the aeroplane nearer*)

NELL RICHARDS: No, I'll sit down by the stream.

CECIL RICHARDS: Good. We'll come back this way. The old man likes his lunch to the minute.

(*As Cecil's footsteps thud away the sound of the aeroplane grows louder for a minute*)

NELL RICHARDS: Horrid thing. Go away.

(*Sound very loud, then suddenly dies as the aeroplane engine is stopped*)

Thank heaven. It's passed.

PETER WELLS: I can't bring the bus down there, Mr Fortune. Why ring the bell? Which was your fancy, the wild woolly woods or that giddy tumble of a split in the air? Nothing doing. Even if you have a date with the lady.

MR FORTUNE: (*Plaintively*) Dullest form of transport yet invented, flyin'. Might be a comely park if one could see it. Did you say there was a lady present?

PETER WELLS: There. Where the jolly old stream falls over the edge. A dainty little piece. Yours, sir?

MR FORTUNE: Peter! (*Reproachfully*) Treatin' serious case with levity.

PETER WELLS: Sorry. She looks lonely. Looks as if she might be waiting for her best boy. He cometh not, she said. Blast him!

MR FORTUNE: Do you pretend to see what she looks like?

PETER WELLS: No deception. Quite a lovely, in a small way.

MR FORTUNE: See anyone else anywhere, young fellow?

PETER WELLS: Not a ghost. It's a blind bit of country.

MR FORTUNE: (*Bitterly*) That's the value of flyin'.

PETER WELLS: You wouldn't see any more on the ground.

MR FORTUNE: I wonder.

PETER WELLS: Not a hope.

(*Faint sound of a shot*)

MR FORTUNE: Hullo! Did you hear that? Crack of a shot. Johnny's got his gun. Pop gun.

PETER WELLS: A shot, Yes. Where did it come from?

MR FORTUNE: You're asking me. The lady's jumped up to look at the wood. I suppose her best boy's having a go at the pheasants.

PETER WELLS: It could be. Get on.

MR FORTUNE: Right.

(*Roar of the engine soon shut off*)

PETER WELLS: Now she'll do. Pretty bit of turf there.

(*Pause. Sound of landing*)

MR FORTUNE: My only aunt!

PETER WELLS: 'S all right. What's the matter? Jolly good landing.

MR FORTUNE: My dear chap! The house. Look.

PETER WELLS: Golly! All that out of Dick's Dainties. The old boy must be rolling. Lucky dog.

MR FORTUNE: Hush!

(*Faint cries from Nell and Cecil*)

Well, well. What do you make of that?

PETER WELLS: It's someone calling in the park.

MR FORTUNE: Two people. Come on.

(*Sound of their hurrying footsteps*)

CECIL RICHARDS: (*Shouting*) Nell! Nell! Where are you? Nell!

NELL RICHARDS: Cecil! Here. What's the matter? Where are you? I can't see you. Are you hurt?

CECIL RICHARDS: No. It's father. Just inside the wood here. Come and help me with him.

NELL RICHARDS: (*With a sob*) Oh my God! I'm coming, I'm coming.

(*Sound of her running*)

Where is it? Where is he?

CECIL RICHARDS: The gate at the corner. Quick.

NELL RICHARDS: (*Panting*) Yes, I am. Cecil!

(*Sound of a gate opening*)

Whatever has happened to him?

CECIL RICHARDS: He's ill. He's collapsed. He can't speak.

NELL RICHARDS: Ill? How? Who was it shooting?

CECIL RICHARDS: I don't know. Him I suppose. I haven't fired a shot. I've only just found him. Here he is.

NELL RICHARDS: Oh, he's been sick. (*In a gasping whisper*) There isn't any wound.

CECIL RICHARDS: What? Nothing of the sort. (*Furiously*) Damn it, did you think I'd shot him?

NELL RICHARDS: (*Faintly*) No, no. Oh, Cecil! Give me your handkerchief. Father!

(*A long groan, a sound of jerking movement*)

CECIL RICHARDS: Stay by him. I'll go and get help.

(*Sound of him running*)

PETER WELLS: There's a bloke going all out, Mr Fortune.

MR FORTUNE: Gentleman in a hurry, yes. Single gentleman. What's he done with the other voice?

PETER WELLS: Napoo. Puzzle, find the lady.

MR FORTUNE: Interestin' problem. There are others. Gentleman has no gun. Might be runnin' away from somebody. Might be runnin' for somebody. I wonder. (*Calls loudly*) Hullo, sir! Where's the trouble?

CECIL RICHARDS: (*Thudding up to them, breathless*) Who the devil are you?

MR FORTUNE: My name's Fortune. Reginald Fortune. And yours?

CECIL RICHARDS: Good God! What brought you here?

MR FORTUNE: I came to see Lord Avalon. Where is he?

CECIL RICHARDS: My father. Why?

MR FORTUNE: Didn't he tell you? Well, well. Then I can't, Mr Richards. Any objection from you to my seeing him?

CECIL RICHARDS: Not the least. I'm damned glad you're here.

MR FORTUNE: Thanks very much. Any particular reason?

CECIL RICHARDS: He's fallen ill. He was out shooting by himself and I found him just now, helpless, collapsed, inside the wood there.

MR FORTUNE: Oh. So you ran away?

CECIL RICHARDS: He can't stand. I couldn't carry him alone. I was running to get help.

MR FORTUNE: You have it. Come on.

(*Sound of them tramping away*)

What's become of the lady?

CECIL RICHARDS: I left my wife with him. Why, how did you know she was in the park?

MR FORTUNE: Didn't know she was your wife. Hadn't a husband with her when we saw her. Where were you?

CECIL RICHARDS: I left her by Rosset water, by the stepping stones there, and went on to join my father. But—

MR FORTUNE: With gun? You didn't want him to shoot by himself?

CECIL RICHARDS: Yes, I had a gun. I was going to join him. But how did you see my wife?

MR FORTUNE: Just passed over the scene of Rosset.

CECIL RICHARDS: You were in that plane?

MR FORTUNE: We were, yes. (*Drawling*) Curious and interestin', wasn't it, Peter?

PETER WELLS: More than somewhat.

MR FORTUNE: Nobody ever knows what he's doin', Richards. Have you noticed that? However. Here's the wood. Lead on.

(*Sound of creaking gate*)

NELL RICHARDS: (*Crying out*) Cecil! Is that you?

CECIL RICHARDS: Yes, darling. Coming.

NELL RICHARDS: He's fainted. I think he's fainted. He doesn't move any more.

MR FORTUNE: Allow me. Oh. Been sick. When was that?

CECIL RICHARDS: I don't know. Before I found him. He was prostrate and groaning then. He couldn't speak.

MR FORTUNE: Too bad.

(*Sound of rustling of Avalon's clothes as he undoes them*)

NELL RICHARDS: (*Whispering*) Cecil, who is this man?

CECIL RICHARDS: (*Whispering*) Doctor of sorts. He does the medical expert work for the police.

NELL RICHARDS: (*Stifled cry*) Police!

CECIL RICHARDS: Be quiet.

MR FORTUNE: (*Sharply*) Peter! Can you get that gate off its hinges?

PETER WELLS: Sure.

(*Sound of creak of gate*)

MR FORTUNE: Put him on that. You and Richards carry him up to the house.

PETER WELLS: Righto.

CECIL RICHARDS: What is the matter with him, Mr Fortune? A fit?

MR FORTUNE: I can't tell you. Where's his gun?

CECIL RICHARDS: I don't know. I haven't seen it. I haven't looked.

MR FORTUNE: This one is yours then?

CECIL RICHARDS: Yes, that's mine.

(*Sound of opening gun*)

MR FORTUNE: Haven't you fired a shot this morning?

CECIL RICHARDS: No, I was looking for my father.

MR FORTUNE: Well, well. Take him along, Peter. Quick as you can.

CECIL RICHARDS: Where are you going? (*Tone of surprise and alarm*)

MR FORTUNE: Goin' to ring up his doctor.

(*Sound of his hurrying off*)

PETER WELLS: Now then, Richards! Coat under his head. That'll do. I'll lead. Lift. March.

(*Sound of slow tramping for a little*)

Keep step, old bean. Pick up the flat feet.

(*More tramping*)

CECIL RICHARDS: I am sorry. (*Breathing hard*) I find it heavy work.

PETER WELLS: You're telling me.

(*More tramping*)

Gosh, do you want your wife to help your end?

CECIL RICHARDS: No, it's all right.

PETER WELLS: Where is the lady?

CECIL RICHARDS: I don't know.

(*Faint sound of a shot through their tramping*)

PETER WELLS: Hullo! Hullo! Where did that one come from?

CECIL RICHARDS: (*Panting*) What one? What do you mean?

PETER WELLS: Somebody else gone gunning.

CECIL RICHARDS: I didn't hear anything. (*Calls*) Nell!

NELL RICHARDS: (*Voice from some distance*) Yes, I'm coming.

PETER WELLS: (*Under his breath*) At the double. (*Normal voice*) Who is the sportsman, Mrs Richards?

NELL RICHARDS: What? What do you mean?

PETER WELLS: Didn't you hear a shot?

(*Tramping unsteady*)

NELL RICHARDS: No. Oh Cecil, let me help. I'll take one side

and you can have both hands for the other. He's frightfully
jolted.

PETER WELLS: Who?

NELL RICHARDS: (*Fiercely*) Father, of course. Don't you see,
can't you feel?

PETER WELLS: Watch your step. Left, right. Left, right.

CECIL RICHARDS: (*Panting*) Stop for a moment, sir.

PETER WELLS: Pull yourself together. Damn it, don't lie down
on him!

(*Tramping more regular*)

That's better! Not much further. Here's the old house

(*Sound of tramping up stone steps and door opening. Tinkle of
telephone bell*)

MR FORTUNE: (*Plaintively*) Can't you get him?

DR SOMER: This is Dr Somer.

MR FORTUNE: At last!

DR SOMER: Who are you?

MR FORTUNE: Rosford House speakin', doctor. Come at once
to Lord Avalon.

DR SOMER: Why, what's the matter?

MR FORTUNE: Up to you. Step on it.

(*Sound of putting down receiver*)

PETER WELLS: Here we are, Mr Fortune.

MR FORTUNE: Good work. Allow me, Mrs Richards. I'll take
this end now. Go ahead, Richards, show us where his room
is.

BUTLER: (*Anxiously*) Can I be of any assistance, sir?

MR FORTUNE: Send up a big jug of hot water and a pot of
tea.

(*Slow tramp of feet going upstairs; door opens and closes. A
pause, then sound of car approaching*)

See who that is, Peter.

PETER WELLS: Female by herself. A mature female.

MR FORTUNE: Might be Lady Avalon. Go down and see the

family reunion, Peter. And make sure the doctor comes straight up when he arrives.

PETER WELLS: I'm on.

(*Sound of his going out*)

LADY AVALON: Why are you sitting in the hall, Nelly? And Cecil too?

BUTLER: My lady—his lordship—Dr Somer has been sent for.

LADY AVALON: Good heavens! Whatever has happened, Cecil?

CECIL RICHARDS: Father fell ill while he was out shooting. I found him sick and helpless.

LADY AVALON: But that's impossible. He was perfectly well at breakfast, you know he was.

CECIL RICHARDS: I don't. I don't think he was at all like himself.

LADY AVALON: Really! You were so pleasant to him. Did you go out with him, you and Nelly?

CECIL RICHARDS: I went after him.

LADY AVALON: Oh, I see. And you found him ill.

(*Sound of a car*)

I'll go up. Why, Dr Somer—

DR SOMER: (*Loud and hearty*) Good morning, Lady Avalon. How is his lordship? I only had the curtest message.

CECIL RICHARDS: Mr Fortune wants you to go to him at once, Somer.

DR SOMER: Mr Fortune! Mr Reginald Fortune?

PETER WELLS: That is the name, sir. Come along.

DR SOMER: What brought him here? (*Defiantly*)

PETER WELLS: You'd better ask him. He's waiting for you.

DR SOMER: Is he with Lord Avalon?

PETER WELLS: Sure. Come on up.

DR SOMER: Very well, I am coming.

(*Sound of their feet on the stairs*)

LADY AVALON: (*Angrily*) Who is this Mr Fortune?

CECIL RICHARDS: (*Bitterly*) Don't you know? He's the medical expert in criminal cases.

LADY AVALON: Cecil! How can you? Is it true, Dr Somer?

DR SOMER: I'm afraid it is. I don't understand.

LADY AVALON: Oh Cecil, your father! When did this Mr Fortune come?

CECIL RICHARDS: I don't know. He was in the park when I found father.

LADY AVALON: And saw you?

CECIL RICHARDS: I was visible.

LADY AVALON: But this is dreadful. Oh, I must go to your father!

(*Sound of her running upstairs and of door opening*)

MR FORTUNE: Dr Somer, I presume. My name's Fortune.

LADY AVALON: (Rather shrill) I am Lady Avalon, Mr Fortune. I—

MR FORTUNE: Please. Quite quiet. Can't let you see Lord Avalon now. In a little while.

(*Sound of her sobbing*)

I'm sorry.

(*Sound of door closing*)

Well, doctor, here's your patient. What are going to tell me?

(*Movement and rustling*)

DR SOMER: Good God, he's dead!

MR FORTUNE: Yes, I know that. When found by me in the wood here, unconscious after violent vomiting. Pulse irregular. Brought him here. Pulse very rapid and feeble. Stopped a few minutes ago. What's your opinion?

DR SOMER: (*Clears his throat. Speaks pompously*) Poor dear fellow. A sad sudden end. Such an energetic man by nature, he could not bear to give up his shooting. I have long feared that it would be too much for him. There can be no doubt of the cause of death—failure of the weakened heart from excessive exertion.

MR FORTUNE: You think so? Lord Avalon rang me up this morning and asked me to see him. I flew down. Not quick enough. Don't like my patients to die without my assistance. I want a consultation with you, Dr Somer.

DR SOMER: By all means, I have no objection in the world.

MR FORTUNE: What was the matter with his heart?

DR SOMER: There were lesions from endocarditis, Mr Fortune, I found some time ago a disturbing murmur.

MR FORTUNE: Oh yes. Lord Avalon told me you sent him medicine.

DR SOMER: Naturally I did, and with excellent results. I am sure he told you so.

MR FORTUNE: Said he felt better for a bit. Lately fresh discomfort.

DR SOMER: He has never mentioned any to me.

MR FORTUNE: Curious and interestin'. Mentioned it to me. What were you sendin' him? Digitalis?

DR SOMER: You are very acute, Mr Fortune. I am so glad to find you agree, digitalis was clearly indicated. I sent him the fifteen minim tincture to be taken three times a day.

MR FORTUNE: Didn't say I agreed. I don't. Shouldn't give digitalis for a heart murmur myself.

DR SOMER: It have Lord Avalon great relief. He told you so.

MR FORTUNE: Told me it did for a time. Also told me lately his heart felt like racing and he couldn't get his breath. Today he collapsed with vomiting, rapid, feeble pulse, and died. What's that suggest to you?

DR SOMER: Clearly overstrain of a weak heart—lesions from endocarditis, you know.

MR FORTUNE: I don't.

DR SOMER: I can sure you that it is accurate. I have attended Lord Avalon for years.

MR FORTUNE: And he called me in. In time to see him die. I should say poisoning by digitalis.

DR SOMER: It is impossible.

MR FORTUNE: You think so? Well, well. Easy to prove. I'll ring up the coroner.

DR SOMER: (*Startled*) The coroner? You are going to ask for an inquest, Mr Fortune? Think of the family!

MR FORTUNE: I'm thinking of the dead.

(*Sound of him opening the door*)

Hullo, Richards!

CECIL RICHARDS: What is your opinion, Mr Fortune?

MR FORTUNE: Somer will tell you.

(*Sound of his going downstairs. Sound of woman hurrying along corridor*)

LADY AVALON: Mr Fortune! Wait, please.

MR FORTUNE: Pardon me, Lady Avalon. Presently.

CECIL RICHARDS: How is my father, Somer?

DR SOMER: (*Clearing his throat*) I am deeply distressed, Cecil. I did not reach your father in time.

CECIL RICHARDS: He is dead?

LADY AVALON: Oh Cecil! It's not true! (*Voice going up to a high note*) Dr Somer, it can't be true. Tell me.

DR SOMER: Dear Lady, you must be brave. When I arrived there was nothing to be done. Lord Avalon had passed away.

LADY AVALON: (*Shrieks*) No! Ah, cruel, cruel!

(*Sound of her staggering and sobbing*)

Don't—don't hold me, doctor! Let me go to him!

DR SOMER: Yes, certainly you shall. But sit down a moment. You must be calm, dear lady.

CECIL RICHARDS: What was the matter with him, Somer?

DR SOMER: His heart was weak.

LADY AVALON: Oh, but he'd been so much better till lately.

DR SOMER: (*Pompously*) I hoped that with care your father would live for many years, Cecil. But the best treatment cannot guard against overstrain. I have no doubt that he died of heart failure. I must tell you, however, Mr Fortune is not satisfied and requires an inquest.

LADY AVALON: How dreadful!

CECIL RICHARDS: Can he force an inquest?

DR SOMER: He asserts that Lord Avalon consulted him and asked him to come today. I have no knowledge of this, but as he desires an inquest to be held I cannot advise you to object.

LADY AVALON: (*Tearful voice*) Ah, what does it matter? Ben is dead. Let me go to him.

DR SOMER: Be brave, dear lady. Take my arm, lean on me. There, there!

LADY AVALON: (*Faintly*) You're so kind.

(*Sound of them going out*)

PETER WELLS: (*Chuckles*) He got the wind up when I told him Mr Fortune was here. Lady Avalon asked him who you were and boy Cecil snapped out your job was Crime, meaning to be nasty, and she had a shock.

MR FORTUNE: (*Dreamily*) Our Dr Somer showed alarm? I wonder.

PETER WELLS: So did Cecil and his little wife when we bumped into 'em in the park.

MR FORTUNE: Cecil and wife in the park—did they go well helpin' you carry Avalon back?

PETER WELLS: Cecil was dying on me all the time, but he did better after she joined up and have a hand. She's got more guts than he has.

MR FORTUNE: Yes. You may be right. But you said 'joined up'. How's that?

PETER WELLS: She stayed behind in the wood for a bit. Now you ask me, it's a rum thing. I'll swear I heard another shot before she caught us up, but boy Cecil said he heard nothing and she stuck to that too.

MR FORTUNE: Curious and interestin'.

PETER WELLS: They're a fishy pair, and then some. It's a blinking maze of nastiness. I—

MR FORTUNE: Hush! Bereaved now leavin' the chamber of the dead. Our Somer with Lady Avalon on his arm.

PETER WELLS: Cecil's lookin' vinegar at 'em.

MR FORTUNE: Yes. You have an eye. (*Calls*) Somer! Want a word with you.

DR SOMER: (*Pompously*) You will be good enough to wait, sir. (*Affectionately*) Now, dear lady.

(*Sound of an opening door*)

I must insist that you rest. I will send you a sedative.

LADY AVALON: You are so kind. But do go to that man.

(*Sound of door closing*)

DR SOMER: Now, Mr Fortune, what is it?

MR FORTUNE: Only wanted to tell you—coroner's sendin' an ambulance for the body. I'm going to do the post mortem tomorrow, eleven o'clock. Like to be there?

DR SOMER: I must insist on being present, sir.

(*Sound of Somer going downstairs*)

MR FORTUNE: Now, Peter.

PETER WELLS: What's up, sir?

MR FORTUNE: (*Softly*) Want to have another look at Avalon. Come on.

(*Sound of door opening and shutting and turn of the key*)

Where did Cecil go?

PETER WELLS: Round the turn of the corridor. To his lady wife, I suppose.

MR FORTUNE: It could be. Anything occur to you?

PETER WELLS: How do you mean? Gosh, has the old man moved? Wasn't he really dead?

MR FORTUNE: Oh yes. I do take my risks. But I shouldn't have left him for dead if he was alive. Not in this house. Bed a little rumpled by the bereaved. Quite natural. I meant his clothes. We didn't leave 'em like that. They've been moved. Not so natural.

(*Sound of rustling clothes*)

Keys left—watch—small change—penknife—wallet. But only money in it. I wonder. What's that other door?

(*Sound of opening door*)

Dressing room. Oh yes. Medicine bottle inscribed: 'One tablespoonful to be taken three times a day. Lord Avalon.' But the bottle is empty. How convenient! Observe also the fireplace.

PETER WELLS: What about it?

MR FORTUNE: Oh my Peter! Look. Fire has been laid, but not lit. Yet upon the tidy hearth there is burnt paper. Why? Very interestin' problem. Who burnt it? Probably fundamental problem. However. Ordinary problem, what was on it? Go to Avalon's study. Get the bottle of gum from the desk there. Don't be seen with it. (*Whistles softly some bars of Handel's Dead March*) Thanks. Now the glass top of the bedside cupboard, please.

PETER WELLS: Here you are. And then what? The paper's burnt to bits.

MR FORTUNE: Imperfect observation. One sheet is. Cheap, thin writin' paper. We don't have much luck. However. Another sheet hasn't crumbled much. Faced paper. Person who burnt it failed to observe it didn't burn so well. Same like you. And underestimated my small abilities. We now make a bed of gum on the glass—(*pause_*)—and proceed—(*speaking very slowly and softly*)—to flatten out on it this crumpled ash of the sheet of faced paper—*very* gently—there—(*pause*) Not too bad. And turnin' it to the light—well, well.

PETER WELLS: Golly, there's a picture. Sort of shadows in the grey.

MR FORTUNE: Yes, that is so. Printers' ink on faced paper. Which was a hand bill. To advertise a young woman in pierrot costume and a male pierrot at a piano. There are also names. Not so good. *Ro* and *air* at the bottom. Suggest anything to you?

PETER WELLS: Nix.

MR FORTUNE: Oh my Peter! Name of a pierrot party above. Probably Canoodlers. Names of the two below. The one remainin' might be Robin Adair. (*Whistles softly the tune of 'Robin Adair'*) '*Oh, I can ne'er forget Robin Adair.*' I wonder. Might get something out of the letter.

PETER WELLS: The letter—the other sheet—how do you know that's a letter?

MR FORTUNE: Natural inference. Only tiny scraps left, as you were sayin'. But try everything. (*Pause*) Well. That is that. *Ife* can be read. Which was probably wife. And *lice*. Which might be Alice. And that is all. But not without interest. Go ahead, Peter. See if any of the amiable family are about.

(*Sound of doors*)

PETER WELLS: All clear.

MR FORTUNE: Good. Stand by. Me for the telephone again. Poor me.

(*Sound of going downstairs. Tinkle of phone bell*)

Is that Kelly's? Mr Patrick Kelly in? Tell him Mr Fortune callin'. Hullo, Kelly. Ever hear of a pierrot troupe called Canoodlers? Ever heard of Robin Adair or Alice Adair in the profession? She sang, he was at the piano. No further description. Small fry, yes. But professionals. What you can't trace never happened. They did. Get a line on 'em. I'll ring you again after five. Rush job. Can't explain now. Good-bye.

(*Sound of receiver clashed down*)

Yes, what is it?

BUTLER: If you please, sir, the Chief Constable, Captain Blackwood.

MR FORTUNE: Good of you to come yourself, Captain.

CAPTAIN BLACKWOOD: I couldn't do less. I liked Avalon.

MR FORTUNE: Me too. He phoned me to come down. Wouldn't say why. Must have been big trouble.

CAPTAIN BLACKWOOD: Yes. Avalon was afraid of being overheard if he talked over the phone. That means somebody in the house.

MR FORTUNE: So we won't talk here.

CAPTAIN BLACKWOOD: Very well. The ambulance will be along in a minute. Are you ready for the body to be taken away?

MR FORTUNE: Sooner the better.

CAPTAIN BLACKWOOD: This is Inspector Cooch. My best man.

MR FORTUNE: Splendid. Just come outside a minute. Want you to put this glass plate in your car, Inspector, and lock it up.

CAPTAIN BLACKWOOD: What the deuce is it?

INSPECTOR COOCH: Burnt paper reconstruction, sir. Does it give us a line, Mr Fortune?

MR FORTUNE: Not yet, no. But it may. Several obscure facts besides Avalon's death. If I may suggest, Captain, Inspector Cooch could stay in the house with Avalon's keys and go through his things—not neglectin' other people's. I'd like to take you to where I found Avalon—takin' the son and son's wife also. Thus givin' the Inspector a fairly free hand.

INSPECTOR COOCH: I see what you mean, sir.

CAPTAIN BLACKWOOD: That's all right. But is there any point about the place he was found?

MR FORTUNE: Several obscure and curious facts about findin' him. While my plane was circlin' round to look for a landin' place we heard a shot. Son Cecil's story, his father had gone off shootin' alone and he followed to shoot also, accompanied by his wife. But when we got to Avalon, only one gun visible and that hadn't been fired recently. Cecil said it was his. I went back to the house. My pilot, Peter Wells, and Cecil carried Avalon up. Wife lingered behind. Peter heard a second shot. Cecil said he didn't. When his wife joined 'em, she also said she'd heard nothing. It could be. Peter's uncommon sharp, eye and ear. They were both dithery. However. Investigation required.

(*Sounds of footsteps*)

CAPTAIN BLACKWOOD: The exact way you went this morning, please, Richards.

CECIL RICHARDS: There is only one way to High Rosset.

(*Sound of footsteps for some moments*)

MR FORTUNE: Richards. You told me the first shot wasn't fired by you.

CECIL RICHARDS: (*angrily*) The first shot?

MR FORTUNE: (*wearily*) That was what I said. Mrs Richards sat by the stepping stones here when it was fired. Where were you?

CECIL RICHARDS: Round the corner of the wood.

MR FORTUNE: And where was the shot fired?

CECIL RICHARDS: It came from the wood. It must have been my father shooting. That's why I went into the wood and almost at once I found him lying helpless.

MR FORTUNE: (*drawling*) Didn't fire his gun though. Mrs Richards, where would you say this first shot came from?

NELL RICHARDS: (*defiantly*) From the wood.

MR FORTUNE: And the second?

NELL RICHARDS: (*fiercely*) There wasn't any second.

CECIL RICHARDS: (*speaking simultaneously*) No other shot was fired.

MR FORTUNE: Oh yes. Rather later, Richards. While you and Peter were carryin' your father to the house. Before Mrs Richards caught you up.

CECIL RICHARDS: I heard nothing.

NELL RICHARDS: Nor did I and I was quite close behind them.

CECIL RICHARDS: What is all this fuss over shooting, Fortune?

MR FORTUNE: I wonder. Any ideas, Peter?

PETER WELLS: Not so easy. We heard the first shot from the air. It might have been in the wood but we only got a crack with a bit of an echo. The second shot was faint, no echo, rather muffled. I'm sure that was a gun from the wood.

CECIL RICHARDS: Nothing of the sort.

MR FORTUNE: You know there's a gamekeeper livin' just beyond the wood. Why didn't you go to him for help? Why didn't you tell me about him?

CECIL RICHARDS: (*stammers*) I forgot. I wasn't thinking.

MR FORTUNE: Well, well. Interestin' witness, the gamekeeper. Might be decisive witness. Run along and fetch the game-keeper, Peter.

PETER WELLS: Righto.

MR FORTUNE: Now here's the gateway. Richards, you'd better tell Captain Blackwood what you did do.

CECIL RICHARDS: I was a hundred yards or so beyond when I heard the shot.

CAPTAIN BLACKWOOD: (*sharply*) The first shot?

CECIL RICHARDS: (*furiously*) The only one I heard. I came back to the gate and there, there by that oak I found my father on the ground.

MR FORTUNE: Avalon'd been sick, Blackwood, you see. Smell of coffee. Notice that? I'm havin' the stuff analysed. However. Also notice, only one gun. And Richards says that's his.

CECIL RICHARDS: He gave me this years ago. It is just like his own.

MR FORTUNE: (*dreamily*) Curious and interestin'. I wonder.

(*Sound of opening gun*)

CAPTAIN BLACKWOOD: This hasn't been fired today, and you say this is yours. Where's your father's?

MR FORTUNE: (*dreamily*) Not visible. As I was sayin'. Strikin' fact. Might be crucial fact.

(*Sound of footsteps*)

Well, Peter?

PETER WELLS: Napoo, the gamekeeper. Only his mamma in the cottage, an old dame deaf as a post. If I got her right the gamekeeper has the weekend off to see his wife who's having a baby in hospital.

MR FORTUNE: Well, well. Gamekeeper was thus eliminated. You didn't know that, Richards?

CECIL RICHARDS: I don't know anything about him.

MR FORTUNE: (*dreamily*) Absence of gamekeeper very convenient. However, problem of second gun still more important. Dense cover this wood with the hornbeam and laurel under the oaks. Avalon must have kept on paths. Path here. Man's footprints on it. Goin' down and comin' up. Let's go down.

(*Sound of footsteps*)

More sickness. What do you say, Blackwood?

CAPTAIN BLACKWOOD: He didn't go beyond this point.

MR FORTUNE: No. came down here. Was then sick, turned back, sick again up there and collapsed. But there's no gun here either.

CAPTAIN BLACKWOOD: Let's look round.

(*Sound of thrusting into bushes*)

No, it's not here. Devilish odd. Are you sure your father took a gun out, Richards?

CECIL RICHARDS: I didn't see him go but he said he meant to shoot and we heard a shot.

MR FORTUNE: Some other footprints about, Blackwood. Smaller feet. Woman's feet. See? Rather faint just here. But they go on down. (*Pause*) Toes deeper. Lady was running. Well, well. Look at that.

CAPTAIN BLACKWOOD: Good God, it's a gun! Now, Richards, do you recognize this as your father's?

CECIL RICHARDS: Let me see.

MR FORTUNE: (*simultaneously*) Careful, Blackwood. Might be fingerprints with luck.

CAPTAIN BLACKWOOD: You can see without handling it.

CECIL RICHARDS: (*Angrily*) I don't want to touch it. It is his.

CAPTAIN BLACKWOOD: Thank you.

(*Sound of opening and closing gun*)

It's been fired today, Fortune. One barrel at least. There's a cartridge still in the other.

CECIL RICHARDS: I told you there was only one shot.

MR FORTUNE: You did, yes. This don't confirm you. Might have been two from the same barrel. See any cartridge case about?

(*Sound of thrusting into bushes*)

PETER WELLS: None.

MR FORTUNE: Well, well. Lady's footprints go on down— running. She came up slower. We also will go down. Where's this path lead to, Richards?

(*Sound of their footsteps*)

CECIL RICHARDS: It will take you to the bridge over the Rosset at the bottom of the combe.

MR FORTUNE: Lady went there—also came from there. If only one lady. Well, well. And where does the bridge lead to?

CECIL RICHARDS: The path forks beyond. One branch goes up to the house, the other to a gate in the park wall.

MR FORTUNE: Well, well. Now we're coming to the stream. My only aunt! What's that?

CECIL RICHARDS: (*supercilious laugh*) A minor outrage. The Victorian idea of a Greek Temple and a Gothic bridge. Designed to dignify the cascade of the Rosset.

MR FORTUNE: (*sighing*) A sad world. However. Sham temple not wholly without interest. Dusty floor smeared. And I should say that is blood. Yes. Provisional conclusion, Somebody was shot here. And then what? No remains left. But the cascade of the Rosset is contiguous.

(*Pause. Sounds of movement. Sound of splashing water*)

Yes. Rush of stream over big rocks and pools good and deep. Just the place to smash up a body.

NELL RICHARDS: Ah, don't be so ghastly!

MR FORTUNE: (*dreamily*) I wonder. (*Pause*) Look, Peter. Under that rock ledge.

PETER WELLS: Golly! Righto. Can do.

(*Sound of scrambling over rock and splashing*)

NELL RICHARDS: (*Moaning cry*) Oh, that's horrible!

CECIL RICHARDS: Don't look, Nell. Come away.

MR FORTUNE: One moment, Richards.

(*Sound of dragging a body up the bank*)

Is the deceased anybody you know?

CECIL RICHARDS: (*Sneering*) That is a fatuous question. Who could recognize a face in such a condition?

MR FORTUNE: (*Blandly*) Face is damaged, Yes. However, oldish man, fat, bald, shabby, flashy clothes. Ever met a man like that before?

CECIL RICHARDS: I have no acquaintance with any man of the type. You will excuse me, I must take my wife away.

MR FORTUNE: See you presently.

(*Sound of Cecil and Nell walking away, she crying*)

CAPTAIN BLACKWOOD: It's frightened her to death. He's as cold as a fish.

MR FORTUNE: Rather bafflin', our Cecil. Far from cool when found with father. Cool enough over this. Only concerned to remove his wife. Well. Deceased's face smashed by charge of shot fired close to it. Features lost in laceration. Low brow. Podgy cheeks. Big mouth. Oh. Wound through left ear not made by shotgun. Bullet wound. Fired very close. Probably from pistol or revolver. That's what killed him. The first shot, Peter. In his pockets—some small change, packet of cigarettes and matches. No papers. Clothes off the peg from a multiple shop tailor. Only a laundry mark on collar. Anonymous fellow. Stand by, Peter, do you mind? Till the police come for him?

PETER WELLS: That's all right by me.

MR FORTUNE: Now then, Blackwood. The sooner it's over the sooner to sleep. Back to the house.

CAPTAIN BLACKWOOD: It is a hell of a case.

MR FORTUNE: Not nice, no. However. Facts are emergin'. Remember what Peter said about the first shot. A crack and an echo. Peter's very good. Our anonymous friend came to the temple. Probably by appointment. There someone met him and fired a pistol into his ear. Small short report echoed from the temple. Subsequently some lady went up into the wood, took Avalon's gun or Cecil's gun, whichever it was that was fired, used it to obliterate the dead man's face, showed him into the stream and brought the gun up into the wood again. Very neat. If Avalon hadn't brought me flyin' down, long odds the deceased wouldn't have been found for days. And we'd never have proved anything.

CAPTAIN BLACKWOOD: (*gloomily*) Can we now?

MR FORTUNE: My dear chap. Oh, my dear chap. (*Soft purring laugh*)

PART II

(*Clock chimes five*)

MR FORTUNE: (*Plaintively*) Five! Oh my aunt! I am empty. Did you have any lunch, Blackwood?

CAPTAIN BLACKWOOD: No, I was just sitting down when I got your message.

MR FORTUNE: (*Sighing*) A hard life, our life. Well, well. On with the dance. Come up to Avalon's study.

(*Sound of them going upstairs and a door closing*)

Tobacco for you?

(*Sound of lighting a pipe*)

(*Speaks slowly through long exhalations of smoke*) Now what have we? Avalon murdered by poison—overdose of digitalis—which took effect—almost simultaneous with murder of unknown man by pistol or revolver shot—near where Avalon was—by someone who used his gun—or Cecil's gun. Woman concerned in that murder—Cecil and Cecil's wife were close by—Cecil is a chemist—Cecil is Avalon's only son—Avalon wanted to consult with me on family trouble. Further to which—

(*Door opens softly*)

Our Inspector Cooch.

(*Door closes*)

A felt want. What are your results?

INSPECTOR COOCH: I can't say I have anything definite, Mr Fortune, but there's points you might call suggestive. Using Lord Avalon's keys I found in his desk a copy of his will, dated August. As I read it, five thousand a year to Lady Avalon for life, all the rest—barring some charity bequests—to his son Cecil.

MR FORTUNE: (*Dreamily*) Is that so? What would you say Avalon was worth, Blackwood?

CAPTAIN BLACKWOOD: He put down a hundred thousand for this place and the land and I've heard that was a fleabite to him.

MR FORTUNE: Yes, made himself and a million. Poor old Avalon. Thus Cecil would get quite a lot by his death. If this will is the last. And it was made in August. And Cecil comes to stay with him in October. Whereupon he dies. I wonder. Anything else of interest?

INSPECTOR COOCH: No, sir. Nothing to signify in Lord Avalon's rooms at all. But going through his son's room I found an empty medicine bottle.

MR FORTUNE: No label on it.

INSPECTOR COOCH: That's what struck me, sir, and Mr Cecil being a chemist.

MR FORTUNE: And bottle not quite empty. Bitter fluid. Could be digitalis.

CAPTAIN BLACKWOOD: (*Violently*) My God, Fortune, that's damnable!

MR FORTUNE: (*Coldly*) As you say.

INSPECTOR COOCH: There's this too, sir. A scrap of paper on the hearth—the rest was burnt to dust—but you can make out a bit.

MR FORTUNE: Four words. 'Go to the devil'.

CAPTAIN BLACKWOOD: It's Avalon's writing, Fortune.

MR FORTUNE: Yes. Interestin' and curious. In Avalon's dressin' room also a medicine bottle and burnt paper. Strikin' a similarity. That bottle was supplied by our Dr Somer and quite empty. But burnin' of paper suggests the same person operated in both rooms.

INSPECTOR COOCH: Was there a letter burnt in Lord Avalon's room?

MR FORTUNE: Letter on cheap, flimsy paper. Not like this, which is good stuff. Only scraps of words legible: *ife*—probably wife—*lice*—probably Alice. Cecil could have burnt it while I was talkin' to our Dr Somer here in the study.

INSPECTOR COOCH: You found something else burnt, sir. The stuff you pieced together on the glass. That's a picture of two pierrots, man and woman.

MR FORTUNE: Yes. Title of picture—from what remains of it—Canoodlers and Robin Adair. (*Whistles softly the tune 'Robin Adair'*)

CAPTAIN BLACKWOOD: Why the devil should Avalon keep a picture of two pierrots?

MR FORTUNE: I wonder.

(*Sound of door opening and shutting*)

Well, Peter, how's it go?

PETER WELLS: The loathly corpse is went. In a plain van. I left coppers buzzing round the scene of slaughter. Do I see a drink there? I need it.

(*Clink of glass and spurt of siphon*)

Fun tomorrow! I say, Mr Fortune, I spotted one cartridge case by the perishing temple. Here you are. Service revolver ammunition.

INSPECTOR COOCH: (*Stiffly*) Excuse me. How does a revolver come into the case? And what is this about a corpse?

MR FORTUNE: sorry. We've all been so busy. Unknown man killed by revolver in the park. Ring the bell, Peter. Butler might help.

(*Door opens*)

BUTLER: If you please, sir?

MR FORTUNE: (*Soft and plaintive*) Wanted to know if Lord Avalon has a revolver.

BUTLER: I could not say, sir. There is a revolver in the gun-room, but that is Mr Cecil's army revolver which he had in the last war.

MR FORTUNE: (*Same plaintive tone*) Might ask Mr Cecil to come here. And Mrs Cecil. And Lady Avalon.

BUTLER: Thank you, sir.

(*Sound of him going out*)

MR FORTUNE: (*Very sadly*) Have to look at the gun-room, Cooch. Oh I say, Blackwood! I must go and phone. That awful phone again!

(*Sound of Cooch and him going out and closing door*)

PETER WELLS: (*Chuckling*) Mysterious bird, isn't he?

CAPTAIN BLACKWOOD: Have you worked much with him?

PETER WELLS: Flown him here and there. It's when he looks like a sad baby and moans I get the jitters.

(*Sound of opening door*)

CECIL RICHARDS: Ah, Blackwood. I thought that fellow Fortune was here.

CAPTAIN BLACKWOOD: He will be.

CECIL RICHARDS: What is this meeting for? Why do you want us?

CAPTAIN BLACKWOOD: There are a good many points we have to check up, Richards. You can all tell us something. The whole family is concerned , isn't it?

CECIL RICHARDS: If you mean in the same way, I don't accept that.

(*Sound of opening door*)

MR FORTUNE: This way, Mrs Richards.

NELL RICHARDS: (*Fiercely*) I'm coming. What do you want us for?

MR FORTUNE: (*Plaintively*) Never can tell what anybody can tell in a case till they all do. Here comes Lady Avalon. Won't be a moment. Pardon me.

(*Sound of shutting door*)

CAPTAIN BLACKWOOD: Please sit down, Lady Avalon.

LADY AVALON: Thank you. I hope you will not keep me long. I ought not to be here. Dr Somer—

(*Sound of opening and closing door*)

MR FORTUNE: (*Short of breath*) You were sayin'?

LADY AVALON: I was saying, Mr Fortune, Dr Somer told me I must rest till he called again. But I felt that I couldn't bear to stay lying down when Captain Blackwood wanted me.

MR FORTUNE: (*Slow and vague*) Glad Somer's comin' back. Want everybody. Must begin somewhere. Begin with breakfast this morning. (*Pause*) What did Lord Avalon drink?

CECIL RICHARDS: Coffee. He always drank coffee.

MR FORTUNE: And the rest of you? Coffee also?

LADY AVALON: I did. Nelly and Cecil had tea. They always do.

MR FORTUNE: Did Avalon eat much?

CECIL RICHARDS: Hardly anything.

LADY AVALON: Really Cecil! That's absurd. You weren't there while he was eating. Actually he ate just as usual.

MR FORTUNE: You differ. Who came down to breakfast first?

LADY AVALON: Nelly.

NELL RICHARDS: I didn't.

LADY AVALON: You were down before any of us. I saw you go into the breakfast room.

NELL RICHARDS: That's what you said this morning. I don't know why. I went straight into the garden.

MR FORTUNE: (*Plaintively*) Wonder why you disputed who was first at the breakfast table. Did Lord Avalon seem quite well?

LADY AVALON: Perfectly.

CECIL RICHARDS: Not at all. My father was nervous and breathless.

LADY AVALON: He was quite himself till Nelly came back and upset him.

MR FORTUNE: What went wrong?

CECIL RICHARDS: Her ladyship tried to make trouble between my father and us.

LADY AVALON: You really are impossible, Cecil. I've hardly been able to soothe your father, you and Nelly fretted him so.

NELL RICHARDS: (*Fiercely*) Sooth! You were always saying beastly things about us.

MR FORTUNE: (*Plaintively*) Could anybody be definite?

NELL RICHARDS: She sneered—Lady Avalon sneered about Cecil and me and I just said that Cecil was the only husband I ever had and then Lord Avalon spilt his coffee and went out.

MR FORTUNE: Oh. (*Pause*) Like that. (*Pause*) Curious and interestin'.

LADY AVALON: it wasn't. Cecil jumped up to give his father some more coffee but his father wouldn't have it and went out.

MR FORTUNE: Why did he go?

NELL RICHARDS: He said to clear up the mess—the coffee on his clothes.

MR FORTUNE: I think he went to phone me. While he was phonin' he thought somebody came near. Who else left the breakfast room?

NELL RICHARDS: I did. He was gone so long Cecil though he might have started for a walk. I met him in the hall.

CECIL RICHARDS: Her ladyship having left the room before you.

LADY AVALON: I went to speak to the butler for a moment to give orders for lunch.

CECIL RICHARDS: The result was he brought more coffee.

LADY AVALON: And when your father came back you'd take my place and gave him a cup.

MR FORTUNE: Well, well. What happened next?

CECIL RICHARDS: More amiable efforts by her ladyship. She attempted to irritate my father and make it impossible for us to stay. He didn't relish it. He told me to stay as long as I liked and told her it was a damned pleasant conversation and went out again.

LADY AVALON: (*Laughs*) Your memory's not very good, Cecil. You were spiteful to me and your father was annoyed. He told you he didn't care whether you stayed or not and you replied by talking about his death. That's what made him say it was a damned pleasant conversation.

CECIL RICHARDS: (*Angrily*) I did not talk about his death. Your ladyship remarked that you understood me perfectly and I answered: 'Perfection is finality and finality is death.' I prefer to be sarcastic when people attempt insults.

MR FORTUNE: Does seem to have been a jolly breakfast for Avalon.

(*Sound of opening door*)

Let me introduce Inspector Cooch. Lady Avalon, Mr and Mrs Richards.

INSPECTOR COOCH: May I have a word with you, Mr Fortune?

MR FORTUNE: (*Affectionately*) My dear chap. Sit down and put it in writing. Revertin' to the breakfast. Are you all agreed after Avalon said the conversation was dam' pleasant he went out? (*Pause*) Oh, don't be shy now!

NELL RICHARDS: He didn't go out at once.

LADY AVALON: (*Laughs*) No, you were affectionate to him, weren't you, Nelly? And he didn't like it.

NELL RICHARDS: I just asked him not to worry then he went off humming a song.

'*She was a miller's daughter,*
She lived beside the mill—'

MR FORTUNE: Oh. (*Laughs quietly. Hums:*)
'*Still and deep ran the water*
But she was—deeper still.'
Song of my vanished youth. Who used to sing that? Hilda Moody, was it? (*Pause*) No answer?
'*She was a miller's daughter*
She lived beside the mill.
Still were the flies on the water
But she was—flyer still,'
Nobody remember? Well, well. On that lyric the breakfast party broke up. Avalon then went out alone to shoot. Was that usual?

CECIL RICHARDS: He often took his gun after breakfast.

MR FORTUNE: You didn't think of going with him, Lady Avalon?

LADY AVALON: I should have gone—oh how I wish I had?— but I had to see my dentist.

MR FORTUNE: And you didn't go with him, Richards. Though you and Mrs Richards followed.

CECIL RICHARDS: We went almost at once.

(*Sound of chair being pushed back*)

INSPECTOR COOCH: Here you are, Mr Fortune.

(*Pause*)

MR FORTUNE: (*Softly*) Good man. One moment.

(*Sound of him rising and going out with Cooch and his return*)
Your Cooch is a hustler, Blackwood. To resume—
'*She was a miller's daughter,*

She lived beside the mill—'
That was the end of the jolly breakfast. What about the beginning? Why the general argument who came down first? Lady Avalon—Mrs Richards? One or other of you, what? Does it matter which? Some question about the coffee?
(*Silence*)
Or the morning letters? (*In a very smooth voice*) Were there any letters for Avalon this morning?
LADY AVALON: Oh, Yes. When he and I came into the room we found some, but they were only beggars and business.
MR FORTUNE: Did Avalon expect a letter he didn't find?
LADY AVALON: I don't know.
NELL RICHARDS: (*Fiercely*) She's suggesting I meddled with his letters.
LADY AVALON: I said nothing of the sort.
NELL RICHARDS: Oh yes you did!
MR FORTUNE: Any letter which you expected missing, Lady Avalon?
LADY AVALON: No, I wasn't expecting anything in particular.
MR FORTUNE: And you, Richards?
CECIL RICHARDS: I didn't expect any—like her ladyship—and there were none for me.
MR FORTUNE: Well, well. Now I'll put my pieces into the breakfast Puzzle. When Avalon phoned me, he wasn't well. Definite symptoms. Also somebody was trying to hear what he said. He asked me to come here at once. He wanted my advice on a family trouble. Anybody goin' to tell me what it was?
(*Silence*)
Richards, have you had a fierce letter from him lately?
CECIL RICHARDS: (*Angrily*) From my father? Never in my life.
LADY AVALON: Wasn't it fierce, Cecil? He told me he meant it to stop you plaguing him.

(*Sound of a motor car*)

CECIL RICHARDS: I give your ladyship the lie.

MR FORTUNE: Like that. Some error. One moment. Who's in the car? Look out of the window, Peter.

PETER WELLS: Old man Somer.

MR FORTUNE: Bring him straight up.

PETER WELLS: Righto.

(*Sound of him going briskly*)

MR FORTUNE: We did want our Somer. Oh, Cooch is first. Well?

INSPECTOR COOCH: (*With gusto*) I've got it, Mr Fortune. This is my note of it.

MR FORTUNE: Splendid. Ah, here's Dr Somer. Do you know Inspector Cooch, Somer?

DR SOMER: (*Haughtily*) How do you do? You wished to see me, Mr Fortune? Lady Avalon! Tut, tut, tut! Really, Mr Fortune, I must protest. I advised Lady Avalon that she must rest in complete quiet. You—

MR FORTUNE: There's been a murder, Somer. Two murders.

LADY AVALON: What? What do you say?

MR FORTUNE: I said two. One at a time. About your digitalis, Somer. Do you know how much you sent Avalon?

DR SOMER: Certainly. I need not tell you I keep records of my treatment.

MR FORTUNE: They will be wanted. Can you account for all the digitalis you ever had?

DR SOMER: (*Stammers*) I—I resent the question.

MR FORTUNE: Think again. Avalon was murdered by digitalis. You sent him digitalis tincture. Two possibilities. You gave him a fatal dose. Or somebody else got hold of digitalis. Not easy to get. Has anybody who could poison Avalon had a chance of gettin' digitalis from you?

(*Silence*)

Oh. You're lookin' at Lady Avalon. Better look at me, Somer. Did you give her some?

DR SOMER: (*Hoarsely*) Never, never at any time.

LADY AVALON: (*Shrill*) Oh, this is filthy! Captain Blackwood, how can you let him?

CAPTAIN BLACKWOOD: (*Sternly*) We want the truth, Lady Avalon.

MR FORTUNE: (*Softly*) What are you going to say, Somer?

DR SOMER: (*Faltering*) I don't know. There's nothing I can say. Lady Avalon is my patient. She's called on me. She has been alone in my surgery.

LADY AVALON: It's a lie. A dirty lie.

CAPTAIN BLACKWOOD: So she could have got at your bottles, Somer. That's your story.

LADY AVALON: (*Gasping*) It was Cecil, he's a chemist.

MR FORTUNE: (*Dreamily*) As you say. When did you first think of that?

LADY AVALON: Why, when you talked of poisoning.

MR FORTUNE: Not before? Not when you made a fuss about who was down first this morning—who had a chance to dope the coffee?

LADY AVALON: I never thought of such a thing. But now of course—

MR FORTUNE: Yes. Now we know. Yes. Evidence of the motive of the first murder in the 'damned pleasant conversation' at breakfast. Mrs Richards happened to say Richards was the only husband she ever had. You didn't like that. No, must have been a nasty jolt for you seein' poor Avalon spill his coffee over it and go out. You had to get him some more coffee. (*Drawls*) So we pass to the second murder, Lady—well, well. What is your real name, Lady Avalon? (*Silence*)

You haven't forgotten? (*Hums*)

'*But now they're cold to me*
Robin Adair.
Yet him I loved so well

Still in my heart shall dwell
Oh! I can ne'er forget
Robin Adair.'
We've found his body—and also his name—Reuben Aarons.
Thus able to prove why you shot him, Mrs Reubens Aarons.
(Shriek. Sound of Lady Avalon falling. Hustle of general move-
ment)
INSPECTOR COOCH: *(Grimly)* I'll take her.
(Sound of her being carried out)
CAPTAIN BLACKWOOD: Good God, Fortune! Have you got
proof?
MR FORTUNE: *(Laughs softly)* My dear chap. Oh, my dear chap!
Quite clear. Avalon wasn't 'the only husband she ever had'.
Woman was a fifth-rate singer. Married Reuben Aarons, in
the same class. The two pierrots. He faded out and she caught
poor Avalon and married him. Handsome female—in her
style. Then Aarons turned up again and no doubt started
blackmailin' Avalon. Wife a bigamist. That was the family
trouble for which he wanted me. I should say Avalon didn't
feel sure what the truth was. But she knew he'd drop her when
he was sure and she'd have Aarons bleedin' her while she lived.
So she arranged to wipe out both husbands. Poured digitalis
into Avalon, stronger and stronger doses with Richards here
for a scapegoat. Final dose in the breakfast coffee. Fixed up
an appointment with Aarons at the sham temple this morning
and shot him with Cecil's revolver from the gun-room, then
obliterated his face with Avalon's gun. Proof of her past from
Patrick Kelly of Kelly's Dramatic Agency. Her special song:
'She was a miller's daughter.' Avalon remembered that this
morning. Proof of the digitalis from Somer. Proof of the
shootin' just obtained by our Cooch. Cecil's revolver's been
fired today but Cecil wasn't by the temple when we heard the
first shot. Lady Avalon left her dentist at ten-forty-five by car.
Lots of time to get to the temple and kill Aarons. Shoes she

wore this morning fit the prints in the wood and they're damp and they have bits of grass and moss on 'em. Clever woman. Searched Avalon's clothes for anything Aarons had sent him. Found a letter and a hand bill of her and Aarons as pierrots. Didn't burn 'em quite enough. Left the essential clue for me to find. Laid a trail to Richards—digitalis bottle and a letter of Avalon's with 'go to hell' in it. I should say Avalon wrote that to Aarons and she took it from his pocket. Well. Sorry you've been troubled, Mrs Richards. Always sure of you. Had to work it out.

CECIL RICHARDS: (*Bitterly*) You weren't sure of me.

MR FORTUNE: You're so superior. Don't make for trust. Rather hard on your wife.

CAPTAIN BLACKWOOD: Damn it, Richards, Fortune has saved your neck. The woman's a fiend.

NELL RICHARDS: Oh don't, it's too ghastly! Let's go, Cecil.

MR FORTUNE: (*Gently*) It's over. Good-bye.

(*Sound of them going out. Sound of him whistling the Dead March*)

Poor old Avalon. Is he satisfied? I wonder.

H. C. BAILEY

Henry Christopher Bailey (1878–1961) was born in London, the only son of Henry and Jane Dillon Bailey. He attended the City of London School, becoming School Captain and winning the Lambert Jones Scholarship, which provided him with an annual grant of £80 (equivalent to around £11,000 or $15,000) and allowed him to go up to Corpus Christi, one of Oxford's oldest and most prestigious colleges.

As Bailey graduated in 1901 with a first-class degree in Greats— Greek and Roman history and philosophy—one would be forgiven for assuming that he had had little time at university for writing fiction, but one would be wrong. His first novel, an historical romance called *My Lady of Orange*, had begun serialization in December 1900 in *Longman's Magazine* and would be available in hard covers before he received his degree. It would be the first of around thirty novels dealing with particular events and personalities of European history.

On coming down from Corpus, Bailey joined the staff of a national newspaper, the *Daily Telegraph*, where he worked in the editorial department for the next forty-five years. In 1908, he married Lydia Guest, the daughter of a Manchester surgeon, with whom he had two daughters. Bailey's role at the *Telegraph* afforded him free rein to muse on anything that interested him—from 'British pantomime in Cologne theatre' to Shakespeare, Wilkie Collins,

Lewis Carroll, the perils of smoking, Christmas traditions . . . the list of topics is almost endless. However, his journalism was necessarily more focused and purposeful during the First World War and later in the Second when his pieces damned in almost equal measure both the Nazis and Labour parliamentarians, a group that included his brother-in-law.

After the First World War, in parallel with his careers as journalist and historical novelist, Bailey began also to write crime fiction. He had written short stories since coming down from Oxford, mostly historical romances or lightly supernatural stories, including a short series about an unusual character called Quintus Harley and 'A Good Place', an eerie story that owes something to Henry James' masterpiece *The Turn of the Screw*.

In 1919, Bailey struck gold with the character of Reginald Fortune, a chatty and amiable surgeon who acts as an adviser to the Home Office. Fortune's laconic style and affected speech would be mirrored by Willard Huntington Wright when he came to create the character of Philo Vance. Fortune appears in nine novels, eighty-four long short stories, one short one and a single radio play. It is a significant and impressive body of work. For his mannerisms, Philo Vance may have needed 'a kick in the pance'—according to the poet Ogden Nash—and Fortune's are similarly grating after a while; even contemporary critics found them wearing. Nonetheless, Bailey's 'specialist in the surgery of crime' remains an important figure in the history of the detective story for the nature of the cases in which he becomes involved and the sometimes unorthodox means by which they are brought to a close. As Cecil Day-Lewis put it, 'Reggie Fortune is a monument of patience and a pillar of detection'.

Bailey also created Joshua Clunk, a pharisaical, hymn-singing lawyer who appears in eleven novels; as with Fortune, Clunk divides critics: if you like him, you like him a lot; if you loathe him, however . . .

After the Second World War came to an end, Bailey left the

Telegraph and settled permanently in North Wales, in the house where he and his wife had holidayed for many years. It was there, at *Bernina* in Mount Road, Llanfairfechan, that he died in 1961.

The Only Husband was originally broadcast in two parts on 14 and 21 June 1941 on the BBC Home Service as the last of a series of plays by members of the Detection Club. This is its first publication.

THE POLICE ARE BAFFLED

Alec Waugh

'There's no motive. That's what makes it so impossible to trace the murderer. There's nothing to hold on to.'

It was the Düsseldorf series of murders they were discussing; that grisly series of crimes committed, apparently by a maniac, upon children and young women that the German police were helplessly investigating. It was in a small public-house off the Tottenham Court Road that they were discussing it. The publican, red-faced, broad-shouldered, his sleeves rolled back above his elbows, leant forward across the bar aggressively voicing his opinions.

'Man's a lunatic, that's clear. Got a lust for killing, same as some people got a lust for drink. War started it, I reckon. Doesn't care who he kills as long as he kills someone. You can see how simple it is for him. He's walking down a quiet lane. There's a girl coming towards him. No one else in sight, no one else likely to be. He strangles her and chucks the body into a ditch. Body won't be found for hours. Days perhaps. He's never seen her before. Hasn't a dog's idea who she is. How are the police going to connect him with the murder? There's nothing for them to start on.'

His cronies, grouped along the bar over their beers and whiskies, nodded their heads approvingly.

Apart from the rest, seated at one of the small tables that

were drawn along the wall, two shabbily genteel men were listening to the conversation. They were in the middle forties. You would have placed them as members of the middle-middle class: commercial travellers, salesmen or senior clerks. One of them was burly, arrogant, wide-jawed. The other small, furtive-eyed, with a long beaked nose. They had never met before. They had just fallen into talk in the way that people do in pubs.

'That's pretty true, that,' the wide-jawed man was saying. 'There's a clear motive behind ninety-nine murders in a hundred. That's how murderers get caught. Someone's killed. It's unlikely to be in the interests of more than two or three people that that person should be dead. The police keep track of those two or three people. Sooner or later the guilty one gives himself away. If it wasn't that people were aware of that, there'd be a good many more murders than there are.'

The small, furtive-eyed man nodded.

'You've said it, you certainly have said it,' he replied.

'I don't suppose,' the larger man went on, 'that there's a person in the world who hasn't got someone in his life who he'd be glad to see well out.'

'No, I don't suppose there is.'

'There's either a relation who one's going to get money from; or a brother who stands in the way of a legacy; or a partner in business one can't get rid of; or a wife one's tired of. We've all got someone who's in our way. I guess you have, too.'

The little man chuckled, knowingly.

'I guess I have.'

'Either a partner or a relation or a wife. Usually it's a wife.'

There was a twinkle in the large man's eyes. The small man's answered it.

'Usually.'

'You're tired of her. She's middle-aged. She's lost her looks. There's another woman, a young woman, in your life. You see a sudden chance of happiness, and there's that ageing woman in the way of it. She won't divorce you, and the young girl, however much she may be in love, is practical. She's not going to give her life up to a man who can't provide her with a home. That's how it is, I reckon.'

'Yes, more or less, that's how it is.'

'And you'd be glad enough to see her out of the way, and no one who's been through the War has any too particular a feeling about the value of human life. But you know perfectly well that if you were to do anything, the police would be worrying round you in a moment.'

The large man leant back in his chair and laughed.

'It's a funny thing,' he said, 'that you, the one person in the world who wants her dead, should be the one person in the world who wouldn't kill her.'

It was said on a note that made his companion look curiously and intently at him.

'What do you mean?'

'What we were saying ten minutes back; that anyone can commit a murder who'd got no motive for doing it. Why are there so many undetected murders in Chicago? Because they're done by gangsters; because people pay other people to do their murdering for them. Take your wife, for instance. I suppose she's by herself occasionally?'

The little man laughed at that.

'By herself. I shouldn't think there was a person in the world who was fonder of her own company. What do you think she does? We live down Chiswick way. Do you know that bit of river front between the Mall and Smith Street? I thought you would. Well, every evening she walks down there alone, because of its quiet, because no one ever goes there. Stays there in the evening till it's dark. Poetic she calls it.'

The large man nodded his head.

'By herself at a lonely part of the river, every day till dark. It would be a pretty easy job for anyone who chose to wait his chance. Anyone could do it. I could.'

The last two words were said after a pause, very quietly, but with an intensity that made the little beaked-nosed man start nervously.

'The easiest thing in the world for me,' the man went on. 'I've never seen the woman; there's nothing to connect me with her. It would be as easy for me as it would be for anyone except me to walk into that small tobacconist's in Chelsea just off King's Road in Merrick Street—scarcely a soul goes in there between eight and nine—and fire a silent automatic at the old man behind the counter. As likely as not they wouldn't find the body for a good hour. In five minutes the man who'd done it would be lost in London. Anyone could do it; you could.'

Again the last two words were said after a pause, very quietly, but with an intensity that made the small man start. The eyes of his companion were fixed on his in a curious, searching stare.

'I suppose,' he went on,' that you'd be pretty grateful to the man who'd get that wife of yours out of the way for you.'

The small man began to stammer. 'I . . . I . . .'

His companion cut him short.

'So grateful,' he said. 'that you'd be ready to do anything in return for the man who did get rid of her: so grateful that you'd do anything in return. Particularly,' he went on, 'if that man were to say to you, "I'm going to do this for you. I rely on you to do the same service for me. If you don't, I shall take such revenge as I think fit." He'd be a resolute follow, after all. The man who's done one murder wouldn't stick at two, and the second murder would be as safe as the first had been. There'd be nothing to connect him with it. I think, don't you, that in those circumstances you'd feel sufficiently grateful to return one service by another?'

He had leant across the table as he spoke. The searching,

intimidating stare of his eyes never for an instant left the watering, furtive eyes of the small man opposite.

'Yes, I think you'd be grateful enough,' he repeated slowly; 'yes, I think you would.'

The little man sat motionless. He could not believe that this monstrous proposal was being made to him by this strange man whose name he did not know; whom he had never met before this night; whom in all human probability he would never see again. He could not believe that this was really happening, here in this familiar bar, with familiar faces and familiar talk around him. But those dark, resolute eyes, as they met his, seemed more real to him than that of the familiar world. He felt himself in the presence of a force that he had neither the will nor the desire to resist.

And there was the man saying, 'I see to it that no one breaks faith with me. I keep my bargains.'

Five days later the body of a strangled woman was discovered on the river front by Smith Street. The body was easily identified. At the inquest it transpired that she and her husband were on bad terms; that he had for the last year been associating with a much younger woman, who had decided, in her own interest only that morning, since the wife would not grant him freedom, to break off relations with the husband. The husband was detained by the police. His alibi was so watertight, however, that he had to be released.

In the following month an old tobacconist in Merrick Street, Chelsea, was found shot behind his counter. His nephew inherited by his death seven thousand pounds. The nephew was proved conclusively to have been that afternoon in Manchester. Quarter of an hour before the body was discovered a neighbour saw from his bedroom window a small man enter and a minute later leave the tobacconist's. He wore a dark coat and a grey felt hat. He carried in his hand a yellow cane. Ten thousand Londoners would have answered to that description.

A year later a burly, arrogant, wide-jawed man in the middle forties entered the small bar of the Trocadero. He wore a flash suit and walked jauntily. At one of the small tables a young, rather flamboyant woman was gazing up adoringly at a small, shifty-eyed man with a long beaked nose. The two men did not recognize each other.

ALEC WAUGH

Alexander Raban Waugh (1898–1981) was the elder brother of the rather more famous Evelyn. Other than for a controversial *roman à clef* about his schooldays, he is best known for *Island in the Sun*, a near 600-page novel that sets crime and romance against the background of Caribbean politics.

Alec Waugh was born in the North London suburb of Hampstead, the son of a publisher. His writing skills were apparent from an early age and his first piece, a play about Robert the Bruce of Scotland, was published in his junior school magazine, *The Jabberwock*, when Waugh was only six and a half years old. At the age of thirteen, his parents sent him to board at Sherborne, a boys' school in Dorset whose ethos and quotidian life he set out to capture in his first novel, *The Loom of Youth* (1917), which was published while he was at Sandhurst Military College. Astonishingly, it had been completed before his eighteenth birthday. Critics were divided over what one described as 'the way in which swearing is depicted as customary among small boys, the manner in which bigger boys have control, the immorality and the persistence of some masters in carrying out their personal hobbies at the expense of individual boyish ambitions'.

While *The Loom of Youth* was being both lauded and slated, Waugh did what young men of his age were expected to do: he enlisted in the Dorset Regiment in May 1917, joining the machine gun corps before heading to the Western Front.

The following March, during home leave, Waugh became engaged to Barbara Jacobs, the sixteen-year-old daughter of W. W. Jacobs, author of the famous short story 'The Monkey's Paw'. He returned to the Front and, within a month, was reported missing. He had been captured by the German Army at Arras in France and was being held in a seventeenth-century military fortress. The Mainzer Zitadelle, styled by Waugh as 'The University of Mainz', would be the focus of his first non-fiction book, *The Prisoners of Mainz* (1920), published by Chapman & Hall, his father's firm. After his release and return to the UK, he joined the firm and he and Barbara Jacobs were married in July 1919 at St Peter's, Berkhamsted. They divided their time between Hampstead and Ditchling, Sussex, and Waugh wrote extensively, contributing short stories, poetry and articles to magazines like *John o'London's Weekly* and *Time & Tide*.

Across the summer of 1920, he wrote on 'This Week's Cricket' for *The Daily Herald* and on 'Life and Letters' for *The Pall Mall Gazette*, but if his literary career was blossoming, his marriage was not; it had not even been consummated, and in February 1923, Waugh was granted a decree of nullity. He drew on the painful and expensive process of disentanglement in *Nor Many Waters* (1928), a novel in which the main character had, like him, spent time in a German internment camp. While that book was also published by Chapman & Hall, Waugh had by this time left the firm to travel. Wherever he went he found something to write about and books poured out of him—eleven in four years—and he also found love.

In Tahiti Waugh had stayed as the guest of Lord and Lady Hastings and, on returning to London, he visited their home where he met Joan Chirnside, the daughter of the owner of the biggest sheep ranch in Australia and among the Hastings' closest friends. For Waugh it would seem to have been love at first sight and, on meeting Joan again in Villefranche-sur-mer, he proposed. The couple were married a month later in October 1932. When Joan's father died in 1934, she inherited the equivalent of £10 million (about $14 million). The couple went to live in Sorrento, a suburb of Melbourne, Australia. After three months, they returned to the UK where they—or rather Joan—bought the Old Rectory at Silchester, renaming it *Edrington* after her father's ranch, in turn named after his birthplace in Scotland. Alec and Joan Waugh were happy. They travelled often—including to Morocco and America—and when at home he wrote and played for the local cricket team, while Joan managed *Edrington* and its extensive gardens. By 1938 they had three children, but the marriage was already in trouble and war was looming.

Alec Waugh rejoined the Dorset Regiment, taking a role in the Counter-Intelligence Corps and spending four years in Iraq, Syria, Lebanon and Egypt. He would draw on the experience in, among other books, *Mule on the Minaret* (1965), set in Baghdad and Beirut, and *Married to a Spy* (1976), which is set in Tangier, where Waugh had learned how to make the perfect martini from a Spanish barman at Madame Porte's famous patisserie. After the war, he returned to *Edrington* and the life he had known before. He renewed his membership of Silchester Cricket Club, meeting much of the cost of the restoration of the green, which had been requisitioned and used for growing corn during the conflict.

Having separated from Joan, more or less officially, Alec Waugh travelled extensively, becoming something of a global nomad. His books became less frequent and, frankly, less interesting until the early 1950s, when he completed *Island in the Sun* (1955), his thirteenth novel and the one that—finally—made his reputation. Set on the fictitious island of Santa Marta, it is a kaleidoscopic love letter to the West Indies, which Waugh had loved ever since his first visit in 1927. With its mix of murder mystery and colonial politics, *Island in the Sun* earned Waugh an enormous amount of money and the 1957 film—directed by Darryl F. Zannuck and starring James Mason and Dorothy Dandridge—earned him even more.

Other books followed, including a memoir of his early years, but Waugh's writing career was on the wane. In 1966 he was made the inaugural artist-in-residence at the University of Central Oklahoma, where he gave lectures as part of their creative studies programme. It was here he met the woman who would become his third wife. After Joan Waugh's death in 1969, Alec married Virginia Sorensen, the marriage taking place on the Rock of Gibraltar. She followed him as the artist-in-residence at Central State and on the end of her term they went to live in Tampa, Florida, where in 1981 Alec Waugh died following a stroke. His body was returned to London and buried in Hampstead, not far from where he was born.

'The Police are Baffled' was published in *The Bystander* on 25 February 1931, and I am grateful to the researcher and bookseller Jamie Sturgeon for drawing it to my attention.

SHADOWED SUNLIGHT

Christianna Brand

PART I

The Guardhouse at Daunton looks down over the little quay and across the bay; a long, rambling, white building tucked away into the cliffside, with a nightmare of steps and terraces and balconies and tacked-on bow windows, all lavishly bedecked with pots and boxes and tubs of flowers.

Mr Thoms was not much interested in flowers but he did like a nice bit of colour and, since 1939 when he had been obliged to lay-up his great shining steam-yacht, the *Ayala*, the Guardhouse had been Mr Thoms's summer home. Now, however, it was 'Britain is Grateful Week' for returning heroes; and though the *Ayala* might not yet be brought into commission, the lovely little racing cutter *Cariad* had been hatched out, white sails a-flutter, from the chrysalis in which she had lain for the past six years; and danced and curtseyed in the sunlit bay to the throngs who crowded the quay to look at her. Mr Thoms and his secretary, on the balcony up at the Guardhouse, also watched her, lovingly. 'She's as pretty as ever she was, Stone. She looks a picture!'

Evan Stone assented with all enthusiasm.

'And I must say, sir, it was an inspiration getting her into commission so as to race her this week—'

Mr Thoms smiled, patting his big fat tummy, stroking his little beard. 'I know the people in these parts, my boy. They've got yacht racing in the marrow of their bones. I knew they'd come flocking just to see the flutter of her sails. And so they have; and all the more pennies in our "Grateful Britain" boxes, to welcome back the boys; and all the more war bonds and saving certificates charmed out of their pockets—'

'And all the less funny questions asked about your getting your boat going.'

Mr Thoms burst out laughing. 'Well, well—I won't say that that hadn't something to do with it, too! Anyway, we shall have some fun on Wednesday; we'll give those kids up at the naval school a run for their money, handicap or no handicap!'

A couple leaning on the rail along the quayside caught their attention, 'It's Truda Dean and the boyfriend, Julian Messenger,' said Stone. 'Shall I signal them aboard for a drink?'

Mr Thoms was delighted. To have young people about him, to have noise and laughter and the gay irresponsibility of youth, was one of the few pleasures left to his rapidly declining years. He was not more than sixty-five; but the long, stern toil through which he had worked his way from pit-boy to millionaire had taken its toll, and no sooner had he retired to the pleasures of wealth and *bonhomie*, in the days before the war, than they had all been snatched away from him again; and at the earnest desire of the Government, he had taken upon himself the onerous duties of Director of Anthracite Production.

This precious week, stolen from Whitehall to be devoted, half in earnest, half in self-indulgence, to the local savings campaign, must live up to all the promise of the glorious regatta weather; and he said joyfully to Stone: 'Yes—run down and make them come in!' and, himself, leaned over the balustrade waving wildly and gesticulating towards the open front door below the level of the terrace.

*

Truda and Julian had been waiting for the bus to Cow's Bay, staring out to sea and holding each other's hands.

'Darling, *what* everyone will think of us, turtle-dove-ing in the middle of Daunton like this—!'

'Who cares?' said Julian. 'I feel absurdly sentimental. Did you know, my love, that you are an extraordinarily beautiful girl?'

She looked at him in astonishment. 'Julian, I believe you really mean it!'

'Of course I mean it,' said Julian, astonished that she should be astonished.

Truda was not a beautiful girl; unless to be radiant with charm and friendliness may be called beautiful. Tall, graceful, slender, it was only in repose that her face lost its loveliness; and since it was alight always with laughter or tenderness, with pity or love, or simply with the joy of living, no one but herself noticed its deficiencies.

Staring into a mirror. she would grieve over it, would wonder what Julian could see in her to admire, he who was so absurdly good-looking with his brown, eager face and his brown, smiling eyes, and the foolish little curl in his hair that he sought so ruthlessly to brush flat . . . And now to be told that he thought her beautiful . . . ! 'Julian, you must he in love, my love, that's all there is to it!'

In love! His heart turned over with the almost sickening intensity of it, and to hide the depth of his feeling he lifted her hand and gave it a mock-gallant little kiss. 'Julian, darling, *don't*, people'll see.'

'What do I care if people see? Let the whole world see!'

'We'll let them see after we've told grandmother, darling; just wait till then.'

'Was ever anything so crazy? Rushing down here to break the great news to her, and finding our trains had crossed and she was speeding up to London!'

'She'll be back the day after tomorrow,' said Truda. 'Meanwhile we'll just stay at home chaperoned by nannie. I couldn't bear for anyone to hear before grandmother.'

Truda's grandmother was also Julian's great-aunt. 'Apart from that, Trudie, she'd never forgive me if she found it out from anybody but me—but *us*. I must just go and make my speech to her and own up like an honest boy. You *should* have told me, darling, about the money—'

'Now, Julian, don't start that all over again. I don't care two hoots about the money. I don't want it, we can manage along perfectly all right—'

'You don't really understand about it, Truda; you've never known what it is to be hard up, brought up to a fortune by a wealthy and doting grandmamma—'

'Much you know yourself, my lad; scudding around on a captain's pay and nothing to spend it on but yourself—'

'Yes, but that's pretty well over now, and I've got to start earning a living; I've got about three hundred pounds in the bank, my love, and my wits; all in all, I think the three hundred pounds is the more valuable.'

'Three hundred pounds is a *lot*,' said Truda, heiress to thirty thousand.

'It *isn't* a lot, sweetheart; you see, you don't understand. I had no idea,' he said, giving way for a moment to a sort of exasperated despair, 'that Aunt Edwina was so *frightfully* against our marriage.'

'It's only because of our being half-cousins; it's nothing to do with you, Julian; she's got nothing against you personally.'

'Not yet,' said Julian, ruefully laughing. 'Just wait till Wednesday evening!'

Mr Thoms's gesticulating arms caught their absorbed attention. 'Oh, look, there's Thom-Thom waving at us.'

'We've got twenty minutes before the bus is due,' said Julian. 'Would you like to go in for a drink?'

'I think it would be fun. You know Jenny Sandells is staying there, though?'

'Oh, yes, that doesn't matter a bit; I mean, she was awfully sweet and nice about breaking off our engagement, it isn't as if there'd been the slightest ill feeling—' (What he could ever have seen to love in harum-scarum little Jenny Sandells when all the time his cousin Truda strolled in and out of his life with her easy grace—!)

'And Roy,' said Truda.

'We haven't seen Roy since he became the "Silver Voice of Radio"!'

'Has anyone ever actually *heard* the "Silver Voice of Radio"?'

'I don't think they have,' said Julian. 'Report has it that he puts on records, without comment, very early in the mornings!'

'You're just jealous,' said Truda, laughing, too . . .

Evan Stone appeared at the door at the Guardhouse and welcomed them in. 'It's ages since we met, Evan dear,' said Truda, her thin, brown face lit with smiles, her thin, brown hands eagerly catching his; and, 'It's *ages* since we met, Mr Thoms!' she cried, almost as warmly greeting the old man as he came forward, beaming, through the drawing-room, and led them out on to the terrace.

Julian shook hands, smiling. 'Awfully nice of you to ask us in, sir. Yes, we'd love a drink; wouldn't we, Trudie? We've got quite a few minutes before the bus goes.'

'Come over to have a look at the *Cariad*, eh?'

Julian and Truda tried to look as though nothing else had brought them into Daunton, all the way from Cow's Bay. 'We heard you were racing her on Wednesday, Mr Thoms?'

'Yes, against those boys from the naval school with their old *Greensleeves*. Mind you, the *Greensleeves* is a pretty craft, there's nothing wrong with her; we're giving them a jolly good handicap, and they'll give us a jolly good race! We thought it would be fun, you see, and bring in a little for the "Grateful Britain week". Lady Audian won't be putting the *Persephone* into commission this year, I suppose?'

Truda's grandmother would put the *Persephone* into commission just as soon as His Majesty's Government told her that it was right and proper for her to do so; no facile, excuses about 'Grateful Britain Week' for *her*.

'I expect we shall all be sailing again this time next year,' said Truda, and for the moment there seemed a flicker of uncertainty in her voice.

Evan Stone sat on the edge of the white balustrade, swinging his one good leg; the other had been injured in a flying accident eight years ago. He seemed to catch the note in Truda's voice, for he suggested suddenly: 'I daresay we could find room for these two on Wednesday, couldn't we, sir?'

'Find room? What, in the *Cariad*? Why, of course, we could! A good idea! You two must come along with us for the race!'

Truda and Julian, their eyes shining, felt it necessary to make some small polite protest.

'But I insist upon it! You'll just complete our party! You know Mr and Mrs Winson are here and the two children . . . ? Jenny and Tiggy are here . . .' Mr Thoms's voice faltered, for he suddenly recollected that the affair between Jenny and this young Julian Messenger had been recently broken off. 'Oh, dear,' he said. 'I hope I haven't dropped a brick. Now that you two are engaged—'

Truda jumped nervously. 'Oh, Mr Thoms, *please* . . .' She flushed and apologized: 'You see, it's all the most deathly secret . . . I mean, I know *you* knew, because of Julian having to—well, to ask Jenny . . . But otherwise, nobody's supposed to know. My grandmother doesn't approve—well, she's against cousins marrying and all that, you know, although Julian and I are only half-cousins; and she—well, we . . .' She broke off awkwardly.

'The fact is, Mr Thoms,' said Julian, 'that we came down to talk to her about it, and we just missed her; so we're waiting till she gets back on Wednesday evening—'

'Well, then, that's just splendid; you can race with us in the morning, and be back at Cow's Bay when she arrives.'

It was a great temptation. 'The only thing is that I don't see how we could get in from Cow's Bay,' said Truda. 'The buses run about once every four hours, and they're always the inconvenient hours! I expect you're starting off early—? '

'Come and stay over Tuesday night,' suggested Stone. 'Then we could all set off together in the morning.'

'Perfect,' said Mr Thoms, all smiles again. 'That's it, of course. Come along to dinner tomorrow night, and stay over Wednesday.' Declining all protestation, he swept his hand towards the pierhead. 'Isn't that the Cow's Bay bus? Much as I hate to speed the parting guest . . .'

As they hurried away he leaned over the balcony and called to them: 'Shall we see you at Lady Templeton's party at the Towers tonight?'

Truda nodded confirmation, turning back to wave at him. She said, laughing ruefully: 'I don't know quite what Grandmamma will say to this jaunt of ours; with "Old King Cole," as she calls Mr Thoms.'

'And all that "riff-raff", as she'd certainly call the Winsons and Roy Silver and Co.!'

'Well, one can't help admitting, darling, that though Geoffrey and Gloria Winson are rather awful—I mean they're the nearest thing to being dishonest without breaking the law—they're full of fun and vividness; and, of course, Jenny is a darling,' added Truda, generously.

'Yes,' said Julian. It was several months since his engagement had been broken off and now it was difficult to remember that he had believed himself in love with that guileless, hoydenish maiden. Since then he had seen service overseas, in France and in Holland and into Germany, and these things changed a man; they had changed a boy to a man, they had taught the man to discriminate between the casual charm of an adoring, dependent child and the true, deep charm of maturity, of poise and balance, of steadfast purpose, of understanding, generous love: of Truda!

In his half-cousin, Julian had suddenly recognized the real answer to his need; and had gone at once to Jenny and told her the truth, because it had seemed the only thing to do.

Jenny had understood and had responded immediately. Her own love for him had been too carelessly given, too adolescent, too purely romantic, to be truly binding and she had told him at once that of course, *of course*, he must be free to go to Truda, if that was where his happiness lay. Perhaps, already, the insidious charm of Mr Roy Silver had been at work with Jenny? Julian had heard that there was at least 'something' between those two . . . 'I hope there *isn't*,' he said to Truda as they jogged homewards in the rickety little old bus. 'I don't think Roy is really much of a chap, you know; and Jenny's sweet; she deserves a better type than that.'

'Jenny takes after her father,' said Truda. 'She isn't like Gloria— there's nothing of her mother in her.'

'John Sandells was a decent chap,' agreed Julian, heaving himself half off the seat to tumble in his pockets for the fare. 'Do you remember that day he died, Trudie? It's the last time we were all together.'

'I remember as if it was yesterday; and it must be—what, nine years ago?'

'Almost that,' said Julian. 'We were playing tennis on the bit of grass out at the back of their house, remember? It seemed so awful to think that, upstairs—'

But the sun was shining, the sea danced in its spangled blue dress far below the winding little road; it was impossible to think for very long of that dark day so many years ago. 'I do *hope*, Julian, that it's a lovely day on Wednesday; isn't it heaven to think that we shall be sailing again—?'

'It's heaven to think that I shall be with you,' said Julian. 'I don't care if it's sunshine or snow, I don't care if I never see a

sail again; and, no, I don't care if the whole of the Cow's Bay
bus is looking on—' It was just as well that their secret was not
to be kept for so very much longer.

Meanwhile, the female 'riff-raff' of Mr Thoms's house-party,
consisting of Gloria Winson, her daughters Jenny and Tiggy,
and Miss Pye, were also jogging home by bus, having monop-
olized, for the entire morning, the beauty parlours of that ancient
town. 'I can't think, Jenny, how you managed to spend eighteen
shillings,' said Gloria, who had spent twenty-five.

Jenny, her dark hair tortured out of its charming natural curls
by the efforts of the Taddlecombe barber, looked. 'It *can't* have
been eighteen shillings. There *must* be another two bob somewhere!'

'And what on earth have you got that mascara on your
eyelashes for? They're quite dark enough as it is.'

'You've got it on *your* eyelashes, mummy,' said Jenny, driven
to resentment.

'What's suitable for me isn't suitable for a child like you.'

'I'm not a child,' said Jenny, indignantly. 'I'm nineteen.'

'Nineteen's nothing,' said Tiggy proudly, bouncing up and
down on the seat of the bus. 'Mummy's forty-two.'

'I'm not forty-two. Pye, I wish you would keep Tiggy quiet
and not let her go screaming out these idiotic things—'

'And Pye's fifty and I'm seven,' continued Tiggy, ignoring this
outburst and bouncing contentedly up and down.

'Well, she *is* right, dear, you *are* forty-two,' said Miss Pye
kindly, for darling Gloria was so dreadfully forgetful. 'I remember
distinctly, you were thirty-four when Jenny's father died—'

'Be quiet, you fool!' cried Gloria, almost screaming it; and,
suddenly conscious of the delighted attention of the bus,
hurriedly switched on her charm, appealing with fluttering white
hands and mascaraed lashes to the bucolic conductor. 'Aren't
children *awful*? I'm forty, every day of it, and not a bit ashamed

of that, but it is a bit hard to have a couple of years tacked on, now, isn't it?'

The ancient succumbed at once. 'Ee don't look forty ter me, no, naw nawthin' loike it,' he assured her handsomely. 'More loike twenty, ee do look to me—'

'There!' said Gloria, fondly. '*Isn't* that kind?' She saved it up to tell them all at the lunch table when they got home. She would smile at Thom-Thom, that funny little crooked smile that turned his old, doting heart upside down with love for her.

She must remember to put some *Nuit de Noël* on her hands—Thom-Thom had said that never before had he met a woman with such exquisite, tiny, scented hands; and since he had kept her in perfume ever since, it was only fair—and cheap—to indulge him in his little idiosyncrasy. She waved them experimentally under the nose of the conductor, but his nostrils were full of the rich, deep odour of the Devon soil and farmyards, and he paid no heed. Jenny's blood-stained fingernails caught her attention in contrast to her own pale petal-tips. 'Jenny! The minute you get home, you're to take off that horrid varnish.'

'Oh, mummy, don't be silly! I always wear varnish in London. This is some of my own.'

Jenny, in London, at her little tuppenny ha'penny job! 'I don't care what you do at the Anthracite office, you're not coming to Lady Templeton's dance like that. Thom-Thom will hate it!'

'I don't see why Thom-Thom should be the judge of how I do my nails.'

'Jenny!' said Miss Pye, scandalized. 'How ever can you talk in that dreadful way? Considering how kind Mr Thoms is, having us all to stay down here for our holidays, taking us all to this lovely party tonight, and actually paying for—well, sending us all off to have our hair done and things—'

The Daunton-Taddlecombe bus hung fascinated upon every word. 'It's only because Thom-Thom's keen on mummy,' said Tiggy gaily, bouncing up and down.

Miss Pye's round, grey-green eyes started like gooseberries out of her circular face. 'Tiggy! Really, Gloria, the things that child says—'

'Well, why don't you stop her?' said Gloria, querulously.

'Now, Charlotte, don't you go saying such things in front of your daddy.'

'Don't call me Charlotte, Pye,' said Tiggy, coolly. 'You know I hate it. And daddy knows perfectly well. *He* doesn't mind.'

'Tiggy!'

'Well, he doesn't,' said Jenny, backing up her small half-sister, unconscious of the greedily listening crowd. 'He says let's cash in on it, while we can —'

At this point the bus came, mercifully, to a stop at the Daunton pier-head, and Gloria, torn between mortification and gratified vanity, allowed herself to be tenderly assisted down the steps by the conductor, and set off to the Guardhouse with her quarrelsome brood. Thom-Thom, watching her from the terrace, thought that she looked like some sleek-feathered, exquisite bird, escorted by her two long-legged scrawny chickens, and a fat little bantam hen.

Tiggy clung adoringly to Gloria's arm, a leggy child with a little protruding belly and two small, fair pig-tails. sticking out almost horizontally from her head; and behind them Miss Pye trudged devotedly, small, round and fussy, buttoned up too tightly in Gloria's cast-off, and highly unsuitable, clothes. Evan Stone, following Mr Thoms's glance, also smiled down at them. 'Gloria looks as though she had stepped out of a band-box, instead of the Taddlecombe bus!'

Gloria looked up and waved to them, smiling the famous crooked smile. '*What* a morning. But we're all too beautiful for words!'

They dived out of sight into the front door under the terrace, and reappeared in the drawing-room, laughing and chattering. Jenny immediately set about her own defence. 'Thom-Thom, look at my lovely red nails! Mummy says I must take the varnish off—you don't think so, *do* you?'

'Thom-Thom, can I come to Lady Templeton's dance . . . ?' demanded Tiggy.

'Dear Mr Thoms, everything has been delightful, so grateful for your kindness, such charming attention . . .' Miss Pye chimed in.

And, above all, Gloria's gentle, affected murmur, recounting the adventure in the Taddlecombe bus. 'No, Thom-Thom. I *wasn't* fishing for compliments—I'm simply telling you that this dear old man actually thought I was the children's sister! Well, very well, Jenny, he didn't *say* he thought I was your sister, but he said he thought I was twenty and since you're eighteen, it stands to reason that—well, all right, you're *nineteen* then —but the point is that's obviously what he thought . . .' She had by now quite convinced herself that this was really so.

Geoffrey Winson and Roy Silver came in from a slightly mysterious expedition referred to casually as a stroll on the cliffs; and now the party was complete. Winson was Gloria's second husband and Tiggy's father, a neat, dark, smiling man, eager and charming. Roy was half a head taller; his air of deliberate over-sophistication belied by a genuine twinkle in his blue eyes and by a small red patch on the back of his neck, which seemed to promise a little-boy-like tendency to start a nasty boil.

At the entreaty of Jenny, Roy had been 'borrowed' from the BBC by Mr Thoms to sing for national savings certificates at Lady Templeton's party that evening; and since the BBC could, all too easily, spare him, he had been granted permission to spend till Thursday morning in being vocally grateful on Britain's behalf in any form he desired.

'Good lord, Jenny,' he said to his love, administering a somewhat roistering pat on her behind. 'What on earth have you been doing to your hair?'

'I had it done at Daphne's, in Taddlecombe, Roy. Don't you

like it?' said Jenny, struggling with her wind-blown locks in front of the drawing-room mirror.

'I like it as it usually is,' said Roy; and he smiled at her and put up his hand and rumpled her hairset into a mass of tumbling curls.

'Like that,' he said. 'You look like Caro Lamb.'

'Caro Lamb? Who's she? One of your BBC girl friends?' said Jenny, naïvely jealous; and could have killed herself immediately, for, of course, Caroline Lamb was one of Byron's girlfriends, not Roy's, and had been dead for a million *years* . . .

'You're not like her at all, Jane,' said Evan Stone, laughing, and put his arm round her shoulders, leading her in after the others, to lunch. 'She was a naughty girl and a foolish girl, and I don't see the slightest resemblance.' Poor Caro Lamb had been deserted by a man she had loved with all the half-crazy passion of her wild, wild heart; the thought of little Jenny Sandells dressing up like a page-boy to stand sighing after Roy Silver, outside Broadcasting House, passed through his mind and gave an ironical twist to his lips. Nevertheless, he looked at Roy Silver very coolly and quietly, and hoped it would not be so worthless a young man who was destined, if anyone was, to break Jenny's heart.

Lady Templeton stood at the head of the great curving staircase of The Towers, receiving her guests. 'Dear Truda . . . Dear Julian . . . Delighted to see you! I'm sorry Lady Audian couldn't be here, and yet . . . What *would* she have thought of some of my guests—?'

'I think it's jolly decent of you, Lady Templeton,' said Julian, cordially. 'I mean throwing open the place like this—'

'Three guineas a head, my dear, for a good cause—'

She swept forward in her ugly, unbecoming green velvet dress to welcome eighteen guineas' worth of savings (dear George had given her an emerald pendant for so splendidly doing her 'bit'—

its value represented nearly half the collected total of the whole week, and she had added the cost of a new dress to go with it, but neither of them were conscious of the slightest inconsistency). 'Mr Thoms, how charming to see you. And your guests, Mrs Winson; Miss Sandells; er— Miss Pye; Mr Winson . . . Ah, Mr Silver, it's you who is so kindly going to sing to us tonight?' The emerald in its platinum setting bobbed and dangled against the chickeny skin of her ageing throat.

The party fanned out, moving towards the ballroom and the buffet. Jenny caught at her mother's arm. 'Oh, mummy, look! There's Julian.'

'Why, we forgot to tell you!' cried Mr Thoms. 'We were all so taken up with the results of the beauty treatments at lunch that we forgot to tell you . . . They're coming over for the racing on Wednesday, he and Truda Deane. They're staying overnight, and racing with us against the *Greensleeves*.' He hurried off to pay his respects to Lord Templeton, leaving Geoffrey Winson and Gloria and Jenny alone.

Jenny put her hand to her mouth. 'Oh, mummy! How frightful!'

'Why frightful?' said Geoffrey, accepting a whisky and soda from the man behind the bar, and leading his family out on to the marbled terrace looking down over Daunton and the bay.

'Well, I mean . . . I mean it's so *awkward*, Uncle Geoffrey! I mean, after all, I used to be engaged to Julian; and now he's keen on Truda, and I'm keen on Roy; and of course Truda's keen on Julian, too, and Roy's keen on me—'

'Do you mean to say, Jenny,' said Geoffrey, staring at his step-daughter with angry eyes, 'that you've definitely released Julian from his engagement? I told you you weren't to.'

'Well, I can't help it, Uncle Geoffrey. He released himself. I mean, the very fact that he wants to marry Truda releases him. It's only a form, asking me to let him go.'

'It's nothing of the sort. Julian Messenger's a gentleman. If you hold him to his engagement, he won't insist on getting out of it. He couldn't.'

'Well, but, Uncle Geoffrey, it's no *use*! I mean, Julian and I thought we were in love, but I suppose we just didn't know, because actually we were getting quite bored with each other and writing terribly feeble letters while he was overseas; and then when he came back, he realized that he was in love with Truda all the time, and anyway, by that time I'd met Roy again, and I was getting keen on *him*.'

Gloria sat perched on the marble edge of the balcony, small and soignée in her straight, white ankle-length frock. 'I do wish, Jenny, that you wouldn't use that dreadful expression! "Keen on him"—it's too awful. And my dear child, whatever Thom-Thom says, that plain green frock does not suit you. It's not your style, it's too old. You may as well remain youthful as long as you *have* youth.'

'Never mind her style,' said Geoffrey impatiently. 'What's all this nonsense about Julian? Did you know about this, Gloria?'

'Well, I knew that Jenny and Julian had broken things off. If he's marrying Truda, Geoffrey, I don't really see what we can do about it.'

'He's not marrying Truda, you can take that for certain,' said Geoffrey, who always knew everything where money might be concerned. 'The old Audian hag would have fifty thousand fits. She controls the money-bags, Truda and Julian being second cousins or whatever it is, and her wards—and she won't let them marry each other, that's flat. You'll see!'

'I don't see why she should be so much against it,' said Gloria, lazily. 'They aren't near enough relations for it to be inter-marriage and dotty babies and all that kind of thing.'

'Dotty babies or no dotty babies, she won't allow it. There's been too much inter-marriage already in the family. Lady Audian kept Julian and Truda apart as much as she could after they were grown up; she won't allow *that* marriage!'

'What's the financial position exactly, then?'

'Lady Audian has control of the fortune till Truda's twenty-five; then she has the power of making it over to Truda absolutely or not at all. One thing or the other. If Truda doesn't have it, it goes to a cat's home, or something.'

'What a peculiar will!'

'Well, it was her own husband's will; and he left that portion of the money to be bequeathed more or less at her discretion. She's as rich as Croesus in her own right anyway. They're all rich together, blast them!'

'I don't think Julian's got much now; and if Truda gets it all he won't have any of it.'

'He's got quite enough to go on with, I can assure you; he may not be rich by Truda's standards—she's been brought up like a princess; but he'll do nicely for Jenny, and incidentally for you and me.'

'It doesn't matter whether he'll do for us or not,' said Jenny. 'Even if he can't marry Truda, Uncle Geoffrey, he still doesn't love *me* any more. Besides, I'm—'

'If you say just once more that you're keen on Roy, Jenny, I shall scream,' said Gloria, languidly sipping hock-cup, looking about her, to see if she were being watched, and down to where the couples strolled on the wide green lawns.

They stood, the three of them, alone on the terrace, in the blue light of the summer evening; and into the gay spirit of the party there began to creep a note of sinister compulsion, which Jenny recognized only too well. 'Uncle Geoffrey, *please* . . .' She stared at her step-father with fear in her wide brown eyes.

Gloria withdrew her attention from the drink and the flirtations on the lawn, and decided that it was time to take a hand. 'This seems an absurd place to discuss it, but while we're on the subject, Jenny, I do think, darling, that you'd better tell Julian you can't let him go. After all, he was in love with you and I daresay, if he did but know it, he still loves you, sort of under-neath! If he can't marry Truda because of the, old lady, then he'll all the more readily stick to you. As for Roy, you know perfectly well that that's nonsense. Roy's got nothing but this fiddling little job with the BBC and how he manages to do as well as he does, I can't imagine. Besides, you've known Roy since you were both kids. You used to be like brother and sister.'

'I've known Julian since we were both kids, too.'

'Don't interrupt when I'm speaking to you, Jenny,' said Gloria severely, switching in a moment from kindly counsellor to outraged maternal dignity. 'That's got nothing to do with it. The point is, that Roy's as poor as—as we are; and Julian's rich.'

'Perhaps Lady Audian will disapprove of me even more than of Truda.'

'Lady Audian doesn't care tuppence who Julian marries as long as it isn't Truda; it's Truda she's thinking of. She'll be delighted to marry him off to you and put a stop to all that.'

All the light had gone out of Jenny's party. She sank back on the marble balustrade, huddled in her slim green frock, her hands to her face. 'But mummy—!'

'I can't think how you can be so utterly ungrateful,' cried Gloria, working herself up by comfortable degrees to one of her well-known rages. 'Here you have a charming, rich, handsome young man, that no time ago you were madly in love with, and you've only to marry him to put us all on our feet again. All these years we've worked for you and thought for you, Uncle Geoffrey and I; there've been times when—well, I won't go into that, Jenny, but you've been too young to know how we've suffered,' said Gloria, whose sufferings had never taken her and Geoffrey further than considerably over-staying their welcome in some comfortable country house.

'You've been too young to appreciate how we've skimped and denied ourselves, always thinking of you, and only of you.

"Darling, she's not *your* daughter, after all," I've sometimes said to Uncle Geoffrey—haven't I, Geoffrey?—but he's always replied the same thing: "If she's your daughter she's mine, and she must be cared for and thought of just as it she were my own—!'"

Geoffrey Winson tried to look as though these sentiments had never been far from his mind. 'And of course there's Tiggy,' he said gloomily.

'*And* Tiggy! Your little sister, Jenny! *She's* got to be educated somehow, brought up as you've been; and how it's to be done, I simply do not know. We're at the end of our tether now, absolutely at the end!' She stared at her husband and daughter with almost genuinely haggard eyes.

'You could borrow some money from Thom-Thom,' suggested Jenny, anxious to be of assistance.

Gloria was electrified. 'Borrow from Thom-Thom! Borrow from *Thom*-Thom! How could we do such a thing—when Thom-Thom's our friend?' She recollected that Jenny was aware of how much the sacred claims of friendship had already permitted her to borrow from Thom-Thom, and added hurriedly: 'I mean, if we borrow any more from him, we might not be able to pay him back.'

'And then he'd stop asking us down here and we shouldn't be *able* to borrow from him,' said Geoffrey.

They could not help laughing at so abrupt a conclusion to all these fine aspirations; and it drew them together a little, formed them into a band of conspirators, battling together in loyalty and unity against an unfriendly world. 'But, mummy darling, I don't see, honestly, what I can do.'

'You can marry Julian,' said Gloria, drawing her daughter towards her and taking her small brown hand in hers.

'But I *can't!*'

'But you must,' said Geoffrey. 'You must.' His jaw was thrust forward in an ugly line, he looked at the frightened girl with hard, glassy brown eyes. 'You'll marry Julian, Jenny; or else . . .'

That threat, 'or else,' had been made many times before. It meant 'or else we will throw you out, you can make your way for yourself without our love.'

Jenny's heart died within her. Gloria's much vaunted education of her daughter had amounted to little more than a few odd terms at convent schools where the nuns turned a charitable eye towards unpaid bills.

Ever since then, Gloria's dread of being recognized as the mother of a girl well out of her schooldays had kept Jenny back in the doubts and uncertainties of adolescence; had kept her unaware and inept, had drained her of initiative to build her own work and her own world. Mr Thoms's influence kept her in a clerical job in the Department of Anthracite, but that would soon now come to a close; and when there was again competition and a struggle for jobs, she knew herself entirely incompetent to take her own stand.

Life, without the sheltering chic skirts of Gloria, without the impatient, quick, half-grim, half-humorous decision of Uncle Geoffrey, was unthinkable. As long as mummy was behind her . . . She blurted out hopefully: 'Perhaps Uncle Geoffrey will make some money again soon on the Stock Exchange . . .' The Stock Exchange held the perennial hopes of the Winson entourage, right down to Tiggy and Miss Pye.

Into Gloria's mind crept a nasty feeling that Jenny might be going to prove too strong for them, after all. Why they hadn't contrived to get the child married off and safe during the long 'unofficial' engagement to Julian, she could not now imagine; but she had been busy attaching Mr Thoms, Julian had gone overseas; and nobody ever did anything for the family but herself. *I am sick and tired of poverty, of scraping and saving and cheating,* thought Gloria; and had the honesty to ask herself whether it was really not the spice of life to her.

They had had fun, she and Geoffrey, poor though they might have been. Every shock to their pride, every shift and contrivance, every shady adventure growing ever more shady as the years went by, every debt, every trick, every subterfuge, all the little cadgings and scroungings, had seemed to draw them ever closer to each other, as the world drew its skirts farther aside.

Geoffrey was nearing fifty now, and his handsome face had grown lined and grey in the struggle of the past six years; she herself, she knew, had worn better, had lost not a whit of her grace, of that facile, fatal charm. Through it, through Geoffrey's own almost equal charm, through the intuitive teamwork developed by years of association together, they had contrived to exist in a sort of unstable luxury, more often up than down. And now the end of all this uphill work was in sight; Gloria had hooked a rich old man, and Jenny had hooked a rich young one. And Jenny must not be allowed to let the young one go free.

In the gardens below the terrace strolled Lady Templeton's guests. The strains of the orchestra floated out to them from the ballroom; Roy had gone off with Evan Stone to supervise arrangements for his song, Miss Pye was, no doubt, tucking in at the buffet as hard as she could go.

Jenny saw Truda and Julian walking far below them, tall and slender and perfectly matched. They were so good-looking! So cool, so confident, so self-sufficient, so utterly unlike herself—she knew that if Julian had not been made for Truda he had not, at least, ever been made for herself. A look of unaccustomed obstinacy came into her eyes. 'I don't care. It's no use. I can't.'

'You must,' said Geoffrey, draining his glass and putting it down on the balustrade with an angry bump.

'I can't. I won't.'

Gloria was bored and irritated. She wanted to go and walk with Thom-Thom through the crowded rooms, with her little white hand in his arm; and tell him how lucky Lady Templeton was to have an emerald pendant, and how she, Gloria, had no jewellery, and sometimes did have a weak little hankering after pretty things, though, of course, underneath, in the real, deep places of her heart, she did not mind one bit.

She said angrily to Jenny: 'You must tell Julian you can't release him from his promise after all. Uncle Geoffrey's right.'

'I can't,' said Jenny. 'I won't.'

'You will!' said Geoffrey.

'I won't, Uncle Geoffrey. I won't. Mummy, *you're* not going to force me to marry Julian, if I don't love him? Surely you're not! *You* wouldn't do such a cruel and horrible thing—?'

An appeal to Gloria's better nature was always too flattering to be denied. 'Of course not, darling; of course I won't. Be quiet now, Geoffrey, Jenny's my daughter and I'm handling this in my own way.

'Nobody shall force you into anything, sweetheart; if you prefer to see Uncle Geoffrey in prison and yourself on the streets and poor little Tiggy . . .' Her voice broke at the thought of the sufferings in store for poor little Tiggy.

A tear trickled down Jenny's cheek, but she did not speak. The fear grew bitter in Gloria's mind that this child might in the end be too strong for her; that Jenny had suddenly grown up, beyond the power of all her delicate bullying, her subtle deception, her camouflaged egotism, her grasping vanity and selfishness. If only Geoffrey hadn't been so stupid attacking the child directly like this, she thought; automatically shifting the responsibility.

A new light dawned in her eyes and the honey returned to her voice. 'Of course she mustn't be forced into anything, Geoffrey,' she went on smoothly, replacing the arm she had withdrawn from her daughter's shoulders. 'I'm going to stand by her and protect her against anything of the sort. Trust mummy, darling; she's never let you down, now has she! You shan't marry Julian, my precious, if you don't want to. But, Geoffrey, I've been thinking, now couldn't we . . . ?'

By the time Mr Thoms came out on to the terrace looking

for them all, Jenny, worn out and bewildered, had promised to take action against Julian, for breach of promise.

In the great ballroom, the couples swayed to the music, the house was alive with sound and colour and bright lights, and outside the evening was a wonder of deep blue sky, and, far below the gardens, the tossing of the restless sea; but Jenny, in tears, pushed past Mr Thoms and fled through the crowding dancers to the sanctuary of a bedroom upstairs. Take action against Julian! And Truda, who detested, above all things, publicity, scandal, gossip and ugliness,

If my father was alive, thought Jenny, *he* wouldn't want me to do such a hateful thing . . . ! But her father had been dead for many years; he had died all alone while she and Truda and Julian and Roy, in brief cotton frocks and untidy flannels, had played noisy tennis on the rough grass court behind the shabby little house on Haverstock Hill.

Even then, Jenny remembered, Uncle Geoffrey had been horrid, he had made a joke while daddy had lain there, dead on his bed, upstairs. She could not remember the joke, only the horror with which she had regarded him because he had made it, because he had been able to think of a joke at such a time. It had not been till Evan came, dear, kind, friendly Evan Stone, summoned over the telephone by a tearful Miss Pye, that she had been able to give way, to cry out her eyes on a friendly shoulder. That had all been eight years ago; and almost ever since, Uncle Geoffrey had taken the place of daddy in all their lives. 'I hate him, I hate him, I've always hated him . . .' she whispered.

Then at last she made her way down the stairs, the green dress clinging, as crisp as a lettuce, to her slender young limbs. Evan Stone met her in the great hall. 'Jenny, my pet, I've been looking for you. I haven't had a dance yet.'

'Neither have I,' said Jenny.

'Not danced yet! Good heavens, and you a young lady at a ball! Come along, let's go!' As they swung into a foxtrot, he gave her a loving little squeeze. 'You don't look too happy, Jenny-pop; what's wrong?'

'Oh, Evan, I can't tell you how awful everything is. I've got to sue Julian for breach of promise!'

Evan was thunderstruck. 'For breach of promise! What on earth do you mean? Who's going to make you do such a thing?'

'It's Uncle Geoffrey, really. I've simply got to, Evan, I've promised now and I can't get out of it.'

'Surely, your mother—'

'Oh, it isn't mummy; mummy was divine!' said poor Jenny, honestly believing it. 'Uncle Geoffrey was going to force me to marry Julian, but she wouldn't let him, and she said she was going to stand by me, like she's always done. In the end, she persuaded him to let me off marrying Julian if I would promise to do this; and by that time I was so muddled up and topsy-turvy that I hardly knew what I was doing, and I said I would. It's all Uncle Geoffrey's fault, he's been doing this sort of thing ever since he married mummy . . . You don't know how awful he is, he gets you all muddled up.'

She rambled miserably on. Evan danced round with her, automatically shuffling his feet in time to the music, his mind a thousand miles away. He was forty-five, with a stubby figure, broad shoulders and a pleasant, ugly face beneath sparse reddy-brown hair. He had spent a life of activity till his flying accident had left him with a slight limp and a tendency to intolerable weariness in the face of overmuch exertion, when he had settled down as private secretary to the management of Mr Thoms's magnificent affairs.

Happy in that job, he had drifted pleasantly along until, one evening in the previous winter, he had found himself at a dinner party, sitting opposite to the woman whom once he had loved. It was twenty years since Evan had first offered Gloria his heart;

she had chosen John Sandells and afterwards acknowledged—but only in half-hints, only in tiny confidences—she had chosen wrong.

Eight years ago John Sandells had died; and he, Evan, had gone off on his record-breaking flight and, coming home, had crashed and lain for long months in hospital—and during that time Gloria had chosen again; and, once again, had chosen wrong.

Geoffrey Winson had been well-to-do in those days, but soon after their marriage and Tiggy's birth, his luck had seemed to run out; and since then—well, Evan hardly knew how they had contrived to live. Facing Gloria across that dinner-table, he had fought against the tide of his returning passion. Gloria had shown no particular enthusiasm for resuming friendly relations.

But Geoffrey Winson, as usual, very much under the influence of somebody else's wine, had hailed their reunion with delight, and persisted in spending the evening in reminiscences which, in Evan's opinion, had been much better forgotten. Gloria, meanwhile, had discovered his connection with a real, live millionaire, the biggest mine-owner in South Wales, and had lost no further time in cementing the reunion.

Evan was very soon her slave again, with all the force of his strong and simple heart. Evan could well believe that 'mummy had been divine'; in his unsuspecting eyes Gloria, for all her little vanities and naughtinesses, could do nothing mean or wrong. He could see that she must have been pretty far driven to have consented to this idea of suing Julian. Not that they'd ever get so far—Julian would simply pay up . . .

He suggested this to Jenny. I should get hold of Julian and tell him all about it. Tell him that your step-father very badly wants two or three thousand pounds, whatever it is Geoffrey needs; and then Julian can decide what he's going to do. I suppose he's got money of his own, I don't know; anyway he'll probably prefer that way out . . .' That the case would ever come into the courts, he did not for a moment believe.

Roy Silver, meanwhile, was singing the first song of the evening, exquisite in top hat and tails, clinging from sheer world-weariness to the microphone, and Edgar Thoms walked slowly through the gardens by Gloria's side, and asked himself what on earth he was to do.

It was years since any desire of his had been denied, and here was one more urgent than any he had known before. To have this exquisite creature always by his side, to warm his declining years in arms so generous and warm and white—he clenched his hairy fist at the thought that only one thing stood between himself and happiness untold. Geoffrey! That charming, feckless, penniless husband, to whom she was bound by ties of pity, and no more. Had Gloria been free she would have come to him; she had admitted that last night.

A tear had crept from beneath her gold-tipped eyelashes as she put aside her dear Thom-Thom's hand and said that, now she had told him the truth, perhaps they must part for ever. Now that he knew that she could never bring herself to desert her—her loyalties, perhaps he would want to break off their friendship . . . It could never be more than that.

Thom-Thom had at once recaptured the hand and vowed that he loved her the better for her courage and self-sacrifice, as indeed he did. He had made, there under the stars, a great and solemn renunciation; but with the morning sunshine came new hopes and new ideas and, with another night of stars, the passion for self-gratification at work again.

Miss Pye stood placidly at the buffet, all alone, eating sausage rolls and eagerly watching the throng. What lovely girls and handsome young men. What wealth, what luxury.

'But it isn't very homey,' said Miss Pye to herself. I daresay when all these people aren't here, it seems pretty empty in these enormous rooms.' Miss Pye's idea of paradise was something small and snug up at Muswell Hill.

It had been a bad day for her, really, when she had met Gloria, and fallen for that easy charm that was as readily extended to women as to men (if a woman could be as much use, for the moment, as a man). Miss Pye had somehow, without quite knowing how it had happened, been added to the Sandells' ménage.

First staying overnight; then spending a weekend; a week; and finally, gradually, moving in for good. Soon her little savings had gone, her annuity was mortgaged, even bits and bobs of jewellery had been put into pawn. '*Such* an adventure, Pye! I don't know how you dared face that awful old man—but you're so brave! And, of course, the minute we have some money, you shall get them all back!' She had got them back; and pawned them again; and got them back again.

The minute Gloria and John—and later, Mr Geoffrey—had had some money, they had all gone deliciously off to the pop-shop to get out 'Pye's crown jewels . . .' It had been fun; she had to admit that with darling Gloria everything was fun; but she was becoming tired now; it was time Mr Geoffrey kept his promise to pay back the sums he had borrowed from her, over the accumulated years.

She knew that a month ago Geoffrey could quite easily have paid her back. He had preferred to gamble with his money—and lose it all on that nasty Stock Exchange. It was too bad. Too bad. Here she was, in the position of a dependant, living on their bounty—or rather on Mr Thoms's bounty—used in a thousand ways by Gloria, nothing more than a governess to Tiggy and receiving as little thanks. It was just too, too bad. I shall speak to Mr Geoffrey tomorrow, thought Miss Pye, emboldened by Lady Templeton's hock-cup. I shall tell him I will not stand it. I shall say he will have to pay.

Roy, his duties at the microphone ended, made his way straight to Jenny. 'Oh, Roy, darling, it was lovely; your song was lovely!'

'My song was damned awful,' he said angrily. 'How can you

expect me to put up a decent show, when you spring these horrible surprises on me, just before I'm due to go on? A breach of promise case! It's too revolting!'

'Roy, please don't be angry with *me*; it isn't my fault—of course, I know it's dreadful . . .'

'On the contrary, Jenny, I think you and your family have excelled yourselves. How much are you hoping to make out of this little enterprise—?'

Jenny stared up at him, white and shaking. 'Oh, Roy—this has been such a terrible evening; I've been wandering about trying to find Julian and tell him, and when I finally saw him he was talking to Uncle Geoffrey and looking dreadfully sort of black and grim, and after that I didn't dare to speak to him about it.'

Roy said stiffly: 'You haven't answered my first question; how much are you hoping to get out of this disgusting affair?'

'I think Uncle Geoffrey needs two thousand pounds,' said Jenny, abandoning herself to the hateful, horrible truth.

'Two thousand pounds! Good lord,' said Roy, shrugging. 'I'm not a millionaire, but I'd have raised that much myself, somehow, rather than see you a party to such an act.'

'Oh, Roy,' cried Jenny, thrilled beyond words at such open declaration of interest by her hitherto somewhat off-hand lover. 'Would you really? Two thousand pounds! Would you really have given all that money for *me*—?'

But he jerked away her grateful, clinging hands, moving his handsome shoulders impatiently. 'You don't seem to realize it, Jenny, but I happened to be—well, genuinely fond of you. I may not make a lot of set speeches like your ex-boyfriend, Julian, I may not go down on my knees and tell you you're all the world to me. Well, never mind.

'I made a grave mistake, that's all. You're not the kind of person I thought you were. It's over. It's done with. I've just been a fool . . . A fool . . .'

The band finished the strains of the last waltz of the evening, and rumbled into a roll of drums to strike up 'God Save the King'. Roy stiffened to attention, padded shoulders well back, hands at his sides.

In the doorway leading out to the terrace, Julian and Truda stood, elegant, rich, well-groomed, with secretly linked little fingers. At the buffet, Miss Pye drained her last glass of hock-cup and drew herself up to attention, carefully dignified. Out in the garden, Gloria and Mr Thoms caught the familiar roll of drums, and hurried forward to put in an appearance before the dance should end; and from their several vantage points on the dance floor, Evan Stone and Geoffrey, bored with their casual partners, watched Gloria's entrance with expressions of amusement, indulgence, and a tiny, ugly pinprick of doubt.

The drums rolled, the conductor's baton lifted, the first violinist stood bow to strings . . . And suddenly, wildly, above the first deep downsweep of the national anthem, ringing through the room, came the voice of Lady Templeton, piercing and shrill and wholly uncontrolled. 'My emerald! My emerald pendant! It's been stolen! It's gone!'

PART II

The guests stood electrified, gazing at each other in stunned silence. Somebody cried: 'Stand back; give the poor lady air!' Another cried: 'The police! Send for the police!' At the door, the ancient butler had already begun, firmly though politely, to decline to allow the guests to leave. 'If I may suggest, madam, it might be better to wait until the police arrive . . . Just in case the pendant isn't found, sir—if you wouldn't mind waiting . . .'

Mr Thoms and his party worked their way towards each other and waited weary and cross until Inspector Trickett arrived and went slowly, with West Country thoroughness, through the events of the evening, the last time the pendant had been seen, the discovery at midnight of its loss. A man stood at the door to take their names, as at last they were released.

At home in the Guardhouse Sparrow was waiting up with hot soup for them. Tiggy heard the noise of their entry, and hopped downstairs on naked pink feet, taking refuge from her mother and Miss Pye behind Evan's chair. 'I only want to hear about the party. I'm not asleep anyway, so you might as well let me stay up and hear about the party . . . Jenny, was it lovely? Did you have a lovely time?'

Jenny could not be said to have had a lovely time. She said, miserably: 'It was a hateful party. We all had a horrid time,' and buried her nose in Sparrow's hot tomato soup.

'But there was a real, proper burglary!' said Roy, laughing to Tiggy.

'A *burg*alry!'

'Yes, a lovely burglary! Somebody burgled Lady Templeton's pendant away, right under our noses!'

Sparrow paused in his handing round of soup, riveted to attention. 'A robbery at The Towers, sir?' Sparrow was a local man, and everything that happened in Daunton was of exquisite interest to him.

'Yes, Sparrow,' said Mrs Thoms. 'Lady Templeton's emerald pendant was taken. It seems his lordship gave her the pendant over the weekend; It's new.'

'She must have had it in time to buy that ghastly frock, Thom-Thom,' protested Gloria, looking over her cup of soup with fluttering lashes. 'It must have been chosen to go with the pendant, it couldn't have been pure chance.

'I saw her coming out of a shop in Taddlecombe today,' said Jenny, briefly.

'A woman with hundreds of pounds' worth of emerald pendant buys her dresses in Taddlecombe!' Gloria shuddered in a manner very unflattering to Lady Templeton.

'So it can't have been a premeditated crime,' said Roy, 'if nobody knew she owned the thing.'

'I don't for a moment believe it was a crime at all,' put in Evan Stone, in his quiet, half-ironical way. 'When the old dame goes to bed she'll fish it out from among her stay-laces, and not be able to *think* how she didn't realize it had just fallen down the front of her dress.'

'No, no!' said Thom-Thom. 'She's already fished the chain out from her stay-laces; and the police definitely say that it's been cut.'

'Cor lummy,' said Roy. 'What fun!'

'And the policeman took all our names and addresses, Tiggy, wasn't that ex*cit*ing?' Said Miss Pye.

'It was intensely boring; and I'm tired and I'm going to bed,' said Gloria firmly. 'And so are you, Tiggy. Sparrow, *thank you* for the soup—it was lovely!' She never spared herself in thanks to servants, so that they forgot to mind when she did spare herself in tips.

'Good night, Roy,' said Jenny forlornly, following her mother upstairs.

'Good night,' said Roy, coldly. He put his hand to the back of his neck where the incipient boil made a scarlet inflamed patch.

Miss Pye hustled Tiggy upstairs, wreathed in good-night nods. 'Did you bring me something back in your handbag, Pye? You promised you would.'

'Yes, I brought you a sausage roll; you shall have it the moment you're back in bed. I hope,' said Miss Pye anxiously, 'that those rolls were all right, though. I wonder, Tiggy, if I'd better give it to you after all? I ate several at the party; and I don't feel well at all; and sausage-meat in hot weather is so dangerous!'

Tiggy decided to risk the peril of sausage-meat in hot weather. 'It's lovely, Pye. I can't find anything wrong with it. Do you think I'll be ill tomorrow?' She wriggled down in bed, her two plaits sticking out wildly over the counterpane. 'Do you think I'll be ill?'

On the morrow, however, Tiggy seemed to have suffered no ill effects from the sausage roll; which was odd, because Miss Pye did not feel well at all!

Julian and Truda arrived at teatime on the afternoon after the dance. Most of the others had left for the quay discussing the readiness of the *Cariad* for racing the following day, and haggling without rancour over the handicap to be given to the *Lady Greensleeves*, their only challenger.

Small boys from the naval college up the hill stood anxiously around estimating their chances against Mr Thoms' steel mast and modern hull, with Tiggy marching about among them, throwing out her legs in a very silly way to attract their attention.

On the terrace, looking down over this scene of remote activity, Miss Pye sat holding her head and still naïvely blaming the sausage rolls. 'Dear Julian and Truda! How nice to see you. They'll all be home soon to tea . . .' Her gooseberry eyes looked languidly out from her flat, round, foolish face. 'A delightful party last night (though I don't know whether quite sufficient care was taken over the catering) . . . And so exciting about the pendant! Any news?'

'No, nothing. We rang up Lady Templeton this morning . . . It was a very good party otherwise,' said Truda, politely making conversation.

'But so dreadful for you, my dears, this horrible breach of promise action Mr Geoffrey's making Jenny take. I assure you, Julian, it's nothing to do with Jenny; it's all Mr Geoffrey's idea.'

'Action for breach of promise?' cried Truda, astounded. 'What on earth are you talking about, Miss Pye?'

Miss Pye goggled distressfully. 'Surely Jenny told you, Julian? Or Mr Geoffrey? Didn't Mr Geoffrey speak to you last night?'

'No,' said Julian. He sat down on the edge of the balustrade with his back to the sea and jingled the money in his pockets. 'I don't think I even saw him.'

Truda began to speak, but stopped herself. Miss Pye wished most earnestly that she had kept quiet; however, having now gone so far, she burst into gabbling confidence. 'It was just that somehow, Julian, the subject of you and Truda cropped up, and Mr Geoffrey made Jenny promise . . . Mr Geoffrey is very difficult to resist, you know, Julian; it's hard for a young girl like Jenny, dependent on him as she is . . .'

Sparrow appeared with a tray of sandwiches and cakes, and unable to bear the sight of a whipped-cream filling, she made an excuse and scuttled thankfully away.

Julian and Truda sat looking at each other. 'Action for breach of promise! Julian, they *can't*!'

'Well, of course they can't,' said Julian, reasonably, trying to appear offhand, to thrust the whole thing aside. 'It isn't a question of whether they would succeed, or even whether they can or not; suppose they even *started*, think of all the horridness and publicity . . . !' And besides, grandmother . . .'

Julian's hands gripped the stone edge of the balustrade, till the knuckles stood out pale against the tan. 'Oh, Trudie, what a mess I've got you into!'

She looked at him, almost surprised. 'You haven't got me into a mess, darling.'

'Yes, I have,' he said. 'I—if Aunt Edwina doesn't come round I'll have done you out of your inheritance; and though I know you don't mind, dearest, *I* do. I mind *for* you.'

'If you go to her straight and tell her the whole story, Julian, she'll forgive us in the end; we've only got to do what we always intended to do anyway—just tell her straight out that we—well, that we're in love. . .'

'But it'll take time to bring her round, Trudie, and with your twenty-fifth birthday so near, when this wretched will is decided one way or the other, time's so important . . . And now if this

ghastly breach of promise thing is started, she'll never forgive
me for getting you into such a mess, she'll never be reconciled
to our marrying each other.'

Julian sat, disconsolate, with bent head, staring miserably at
the stone floor of the terrace.

'I meant to be so good to you, Trudie darling. I meant to look
after you and—and guard you, and never let you be worried or
upset; and now the very first thing I do is bring this beastly
sordid affair on you . . . And it's more than that. I know how
fond you are of the old lady, I know you don't want to hurt her
feelings by going against her.'

She got up and came and stood close to him, half leaning
against him. 'That's true, darling; it isn't the money, not a bit,
really; but I know I'm the most important thing in her life—
everything she does is for what she thinks is my good, and it
is rotten to think I should have to hurt her and upset her . . .
She's—she's old; and though she's autocratic and wants
everything her own way, well, she's awfully sweet really, and
awfully kind . . .'

She bit her lip, turning away her head so that Julian should
not see the tears that were welling up in her eyes.

'Action for breach of promise! Of all the sordid . . .' He turned
away in disgust. 'Anyway, she'll be here tomorrow evening; he'll
keep quiet till then.'

'I suppose it wouldn't be worth our rushing up to London
today and catching her . . . ? No, it's too late, the trains and
things won't do. I suppose we could ring her up, but one couldn't
possibly explain on the telephone.' She paused. 'I suppose
Geoffrey won't try anything like that? I wouldn't put it past him!'

'No, no,' said Julian quickly. 'He —he'd never dream of such
a thing. He doesn't even know where she is.'

'He'd ring up the flat; anyone can know where she lives when
she's in London. It's in the directory.'

'He won't,' said Julian, reassuringly.

Truda stared out unseeingly at the bay, sparkling beneath them with the little white yacht moored out in the centre. She said slowly: 'I suppose, Julian, it wouldn't be possible to—to buy him off?'

'Oh, *no*,' said Julian. 'I—I couldn't.'

'It would save so much distress and horribleness, darling. This is only just a try-on; he'd probably keep quiet for a couple of hundred pounds and that would be the end of it. I know it's beastly and blackmail and all that kind of thing,' but it it'd save grandmother so much extra pain on top of what we've *got* to cause her . . .'

'I haven't got the money,' said Julian.

'You've got three hundred, darling.'

'No, I haven't,' he said. 'I haven't got a bean. Well, perhaps fifty pounds, but that's all; really it is.'

'I thought you said yesterday . . . ?'

'I was just talking metaphorically,' said Julian, quickly. 'I was—I didn't mean it in exact figures . . .'

Truda went a little white, looking down at her brown hands braced against the stone parapet; but she said simply: 'Well, then, that's out darling. The only thing to hope for is that Jenny won't consent. And surely she won't? Surely she'd never do such a thing?'

'Poor Jenny's so completely under Winson's thumb; and Gloria's. That woman's absolutely unscrupulous . . .'

Truda was silent, hardly hearing what he said. Poor Julian, heart-breaking Julian with his troubled eyes and trembling mouth, who wanted so passionately to 'guard' her, as he had said, and whom she would always, delicately, imperceptibly have to 'guard'.

She was well aware that she should have told him earlier that her grandmother had declared her intention of disinheriting her if the love affair with her cousin progressed any further; but she had believed, and rightly, that he would not have allowed her to make what he thought too great a sacrifice; though she counted the loss of her wealth no sacrifice at all.

Now for Julian to feel that he had brought ugliness to their happiness, the sordid ugliness that such a man as Geoffrey Winson could throw across it, whether or not he could succeed in bringing his action . . . Poor Julian; she knew that he was blaming himself, who was blameless; and longed to tell him so, and could not because her longing was so great. Side by side, they stared silently across the bay, and saw nothing of the blue water and the blue sky; their thoughts, divided for the first time in many days, and far away from the sunshine and the coming yacht race, and the chatter and laughter of the family party strolling back along the quay.

Sparrow had seen them, however, and though Sparrow had troubles of his own, his thoughts were concentrated upon his work with all the fervour of his conscientious soul. He came out on to the terrace with the rest of the cakes and sandwiches; already he had put the kettle on the gas in his orderly little kitchen. Mr Winson and Mr Silver appeared to be taking leave of the rest of the party and branching off towards the road that led to the cliff tops over towards Cow's Bay; they were evidently going off for a walk and would not be back to tea, so Sparrow picked up their two cups and returned them to his tray.

Mr Winson and Mr Silver were pretty thick these days; there was that about Mr Winson, thought Sparrow shrewdly, that made him contented with the society of young people less sophisticated and worldly than himself; not that you could call Mr Silver unworldly, a proper lad he was, but he couldn't hold a candle to Mr Winson in knowledge and general information and experience. But Mr Winson didn't mind that. The young were easily impressed by his wit and cleverness and it didn't bother him that they were not really worth the pearls he flung. He had so many pearls; it was a pity some of them couldn't be translated into good hard cash.

Sparrow, retreating with the tray under the mute observation of Miss Deane and Mr Messenger (those two looked a bit white and funny; he hoped that nothing was wrong), wondered idly what took Mr Winson and Mr Silver up to the cliffs so much. Long country walks were not really in their line, and the pubs would not be open for another two hours. Girls, was his guess.

There were several young things up at Cow's Bay who wouldn't be above a bit of skittishness with the local rich gentry. Sparrow, though he was now obliged to live in at the Guardhouse, owned a little cottage at Cow's Bay, where his pretty little wife lived all alone, and he knew all about the lovelies of that seaside village. He speculated without much interest as he rattled about in his tidy pantry, as to which of the local bits might he luring the gentlemen so far from home on so hot an afternoon.

Dinner that evening was not a very festive affair. Julian and Truda, for all their automatic good manners, were frightened, angry and disgusted, and only just concealing it. Miss Pye had one of her periodical rows with Geoffrey, this time over his (imaginary) ill treatment of Gloria, which had ended, as they invariably did, in Gloria turning the tables in her husband's defence and siding with him against her champion. Roy, usually so full of sparkle, was black-browed and silent; the boil on his neck, now mercifully plaster-covered, was evidently coming to a head.

Mr Thoms was unhappily watching Gloria and trying to accustom himself to the idea that she could never be more at his table than a guest. Tiggy, allowed to stay up to dinner for a treat, maintained a ceaseless gabble about the doings of the girls at St Hilda's, where she had recently spent a much interrupted, and not yet paid for, term; and as soon as she had finished her pudding was banished to bed.

However, the evening was lovely and, Evan Stone suggesting a stroll along the quay, they dribbled out in twos and threes, driven to organized action by their own indifference.

Out in the sweep of the bay, the *Cariad's* white hull caught the gleam of the dying sun as she lay like a moth asleep with her white sails furled; astern of her, a little larger, shabbier, less lady-like, but polished and trimmed to mirror brightness by the boys from the naval school up the river, the *Greensleeves* also rocked herself to sleep.

The party straggled along the flat pebble road separating the beach from the land, kicking stones ahead of them, hands in pockets, slouching moodily along. Evan Stone, apparently conceiving it his duty to try to entertain them, drew them into a more compact bunch, by a description of a long-distance flight which he had undertaken early in his career, with unhappy results.

'Mercifully the natives there were very pleasant, and they looked after me till help came . . .' Geoffrey responded to his lead with interest, alone of the party quite free of self-examination, envy or distrust. What type of natives were they? Had Evan been with them long enough to get any insight into their habits and super-stitions? Jenny, trailing along, avoiding Roy and keeping to her mother's side, looked up to ask what would have happened if the aeroplane had come down on a cannibal island . . .

'I took care not to fly over cannibal islands,' said Evan, laughing.

'And anyway, there aren't any left,' said Roy, loftily.

'Oh, well, I wouldn't say that. No small islands, perhaps, but in parts of New Guinea the people are supposed to have the most disagreeable habits.'

'Besides, not only cannibals, but there are head-hunters in Borneo and things like that,' said Jenny, aggrieved at doubts cast upon the good sense of her suggestion.

'Yes, indeed; however, I've never come down among any, so I can't tell you how one would organize such a situation. It must be a nasty experience.'

'Horrible,' said Gloria, pushing her way into the limelight,
with a realistic shudder. 'One can't bear to think of it! What
would you do, Evan? I mean to say, you wouldn't have a chance
in the end, would you? So would you just kill as many as you
could before you let them get you?'

'I don't know; I suppose I would. It would be one's first instinct,
wouldn't it? Of course, there's always the chance that they might
turn round and be friendly.'

'Yes, but suppose they obviously weren't. Suppose they came
rushing at you, quite frankly waving spears, with the cauldron
bubbling away like mad in the background . . . ?' Gloria, finding
this somewhat speculative discourse on cannibals more entertaining than heavy silence, flogged it resolutely.

'Well, then, of course, the tradition is that you should take
out your false—er, take out your glass eye,' said Evan, suddenly
remembering his employer's full equipment of dentures, 'and if
that didn't work, well—you makka da firestick speak.'

'Reserving the last bullet for yourself,' suggested Julian,
looking up, smiling.

'Well, I always used to carry poison,' said Evan more seriously.
'A gun isn't fool-proof. Anything might happen to it if you
crashed; it might get burnt up with the rest of the machine, or
simply fall out as you went down. Or supposing you managed
to keep it, your arms might be damaged and you might not
make a very good shot—I should hate to add a half-successful
attempt to shoot myself to the rest of my troubles if I had to die
slowly in the desert.'

Gloria thought it was all too, too thrilling, 'Do you mean to
say, Evan, that you take a dose of poison with you every time
you go on a flight? Just cold-bloodedly like that?'

'Well, my flying days are over now,' said Stone, ruefully,
walking along tossing a handful of pebbles one by one into the
sea, listening between his sentences to their pleasant plops. 'But
I certainly always used to take some stuff. At least, I didn't so

much take it, as it just went with me. I kept it in my notecase, and I simply shoved the whole thing into my pocket before I started off, and there it was.'

'What did you take?' asked Mr Thoms, interested. 'Something quick, I suppose?'

'Oh, yes, it's instantaneous. They say people die as they open their mouths to gasp. My brother gave it to me during the last war; he was a doctor as you know, sir, and he made up a couple of doses and gave me one and kept one for himself. *He* wasn't going to die in agony on any battlefield, and it was so small that he said he could have secreted it into a German prison camp in case he couldn't stick things there. As it happened, he died instantaneously, shot through the heart at Zeebrugge, so he never had his dose.

'But I had mine, and the first time I went on one of these trips, I took it along just in case. I've never really given it a thought since then.' He fished out his wallet and hefted it in his hand, with a laugh at Jenny's round-eyed amazement 'It's in here now! I suppose I really ought to get rid of it.'

'You should throw it away, my boy,' said Mr Thoms. 'You should throw it away at once.'

'Yes, I know; and I will. I'm always meaning to, but somehow it never seems just the right moment, and each time I get a new wallet, I transfer it with the rest of the stuff and forget it again. Take now, for instance,' said Evan with a wave of his hand to the flat, pebble road, the little wooden fences dug into the shingle, protecting the cottages to their left, and the stony beach, sloping down to the sea a dozen yards to their right.

'You might say, chuck it away now. But it would lie about on the beach and some dog would come ambling along and lick it up; or a child might pick it up and eat it. One never knows . . .'

'You should burn it, Evan,' said Jenny earnestly.

'Yes, I know I should. And I really will, I promise you.'

Miss Pye trotted along beside Jenny, irritatingly hooking a

hand into her arm. 'Yet it seems a waste, Mr Evan. You might yet want to commit suicide!'

'So I might,' said Evan, laughing. 'It does seem a waste under that happy supposition.'

'No, but you might, Evan,' insisted Gloria. 'We might have a shipwreck tomorrow, in the *Cariad*: now wouldn't that be exciting? If everyone sinks to the bottom except you and me, Evan, and we're carried out to sea on a raft, dying of starvation and thirst, I shall expect you to share your last crumb of poison with me. *Will* you?'

Jenny pulled herself away from Miss Pye and, slipping along-side Roy, managed at last to detach him from the crowd. 'Oh, Roy, I *have* been wanting to talk to you. Why did you stick with Thom-Thom all the time? Now there's only a minute left.'

'I don't particularly want to talk to *you*, Jenny, if you want the truth.'

'Oh, darling, *why*? Why should you put all the blame for this horrible case on to *me*? After all, it isn't my fault . . .'

'I simply don't wish to discuss anything about it any more,' said Roy, coldly. 'It's nothing to do with me.'

'But it is something to do with you if it's—if it's coming between us. Please talk to me; please come and talk to me alone!'

They had come to the steps of the Guardhouse. 'How can I?' said Roy. 'Don't be silly. We shall have to go in now with the others.'

Gloria called to Jenny to come along. They were all going to have some drinks in the drawing-room. 'I shall come to your room tonight, Roy,' said Jenny, one foot on the steps.

'Don't be so damn silly, Jenny! Of course you can't.'

'I simply must talk to you, I shall *die* if I don't. Half an hour after everyone's gone to bed, I'll creep along the passage: be waiting for me!'

'Now, Jenny, don't do anything of the sort! What on earth sort of scene do you think there'd be if you were caught coming to my room?'

'We can go out on your balcony and talk in whispers there,' said Jenny. 'Then nobody can make a fuss. Anyway, I don't care—I must see you!'

Anything was better than this. He hesitated; made as though to go down towards the quay again; but as she followed him, returned. 'No—we must go in now! Look here, Jenny, I'll talk to you in the morning—I promise I will!'

'We'll be racing in the morning,' said Jenny. 'There won't be any opportunity; and then there'll be all the fuss of after-the-race drinks and people coming in and things; and Thom-Thom's got a whole crowd coming in to dinner. I shan't be able to see you alone for a minute . . .'

'I'll make time, I promise you I will.'

Gloria came out on to the terrace above them, and called to her daughter with a peremptory note in her tone. The less Jenny fooled around with Roy Silver the better, with this breach of promise thing on the cards; and anyway, the wretched boy was no use to her. She waited until Jenny reluctantly came up the steps at last and into the house and then returned to the tray of drinks in the drawing-room; when Roy and Jenny came in, she was already officiating with the siphon of tonic-water.

Evan poured out the gin. 'For you, Gloria? And gin for you, Miss Pye? Whisky for you, sir, or lager?'

Apparently they were still discussing the division of the poison on the raft with Evan and Gloria alone on the boundless ocean. 'Now, Evan, I must have a straight answer,' said Gloria gaily, but evidently bent upon extracting every ounce of flattery from this particular orange. 'Half the dose for me and half for you?'

Evan continued to measure out drinks. 'Well, actually, Gloria. it would be rather difficult to *divide* the poison.'

'Mummy,' said Jenny. 'You've gone and put tonic in my gin and you know I hate it.'

'Hush, darling, mummy's talking. Why would it be difficult, Evan?'

'But, mummy . . .'

Evan's voice deafened Jenny's protestations. 'Well, it's a tiny matchhead of stuff, Gloria, and I'm afraid it would get blown away by the gale—of course, there would be a gale!—while we tried to cut it in half. You shall have it and I'll die in slow torment, glad to play the hero for your sake.'

'*Mum*my!'

'You'd probably get picked up at the last moment, and that would be unselfishness rewarded,' said Truda, accepting her glass from Roy, and refraining from adding what it would be for selfishness.

Sparrow stood quietly in the background, ready to intervene if the laity suddenly grew tired of waiting upon each other, and somebody got left out.

'Oh, mummy,' said Jenny, finding a moment of silence at last, in which to make her claim heard. 'Now *look* what you've done! You've gone and done all the Gin's, and here I am landed with this beastly old tonic, just because you won't listen when I ask you.'

'What *is* the matter, Jenny? If you didn't want tonic, why didn't you tell me before?'

Julian, glass in hand, came up beside Evan. 'I wish you'd let me have a look at that poison, would you? I—I ask for a particular reason. My—my cousin died in a prisoner-of-war camp in Germany. We're still trying to find out what happened and it all seems rather mysterious. He had a girl friend who was a military nursing sister. I just wondered if she could have given him anything of this sort . . .

Evan good-naturedly opened his pocket book and displayed a white square of paper folded over the tiny pellet of poison within. Miss Pye meanwhile had come to Jenny's rescue with her own glass of gin, which, being among the first, had escaped Gloria's tonic syphon in favour of ginger ale. 'Here, you have mine, dear. I don't mind tonic a bit.'

'Now, Pye, don't spoil her. If you didn't want tonic, Jenny, you should have said so before . . .'

'Oh, good *lord* . . . !'

Roy looked on crossly. 'It doesn't seem to matter if poor Miss Pye had chosen ginger ale . . .'

'Now, now, say nothing more. Look, Jenny, I've drunk from the tonic one now; so it's too late. You have the ginger ale—I don't mind a bit.'

Mr Thoms yawned hugely. 'What a sleepy evening it is! How do we all feel about having an early bed before the race?'

Evan caught the infectious yawn. 'I think it's a good idea.'

'What time is the starting gun?' asked Geoffrey, who had kept his ears open for racing jargon all day and was entering most fully into the spirit of the thing; thus ingratiating himself with Mr Thoms.

'Midday. We shall have a snack aboard, just a rough, homely picnic,' promised Mr Thoms, whose homely picnics were attended by Sparrow and included every procurable delicacy that the hungry heart could desire. He yawned again. 'Yes, I think bed for us all.'

Miss Pye patted her mouth with a plump, speckled hand. 'I for one shan't be sorry to seek my little bye-byes. I don't like to say anything against Lady Templeton's catering, Mr Thoms, but I really do not think those sausage rolls were quite fresh. I haven't felt well all day.'

'I wonder if anything's turned up about that pendant of hers?'

Sparrow interrupted with a deprecatory cough. 'No news, sir. I spoke to the constable this evening, meeting him on the quay. The police have no clue.' He collected the empty glasses on to his silver tray; and the party, in a positive epidemic of yawning, made their way upstairs to bed.

Next morning Geoffrey Winson ran whistling down the narrow built-in stairs of the Guardhouse, 'Perfect day!' he remarked to

Sparrow, looking out at the glorious sunshine glinting over the blue water and the pretty little yachts dancing with joy at anchor in the bay. He stood in the front doorway at the top of the steps leading down to the quay, tittupping back and forth from his heels to his toes, his hands in his pockets, whistling a merry tune. Really, after all, thought Geoffrey, an excellent old world!

Upstairs, the rest of the party dragged themselves from their beds, and bathed and dressed. The house was tall, sprawling along the cliff-side and dug back into it to three storeys high. The reception rooms were on the first floor, on a level with the terrace; Mr Thoms had his suite on the second, a large roomy study, all set about with the trophies won for him in three racing seasons by the *Cariad*, his bedroom and bathroom, and his secretary's bedroom and bath; Harley Street had suggested somebody always near at hand, for the old man's heart was 'not what it used to be'.

Above this suite were the guest rooms, each with its own bathroom, one for Gloria and Geoffrey, one for Jenny, a tiny box of a room for poor Miss Pye; Tiggy had been put on a sofa in Jenny's room to leave the three remaining rooms free for Julian and Truda and Roy. Roy, who had come down for the weekend and would be leaving soon after the race, could, compared with the Winson family, be classed as a mere passing guest.

The Winson family had been there for nearly two months, Jenny coming down for weekends; and intended to remain, when Thom-Thom and Evan went up to London during the week for their duties at the Ministry. And so, it seemed to Geoffrey, they might very comfortably go on. 'In fact, I don't see why the old boy shouldn't open up the London house and have us all there. It's absurd, living perched in a flat now, as he and Evan do; Gloria could see to things for him. I must tell her to put forth a casual suggestion . . .'

Geoffrey rocked to and fro quite gaily at the thought, smoking a cigarette while he waited for his breakfast. 'If only Gloria can string the old chap along and keep him at a sufficient distance not to start complications, everything will be dandy. Then if I can screw something really decent out of Messenger over this breach of promise business, I can stall off old Pye with a few pounds and get the rest of my stuff paid up, at least whatever's clamouring for immediate attention. Really, that had been an inspiration of Gloria's, and Julian could easily afford it; it wouldn't hurt him to go short for a bit.

'And damn this ridiculous yacht race today,' thought Geoffrey, his mind wandering off after a secret and delightful new hare. 'I promised the little girl at Cow's Bay that I'd meet her on the cliffs at five, and I don't believe, with all this fuss and prize-giving and rubbish, I'll be able to make it. Pity Roy's going. He's an amusing young devil, and a party of four is more fun; the girls egg each other on! However . . . !' He shrugged philosophically, glancing out over the bay. 'The sea looks damn restive—I don't like those nasty little white waves one bit!'

He had a morbid horror of sickness, of the ills of the flesh; he could not endure that anyone should see him less than his smart, sure, self-composed, sophisticated self: in his wit and smartness and invulnerability lay all his strength. 'I wish my ruddy tummy wasn't so weak!—a nice thing if I sick up all down my nice new coat!' Ugly memories of cross-channel trips obtruded themselves with such nostalgic force that for a moment the smell of frying bacon filled him with nausea.

Miss Pye interrupted a tête-à-tête with Sparrow, and stood still for a moment listening, herself unseen. Geoffrey looked a trifle guilty when he finally caught sight of her, and advanced upon her with ingratiating smiles. 'Oh, hullo, Pye! Ready for brek?' The old hag had recently become dangerously tiresome about her fiddling little pennies. Nothing, thought Geoffrey, is so endearing to a woman as the dependence of a male; and he took a sudden resolution.

'Come down here for a minute, I want to talk to you; I want

to ask advice . . .' He handed her down the remaining few steps and pulled out a chair for her.

'I'm telling you this in complete confidence, Pye, of course, don't you dare let me down!' He gave her a conspiratorial wink as the rest of the party came trooping downstairs, remarking upon the beauty of the day but not yet sufficiently full of toast and coffee to enter into all its promises to themselves.

Thom-Thom, indeed, was for him quite crochety and disagreeable, he who was usually so benignly good-tempered. 'Throw open the windows, Sparrow, it's a disgrace to keep the room like this. It's an oven!'

Sparrow went tactfully to the windows which were already wide open, and made passes with his hands.

'That's better! What a fug!'

'It is a bit stuffy,' said Evan. 'It must be the day; however, it'll be lovely on the water. How did everybody sleep?'

Nobody looked as though they had slept very well. Miss Pye, for her first part, had hardly closed her eyes all night. 'But then I never do. I'm such a wretched sleeper . . . Insomnia; it's a dreadful thing . . .'

'You keep yourself awake, grumbling because you can't sleep,' said Jenny, who had often suffered from Pye's bad nights.

Tiggy arrived, flying down the stairs with one sandal in her hand and her parting most strangely zigzagging down the back of her head, shooting off into the two tight pigtails, one tied with red ribbon, the other with a piece of white tape. 'Well, I can't help it, mummy, Pye always does it for me in the morning, and today she wasn't in her room when I got there . . .'

'I thought you had already gone downstairs,' said Miss Pye who, having felt cross and out of sorts this morning, had summoned up courage to declare (to herself) that she would no longer be an unpaid lady's maid to Gloria and her children. She could not meet Gloria's eye, however, and repeated with a hangdog air: 'I thought you were already up.'

'Well, I wasn't because I am very tired this morning,' announced Tiggy severely. 'I had a most peculiar night . . .' She broke off suddenly.

'Jenny! You promised to keep me some strawberries from after dinner and put them beside my sofa for me in the morning and you didn't!'

'I'm sorry,' said Jenny. 'I forgot.'

'Well, you shouldn't forget. I woke up in the night and looked for my strawberries by my sofa and they weren't there . . . Oh, Sparrow!' cried Tiggy, overjoyed, 'you've remembered! 'You've kept some for me! Oh, heavenly Sparrow! Darling Sparrow!'

Geoffrey Winson stood at the helm of the *Cariad* alone with Turvey the skipper, for all the others had gone below for lunch. The long silver—grey deck with its inward-curving dark lines, stretched out before him, the crew lying face-down to lessen windage. Above him the steel mast reared, tapering, towards a cloudless sky.

The wavelets rippled and sparkled at the waterline casting up delicate feathers of spray at their bows, and astern of them came a great bellying white sail as the *Greensleeves* forged through the blue water, coming up on the weather side. Geoffrey Winson made an entirely characteristic remark. 'I could do with a drink,' he said.

Turvey smiled and a thousand wrinkles gathered about his bright old eyes. 'Better not let Mr Thoms, hear that,' he said. 'Mr Thoms don't approve of drinking aboard the *Cariad*. Many's the time I've heard him say to the young gentlemen, "A glass of sherry perhaps," he's said, "but I don't like more. Spirit warps your judgment," Mr Thoms says, "and the beer makes you sleepy." And he's right, sir, at that. I wouldn't take anything myself, not during a race I wouldn't. When it's all over—ah, that's different!' He smiled again.

Evan Stone's head appeared over the top of the companionway which led to the saloon below decks. 'I won't be long, Winson.

How are things going? Oh—oh! Coming up, isn't she? I think they were a bit generous with that handicap . . . I expect you're dying for want of food?'

'Dying for want of drink,' called Geoffrey, laughing.

'Well, give the helm to Turvey and come on down. I'll be up in a minute, Turvey.' He cast an experienced eye at the oncoming *Greensleeves*, glanced up at the sky, and as Winson handed the wheel to the skipper, turned and went below. Winson followed.

Nine smiling faces were raised as his ankles came into view on the companionway. 'I'm starving,' Geoffrey said. 'I couldn't wait another minute. The *Greensleeves* coming up, sir,' he added addressing Thoms, having carefully learned off a piece from Turvey for the purpose, for his experience of yacht-racing was less than he would have had the old gentleman believe it was. 'But she won't catch us before we've rounded the North Buoy, and after that we shall be hard on the wind. These kids from the naval school know their onions, though!' He pulled out a chair and sat down.

There was a little pile of paper napkins in the centre of the table. Miss Pye reached for one and passed it to him—with a significant smile. He gave her an almost imperceptible wink and put the napkin on the plate beside him. Tiggy appeared, making her way crabwise round the too-crowded table.

'I've been keeping an egg sandwich for you,' she recited reluctantly, holding out a plate upon which reposed the ragged remains of two shell-egg sandwiches—no powdered cardboard for Thom-Thom!

'*Two* egg sandwiches, Tiggy,' said Gloria firmly.

'I've eaten eight.' said Tiggy, ignoring this amendment; 'but I've still got room for more. I do love egg sambwidges.'

'I don't suppose the poor kid's ever had such a thing before,' said Geoffrey. 'No, I won't deprive you. You have them, baby.'

'No, Geoffrey, no,' insisted Gloria. 'She's been keeping them

for you and you must have them. She must learn to be generous,'
she elaborated to the table at large. 'She must learn to give carelessly and open-handedly, without thinking about the cost to
herself . . .'

'She must learn to be just like her mother,' said Thom-Thom
handsomely.

This was all as intended. Gloria launched into a little disqui-
sition upon her own natural generosity. 'It's nothing to be in the
least proud of. It's just the way I'm made, that's all . . .'

Julian and Truda exchanged a tiny glance, sharing the
common joke of Gloria's fantastic egotism.

'It looks as though you'd been saying a very loving farewell
to them,' said Geoffrey to Tiggy, looking distastefully at the
sandwiches. 'I'll tell you what, Tigs; you have one and I'll have
one; then we'll all be satisfied.' He crammed one of the sandwiches into his mouth and Tiggy wasted no time in following
suit with the one left on the plate.

'What'll you have, my boy?' asked Mr Thoms from the head
of the table. Sparrow, who knew Mr Winson's habits, stood ready
with a bottle of gin.

Geoffrey, however, remembered his conversation with Turvey.
'I'll just have a sherry, sir, thank you,' he replied, piously. Mr
Thoms beamed approval.

Sparrow began hastily to open a fresh bottle of sherry. Geoffrey
looked round the table, thirsty and impatient. 'What's that you're
drinking, Jenny?'

'Iced coffee,' said Jenny ungraciously, putting down her
tumbler with a little thump; during these last two days she found
it barely possible to be civil to her step-father.

'Well, I'll have a spot to wash down the egg sandwich,' said
Geoffrey, completely ignoring her sullen resentment. 'Never
mind about a glass, Sparrow—you carry on with the sherry.' He
picked up Jenny's glass, drained off what little remained in it,
and looked round for more.

Evan Stone passed across the heavy vacuum jug, and Geoffrey filled up the glass and drank it down. Evan, already on his feet, reached for the jug again, replenished his own glass, and, having gulped the contents, ran off up the companionway, and Sparrow put the newly decanted sherry at Mr Thoms's elbow. Thom-Thom poured a spoonful into his sherry glass and solemnly tasted it before passing the decanter up the table. There was a tiny speck of dust in Geoffrey's glass and he inserted the tip of a fastidious finger and brushed it out, before pouring a glass of sherry for himself.

'I think I'm still hungry,' said Roy, patting his stomach and looking round the table. Could I have, a bit more pie?'

Julian cut several slices and passed the pie across to him. Roy helped himself and passed the dish along to Winson; they each settled down to a large plateful.

There was a bowl of salad in front of Geoffrey. He helped himself liberally and handed the bowl on down the table. 'I'll make you a dressing,' said Truda who had finished her lunch.

'Will you? That's very handsome of you.'

'And Jenny will oil your lettuce for you,' said Gloria, whose careless generosity was frequently at somebody else's expense.

Jenny jerked the plate ungraciously towards her, and began pouring the oil—real olive oil!—on to the leaves, turning them over and over with a spoon and fork. Truda mixed her dressing in a tablespoon and tipped it carefully on. Tiggy, hanging lovingly round the back of Winson's seat, eyed every mouthful as though she had not already eaten a meal sufficient for a labouring man. 'That looks lovely,' she said.

'You wouldn't like it, darling,' said Geoffrey, smiling at her over his knife and fork.

'Yes, I would. I'd love it. Can I have a bit to taste?'

'No,' said Geoffrey, firmly.

They began to discuss the race. 'We'll be all right once we're round the next mark. All the same, I'm not sure that we haven't been a bit kind to them over that handicap, sir . . .'

Geoffrey paraphrased what he had picked up from Evan a few minutes before, laying down his knife and fork to explain.

'Oh, daddy, can I finish up this bit of salad?'

'No, Tiggy. Daddy hasn't finished yet,' said Gloria firmly.

'Yes, I have,' said Geoffrey unexpectedly. 'I don't think I'll have any more.' Confound it, he thought, I hope I'm not going to be sick after all!

Tiggy joyfully scooped up the remains of the salad dressing. 'It's lovely,' she said, rather pink in the face, for Truda had been generous with the mustard. 'When I get back to school, I shall tell Mother Madeleine, I shall tell her that we must always have salad and lovely salad dressing. I shall tell all the girls to have a mutiny unless we have lovely salad and lovely, lovely salad dressing . . .' She broke off suddenly, staring. 'What's the matter with daddy?'

The glass broke under him as he fell; and a trickle of blood spurted, bright and fluid, across the white tablecloth.

PART III

They had not known that human blood could be so bright, so blue-bright, spurting horribly from the severed vein, as the glass broke under the heavy head. They sat motionless, staring; only Tiggy screamed shrilly and scrambled round to her father, clasping the lolling body in little, reedy arms. 'Daddy! Daddy! What's happening to daddy? Daddy, wake up, wake *up*—!'

Julian caught her up and half carried her up the companionway to the deck. 'Tiggy, darling, don't cry, *don't* cry! It's all right, it'll be all right, there's nothing to be frightened of. Daddy's fainted, that's all, and cut his head in the broken glass. We'll look after him, we'll bandage him up and make him well . . . You stay up here on deck like a good girl, while I go down and see to him—' He caught sight of Turvey, the old skipper, standing at the helm beside Evan Stone. 'Turvey, look after the child; keep her with you and look after her. And turn back to shore at once. Make a signal that you're giving up the race. We must stop at once. Evan, come below, there's been—an accident.' He pushed the howling Tiggy into the old man's arms, and ran down to the saloon.

They sat round the table, staring. There was nothing to do, for they knew that he was dead. Jenny sobbed dreadfully, peering out at her step-father from between her fingers as though by covering her face she could blot out the dreadful sight; Gloria sat motionless. her hands to her throat in a gesture that for once was unstudied. Truda and Julian drew close to each other, with strained, white faces; Roy's blue eyes were blank in his staring face. Only Miss Pye pulled herself together with a little shake. 'We shall have to do something. We must get him down on to the bunk. Move, all move and let us get a bunk free to lay him down—come, Jenny, move—'

Jenny, stumbling from her seat, picked up the folded paper napkin on Geoffrey's side-plate and, prompted more by instinct than by sense, dabbed nervously with it at the cut, from which the blood had died down to a trickle, congealing as it dropped. Something fell to the floor, something tiny and white, but she hardly noticed it. Her foot crushed it to powder as, sobbing uncontrollably, she struggled out from the table, and put her hands to her step-father's shoulders. 'I'll help you, Pye. I'll do it.' Sparrow stepped forward with a cloth and began to clean up the table where, bleeding and vomiting, Geoffrey Winson had given up his unworthy soul; he heaped the filthy plates and broken glass on to a tray, and carried them up to the deck and tipped the whole lot into the sea. Tiggy tore herself from Turvey's kindly grasp, to run to him. 'Sparrow, Sparrow! What's happened? What's happened to my daddy?'

He wiped his hands on the cloth, seemed to polish them clean on the sides of his short, white coat, and led the child into the well, where he sat down on the leather-cushioned seat and took her between his knees.

'You'll have to be a good girl, Miss Tiggy, and a brave girl, too. Your poor daddy's gone, see? No use pretending, Miss Tiggy, is there? Your daddy was happy and jolly, racing on this lovely day, and all of a sudden, he isn't racing no more; but *he* doesn't miss it. Miss Tiggy—he don't know it's gone, and he didn't have no pain nor no fear, he didn't know what was going to happen. We don't know about heaven and that, do we?—not really; but whatever there is up there, why, your daddy knows now, and maybe he's enjoying it, maybe it's fun.

'He'll miss you all, you and mummy and Miss Jenny, but one day you'll be going to join him too; and till then I expect he'll be busy getting to know the place and settling in. For all you know, there's racing there, Miss Tiggy; maybe he has a boat of his own now, with a silver hull and sails of white clouds, scudding through the blue skies like it might be the seas down here . . . I wonder what he'll call his boat, Miss Tiggy? Maybe he'll call it after you; the *Tiggy Winkle*, eh? How would you like that, to have a racing yacht up in heaven called the *Tiggy Winkle*?'

'I expect he'll call it the *Gloria*,' said Tiggy, sniffling dolefully, but no longer abandoned to her grief.

Sparrow was much struck. 'Well, there! I never thought of that; what a silly I am! The *Gloria*; he'll call it after your mummy, won't he? But then there's the steam yacht to be thought of, Miss Tiggy. You never saw Mr Thoms' *Ayala*, what I was steward aboard; but you'll see her one day—a great white ship she is, more like a liner nor a yacht, and cabins, Miss Tiggy, why they're like little bedrooms, perfect, all tricked out in their special colours . . . And bathrooms: the very bath salts is pink or blue to match the curtains at the portholes . . . And the saloons, they're like the grandest drawing-rooms, Miss Tiggy—you wouldn't believe. Now, how would you like to have the *steam* yacht named after you?' Tiggy leaned against him, half enamoured of the visions conferred by his wheedling voice.

Gloria came up on to the deck and found them there. Sparrow jumped to his feet. She went to the head of the companionway, tearless, her face very pale. She said, woodenly: 'Thank you, Sparrow,' and put out her hand to her child. Tiggy crept to her side and stood there, her fair head gently butting her mother's shoulder as she struggled with her tears. Gloria put an arm round her.

'What has Sparrow been telling you, darling?'

'He says perhaps daddy has a silver boat in heaven with clouds for sails and the sky for a sea. Sparrow thought daddy would call it the *Tiggy Winkle* after me—but *I* think he'll call it the *Gloria*, mummy, after you. Don't *you* think he'll call his lovely new boat in heaven after you?'

Sparrow waited humbly, deprecatingly, alarmed at the endurance of his simple thought. Gloria stood, erect and quivering, staring up at the sunshine, choking back her emotion, forcing it down; and then, suddenly, as though through the blue skies she saw the glint of a silver hull and heard the long hail of farewell, she put her face in her hands and at last burst into tears.

Colonel Potts, the chief constable, was at the station on Thursday morning to meet the detective they had sent down from Scotland Yard. 'Best to hand the matter over at once and then we can't have any blame,' he confided to Inspector Trickett. His face was scarlet and his little black moustache looked as if, with a really good, big sniff, it might disappear up his nose and never be seen again.

Trickett, an enormous man with a broad, deep chest and bow-windowed stomach over thick legs in stove-pipe trousers, smiled polite agreement. He would have liked to have had a shot at the case, unaided, but old Potts was already terrified by the

theft of the emerald up at The Towers, and had insisted on the
Yard. He hoped the visitor would not be one of them university
pups, all polish and no experience . . .

Mr Dickinson was a university pup with very little experience
indeed; but at least with no polish. A straightforward poisoning
in a yacht, where, of necessity, the suspects must be few and the
solution merely a matter of motive and opportunity, had seemed,
to the simple hearts of his superiors, a cinch; and thereupon
they had put him on to it as his first solo murder case.

He shook hands nervously with Colonel Potts and Inspector
Trickett, a slender young man with bright, blue eyes and crisp
red hair and a manner half bold, half shy.

'Detective Inspector Dickinson, sir. You see we haven't wasted
any time, sir! They're checking up on the suspects and sending
the reports after me; I just had time to catch my train . . .' Thank
heaven the local chap, Trickett, looked a good old stick, a trifle
dense, perhaps . . . And could the chief constable's moustache
be real?

The *Cariad* tugged gently at her moorings thirty yards from
the quay, her mast standing naked against the summer sky;
Trickett with all his bulk disturbed her less as he clambered
aboard than Dickinson's light but land-lubberly foot. The launch
nosed gently against her sides, like a foal softly nuzzling its
mother. 'Here we are, Inspector Dickinson; scene of the drama
. . . The well, where they'll all have been sitting to watch the
race . . . The saloon . . .'

Inspector Trickett led the way down to the saloon. 'They all
sat round the table here, having their lunch. Mr Winson came
down the companionway and sat here at the head of the table;
he started on his lunch, apparently quite healthy. Ten minutes
later he vomited all over the table; and in a couple of minutes,
or less than that, he was dead.'

'What's this blood?' said Dickinson, flicking a forefinger at
the half-cleaned table.

'The glass beside him broke as he fell; he cut his head—nothing to do with the cause of death.'

'What *was* the cause of death?'

'Well, the police surgeon said it was poison: something like cyanide. He's doing the post-mortem now—we shall hear the result this afternoon.'

'Cyanide would be instantaneous death.'

'This seems to have taken a minute or so,' said Trickett, slightly puzzled. 'I suppose it might depend on the size of the dose?'

'It *might*,' agreed Dickinson, who knew nothing whatsoever about it. To change the subject he asked abruptly: 'Why murder? Why not suicide? Or accident?'

'Well, we only said query murder,' said Trickett, deprecatingly. 'But on the face of it, the alternatives seem unlikely. I mean there wouldn't be much in the way of poisons lying around in a racing yacht, one would think; and as for suicide—they were in the middle of a race. He'd surely have waited to know the result!'

Dickinson, being anything but a yachtsman, felt that with self-destruction in his mind, he himself would hardly have let the outcome of a race affect the timing of the event. He said: 'It seems such a rummy place to pick for a murder!'

'Well, I think that's rather different,' said Trickett, thoughtfully. 'These rich folks, inspector—it isn't so easy for them to poison each other at meal times, when you come to think of it . . .' (He spoke as though among the poor this was a frequent enough pastime, easily arranged.) 'Suppose it was only possible to administer the stuff in the food—why, you couldn't do it. The man sits down to table. His savoury's put in front of him by the butler, or the steward or such,' explained Trickett earnestly, having apparently but a vague idea of the progress of a well-ordered dinner.

'Then the soup, not ladled out as you or I might do it. The fish'll be handed round, the meat the same, and the vegetables too . . . No helping each other, no passing of things to one another, no forcing a certain portion on the victim ... The pudding the same. Then the horse durves.'

He looked a little puzzled. 'Have I gone wrong somewhere?'

'You want to switch the savoury and the *hors-d'oeuvres*,' said Dickinson helpfully. 'And anyway, isn't all this a bit pre-war standard?'

'Not much wartime standards about Mr Thoms,' said Trickett, grinning. 'My point was that it would only be at a picnic that rich people like these—well, living rich, anyway—would be able to poison each other in the course of a meal.'

He ran through a list of things the dead man had had to eat and drink. 'He had an egg sandwich; he drank some iced coffee; he had a glass of sherry. Some pie, some salad, and the salad dressing. That's the lot. Somehow or other, into something he ate or drank, the murderer had inserted poison.'

'What about the plates and glasses?' asked Dickinson.

Trickett confessed Sparrow's action in disposing of them all. 'It looks odd; and it's hell for us—but actually it was a natural enough thing to have done. He'd been very sick, you see. And there was the blood. The stuff was nothing valuable, just cheap crockery bought for the yacht, because it so easily gets broken in a rough sea. I suppose the man simply scooped the whole lot up and chucked it overboard. No one would quite fancy using it after a thing like that had happened.'

Dickinson shrugged. 'Well—we must talk to the steward; it could be quite natural, it could be exceedingly odd. But we shall never be able to check now where the poison was; the glasses might have told us, even if the plate didn't.' He turned to the little crowd of constables and various experts who stood at a respectful distance waiting for a signal from the great man from Scotland Yard,

'I want fingerprints and photographs—I can't have too many; you can really let yourselves go—money no object!' Under his breath he said to Trickett: 'Do they know their stuff?'

'They're the Taddlecombe police,' said Trickett, reverently; for dang it all! Taddlecombe is a town of twenty thousand souls!

The house-party sat over a listless luncheon, at which Gloria had not appeared; and only Truda showed no sign of the terrible time through which they had all passed. Her rich hair shone, as glowing and smooth as the coat of a chestnut, rounding her shapely head; her brown hands were still against the dull white of her frock, her eyes were kindly, sympathetic, sorrowful, but looked out steadfastly and without fear,

No so the rest of the party. Mr Thoms was a wreck of the fat, jolly man who had chivvied them all from that table only a little more than twenty-four hours ago; the heavy pouches under his eyes were dark with lack of sleep and his fat fingers rapped on the table a ceaseless tattoo.

Stone looked really tired and grey; and for the first time she realized that he was no longer a young man. Roy and Julian were silent, looking down at their plates as though ashamed of their hearty appetites, yet longing to eat; she thought that both of them avoided the eyes of their fellows. Jenny was puffy and tear-stained after a fresh bout of weeping, Miss Pye a mass of nervous irritation, and Tiggy looked white and frightened, a ghost of a child.

Gloria, in her room, was surreptitiously reading a novel, but even her face was lined with worry. She had paid her tribute to Geoffrey in that outburst of tears that had followed his death; but it was impossible to cry for more than an hour or two. She stuffed the novel hastily under her pillow as Evan knocked at the door; and called in a trembling voice: 'Come in!'

He came in hesitantly, and stood by the bed, holding her languid hand in his.

'I didn't sleep all night, Gloria, thinking of you and wondering if you were unhappy and—and lying awake too. You look terribly washed out. I hope you're not feeling too bad'

'No, I'm all right, Evan dear. I haven't slept, of course; but didn't exactly expect to!'

She lay back against her pillows and a perfectly genuine tear made a tiny trail down her face.

Evan gave a sort of groan, and fell on his knees by her bed. 'Don't cry, Gloria; don't cry! I—I can't bear to see it . . . It's been a shock to you, of course, but you'll get over it. You—you didn't love Geoffrey; he was only a drag on you . . . Don't let it upset you too much.' He turned his head aside, his fists closed, his nails digging into the palms of his hands.

'It—it seems wrong to say so just at the moment, Gloria, but—but one day, Gloria, you and I . . .'

'You're so sweet, Evan dear,' said Gloria, putting out a hand to his sparse brown hair and giving it a little, loving tug. She looked at him with something of real affection in her eyes.

'We can't talk about these things, as you say, with poor darling Geoffrey lying—lying dead, and having died in such extraordinary—such utterly fantastic circumstances; because, honestly, Evan, I simply *can't* understand what happened. But—well, later on, when everything is settled, we'll think about it again . . .' She left the air warm with unspoken promises.

The love and service of any man was too good to be refused, and for twenty years this man had kept alive his love for her. She watched him go with a smile; if anything went wrong between herself and Thom-Thom—and there were dangerous and difficult days ahead—the devotion of even a secretary might come in useful. She did not know that this thought was in her mind; hedged about by vanity from recognition of her nature as it really was, she only knew that Evan was honest and true and dependable and a dear—if rather dull; and that marriage with Thom-Thom, if she could attain it, was the irresistible prize; and that, if Thom-Thom failed her, she might reward Evan. Unless, of course, in the meantime someone else came along. She started to read again.

Meanwhile Jenny wept drearily in her bedroom with Miss Pye in blubbering attendance, imploring her to control herself or she would be ill. 'It was so dreadful—so *dreadful*,' sobbed Jenny, and would not be consoled.

Julian and Truda sat in the little back garden out of sight of the curious stares of the local inhabitants. 'At least now this ghastly business about the action won't come off,' they said, and eyed each other unhappily.

Roy, by the telephone in Mr Thoms's study, irritably wrangled with Trunks, who would not get him through to the BBC. 'For heaven's *sake*, don't you understand? I'm an artist, an *artist*, and I'm due for a show tomorrow morning. You must get the call through. For the lord's sake, do try again . . .'

Mr Thoms stood with his back to him, staring out of the window across the bay, and wondering when he could, in decency, speak to Gloria.

Downstairs, Tiggy, on her fairy cycle, pedalled madly through the french window of the drawing-room out on to the terrace, and back through the second window and round again.

Mr Dickinson, with Trickett cumbering at his side, came up the steps and paused for a moment to look out to where the *Cariad* nosed at her moorings across the bay. 'It's very lovely. Talk about peace . . . !' he said.

There was a piercing scream and something hit him violently in the rear. He found himself sitting in the ruins of a miniature bicycle with a small girl of repellent aspect glaring at him across the wreckage. Trickett, leaning back against the balustrade, grinned.

Dickinson hoisted himself gingerly out of the mass of pedals and handlebars and slowly rotating wheels and turned upon his assailant. 'And what the devil do *you* think you're doing, crashing into me like that? You might have knocked me over into the harbour.'

'What about what you've done to my fairy cycle?' said Tiggy

calmly, lugging the battered machine into her arms and pushing the front wheel up into his face.

Dickinson could not repress a grin. 'Well, of all the infernal cheek!' To Trickett he murmured, 'I take it this is one of the prostrate relatives?'

'It's not very bad really,' said Trickett, still laughing. He squatted down on the stone terrace with Tiggy earnestly squatting beside him, and wrenched with expert fingers at the tiny frame. 'There you are, puss; it's as good as new!'

'It *is* new,' said Tiggy, pedalling unsteadily off without further acknowledgment. Two minutes later, however, she was round again and continued as though there had been no interval; 'Thom-Thom gave it to me. It's blue.'

'You don't say so,' said Dickinson.

'One of the girls at school has got one and it isn't blue,' went on Tiggy, unruffled. 'I should think she'll be jolly sick when I come back with this one.'

'I should think so indeed,' agreed Dickinson, gravely.

Tiggy abandoned her fairy cycle and with it all ill-feeling, and thrust her arm through Dickinson's. 'Who are you?' she demanded.

'Adolf Hitler,' said Dickinson, regarding her with repulsion. 'Who are you? Are you Charlotte Winson?'

'Yes, I am, but I'm really called Tiggy because my little eyes go twinkle, twinkle, twinkle,' said Tiggy gaily, and added in gabbling recitative: 'And Mrs Tiggy Winkle's eyes went twinkle, twinkle, twinkle, and her nose went snuffle, snuffle, snuffle, and she ironed out pocket handkersniffs for henny-pennies. Isn't it *sweeeet*?'

She went out into the centre of the terrace, and there performed a couple of somersaults with an air of great unconcern. After a moment she struggled to her feet with an ample display of cotton knickers and, coming quietly to Dickinson's side, put an arm round his waist and said disarmingly: 'I'm only showing off.'

'Good lord, this is frightful,' said Mr Dickinson wildly to Trickett. 'Has the damn child fallen in love with me?'

'Yes, I have,' said Tiggy uncompromisingly. 'I love you better than anybody else in the world. Better than Thom-Thom and better than Evan and better than Roy; but I don't love you better than mummy.' She paused a moment: 'My daddy's dead.'

'Yes, we know,' said Trickett kindly.

'We think he was poisoned,' said Tiggy in a chatty, off-hand voice.

Trickett was slightly shocked. 'Perhaps he ate something that upset him.'

'No, because we ate all the same things, so if there'd been anything wrong with them we'd have died, too. He ate a egg sambwidge, but then I ate the other one,' said Tiggy, nodding a wise yellow head, 'and he ate a bit of pie, but Roy or Julian—I forget who it was, but one of the boys—ate another piece after that. And he ate some salad, but I finished up what he left on his plate, and *I'm* all right, aren't I?'

'You are indeed,' said Mr Dickinson.

'And he drank some of the iced coffee, 'but we'd all been drinking it,' continued Tiggy, faithfully paraphrasing the conversations of the grown-ups during the past twenty-four hours, 'and Evan drank some more from the jug afterwards. And he drank some sherry, but Thom-Thom tasted it first to see if it was all right—and it was, because Thom-Thom is.'

'Didn't he drink anything but the sherry?'

'No, because beer in the middle of the day makes you sleepy, and spirits warps your judgment,' recited Tiggy solemnly. 'That's what Thom-Thom says, and daddy said he'd better play up to the old buffer. What's a buffer?'

'A thing a train bonks into at the station,' said Dickinson. Over the fair pigtails he commented to Trickett: 'What the kid says is true, you know. Everything the man ate was sampled just before or just afterwards. You don't think by any chance this may all end in a mare's nest? Not poison at all, I mean?'

A man appeared on the quay below the terrace, waving up to attract their attention. 'Is that your chap, Trickett, with the results of the post-mortem?'

Trickett's backside waggled a confirmation as he hooked himself over the balustrade to speak to the man. He stood up again and turned round. Tiggy, watching open-mouthed, saw that his fat, round face was grave. 'Yes. Cyanide!' he said.

One by one the household was summoned. Dickinson patiently interviewed them in the dining-room, giving away nothing himself, patiently extracting every detail of the scene in the saloon of the yacht, fishing meanwhile for underlying motive beneath the straight narrative. Mr Thoms, Gloria, Roy, Jenny, Julian . . .

Truda, restlessly pacing the house as Julian remained longer and longer closeted in the dining-room, came at last to Mr Thoms's study where Evan Stone sat at his desk. 'I'm sorry, Evan; have I disturbed you? I'm so fed up waiting for Julian that I thought—I thought I'd have a look at Mr Thoms's trophies,' said Truda, nervously fingering the silver vases and cups. She added, hardly changing her voice, but with a look of concern in her eyes; 'You don't seem a bit well, Evan. Are you all right?'

Evan put his head down in his hands. 'I think I'm just tired,' he said.

'Did you have a rotten night? Your leg keeps you awake, doesn't it?'

'It does usually; but last night—it wasn't that.' He must talk to somebody; and he had known Truda Deane since she was almost a child, and had loved her always. He said: 'This is all rather a special hell for me, Trudie, you know.'

'I know, darling,' said Truda.

'He looked so—sort of surprised, Trudie! Sort of pained and surprised . . . It made him look dreadfully young and—well, somehow, vulnerable; and he wasn't a vulnerable person, really not at all.'

'No,' said Truda. 'He was like a—well, he was like a smooth, polished stone; emotion just skidded off the surface of him. You couldn't touch him; not really.'

He gave her a grateful look for her ready comprehension, her translation of what his hesitant speech could not put into words. 'It made it just that much worse, to see him beaten at last. God knows I didn't like Winson; I think I hated him—but I can't forget the look on his face as he lay there dead . . . It was almost—well, almost ludicrous; that's what makes it so horrible—'

Truda leaned against the window seat, turning her head to look out over the smiling sea, away from the sight of his face, from the pain and weariness and horror in his eyes. She said, knowing even as she spoke that words were vain: 'Try not to remember it, Evan dear,' and added the age-old comfortless words of comfort: 'After all, it can't do *him* any good, to distress yourself—'

He seemed hardly to hear her; at any rate, he took no notice; but after a while he said, in his groping way: 'You see—I mean, I suppose you understand about me and Gloria, Trudie? Everybody knows, of course; everybody's known for years. Even in the old days at Haverstock Hill—even in those days, Truda, though you were a child, almost—I suppose you knew—?'

'We all knew you were keen on Gloria, Evan, as Jenny would say; but so many people were! And then when poor John Sandells died, she married Geoffrey—'

'Yes, she did, but—but now Geoffrey's dead, Trudie. He's murdered! And what seems so ghastly is that I should benefit by his murder!'

Truda stared at him. 'That you should benefit?'

Was it possible, could it be possible, that Evan in his blind devotion could really believe that now Geoffrey was dead, Gloria would turn to *him*? Would give her charms to dear, dull Evan Stone with his secretarial salary, when Edgar Thoms held out plump hands, dripping with the wealth and luxury that was all her mean little soul desired? She could not believe it; and yet . . . She knew that Gloria, not dreaming that Geoffrey would soon be dead, was perfectly capable of making vague half-admissions of affection for the man who might, at some time or other, prove useful; who might, as well as not, be kept tied to her.

She looked at him, shocked and pitying; but knew that this was not the moment for even the gentlest whisper that he must not cling to such hopes. She said, playing for time: 'Well, never mind, Evan. A lot of time must pass before Gloria's out of mourning' (Gloria? Mourning!) 'and you'll feel better about it all and be able to see straight again. I mean, after all, it's not as if *you* murdered Geoffrey Winson so as to be able to marry his wife!'

'No,' he said. 'God knows that's true!' He got up from the table and came and stood beside her in the bow window, put a hand on her arm for a moment in his quiet, undemonstrative way. 'Thank you, Trudie; you're always such a clear-sighted person. It's always good to talk to you.' And, turning his back on the room, looking out over the shining bay, he said: 'I'm glad that out of all this horror and wretchedness, there is *one* gleam of brightness. You and Julian will be free now of the frightful threat of the breach of promise action—'

She stared at him, as though a ghost had suddenly opened the door of her mind and walked in; and turned and rushed out of the room.

The Daunton 'Britain Is Grateful week' went relentlessly on. The quay was left deserted of all but stolid policemen, keeping an eye on the incomings and outgoings of the party; which, since they had been, to all intents and purposes, forbidden to leave the house, were few.

Jenny came down the steps with Roy, and in silence they walked along the quay in the evening light, kicking an occasional pebble in front of them, gloomily. Thom-Thom had sent to London for mourning clothes for the widow and her children, and placed his well-filled coupon book at Gloria's disposal.

In the meantime, Jenny was clad in a georgette frock of her mother's which she had long ago passed on to Miss Pye, who had let it out in a dozen different places, and home-dyed it black. Poor Jenny had gathered it in again at the waist with a piece of tape, hidden in its turn by a white cloth belt, which had not been designed for wear with georgette, and she carried a white handbag to show that it was 'meant'.

She looked a pathetic and incongruous figure, though she was unaware of it, and her shining brown eyes were troubled by other things. She walked along gravely by the young man's side, not attempting as in other more carefree days to cling, irritatingly but adoringly, to his arm.

'Thank heaven to be out in the open, anyway,' said Roy, at last. 'I hate being stuck in the house.'

'When do you think they will let you go home to the BBC?'

'You talk as though I literally dwelt at Broadcasting House,' said Roy, crossly. 'As to when they let me go back, I can go this minute if I choose. The police have no power whatsoever to keep me here.'

'Then why don't you go?' asked Jenny innocently.

'Because it would give a damn bad impression and they've as much as said so. What did that chap Dickinson say to *you*?' asked Roy, changing to a more off-hand tone. 'You were in with him for hours.'

'Oh, he didn't say much,' said Jenny, also very off-hand.

'You—er—you *didn't* come to my room on Tuesday night by any chance, did you?' asked Roy, carelessly. 'I mean, I thought

you might have, like you said you would, to go on talking about
that breach of promise case, and all that business. I—I shouldn't
have heard you; I slept like a log that night—'

'Good *lord*, no!' said Jenny, tremendously surprised. 'Of
course, I didn't come. I mean, you said you'd talk to me about
it next day.'

'Oh. I thought you might have. I mean, you did say that the
next day we should be sailing and then I was going back to town,
and we wouldn't have a chance. And you did say you'd come.'

'Well, I—I decided not to bother,' said Jenny. 'Anyway I was
nowhere near your room,' she spoke emphatically and glanced
quickly at him.

Roy wondered who had been there that night. Someone had
dropped a small, rather grubby handkerchief; it hadn't been
there—well, it hadn't been there at midnight; and at half-past
twelve, it *had*. Between twelve and half-past, someone had come
at least to his door; and there had dropped that handkerchief
and come away. If it hadn't been Jenny . . . ? He glanced at her
face. She looked very odd. 'You look very odd,' he said.

'Odd? Why should I look odd? I'm perfectly normal.'

'Oh, perfectly,' said Roy, dryly. He took a sudden resolution.
'Jenny—you do love me, don't you?'

Jenny stopped abruptly, putting out a hand to clutch at the
rail running along the quay. 'Of course,' she said.

'I know that I said some rather hard things to you that night,
about—about the case; you must try to understand—I was so
absolutely bowled over by the whole affair. To think that you
could even contemplate such a thing; oh, I know it wasn't really
anything to do with you, I know it was Geoffrey's fault and I
knew it then; but—well, I loved you so much, Jenny, that it quite
knocked me sideways to—to see you mixed up . . . To think that
your step-father could force you to do such a thing!'

'Oh, *don't!*' cried Jenny.

'But to think that you—you having all that mud thrown at

you, written up in the papers, and made cheap and vulgar and horrible . . .'

'Oh, don't, Roy, don't,' implored Jenny again. 'Don't say anything more about it. I—it's dangerous. Everybody's forgotten now about the action, that's all over . . . Let it be forgotten, just go on letting it be forgotten.'

Roy stood staring at her terrified face. 'What do you mean?'

'I don't mean anything; I don't mean *any*thing. I'm just talking stupidly . . .' She suddenly caught his hand, looking up beseechingly into his face. 'Roy—do understand! Do try to understand! The thing about the breach of promise case is forgotten. I—well, I was angry with Uncle Geoffrey and I didn't want to go through with it and of course I should have suffered; but now—well, by some extraordinary—accident—it's over. That's the end of it as far as we're concerned. You know what I mean, Roy?'

They stood facing each other, their minds awhirl with distrust and suspicion, two young people more frightened than they ever had been before.

While Sparrow was closeted with Dickinson the family assembled on the terrace. 'Mummy,' said Tiggy, hanging lovingly over the back of Gloria's cane chair, 'what's cyanide?'

Gloria, who had decided her own official attitude to her husband's death, was intent on instructing the others before Mr Dickinson could infiltrate his ideas on the subject.

'Hush, darling, mummy's talking. Now, my dears, what I mean is this: we can't any of us believe that Geoffrey was really murdered, and I think we should go all out to prove that there was some sort of accident. I mean, after all,' said Gloria, gazing with determined courage into each of their faces, one by one, 'I mean, who out of all of us could possibly have wished poor Geoffrey dead?'

Who indeed? Mr Thoms, for one, shifted his gaze, looking down at his fat hands folded on his fat stomach; his prominent pale blue eyes flickered as he watched his twiddling thumbs. Evan stared at his changing countenance, and for the first time suspicion entered his soul. What meant this evasion of all their eyes? Surely old Thoms could not fancy himself suspected of any real reason for wanting Winson out of the way? Damn it all . . . He was devoted to Gloria, of course, with an old man's doting indulgence, but surely he didn't for a moment suppose . . . ?

Evan had known Gloria and Geoffrey too long to believe that Gloria's pandering to the old boy's infatuation meant anything but that Geoffrey was hard up and that it behoved her to cash in on anything she could get in the way of a home for herself and her family.

There had been several other rich men for her to batten on before. It might not be pretty, but it had become a necessity to them, and of course Geoffrey drove Gloria to it, had driven her for so long that it had become almost natural to her to play up. But if poor old Thoms really thought . . . All the same, a small needle of disgust and anger welled up in Evan's heart. Of anger. Not of doubt.

Mr Thoms looked up and caught the wondering glance. Poor Evan, poor boy, he looked a wreck; and Thom-Thom did hope there was not too much of a shock in store for him. He had been in love with Gloria for many years. One knew . . . one hoped he had not dreamed himself into false hopes, that he did not seriously suppose that Gloria would look at a tuppenny-ha'penny secretary, good chap though of course he was . . . Jenny, watching the two alert, suspicious faces, shuddered in her soul.

Roy, in his turn, lifted an impudent eyebrow in Julian's direction: anything to shift suspicion—if only he had not made so public his break with Jenny over the breach of promise affair; if only he had not allowed the world to think that he cared so much . . .

How the hell, now, was he ever going to get away from here, with that wretched police fellow asking them all to remain in the house, and politely hinting that though he had no powers of compulsion, it would be—well, politic to obey . . . ?

Julian caught the glance, the uplifted eyebrow, and recoiled under it. His eyes met Truda and they looked away. If only, thought Julian, if only he had not denied speaking to Geoffrey Winson at Lady Templeton's dance that night . . . Dozens of people must have seen them talking there.

Jenny, he knew, had seen them, had seen Geoffrey arguing, threatening . . . Why, in heaven's name, had he blurted out to Truda and Miss Pye the next day that he had not spoken to Winson at the dance? Why had he not had the wit to admit that he had had a few words with him, had just chatted to him casually . . . ? But, then, how could he have known that it would all become so important that he would have to—that this would happen . . . ?

And what, thought Truda, had happened to the money that Julian had had in the bank? The three hundred pounds that had been there on the Monday evening when he mentioned it to her; and had all been spent in some way that he could not admit, not even to her, over twenty-four hours in quiet little Daunton Bay! What had Julian done with that two or three hundred pounds . . . ? The filthy word 'blackmail' stole into her mind; and, banished by the loyalty of her heart, fled out again, but left a trail of slime . . .

Oh, Julian, my love, my darling, was it because of the money—the wretched old money that I don't want, I don't need? If only I can have you, and know that you keep no secret from me . . . In the depths of her heart she knew that Julian had known about the breach of promise action; that he had not been genuinely surprised when Miss Pye had told them of it on the afternoon following the dance. Had Geoffrey threatened him that night—was that why he now denied a meeting she knew there had been? Had he paid over money to shut that ugly mouth?

If Julian submitted to blackmail to safeguard the money

which she had told him repeatedly she did not care about—could that be all for herself alone? Was it not possible, horribly, heart-breakingly possible, that Julian cared more for the money, himself, than he had ever owned?

Julian also was not used to poverty: had he perhaps wanted, more than he himself realized, on sharing her fortune after they were married . . . ? She thrust aside the terrible, teeming thoughts and concentrated only upon the danger that threatened him.

If he had actually given Geoffrey his cheque and now, Geoffrey being dead, that cheque was found . . . If his bank revealed the recent, the significant, withdrawal of such a sum, and Geoffrey was discovered to have suddenly grown flush with money . . . As long as we hang together, she thought, as long as we have no secrets from each other, I can bear everything; only let him trust me, let him confide in me . . . She lifted her head suddenly, and gave him across the room her warm and lovely smile; and he turned away his face and would not meet her eyes.

Miss Pye wasted no time in self-examination. She said, 'There's no mystery at all. It was Sparrow. I explained it all to the detective this afternoon.'

Sparrow! But why on earth should Sparrow want to murder Geoffrey Winson, who, beyond tipping him rather ungenerously, had done the little man no harm.

'I don't know why he should wish to do it,' said Miss Pye firmly, in reply to, protestations, 'but I heard him whispering to Mr Geoffrey in a threatening way only an hour before we went aboard.'

'He always whispers,' said Mr Thoms. 'He's deaf and he's afraid of raising his voice in case he should be speaking more loudly than he thinks he is.'

'It wasn't so much the way he said it,' said Miss Pye, 'as what he said.'

They were all irritable and impatient.

'Well, go on—what *did* he say?'

'It was when I went down to breakfast. I stood on the stairs and watched them talking; they didn't know I was there. And Sparrow leaned forward and whispered in Geoffrey's ear: 'It's a drug!'

'That sounds more like a warning than a threat.' All the same it was strange.

'And three hours later poor Mr Geoffrey was dead,' said Pye, ignoring interruptions. 'Sparrow *mur*dered him!'

Sparrow stood in the doorway leading out from the drawing-room. He advanced into the little group, suddenly silent. He said quietly to Mr Thoms: 'May I speak, sir?'

Thom-Thom was like a schoolboy caught passing rude notes to his neighbour. 'Well, Sparrow—what is it?'

'I'm a little deaf, Mr Thoms, sir,' said Sparrow, addressing himself to a master from whom he had always received kindliness and justice. 'But not so deaf that I couldn't hear what Miss Pye has just said: that I murdered Mr Winson. I can't let that pass, can I?'

'No, no. Get on with it, man.'

'I just wish to say that I had no motive to murder Mr Winson, sir; and I did not do so. I had no means of doing so. But, since Miss Pye thinks fit to accuse me, sir, I think I should be permitted to point out that Miss Pye had a very odd conversation at breakfast on the morning of the death. She and Mr Winson were whispering together at the table, before the rest of the party came down; I did not listen to what they were saying, naturally, Mr Thoms—but there's no doubt Mr Winson did say: "I trust you; don't tell anyone else"—or some such words. I wouldn't have said anything about it, if Miss Pye had not thought fit to say what she has about me.' He gave a little half bow to his employer, and looked straight into Miss Pye's face.

Tiggy was playing with an aged rag doll to whom she was administering choking doses of earth from the geranium boxes that bordered the terrace; tipping it forward on to its face with a frightful, slumping collapse. So did she exorcize from her subconscious that haunting memory of her father's death. She left her play to stand staring solemnly at Sparrow, her arm hooked over the back of her mother's chair. 'Mummy—was it Sparrow who gave daddy cyanide?'

'Tiggy, be quiet. Sparrow, I'm sure,' said Gloria earnestly, 'I'm *sure* that Miss Pye didn't mean to accuse you of anything. We're all upset and nervous over this dreadful thing that has happened, but of course we know it was nothing in the end but an accident. We've quite decided that. What the detective thinks, we don't know and we don't care,' said Gloria, dismissing Mr Dickinson with a wave of her hand, 'but we who knew him realize that poor Mr Winson just took something by mistake, thinking it was something else. Perhaps a chocolate or something, while he was up on deck with Turvey.'

'What did he mistake the chocolate for?' asked Roy, politely ironical. 'And besides, Turvey says that Geoffrey ate nothing while they were on deck together. No, I don't think that will work!'

'Perhaps Turvey himself . . .' suggested Miss Pye, evidently determined to confine the subjects to the lower deck.

Roy swivelled round upon her. 'Really, Miss Pye, you put my trusting heart to shame, indeed you do. Dear old Turvey, with his blue, blue eyes and his face like Hamm marshalling yards without their rolling stock . . . The vision of Turvey, fishing in the recesses of his oilskin for a lethal dose of poison, is really rather sweet . . .' He tipped his chair gaily backwards.

'I can't think why you want to suggest that *any*one murdered him,' said Gloria, plaintively. 'It is so tiresome of you, Pye, when we're just getting it decided that the whole thing was an accident . . . I think we should all just sort of suggest to the inspector that Geoffrey suffered from—from indigestion, or something like that; and that he probably took some stuff aboard with him and took a dose . . .'

'But Uncle Geoffrey never *did* get indigestion,' said Jenny; and under her mother's indignant eye fell silent.

'So that's what *I* think happened,' said Gloria, firmly fixing them all with a bright, compelling eye. 'I think darling Geoffrey smuggled some indigestion stuff aboard, and the chemist had given him the wrong thing, some chemist in London, that we've quite forgotten about . . .

'Mummy,' said Tiggy. 'Do answer me—*what's* cyanide?'

Evan Stone with a sudden, swift gesture, tore the wallet from his breast pocket, and opening it out on the table before him, searched through it with shaking hands. Letters, photographs, two or three bills, a couple of five-pound notes . . . 'Cyanide! It was cyanide that my brother gave me, it was cyanide I carried with me on my flight to the Cape . . . I didn't realize, I didn't think, I'd forgotten all about it . . .' His pleasant, ugly face was scarlet by the time he had found what he wanted and spread it out before them: a tiny square of paper that had been folded into a sort of envelope, but now lay creased and empty before their eyes. 'It was cyanide! And it's gone!' he said.

PART IV

The little square of paper lay on the table, its creased corners fluttering in the breeze. Evan Stone put out his hand to hold it still. He said again: 'It's gone! The poison's gone!'

'It was there that night,' said Julian, rushing without reflection into speech. 'The night you told us about it. The night before— Geoffrey died. I saw it. You remember, after we came in from our walk? You showed it to me.'

They turned upon him curious eyes; faintly hostile, faintly frightened eyes. Gloria put the thoughts of them all into words when she said—but deprecatingly: 'So actually *you* were the last to see it, Julian!'

'Except me,' said Evan swiftly. 'I wrapped it up again in the paper and put it safely away in my wallet. *I* was the last to see it, or touch it. And now it has vanished!'

'Who else knew you had the stuff, Evan?' said Roy, in a consciously conversational tone. 'Besides us, I mean, of course.'

'I don't suppose anyone knew,' said Evan at once. 'I'd forgotten about it myself till the subject cropped up on Tuesday night. I don't suppose I'd mentioned it to a soul for years.'

'So that only us . . .' Jenny looked round at the little group on the terrace, clustered about the table. Gloria, Mr Thoms, Evan, Julian and Truda, Roy and Miss Pye . . . . Only the eight of us knew that it was there?'

'And Sparrow,' said Roy. 'Poor old Sparrow keeps getting himself accused of all sorts of things, so he may as well come in here too. He was standing by with the drinks when Evan showed the poison to Julian.'

There was no pretence any longer of its having been an accident. Murder stared them in the eyes, and they dropped their own before it.

'So that between—between ten o'clock that night and lunchtime the next day—somebody went to Evan's pocket-book. One of *us!*'

'I don't know how you can say such things, Jenny,' said Gloria, almost tearfully. 'How can you be so—so *crude*?'

'Uncle Geoffrey was murdered.' said Jenny sternly. 'We all saw him die, and it was—horrible. I'll never forget it. And I don't think we ought to pretend about it any more. If one of us killed him I think we ought to let it be found out.'

'You didn't exactly love him yourself, Jenny,' said Roy.

'No, I didn't sometimes. But usually I did; usually I was quite friends with him . . . Wasn't I, mummy?'

'He was like a father to you, Jenny. "Geoffrey," I've sometimes said to him, "it isn't as though Jenny was your own daughter," but he's always said . . .'

'"Jenny's your daughter—I look upon her as my own,"' finished Jenny, with a gleam of irony.

'Yes. Actually,' said Miss Pye, raising green gooseberry eyes nervously to Gloria, 'what Geoffrey always said on these occasions was: "She's *John's* daughter—and I'll look after her as though she were my own." Jenny's father was so fond of Geoffrey; and of you too, Evan dear,' said Miss Pye hurriedly, as though Evan might feel aggrieved at this preference between the three friends.

Evan did not seem inclined to discuss the subject. He returned to the disappearance of the cyanide from his pocket-book.

'It was there in my pocket-book that evening; Julian saw me put it back. My pocket-book was in my brown coat all night, hanging over the back of a chair, and in the morning I moved it to my reefer jacket, when I was dressing to go sailing. After that . . .' He shrugged. It was obviously impossible that the poison could have been taken from him while he wore the coat.

Sparrow emerged from the drawing-room with the silver tray of drinks and put it down on the table; he noticed the little square of paper and, apparently without recognition, picked it up and was rolling it into a ball preparatory to throwing it away when Evan Stone caught his wrist. 'Better leave that, Sparrow. It's . . .' He glanced at Mr Thoms. 'We're all in this; I'd better tell Sparrow, sir, I think . . .

Evan gave the little man a rapid outline of the discovery that the poison was missing.

Sparrow was thunderstruck. 'Good *lor*', sir!' He stood by quietly, his hands hanging, twitching a little, at the sides of his coat. 'That'll mean, sir, that the stuff was took overnight from your room.'

They had not had time yet to think of that.

'Do you really mean to suggest,' cried Thom-Thom in despair at these dreadful goings-on in his quiet house, 'that somebody went along to Mr Stone's room and *stole* the stuff . . . ?'

'It does seem like that, sir,' said Sparrow humbly, rather shaken by the storm he had caused.

'Come to think of it,' said Evan, 'I did sleep very soundly that night. Usually I lie awake a lot because this ruddy leg of mine begins to ache . . . But on Tuesday night, I do believe that anyone could have come into my room and I shouldn't have heard a thing.'

Jenny sat with her hand to her mouth, staring horrified at Evan's face; Julian and Truda exchanged a look, which, for the first time in many hours, held something of frankness, something of renewed understanding and trust. Roy perched on the edge of the balustrade jauntily swinging a shoe. His face was white and somehow rather ugly, and the boils on the back of his elegant neck—there were two of them now—retained in him that engaging, slightly pathetic little-boy air.

Mr Thoms said: 'So that really anyone . . .'

'Any of *us* . . .' said Julian steadily; but he did not look as though the words meant anything to him.

Any of us! They stared at each other anew. *Any of us!* Mr Thoms said abruptly but carefully: 'Were you in the house on Tuesday night, Sparrow?'

No offence taken where none intended, Sparrow said quietly: 'No, sir. If you remember I had permission to go home for the night. I waited till the drinks had been cleared, sir, and then I bicycled out to Cow's Bay.'

'That's where your home is, isn't it, Sparrow?'

'Yes, sir. I slept at home that night and bicycled back in the early morning to get the breakfast.'

'Well, that lets *you* out, Sparrow,' said Evan with an air of relief. 'I daresay your wife can confirm your having spent the whole night in the cottage.'

Sparrow's face changed a little. 'Well, no, sir. Mrs Sparrow did not come home that night.'

'You mean you spent the night there alone?'

'Yes, sir,' said Sparrow.

It seemed an odd idea to bicycle ten miles out to spend the night by oneself in a lonely cottage, and bicycle back ten miles in the early dawn. Evan suggested as much, but kindly, to Sparrow. 'The police will ask you this, you know. What was the idea?'

'I expected Mrs Sparrow to be at home, sir.' The little man gave a sort of gulp. He repeated stiffly: 'I stayed in the cottage alone.'

Evan did not press his questions; that was up to the police if they cared to try. He said to Mr Thoms: 'You didn't hear anything that night, sir? Your room being opposite mine you might have heard someone in the corridor . . .'

'No. I also slept heavily that night,' said Thom-Thom, wheezing a little, putting out his hand to his dry martini, which up till now he had entirely forgotten.

Everyone, it seemed, had slept exceptionally well that night. Miss Pye, usually such a martyr to insomnia, confessed that she had dreamed the whole night through. 'Quite extraordinary for me,' she declared, looking at them over the rim of her glass.

'Of course, I must admit I had not felt very well all day. I fear there was something *not* quite right with those sausages at Lady Templeton's ball; I've said so all along; I felt quite unwell all Tuesday, and even on Wednesday morning I woke up still feeling stuffy and headachy . . .'

Stuffy and headachy . . . 'Open the windows, Sparrow, this room's like an oven . . .' That had been Mr Thoms. Evan had said: 'It does feel a bit stuffy; it must be the day . . .' And yet the windows had been wide open all the time. Mr Thoms, with his uneasy heart that so often kept him breathless and awake; Evan, with his aching leg; Miss Pye, 'a martyr to insomnia'—they had all slept heavily that night—that particular night of all nights in the year—and awoken 'stuffy and headachy . . .'

*

Mr Dickinson, arriving next morning to conduct them to the inquest upon the remains of Geoffrey Winson, was met by their united insistence that on the evening before the murder, some at least of the party had been drugged!

'Drugged! When on earth could you have been drugged?'

'Somebody must have put it in our coffee after dinner,' said Gloria.

'But you all went out for a walk after dinner; you'd have felt drowsy early on in the evening. *Did* any one?'

Everyone immediately had a distinct memory of being particularly drowsy on the walk along the seashore that night; the pictures faded quickly, however, leaving them all with sensible convictions that nothing of the sort had happened. 'But we all had drinks when we came in,' said Mr Thoms. 'It's more likely to have happened then.'

'Who dispensed these drinks?' asked Mr Dickinson, glancing at his watch, for it would soon be time to start.

Everyone had dispensed the drinks: poured them out or passed them or exchanged them, or even just been near enough to them to slip in a few drops of fluid, a quick-dissolving tablet. They went hurriedly through the history of that half-hour before they had all gone up to bed. 'Did anyone go to their room between the walk and you all meeting in the drawing-room for drinks?'

But nobody had. They had all gone together up the steps and into the drawing-room, except for Jenny and Roy, who, however, had been together till they also had joined the party. Mr Dickinson scratched his wild red head and admitted that it was really most extraordinary: *most* extraordinary! In his heart he was inclined to consider it the most extraordinary thing that had happened yet. 'However, I really think we all ought to be getting along . . .' He tucked it away for discussion with Trickett later on.

*

Left at home, Tiggy squatted happily on the bed in Roy's room, applying a moustache of vermilion lipstick to her upper lip. At the sound of approaching footsteps, she dived beneath the eiderdown in an ostrich-like effort at concealment, but it was only nice, fat Inspector Trickett, who smacked her resoundingly on her up-thrust behind and asked her whatever she was a-doing-of-here.

He appeared terrified when she unveiled her appalling countenance, and would probably have died of terror on the spot if she had not burst into an ecstasy of uncontrolled giggling and revealed to him that it was only her, Tiggy, with a red lipstick moustache.

'Did you think I was somebody terrible?' she demanded gloatingly, bouncing up and down on her knees on Roy's bed. 'Did you think I was a monster? Did you think I was going to eat you up?' Regretting her weakness in unmasking herself so soon, she sought belatedly to heighten the effect by the addition of a scarlet beard, and burst into a series of loud, rude noises, horrible to hear.

Trickett, a family man, continued automatically to register horror and dismay, while giving his entire attention to the purpose of his visit, which was to take a dekko at Master Silver's room. As the party drove off to the inquest, nicely out of the way, he had murmured a word which might have been taken as a request for permission if there had been any time to refuse it, and he had already visited Truda's and Julian's rooms, and Miss Pye's.

Truda's and Julian's rooms appeared remarkable only for the universal excellence of their possession; in Miss Pye's were amassed more bottles of patent medicines and cures than he would have thought possible, but none of them having the smell of bitter almonds usually indicative of cyanide.

Roy's possessions, though not numerous, appeared to be of excellent quality. Trickett, glancing down at his own well-worn off-the-peg suiting, thought for a fleeting moment that it was hard that these young fellows should have life made so entirely easy for them. He gave up his search and turned to the rescue of Roy's sponge bag, which Tiggy was now engaged in forcing upon her head.

'Here, you're wrecking it, you little toad! And where did you get that lipstick? *Some*body won't be too pleased when they see what a mess you've made of it. These things aren't too easy to get these days.'

'I found it in here,' said Tiggy, reluctantly removing the sponge bag from her head and dropping the lipstick into it.

'In there? You can't have. That's Mr Silver's sponge bag.'

'Well, I did.'

'Where did you find the bag?'

'In here, of course,' said Tiggy, hanging it carefully over the bathroom taps in such a way that the thin strings became inextricably tangled together.

'And the lipstick was in it?'

'Yes, it was,' said Tiggy. She took his hand confidingly and announced her intention of remaining with him for the whole of the rest of the day. She trailed after him, blithely ridiculous with her encarmined face and a little square of waxy pink paper sitting flat on the top of her head.

'Don't you like my hat?' she asked at last, Trickett having failed to pay tribute to this exquisite joke.

'It's beautiful,' he said absently, casting a look round Jenny's room and backing out again. Jenny's possessions and her mother's were sharply divided into the pre-Thom-Thom era and the present, but held no further significance.

'I got it in Bond Street, my dear,' said Tiggy in a voice of great affection. She hooked herself on to his coat tails as he made his way down the main stairs and along the corridor to Mr Thoms's quarters on the first floor. 'Do you like it, Inspector Trickett? Do you think I look nice in it?'

'I think you look lovely,' lied Trickett, throwing open the door of Mr Thoms's bedroom.

'Oh, *great* compliments!' said Tiggy, folding her hands across her flat little bosom and looking up to heaven, apparently overcome by this laboriously extracted expression of admiration. She added in her normal voice: 'Of course, I didn't really get it from Bond Street, Inspector Trickett. I got it out of Roy's sponge bag, too.'

Nothing in Thom-Thom's room, nothing in his study, nothing in Evan Stone's. Trickett sniffed himself into a coma, but failed to detect anywhere the odour of bitter almonds; and certainly there was no trace of the emerald stolen from Lady Templeton at her dance.

Making his way down the front door steps he shot out a foot to trap Tiggy's 'hat' as it blew off her head and bowled merrily along the quay.

He made his way slowly back to the police station; and did just idly wonder as he went why Roy Silver should keep in his sponge bag one lipstick and the paper off a stick of chewing-gum.

The inquest proved an unexciting affair and ended in a draw—proceedings adjourned for further evidence from the police.

'I can't say I feel I'm any forrarder,' confided Mr Dickinson to Trickett, his red hair standing up like a little boy's all over his head. 'And that drugging business—that's got me foxed, it really has! I think I shall go up to the house this evening and invite myself in for a drink and a chat with the assembled family—*you* know, wheedle my way into their confidences, intercept veiled glances and things, and let the little grey cells get cracking . . .' He looked at the stolid inspector rather wistfully. 'Though it never really seems to work for *me*,' he confessed and drank down a cup of tea.

*

Truda's grandmother clambered stiffly into her ancient pony-trap and had herself conveyed down to Daunton Bay. Here, to the speechless astonishment of the inhabitants, who had never seen her except apparently glued to the seat of her car, or its wartime substitute, the trap, she lumbered laboriously down, evaded payment of a penny after a sharp argument with the misguided young man at the end of the quay, and stumped along towards the Guardhouse.

The antique feather boa she wore round her shoulders gave her the look of a predatory eagle.

Truda and Julian ran down the steps of the house to meet her. 'Oh, grandmother darling, I'm so thankful you've come! We've been ringing up home and nannie said you hadn't got back yet . . .'

'I stayed up in London for a couple of nights longer; your Aunt Sophia has been ill and I went there on Tuesday . . .'

'That explains why we couldn't get you at the flat . . .'

'Well, now, Truda, what is all this terrible news?'

'Oh, it's been awful, grandmother; you see, we came over here to stay with Mr Thoms, as I told you in my note . . . But look, come inside, darling, we don't want to stand here on the steps . . .'

'I suppose Mr Thoms won't mind?' said Lady Audian, preparing to mount.

'No, of course he won't; he'll be only too pleased. We can't get away, granny; you see, Mr Dickinson—he's the policeman— won't *let* us . . .'

'The police have no right whatsoever to keep you here.'

'They keep saying that we shall oblige them very much by staying,' said Julian. 'They sort of hint that it'll look funny it we refuse. As you weren't at Cow's Bay we thought we'd better just stay here, at any rate till you got back.' He said, stammering: 'We've been wanting to see you and—and talk to you . . .'

Mr Thoms came out into the hall. 'Lady Audian! Most

honoured to have you in my house! Come in, come in, and sit yourself down . . . ' He led her into the drawing-room, where the others sat about idly, with Mr Dickinson perched on the arm of a chair trying valiantly to invite their confidences and intercept veiled glances; and, handing her to an armchair, Thoms asked purely by force of habit: 'What'll you have to drink?'

Mr Dickinson's swinging foot arrested itself in mid-air. 'I'll have a nice strong whisky and soda, Mr Thoms, if you'll be so kind,' said Lady Audian. She was tired and cold and very anxious; for what was her darling doing here among all this riff-raff, these ne'er-do-well Winsons and that cocky, over-smart Silver boy . . .? Mr Thoms was all right, a good-hearted, kindly old man; and Evan Stone she liked and respected; and of course, now Geoffrey Winson was dead, poor fellow, but the wife . . . The *wife* . . . ! She said to Gloria in her direct way: 'Have I met you somewhere before?'

'I don't think so,' said Gloria. She added archly that she was sure *she* would not have forgotten, if they had ever met!

Lady Audian continued to look puzzled. 'Perhaps you saw us at Lady Templeton's dance?' suggested Thom-Thom.

'I was not able to be at Lady Templeton's dance,' said Lady Audian. 'I've only just returned from London.' She refrained from comment upon Lady Templeton's fall from grace in actually giving a subscription ball.

'Did you hear about her having her emerald pendant stolen, grandmother?'

'Yes, it's very distressing for Mabel. George had just given it to her . . .'

'It was a lovely thing,' said Gloria, carefully keeping her eye from Mr Thoms.

'Just one big stone, set in a border of sort of filagree work in platinum. I adore emeralds; really I think they are my favourite stone . . . I wonder if the police have any trace of the thief . . .?'

'I daresay the inspector knows all about it,' said Miss Pye, rolling her gooseberry eyes at Dickinson, to whom she had taken an old maid's fancy.

Mr Dickinson was far too much preoccupied with the murder to have paid much attention to Trickett's occasional groans about the jewel theft. 'I know the local police have the matter in hand. I've got nothing to do with it . . .'

Lady Audian, understanding for the first time whom he was, immediately lost interest in Mabel Templeton's emerald pendant, and turned upon him the full battery of her commanding presence in an endeavour to induce him to give willing permission for her granddaughter—and her great-nephew too, if possible—to return home with her that night.

'Mr Thoms will understand, I'm sure, that I haven't seen anything of these children yet, and I don't want to miss more of their visit than I must . . .' She gave old Thom-Thom her little, hardly perceptible yet infinitely gracious bow. Mr Thoms bowed gravely back.

'Sorry to lose them, of course, Lady Audian, but I quite understand your feelin' in the matter . . .' Because he was not quite at his ease, the strong Welsh accent of his childhood forced its way up.

Mr Dickinson, however, was adamant; and for the first time Lady Audian realized that her chickens had not only been present at the murder, but were to some extent involved in the investigation. Her brow grew terribly black. She retreated with Truda and Julian to Mr Thoms's study, kindly placed at her disposal. 'Julian—what have you let Truda in for, bringing her to this house . . . ?'

'Darling, he didn't bring me. *I* accepted the invitation, *I* . . .'

'Hush, Truda. Now, Julian . . . ?'

Julian looked unhappily at Truda. Now was the moment for the great speech, for the great declaration, the great confession they had come all the way to Daunton to make; and a moment more unpropitious it would be hard to imagine. 'I'm terribly sorry, Aunt Edwina. You can't feel more awful about Trudie being here than I do, and that I'm responsible for—for letting her get mixed up in it . . .'

'Grandmother darling, I'm perfectly capable of coming to the Guardhouse on my own; it was nothing to do with Julian.'

'It's always the gentleman's part to look after the lady. You knew perfectly well that I wouldn't approve of your coming here. I hear that that man Winson was on the black-list of every reputable club in London, and as for the woman . . .'

'Just because Thom-Thom's rather a rough diamond . . .'

'It has nothing to do with Mr Thoms; if Mr Thoms is rough, he is a diamond, and I have a great respect for him. But the Winsons were actually bad, actually dishonest . . . Besides, Julian, I think it hardly delicate of you to be staying in the same house with a young woman you were so recently—involved with.'

'Look, Aunt Edwina, I—I want to talk to you. I came down here to talk to you, and though, goodness knows, this isn't the moment I'd have chosen . . .'

Mr Dickinson had left the family in the drawing-room, and wandered out on to the terrace; standing there, busy with his own thoughts, he was suddenly interrupted by voices, unconsciously perhaps a little raised, from the balcony above. '. . . this isn't exactly the moment I'd have chosen . . . Yes, I was more or less engaged to Jenny Sandells . . .'

'Sandells!' cried Lady Audian, and her voice rose almost to a scream. She lowered it, immediately. 'I knew I had seen that woman before. Gloria Sandells! Gloria Murray!'

Truda stood beside Julian in her slender, patterned summer frock, very tall and straight, her eyes very bright because now Julian was going to tell grandmother outright; now the wretched old business of the money could be tossed aside, now the all-important business of seeing to it that grandmother's feelings were not hurt by unnecessary concealment and deception was at last to be undertaken; that it had been too long awaiting had been no fault of her own or of Julian's. 'Never mind about Gloria, granny. Julian wants to tell you . . .'

Lady Audian did not even hear her. 'Do you mean to say these are the people you knew that summer in Hampstead, when you were staying with your Aunt Elizabeth? The woman whose husband died?'

'Well, yes, granny, I thought you knew . . . We met them again in London at a party Mr Thoms gave . . . Julian met them several times . . .'

There was a long pause; so long that Mr Dickinson, shamelessly eavesdropping on the terrace below, thought they must all have returned to the study behind the balcony. But Lady Audian spoke at last, and though she spoke very quietly now, her clear voice carried down quite clearly on the still evening air. She said: 'Gloria Winson's husband has died; and it is suspected—more than suspected—that he was murdered. In 1937, Gloria Sandells' husband died; and at that time it was more than suspected that he had been murdered too!'

Saturday morning dawned. More interviews, more questioning, more discussion, more trunk calls, more examination of photographs and fingerprints. A great deal more fuss from Chief Constable Colonel Potts, his face scarlet with anxiety.

'If that moustache once gets loose,' said Mr Dickinson to Inspector Trickett, 'we shall have to put a ferret up after it. What's the flap about? We're getting along all right.'

'*Are* we?' said Trickett. trudging along beside him to the Guardhouse, for yet more interviews.

'Well—good enough for the job. The chap only died on Wednesday; what does Potts expect in three days?' Mr Dickinson's hair glowed, crinkling in the sunshine, and his blue eyes danced in tune with the dancing waves. Jenny, watching him from the terrace with Miss Pye, said with the first gleam of interest she had shown since her stepfather's death: 'He *is* rather nice.'

Mr Dickinson demanded to see Mrs Winson. Mrs Winson was not up yet. 'Tell her I'd like an interview with her as soon as she is,' said Dickinson, and settled himself with Trickett in the dining-room, opening out his untidy little note-book on the table before him with an air of stern importance most ill-becoming his usually open and unclouded visage. 'Meanwhile, let's see what we've got so far. This thing about the first husband is a bolt from the blue!'

'You rang up London last night?'

'I gave 'em no peace; but it seems that it wasn't a police affair and the whole thing was simply nosed out by a private investigator. Apparently old Lady Audian's niece, the aunt of the present young people, had a friend called Mrs Murray, whose daughter was this Gloria, who married John Sandells. While young Messenger and Truda Dean were staying with this aunt, they got to know the Sandells and Roy Silver, who was also a friend, and they were all young things together for a few weeks one summer.

'On the last day of the holidays they were messing about in the garden of the Sandells' house, and Gloria came out to tell them that she had found her husband dead in bed. Truda Deane and Messenger came away at once, and they heard no more about it, but their aunt wrote to the old lady afterwards.'

Dickinson picked up his note-book and thumbed through the pages and continued: 'It appears that the nurse got suspicious, and finally a private chap was put on to try and smell out the rat, but nothing ever came of it; John Sandells was very ill and he was alone upstairs in his room, and there was some suggestion that he might have been—well, smothered or something; There were several admirers around, including Evan Stone and Geoffrey Winson, whom she afterwards duly married, and it was suggested that the death was very convenient for all concerned.

'Nothing could be proved, though, and a death certificate was granted, and that was the end of it; it never came into the hands of the police, and that's why I didn't get to know about it until I rang up last night and they began digging things out . . .'

He shut his book and got up. 'I shall face her with it this morning and see what I can get. Meanwhile, whether or not Sandells was murdered, Geoffrey Winson quite definitely was; and whereas, apparently, anyone could have murdered Sandells, only one of nine people could have murdered Winson; unless, of course, the poison could have been planted on him earlier, which seems hardly practicable. The stuff is instantaneous: he couldn't possibly have taken it before he sat down to that table.'

'It wasn't as instantaneous as all that; I thought cyanide snuffed you out at the first gasp,' remarked Trickett.

'It loses its potency a little with keeping, and this had been kept since the last war; more proof, if proof were necessary, that it was Stone's that was used. The witnesses seem to have been spared the worst of the symptoms; but they all said how bright the blood was—that's a peculiarity of cyanide poisoning.'

'How well-informed you are,' said Inspector Trickett.

'I looked it up in Murrell's on the way down in the train,' said Dickinson, with great frankness. 'Well now, the point is that Winson must have been given something at that table by one of those nine persons. The question is—how?'

'To which you do not know the reply!'

'Well no, I don't,' said Dickinson, laughing. 'The chap came running down the little staircase—sorry, companionway!—and sat down in his place. Miss Pye passed him a paper napkin from a heap on the table. That was the first thing.'

'Impregnated with poison,' suggested Trickett brilliantly.

'All too likely, but unfortunately he didn't use it. The step-daughter mopped up some blood with it afterwards, and she says it wasn't unfolded. A nice kid that,' said Mr Dickinson inconsequently.

'Yes, she is. Well, that lets Pye out. Who's next?'

'The child, Tiggy, went to him with two egg sandwiches. Mrs Winson had made her save them for him. He took one and the child ate the other. Mrs Winson seems to have made no real attempt to stop her; it's inconceivable that if she had poisoned either of them she'd have let the little girl take one at random.'

'So the widow's out.'

'M'm. Next thing, Winson takes Jenny Sandells' glass, from which she has just been drinking, so it must be all right; he drains off what remains in it. Stone passes him a vacuum jug of iced coffee from which they have all been drinking. Winson himself pours out some coffee into the glass and drinks that too. Stone takes back the jug and pours out some more for himself and drinks that. So the coffee must have been O.K.'

'Exit Stone.'

'Meanwhile, Sparrow has opened a new bottle of sherry and he decants it. Mr Thoms tastes the sherry from the decanter. So *that* must be all right. The decanter is passed up the table, and as there is a heavy glass stopper in it, can hardly have been tampered with on the way. Winson sees a spot of dust in his wine glass and fishes it out with his finger before pouring in the sherry. So there was nothing in the glass or he'd have noticed it. That seems to let out Thoms and Sparrow.'

Trickett nodded, and ticked them off on his fingers. Dickinson continued:

'Julian Messenger and Roy Silver; Messenger cut several bits of pie, Roy helped himself at random. Nobody could have doctored an odd piece and left it at that. Too damn dangerous to themselves and to other people.

'Jenny Sandells put oil on some lettuce for him, and Truda Deane made up a salad dressing. The kid, who seems to have constituted herself King's Taster on this occasion, ate up some of the salad from Winson's plate, and even scooped up the dressing with a spoon; so that lets out little Sandells and Miss Deane.'

'Who's left?' said Trickett, rumpling his short, springy hair.

'Nobody's left. Somebody poisoned that man at the table; and nobody did. Think it all over carefully: can you see any flaw?'

Trickett had been thinking it all over carefully before Mr Dickinson had ever been heard of in Daunton Bay. He mumbled into his chin, however, and emerged to say flatly: 'No.'

The room they were in was panelled in pale oak, and curtained in a velvety, midnight blue, the better to set off the silver trophies ranged round the walls. They amounted to a total value of something like five hundred pounds, and it had cost Thom-Thom a cool hundred thousand to attain them. Mr Dickinson, roaming aimlessly about, caught up a figurine and brandished it at Inspector Trickett. 'Somebody poisoned Geoffrey Winson—and nobody did. And I'll tell you something else—somebody drugged Thoms and Stone on the previous evening and nobody did that either.'

'Thoms'll drug you and poison you too, if you wreck that figure in your hand. For heaven's sake put it down, man, and detect like a Christian.'

Dickinson put down the figurine and perched himself on the window-sill, his back to the beckoning blue of the sea. 'That drugging. They walked together the sea road and Stone mentioned to them the presence of the poison in his coat pocket. Nobody left the party on their return to the drawing-room. Sparrow joined them there, and as the conversation was still going on, he too learned about the cyanide. They all had some drinks; and that is the last thing any of them ate or drank that night. And yet in those drinks Thoms, Stone, and possibly old Pye (though that may be only nonsense, because she says anything that comes into her head)—anyway, Thoms and Stone were drugged.'

'Well?' Trickett was a bit bored by this sustained monologue.

'Well, where did the druggist get the drug? *When* did he get it? Are you going to suggest that someone in this party went round with a carefully prepared dose of sleeping draught in his pocket? It doesn't make sense. And from the time they all learned that the poison was there—from the time, that is, that the criminal learned that it would be convenient if Stone and Thoms slept heavily that night—there was no opportunity to get any stuff to put in the drinks. So there!'

'It's conceivable that someone used sleeping tablets and happened to have them in his pocket.'

Dickinson was slightly flattened out by this reasonable suggestion. 'I suppose it's just possible . . .'

There was a sound of pounding feet in the passage outside, and the door was flung open by Tiggy, one plait standing out like a windsock from her head, the other hanging limply over her ear. In her hand she carried a crumpled ribbon and this she offered to Dickinson, advancing upon him with ecstatic cries.

'Go away,' said Dickinson severely.

'I can't,' said Tiggy. stopping in mid-career. 'Sparrow's fed up with having me hanging round while he tries to get on with his work, and he told me to go and get someone to do my hair. I think it was only an excuse to get rid of me,' she added, without rancour.

'What have I done,' Dickinson sighed to Trickett, 'to be cursed with the devotion of this female?' He grabbed at the soft, fair hair with unaccustomed hands.

'Anyway, we'd nearly finished,' said Trickett, resigning himself to Tiggy's company during the rest of the discussion. 'We're stuck. We don't know who administered the poison, or how; we don't know who administered the sleeping drug, or how. And nobody heard a thing that night before the murder, and nobody left their rooms from the moment they went to bed—or so they say.'

'Except me,' said Tiggy.

'Oh, you did, did you?' said Dickinson, still struggling with the plait. 'And what were *you* doing out of bed?'

'Looking for Jenny,' said Tiggy.

'I thought you slept in her room?'

'So I do,' said Tiggy. 'But she wasn't there.'

'Why—hadn't she come to bed yet?'

'Good gracious yes, of course she had,' said Tiggy scornfully. 'It was twelve o'clock in the miggle of the night. I saw it on her clock.'

'Twelve o'clock. Nonsense. You made a mistake in the time!' declared Dickinson.

'I did not,' said Tiggy indignantly. 'Do you think I can't tell the time? Besides, she'd come in long before; I woke up and I saw her and I said: "Have you brought some strawberries for me from dinner?" and she said: "No, I forgot, go to sleep," and then I went to sleep again.'

'But later you woke up and she wasn't there?'

'That was at twelve o'clock in the miggle of the night,' insisted Tiggy.

'Yes, yes, we quite realize that now,' said Dickinson humbly. 'She wasn't there—so what did you do?'

'I went to ask Pye where Jenny was, but *she* wasn't there either. At least I banged and banged on the door and she generally wakes up if you even whisper, but she didn't seem to hear. I couldn't go in because she keeps her door locked because of burglars,' added Tiggy, contemptuously.

'So then what did you do?'

'So then I thought I would go and ask Truda where they could be, so I pushed on Truda's door, but she wasn't there. So then I couldn't think *where* they could be, so I went to Julian's room and *he* wasn't there. So I thought they must all be in Roy's room, but I couldn't open his door properly, and I could hear him snortling a little bit inside, but he wouldn't wake up.'

'Well, it's nice to think that *some*body was in his room,' said Dickinson, grimly ironical. 'What happened then?'

'I thought they must be downstairs, so I looked in the drawing-room and the dining-room, but there was nobody there. So then I went back to bed.'

'You didn't go to your mother's door by any chance and find her missing too?' said Dickinson to Trickett, over her head.

'Well, I did rattle at the handle a little teeny bit, but the door was locked, and I was afraid to make a noise because mummy gets terribly cross if you wake her up early,' said Tiggy innocently.

Dickinson, in a dream, tied the ribbon tightly round the end of her plait, and turned her round towards him. The little face, without its disfiguring goggles, was as lovely and fresh as a flower, 'You're sure of this, Tiggy?' he said gravely. 'It wasn't a dream? It isn't made up?'

She rammed on her glasses and stared at him, a hideous little tadpole with two great swimmy blue eyes. 'Of course it isn't,' she said indignantly. 'I was for hours and hours trying to find them.'

'It might have been a nightmare,' said Trickett pacifically. 'My little boy dreamt once that he saw a blue bull and he won't believe even now that you can't have blue bulls; he still thinks he's seen one.'

'He must be very silly,' Tiggy said candidly. 'I wouldn't believe a thing like that. Besides,' she added, fishing up the leg of her bloomers and producing a small dank object, 'besides, if I hadn't been in the dining-room that night, how could I have found this?'

Mr Dickinson caught it from her hand. 'It's a rubber container, Trickett, the sort you get for petrol lighters . . .'

'It's a darling little bottle for a baby fairy,' corrected Tiggy in a voice of sickening sentimentality.

'. . . pierced at one end; and empty,' continued Dickinson. '*Where* did you say you found this, Tiggy?'

'I found it in the miggle of the night under the sideboard in the dining-room. I thought they must all be hiding so I looked under the table and behind the chairs and things, and then I lay down flat on my tummy and looked under the sideboard . . .' They could imagine her, rather pathetically scrambling to her feet, crestfallen at the failure of what had promised to be so splendid a joke.

'What have you been doing with it?' said Dickinson swiftly. 'Feeding dolls with it? Or—or filling it up with water and squirting it . . . ?'

'No, I haven't,' said Tiggy regretfully. 'I didn't know it would squirt. Can I have it back now?'

'I'll give you mine instead,' said Trickett, producing one from his pocket. He pierced the end and emptied the contents into a vase of flowers. 'There you are, Tigs.'

'It smells of petrol,' said Tiggy, wrinkling her nose but tucking the container away, nevertheless, in the leg of her knickers.

'And this one doesn't,' said Dickinson to Trickett, joyfully. 'It's been emptied and washed out and used—and used to squirt liquid sleeping stuff into the drinks.'

No question now of an odd couple of doses carried by chance on the person and used when the occasion suddenly presented itself. 'Nobody could have administered the poison; and somebody did. Nobody could have had the sleeping draught ready; and somebody had.' His blue eyes shone.

They sent for Sparrow and examined him minutely on the events of that evening when they had all had their drinks in the dining-room after their walk. Miss Pye, in search of Tiggy, blundered in on them, and looked daggers at Sparrow who, with cool scorn, looked back.

'Just a moment, Miss Pye,' said Dickinson, as Tiggy fled to the garden away from the compulsory walk up and down the quay. 'Among other things, we've been asking Sparrow about those conversations at breakfast on the morning before Mr Winson's death . . .'

Miss Pye went rather white. 'I heard Sparrow say threateningly, "It's a drug."'

'I've explained that to the inspector,' said Sparrow calmly. 'Mr Winson told me he was afraid of being seasick; and I advised him to get some stuff from the chemist before we sailed. I may have said "It's a drug." He added, with something like a sneer: 'I don't know why Miss Pye should think I would want to murder Mr Winson; Miss Pye herself had some quiet words with Mr Winson that morning . . .'

'I had not,' cried Miss Pye, trembling.

'And some very noisy ones with him the evening before,' added Sparrow.

'I may have . . . I did speak to Mr Geoffrey . . . It was all nothing to do with me, inspector,' cried Miss Pye in an agony. 'I mean I had words with Mr Geoffrey, but it was nothing to do with me! It was all for Gloria. He was off up on the cliffs with Roy Silver again, with a couple of girls from Cow's Bay . . .'

Trickett glanced at Sparrow who suddenly went first scarlet, and then a deathly white. He seemed about to say something, but stopped, and assumed an air of dignity.

Miss Pye, fumbling in her bag for a handkerchief, let it slip from her trembling, pudgy little hands, and spilled the contents all about the floor. Trickett and Dickinson, still lost in astonishment at the guilty appearance of the pair, dived after it, handing up the articles one by one as they found them scattered about the floor. Purse, powder-box, notecase, pencil, a grubby swansdown powder-puff, and a twisted piece of metal that had once been a delicate oval of filagree: the setting from Lady Templeton's emerald pendant—with the emerald gone.

PART V

Dickinson stood among the scattered contents of Miss Pye's handbag, the twisted setting of the pendant in his hand. Trickett said, 'Good lord,' and snatched it from him.

'What is it?' said Miss Pye, still very white, but now with an air of curiosity.

'It's the setting of Lady Templeton's emerald, which was stolen

at the dance on Monday,' said Trickett, staring down at it as
though he could not believe his eyes.

After a moment in which they all stood silent, he said: 'You
were there, Miss Pye, weren't you?'

'Yes, I was but . . . Good gracious, Inspector,' cried Miss Pye,
beginning to gobble, 'you don't think that *I* stole . . . That *I* took
. . . You can't possibly imagine . . . ?'

'What were you doing with the setting in your handbag?'

Miss Pye begun to weep. 'I don't know anything about it. I
don't *know*. I never saw the thing before!'

'You didn't know you had it?'

'Of course I didn't,' cried Miss Pye through her tears. 'I just
. . . I can't think how it could possibly have got *into* my bag . . .
It may have been there for—well, I don't know how long. It
would be right down at the bottom. I would never notice it . . .'

'Whom did you speak to at the ball?'

'I didn't speak to anybody,' said Miss Pye truthfully. 'Except
the man behind the buffet. And once Jenny said something to
me. Otherwise I just—just watched the people enjoying themselves and had my supper . . .'

'Did you speak to Lady Templeton?'

'I said "How d'you do?" to her, and she waggled my hand as
though it were a bit of fish off a slab,' said Miss Pye with some
spirit. 'I never saw her again the whole evening, till she suddenly
cried out that the emerald was gone.' She began to weep afresh.

Dickinson abandoned her to the tender mercy of Inspector
Trickett, whose case the theft of the emerald really was. 'I want
to see Mrs Winson now,' he said firmly, and this time took no
rebuff. 'It's eleven o'clock. I think she should be up by now . . .'
He waited for her in the dining-room where he might talk to
her undisturbed.

Gloria had put no eyeblack beneath her eyes this morning, and
she needed none; but she managed to assume the famous crooked

smile as she sank into a chair and arranged to the best advantage
her scented white hands. She was dressed from head to foot in
white, with a little black belt to show that, as Jenny would have
said, it was 'meant'; real mourning did not become her, and after
all the weather was dreadfully hot. 'Geoffrey would not have
wanted a parade of feeling,' she explained soulfully to Mr
Dickinson, whose susceptible heart missed a beat; but with an
effort caught up on itself. He said, very sternly, 'Mrs Winson—I
want to ask you some details connected with the death of your
first husband.'

Gloria went deathly white.

'My—my first husband? Details about his death?'

'Isn't it true that there was some investigation into the circumstances of his death?'

'There was a little question about it, yes. It was all nothing,
inspector, nothing but ill-feeling and—and jealousy and horribleness . . . just because I had men friends . . . I've always had
men friends, I'm a woman who collects men, I can't help it, it's
just the way I'm made . . .

'My husband was an invalid. He was ill, and he got worse and
he died; but because there were other men who—who cared for
me—immediately it was assumed that I was—was glad to be rid
of him. Some snooping old woman friend put on a so-called
private investigator; he came round and asked a lot of questions,
but he soon realized the truth, that it was nothing but a lot of
ill-natured, wicked gossip and jealousy; and he went away and
my husband was buried and that was the end of it. Surely you're
not going to take any notice now of a lot of ancient, wicked
scandalmongering rumour?'

'I'm afraid we must take a great deal of notice of it. London
has traced the nurse who attended your first husband on his
death-bed and the doctor who signed the certificate. The doctor's
vague; but the nurse remembers the whole case perfectly.'

'She would!' said Gloria spitefully. 'The truth is that that woman went out and left my husband, and he died and it was all her fault.'

'Where were you at the time?'

'I was in the kitchen,' said Gloria impatiently, 'and as a matter of fact I did leave the house for a few minutes, to run down to the shops. I suppose we weren't all to *starve* because my husband was ill?'

'Your husband was lying upstairs, very ill, in bed. He'd been bad for several years, and you'd had this trained nurse for him for the past two months.'

'Yes. We were as poor as church mice, because he hadn't earned anything since heaven knows when, but . . . but I couldn't grudge him that luxury,' said Gloria, recovering something of her normal stride at the thought of the sacrifices involved in nursing the stricken invalid. "'John must come first," I said and I scraped and saved. I denied myself and Jenny—though she was only a child then—we were willing to go without so that John should have all he needed . . .'

Mr Dickinson's blue eyes took it all in without a blink. He waited patiently to the end and then steadily pursued his course; 'On that afternoon, your daughter, Jenny Sandells, was out at the back of the house playing tennis with Mr Julian Messenger, Miss Truda Deane and Mr Roy Silver, who would all be in their teens, I suppose, in those days?'

'Well, that or a bit more; they are all older than Jenny.'

'Yes. Well, the nurse went out for some fresh air. She was gone for about two hours. Meanwhile you were in and out of the house. Was the front door locked?'

'No,' said Gloria sullenly. 'It was left open. The children were in the back garden; and all our friends used to walk in and out anyway, people were always running up to see John . . .'

'I see. Did you go up and see your husband at all while the nurse was out?'

'Yes, I did,' said Gloria. 'I went up after I got back from my shopping. He was all right. He was asleep and I crept away and left him.'

'You're sure he was only—asleep?'

She stared at him blankly. 'Yes, I am. I'm certain.'

'Now, the nurse says that when she went out the bedclothes were rather untidy; but she didn't want to disturb him and she left them. She says that when she came back the bedclothes had been pulled straight. Did you tidy them up when you went in?'

'I don't remember,' said Gloria. 'I may have.'

Young Mr Dickinson began to be a tiny bit frightened; with a chill, impersonal fear that closed for a moment about his heart. For either this was a murder, or second murder, out of the dim past; or it was not. And this woman was being deliberately evasive. If it had not been murder, why was she dodging his questioning, bright eyes wary? If it had been murder, if the invalid had been stifled on his bed of sickness, as he strongly suspected, why, also, was Gloria being evasive?

He said sharply: 'Mrs Winson—you must remember! The question is all-important, and it must have been put to you when this happened. Did you or did you not straighten out those bedclothes?' As Gloria opened her mouth to reply he reminded her: 'You say your husband was asleep; or anyway you thought so. Now in the light of that—did you or did you not touch the bed?'

'No,' said Gloria. 'I don't think I did.' And he knew she had changed her mind, that that had not been what she was going to say.

He was silent for a moment. 'The nurse says,' he continued at last, 'that when she returned from her outing she knew at once that somebody had been smoking Virginian cigarettes in your husband's sickroom.'

'She said so at the time,' said Gloria angrily, dismissing the whole idea. 'The woman was a fool. I've told you I was in the room; I used to be a chain-smoker. It was my smoke she smelled.'

'She said you never smoked anything but Turks. She said she couldn't mistake the smell. It wasn't your cigarette-smoke.'

'I don't see what it is that you're suggesting,' said Gloria. trying to be calm.

'I'm suggesting what the nurse suggested then: your husband was very weak, so weak that if anyone had held a hand for a minute over his mouth and nose—that would have been enough.' There seemed no need between them for any apology in bringing forward matters that to other women might have been too harrowing.

Gloria said coldly: 'The doctor gave a certificate; he saw nothing wrong. My husband had had a heart disease for years, and he finally died of cardiac failure.'

'Everybody dies of cardiac failure in the end,' said Dickinson, rather grandly. 'The doctor hadn't expected your husband to die so soon, but he was ill, and one couldn't be surprised; there was no post-mortem; and anyway the signs of stifling would have been imperceptible.'

'So nobody could prove anything then; and they can't prove anything now,' said Gloria with a hint of triumph that sat ill on her handsome face and tiny, erect, impregnable frame.

It was frightening. It was really frightening, however old a hand you might be at the Yard, however many cases you might have been on before (though never alone!), however many suspects you might have interviewed, doggedly, coldly, relentlessly wearing them down. It was frightening. She was so small, so beautiful, so terrified—and so strong.

He said shortly: 'Your husband has just been murdered. Your first husband died eight years ago under suspicious circumstances. Many of the people concerned in Mr Winson's death were present at the time of Mr Sandell's death; yourself, of course, and Miss Pye, and Julian Messenger and Miss Truda Deane, and Roy Silver, and Jenny, your daughter.'

'Jenny was a child. Surely you're not suggesting . . . ?'

Mr Dickinson knew that he was absurd in feeling reluctant to suggest anything so ugly against Jenny Sandells, that guileless creature with the bright brown eyes and curly hair, either then when she was a child, or now when she was supposed to be grown-up. 'And then there was Mr Stone.'

There was a silence. Gloria said: 'Mr Dickinson—you've met Evan Stone. Does he strike you as the sort of man who would murder his best friend?'

'No, he doesn't,' said Dickinson. He added: 'He seems to have offered no alibi at the time.'

'Ordinary people don't have alibis every minute of the day,' said Gloria.

Jenny Sandells, Julian Messenger, Truda Deane, Roy Silver— all kids or in their early twenties; Miss Pye; and Gloria herself. Or Evan Stone. 'Mrs Winson,' said Dickinson, gathering his papers together, shuffling them into an untidy heap, stowing them into the pockets of his jacket, 'I'm going to ask you one more question and let you go. Was Mr Evan Stone in love with you in those days?'

'No,' said Gloria. And still there was that false note in her voice.

Evan Stone stood alone on the terrace, his hands in his pockets, looking out to sea. To him came that detective fellow, Dickinson, a nice little chap with his blue eyes and fierce red hair; but Evan did wish he would clear out and leave them all alone. He advanced, however, resolutely. 'I say, Mr Stone—I've been looking for you. I've been talking to Mrs Winson, and she's been telling me about her first husband's death. You were a friend of Mrs Winson's at that time—?'

Evan turned his ugly face away and fiddled with the geraniums growing in their gay boxes round the balustrade. 'Yes, I was,' he said.

'You were questioned by the private investigator fellow?' Dickinson continued resolutely.

'I was, yes. I was training for a long-distance flight just then, and the evening John Sandells died I was messing about with my machine. I was twenty miles away, if that's what you're interested in; but I didn't have a whole row of witnesses ready for the occasion, so you'll have to take my word.'

'You went on your flight, and you crashed?'

Evan said shortly: 'Yes.'

The red hairs seemed positively to sparkle. 'I don't like to ask you this, but it's part of my job—was your crash a mistake?'

'My surviving it was, if that's what you mean,' said Stone.

'You do admit that?'

Confound the man, thought Evan. Is he going to pull my soul up by its roots . . . ? He said at last: 'Listen, inspector. I had nothing to do with Sandells' death. I loved him dearly—he was one of my greatest friends. But I was in love with his wife, I always had been, and I'm in love with her now. I didn't make love to her during his lifetime; and after his death . . .' He paused for a moment, and went on, rather stiffly: 'After his death, she chose someone else. My flight was all fixed up and I decided I ought to go ahead with it. Other people's money was at stake—I couldn't let them down. I got there all right, and that was the end of my responsibilities. It was my own machine and nobody would be any the worse off if I died—so on the way back I let the thing crash. Some interfering busybodies picked me up and put me together again, and by the time I was out of the wood, Gloria was married and that was the end of it.'

'I'm sorry.' said Dickinson sincerely, and turned on his heel. After a moment he came back. 'You could have taken the poison,' he said.

The chap's bewitched, thought Evan wearily. He explained, embarrassed: 'It seemed rather an unsporting way out. I mean, I know that suicide is a cowardly thing really; but it takes a bit of courage deliberately to crash yourself, and that seemed to sort of cancel things out, if you know what I mean . . .' He remembered the struggle, the hideous decision, the deliberate choice. The little dose of poison that would have ended all things in a moment of time; the terrible, hurling of his machine through the downward air, the deafening impact with the earth, the reeling purple of pain and fear and unavailing regret . . . 'I knew I was a coward to kill myself; but it seemed better if I chose the least cowardly manner of doing it. You do see what I mean?'

Mr Dickinson saw what he meant. It seemed very improbable indeed that this man had murdered a helpless invalid.

Truda and Julian wandered about the house together like two sad ghosts in search of a resting-place. Inspector Trickett was in the study with Miss Pye, whence came the sound of tearful and vehement denial; Dickinson was monopolizing the dressing-room in tête-à-tête with Gloria; Jenny and Roy were sitting miserably in the drawing-room, nervously playing a sort of hideous game of being in love all over again.

Julian and Truda sat down at last, forlornly, at the top of the stairs. 'To think that all my fine ideas of loving you and looking after you should bring you to *this*!' He hunched his knees up under his chin.

Truda turned towards him, pushing back with a loving hand the short-cropped curly hair at his temple.

'My dearest one; *don't* torture yourself with this fantastic idea that any of it's your fault—'

'But it is,' he said gloomily. 'You don't know, Trudie. You don't understand. Oh, I know that I wasn't responsible for our being here in the first place, and all that—but since then . . .' He broke off and then said wretchedly: 'If it wasn't for me, Dickinson wouldn't be keeping us here.'

'Oh, nonsense, Julian; everyone at that lunch-table is suspect, just by reason of their being there—he'd keep us both here anyway. Of course, now that this new complication about Gloria's first husband has come out . . .'

'It may make a difference. We were all there, too, when it happened.'

'He surely can't think for a moment . . . ? Why should we have? Anyway, we were only kids.'

'In fact, I was twenty-one,' said Julian gravely. 'As to why—well, Dickinson isn't to know that we had no earthly reason to do it. Oh, lord, what a mess! As if things weren't bad enough already.'

'And *still* we haven't told grandmother!'

'Darling, I did my level best. It was a hopeless moment to come blurting out with it, but I went ahead; only suddenly she thought of this thing about Gloria, and that was the last straw. I simply couldn't start a long family argument on top of that. I suppose she'll be angrier than ever after all this extra delay.'

'It isn't her being angry I mind, Julian; only she'll be so dreadfully hurt and upset. I'm so afraid it'll all come out through this wretched inquiry, and she'd just never get over it. I wonder,' said Truda thoughtfully, 'whether it would be best to go and talk to Mr Dickinson and ask him to let us have a chance to go and see granny; or at least ask him to keep this side of it quiet . . . ?'

Julian sat up. He said, almost violently: 'You mustn't tell Dickinson!'

'Not tell him? If he keeps it secret?'

'No, no, Truda, you mustn't tell him. You mustn't say a word to him about us. He mustn't know!'

She was astonished and a little bewildered.

'Why on earth not?'

'He mustn't, definitely. Promise me you won't say a word!' His voice was tense, almost harsh.

She sat staring at him. 'I don't understand you, darling. Why not? Anyway, he knows about the breach of promise action.'

'He doesn't necessarily know that *you* were involved in that. People bring breach of promise actions without there being a second girl in the case; just for refusing to marry the first.'

'But, Julian, everybody here knows that we're—that we're in love. Mr Dickinson *must* know by now.'

'Well, he needn't know any more than that. He asked me if I was engaged to you and I said I wasn't. I said your grandmother disapproved; which was all quite true.'

Truda was silent again. She said at last: 'Julian, there's something you're not telling me.'

'No, there isn't.' The reply was quick . . . too quick?

'Darling, I know there *is*. Julian, do trust me; do tell me! Surely we can't have secrets from each other . . . ? Even if it's ugly and horrid, dearest, I don't mind; I understand. I'll be on your side, I'll share it with you; anything's better than that we shouldn't trust each other.'

'There's nothing,' he said.

She took a deep breath. 'Julian—you paid Geoffrey Winson money to stop him from bringing that breach of promise action, didn't you?'

'No,' said Julian. 'It wasn't that.'

'Julian, for *God's* sake tell me the truth!'

'Geoffrey Winson could never have brought any breach of promise action,' said Julian impatiently. 'The whole thing was nonsense.'

'And you didn't buy him off? You promise me, Julian, you *promise* me, that you didn't give him your money—your three hundred pounds, or whatever it was, to stop him from bringing the action, even from trying to bring it? You promise me?'

'I promise you I didn't,' he said. 'I give you my word of honour.' She knew that he was telling her the truth; and yet she could not be sure it was the whole truth.

They sat silently, side by side, staring down the steep stairway into the hall; together, and yet divided, passionately desiring each the love and trust of the other, and yet unable to give or demand that trust.

*

Murder will always out; and in murder's train march always these ugly progeny: distrust, fear, concealment, untruth; pain and sorrow and disillusionment and regret. A thousand fears and diffidences beset them, too delicate and complicated for their own comprehension, too purely of instinct and impulse, too purely emotional to be brought out into the world of hard treason and examined and resolutely thrust aside again.

'There doesn't seem to be any trust left,' said Truda at last, sadly, following her own unspoken train of thought. 'We all go about uneasily, not looking straight at each other . . .'

'I suppose the others feel the same about us. I suppose,' said Julian deliberately, looking unseeingly before him down the stairs, 'I suppose we even feel the same about each other!'

Her mind was too delicate, too scrupulously honest, to blot out the knowledge of her own distrust; the conviction that he had not told her the whole truth. She hesitated; and immediately he knew. 'My God, Truda—you actually were, you actually were suspecting *me*!'

'Oh, Julian, darling, never, never in my life! Suspect *you*—of murder! I would as soon suspect myself, I would *rather* suspect myself. I would rather believe that I'd gone mad and didn't know what I'd done, that I'd been sleep-walking and done it in my sleep! Suspect you of killing Geoffrey Winson—as if I *could*!'

'Then why didn't you answer at once?'

'I was thinking—well, obliquely; I wasn't thinking about the actual answer to what you said.'

He was bitterly hurt, wounded and frightened, and his heart was sick with the loneliness of his pain and fear. He had let her down, hopelessly, all along the line; he had acted wildly, rashly, madly, he had landed them both in horrible danger, a danger of which no confession of his own would serve to clear her. He knew that he must carry the burden alone; and yet, if Truda deserted him, if Truda turned away her love . . . He said coldly and roughly because he was so much afraid: 'You're making excuses.'

Distrust, fear, concealment, untruth; pain and sorrow and disillusionment and regret . . . Like two unhappy children Truda and Julian sat at the top of the stairs, together and yet a thousand miles apart; and down in the drawing-room, together also, but yet farther apart, Jenny and Roy went through a ghastly make-believe of love. In her bedroom, released at last from her inter-view with Dickinson, Gloria relieved her feelings at the expense of Miss Pye. 'Well, how do I know that you *didn't* steal the emerald pendant? After all, none of us saw much of you at the dance. Well, all right, I don't suggest that you were part of a tremendous plot to steal the thing, Pye, but after all here you are discovered with the setting in your handbag . . .' And Miss Pye was flaring back with ugly accusations about that day nine years before. 'You were in the house alone with John, Gloria; I'm not saying anything, I'm not *suggesting* anything. I'm merely putting it to you that you had the most reason to get rid of him, poor useless creature that he was . . .'

Out in the garden Mr Thoms, with heavy pouches under his eyes, was saying peevishly to his secretary: 'Well, my dear boy, *you* wouldn't have had to steal the cyanide, would you? For all we know, we may all have slept quite normally that night, it may be purely coincidence that I had a headache when I woke . . .'

And Evan, suspicious and jealous also, his head in his hands and listening with only half an ear, was thinking: Gloria might have confirmed my alibi for that day that John Sandells died; if she loves me surely she might have told the detective *that*!

Distrust, fear, concealment, untruth; pain and sorrow and disillusionment and regret. Murder will out!—and murder's ill-favoured offspring will not be far behind.

While fear and tension mounted, Inspector Trickett and Dickinson laboriously searched the rooms and belongings of the household. Dickinson distastefully perused private correspondence, bills, business documents, anything that might throw further light on the motive, if not the method, of Geoffrey Winson's death; Inspector Trickett tapped at the handles of hair-brushes, prodded through cakes of soap, prized loose the heels of shoes, but the emerald was not to be found. They moved down to the second and first floors, and ransacked the rooms there.

'It must be somewhere—they can't have got rid of it in the time,' insisted Trickett, ever hopeful. 'The murder took place the morning after the dance; and nobody's left the house since then— except Sparrow whom we've let exercise Tiggy for an hour—and nothing has been sent to the post without being examined by us.'

'They may have got frightened and chucked it into the sea,' suggested Dickinson, rather wishing that Trickett would let him concentrate on his own trouble, which, being murder, was surely of major importance.

'Not on your life! Did you ever hear of a thief disposing of five hundred pounds' worth of stuff where he couldn't one day recover it? Why, he didn't even throw the setting away—five pounds' worth of platinum!'

'Perhaps he didn't get the chance.'

'If he didn't get the chance to throw away the setting, he didn't get the chance to throw away the emerald either. Either it's Miss Pye,' said Trickett, ponderously working it out for himself, 'or someone got frightened that day on the yacht when Winson died and he saw that there would be unwelcome investigations and so he planted it on the old girl. Actually, I'm inclined to think that that's what happened.'

With some trepidation he invited the suspects to allow themselves to be searched. Mr Dickinson, looking on with a wicked gleam in his eye, thought that this time Mr Thoms really would blow up and bust. But neither among their clothes nor about their persons was any sign of the emerald to be found.

Tiggy, who had been permitted to accompany Sparrow on an outing chiefly because Dickinson could bear her company no longer, arrived back by the time the party, mostly trembling with outraged dignity, had reassembled in the drawing-room. She was full of her outing, but no one had ears for Tiggy's affairs.

Truda felt that she could not endure for one more moment the bickering and recrimination, the ill-feeling and mutual distrust. The knowledge that she herself was unreasonable, irritable and on edge, made it no easier. She sought out Mr Dickinson. 'Do *please* let me and Julian go home! We won't budge from my grandmother's house, I promise you. We'll come to you for questioning, we'll do anything you say; but we're all getting on each other's nerves, boxed up here, and I know it would be easier all round if at least two of us went away.'

'I should be very much obliged, Miss Deane, if you'd just stay over the weekend. This is Saturday evening. On Monday,' promised Mr Dickinson suddenly, taking a chance which astonished himself beyond words, 'I'll let you *all* go!' He raised his voice and went forward to the rest of the party. 'I've decided that after Monday I won't keep any of you here against your wishes.'

Roy had been the most vociferous of all in his objection to the search. Still sick with rage, he announced that he was not waiting for Monday or any other day. 'I'm catching the morning train back tomorrow.'

'I'd rather you stayed, Mr Silver.'

Roy looked for a moment as if he were about to resort to the small-boy vulgarity of: 'Well, I'm not going to, see?' but controlled himself and said in a whining voice that he had stayed on and on since Wednesday at Inspector Dickinson's request, and that he couldn't keep it up much longer. 'I happen to be a radio artist, perhaps you have forgotten? I had to cut a broadcast on Thursday morning, and I'm due for one on Monday morning. Who's going to do *that*, may I ask?'

Mr Dickinson looked volumes. Roy said hotly: '*You* may not think it so very important, but other people . . .' He blathered into impotent rage.

'I won't keep any of you after Monday,' promised Dickinson again. 'I—I think we might have a little expedition tomorrow; it'll be a good day, Sunday, when everyone's at the "Salute the Soldier" Service up at the church; we can all go aboard the *Cariad*, and I think we might just run through what happened that day at lunch . . .' Scotland Yard does not encourage its young officers to stage dramatic 'reconstructions', and he avoided that sinister word.

He caught the speechless amazement in Inspector Trickett's eye and for the life of him could not help adding airily; 'I think we can then "unmask the criminal", as they say, and you will be able to go home on Monday as you wish.'

Tiggy, making a round of boisterous good nights, received little attention. She bestowed moist kisses on Mr Thoms and Evan, who sat through the ordeal as though turned to stone; clasped Roy round the neck, and he hardly seemed to notice her; gave Jenny and Truda brief pecks, and they returned them automatically, their eyes on Dickinson's face. Gloria forgot her customary role of indulgent mama and almost pushed the child aside, and Julian patted her on her flat little behind and said: 'Good night, Tigs,' in a voice that showed that he spoke merely from the habit of polite acknowledgement. Trickett, most astounded of all, bent his heavy head to her tender embraces; Miss Pye got up automatically and stood waiting for her at the door. Tiggy advanced upon Dickinson.

It was rather a relief to take his mind for a moment off this frightful folly to which he had committed himself. What on earth had possessed him to make such a promise? It was Trickett, looking so round and bewildered—the temptation had been too much. What an *ass* I am, thought Mr Dickinson holding out a hand to Tiggy who advanced upon him with animal cries of affection. He lifted the child off her feet and she wound her skinny arms about his neck. 'Good night, fish-cake!'

Tiggy screamed with laughter. 'Fish-cake! Fancy calling me Fish-cake! I shall call Mother Madeleine Fish-cake when I get back to school, and Fish-pie, and Boiled-fish, and Old Fried Cod—I shall call her Old Fried Cod . . .' She went off into fresh peals of laughter at this exquisite wit, clasping him tightly about the neck and waiting, in an ecstasy of apprehension, for the tickling which would surely follow.

Mr Dickinson, however, proved disappointing. 'Ow—don't! You're strangling me.'

'I always strangle people when I kiss them,' said Tiggy cheerfully. 'Once at the convent . . .'

But the doings at the convent passed harmlessly over Mr Dickinson's head. He set her down on her feet and, like a sleepwalker, advanced into the middle of the room. She always strangles people when she kisses them! Her thin little arms quite hurt when she puts them round your neck! He turned round and said to Roy Silver in a voice of honey which even that BBC young man could not have rivalled: 'She put them round *your* neck just now. Didn't she hurt *you*?'

'Hurt me? No—why should she?' said Roy bewildered, taken unawares.

'Because at your boils,' said Mr Dickinson, and stripped off the plaster.

Trickett caught the young man as he turned to bolt through the door. On the back of his neck were two red rings; Dickinson held in one hand a hard lump of chewing-gum; in the other, firmly stuck to the plaster, an emerald the size of a bean.

And at last, looking at those red, seemingly inflamed patches of skin, Inspector Trickett understood the ingenious use of the lipstick in Roy Silver's sponge bag—and the reason for the small piece of waxy chewing-gum paper.

Trickett muttered the regulation warning. Jenny struggled to her feet. She said, holding out piteous hands: 'Oh, Roy—no!'

Roy stood still, controlled by Trickett's strong right arm. He said, mocking her tone: 'Oh, Jenny—yes!'

'A—thief . . . ?'

'A common thief—but better than a murderess!'

'A murderess—?'

'Aren't you?' said Roy in a tone of conversational surprise. Dickinson made a sign to Trickett to allow this possibly informative dialogue to continue. 'If not, why all that to-do the day after your step-papa's murder, about forgetting that he had ever threatened you, etcetera, etcetera . . . ?'

'I—oh, Roy, I thought *you* had done it. I wanted to protect *you!*'

'Why the hell should *I* murder Geoffrey?' asked Roy, astonished. 'He was a pal of mine; we had a lot of fun together.'

'I—I thought that it was because you loved me. I thought you did it to save me from getting mixed up in the breach of promise case. You were so disgusted with it—you were so upset . . .'

'Good lord!' Roy sneered. 'I didn't care two hoots about the breach of promise case; I thought it was a jolly good idea, actually, to get some money out of that stuffed fish over there! And it was an excuse for getting rid of you. I wanted to get invited down here and I wangled it through making passes at you! And then I wanted to vanish from these parts, and I couldn't do it while we were still playing turtle-doves.'

It seemed that Mr Dickinson would never cease astonishing himself that night. He stepped forward suddenly and said to Trickett: 'Let go of his arm!' When Roy stood free, he lifted one hand and hit him with a pleasant crack beneath the jaw. so that he staggered back and almost fell into the inspector's arms. 'You can hit back,' Dickinson said coolly. 'For the moment I'm not the police.'

Roy Silver, however, did not choose to hit back. He stood nursing his chin, and merely essayed a sneer. 'Change your tone then, when you speak to Miss Sandells,' said Mr Dickinson.

'I was merely saying that I used her to get to know Thoms,' said Roy sullenly. His vanity, wounded in one place, struggled forth from another. 'The emerald—that was nothing; I saw it dangling against the old girl's chest and I just couldn't resist the impulse; when I saw that Winson's death was going to cause awkwardnesses, I fished out the setting and shoved it into old Pye's bag. But it wasn't the little stuff I was after.'

Dickinson looked down at the lump of hardened chewing-gum in his left hand. In it were a number of deep clefts. He said: 'What's this? It looks like the impression of a key.'

'It is the impression of a key,' said Roy, with a sort of cool impudence that was not pretty to see because it was cheap and vain and far removed from the élan and daring of the 'big fish' whose manners he aped. 'It's the impression of the key to Mr Thoms's safe in London!' He stood with his head on one side, inviting admiration.

'You came down to get a copy of the key of my safe?' cried old Thoms.

Roy bowed grandly. 'That's right. I looked up the Winsons again when I heard they'd landed you—you'll pardon the expression, sir—and I clung to you all like a limpet till the opportunity came; then I planned to drop out so that when eventually your London safe was opened and robbed you'd never connect it with that charming boy, Silver, who used to be a friend of little Jenny's.' He paused deliberately and pulled out his cigarette case. This was his dramatic moment, and in a macabre way he was enjoying it.

'You remember the Grosvenor Square robbery just pre-war?' he demanded of Dickinson; and added, laughing: 'Well, I didn't do that! But I was doing this kind of thing for ages before the war—all right, you just try and pin anything else on me—you won't be able to! And I was getting fed up with tuppence a week from the BBC, so I thought I'd put through a job of my own.

'I drugged your drinks that night when we came back from

the walk along the sea shore—Jenny had insisted on saying she'd come to my room and talk to me about her precious breach of promise case, so I dosed hers, too, with a drop I had left over; and I could have killed Pye when she went and changed drinks with her! It was my last night and I had to go through with it. I chanced Jenny not coming and went down to old Thoms's room at about midnight . . .'

'I went to your room then,' said Jenny. 'You weren't there. Someone came to the door, but I held it from the inside and pretended to be you, breathing heavily in your sleep, and they went away. I waited and waited; I couldn't think where you could be; and at last I just went back to bed. Afterwards, when I found out the poison had been stolen . . .' Then she said, with a little, forlorn dignity: 'So you didn't love me at all, Roy? You were pretending all the time?'

Just for a moment Roy had the grace to look a little ashamed. 'Yes. I'm afraid so, Jenny; all the time.' He added to the others, as though he really owed it to himself to explain matters: 'When I thought afterwards that she'd killed Winson for love of me, I got the wind up vertical, I can tell you! I didn't know what such a virago might do to me next if I didn't play fair; so I tried to revive the affair till I could get safely away . . .

'You'd better get safely away now,' said Dickinson, 'before I hit you again.'

Sparrow, coming to the doorway to announce dinner, stood in amazement at the sight of young Mr Silver being hustled down the front steps with a police hand heavy on his shoulder.

He recovered from his shock sufficiently to announce that dinner was served. 'You'd better stay and have something with us, Inspector,' said Mr Thoms, cocking an eye at Dickinson.

Miss Pye was voluble over the soup, full of rather obvious digs at Inspector Dickinson who had actually questioned *her* in relation to the jewel theft. 'I always knew Roy was not to be trusted,' she declared. 'There was always something not quite frank about that boy . . . If only you could make out that he killed poor Mr Geoffrey too, Inspector, how very convenient that would be, now wouldn't it . . . ?'

'It might be convenient, Miss Pye, but I don't think it will work.'

Gloria had also privately thought it would be an excellent idea. 'I don't see how you can be so sure . . . ?'

'He simply had no motive,' said Dickinson firmly. 'The only possible reason would have been if he—if he really loved Miss Sandells; and even that was far-fetched. Besides, if he'd had murder planned for the following day, do you think he'd ever have bothered to take that pendant the night before?'

Miss Pye veered round to her earlier theory, going through an elaborate pantomime, forefinger jabbing in the direction of the serving door through which Sparrow had disappeared in search of the fish. Truda and Julian, miserably aloof from each other, aloof from all the world, looked on at this ugly exhibition with disgust. Evan Stone said mildly: 'Oh, I don't think so, Miss Pye. He's a dear little man, he wouldn't do harm to a soul—and why, anyway, to Geoffrey?'

Gloria had no nonsense about *noblesse oblige*. She thought if anyone were going to have the blame it might as well be Sparrow, who might be a dear little man but was after all only a servant and so didn't have *feelings* like real people. Into the bowl of discussion she tossed an ugly little pebble. 'What was that you were saying to Geoffrey the night before he died, Pye, about some girl at Cow's Bay?'

Miss Pye also was anxious to make amends for hasty words that afternoon. If darling Gloria was still angry with her when the marriage with Mr Thoms came off, then good-bye to all hopes of ever getting back her money.

She hastened to catch up the pebble and toss it back. 'It was all for your sake, darling; Mr Geoffrey and Roy were meeting a couple of girls on the cliffs and I didn't think it was right . . .' As Sparrow returned with the fish, she added: 'The girls came from Cow's Bay.'

'Sparrow lives at Cow's Bay,' said Tiggy, trailing lovingly after the steward.

'Your wife's there alone, is she, Sparrow, while you're on duty here?' asked Gloria sweetly, leaning sideways to allow her plate to be placed in front of her. Sparrow put it down with a little clonk. He said briefly, 'Yes, madam.'

'I expect she's *very pretty*, Sparrow, isn't she?' asked Miss Pye, leaning forward.

Sparrow continued steadily with his duties. 'Mrs Sparrow is a nice-looking young woman, miss,' he agreed with a sort of deliberate modesty, as though to shame the questioner by his own humility.

'Had Mr Winson ever met Mrs Sparrow to your knowledge?' asked Gloria; they were like two sleek, female cats watching a mousehole, waiting for the first faint flicker of a whisker.

'Not to my knowledge, madam,' said Sparrow.

Dickinson looked appealingly at her; Evan made a little sign begging her to desist. Mr Thoms said heavily: 'Well, never mind that now.' To Sparrow he said, with a hint of apology in his voice: 'Go on serving the dinner, Sparrow. All this can be discussed another time.'

But Sparrow could no longer control his indignation. 'It's the first I've heard of the matter too, Mr Thoms, sir, and if you'll excuse me, sir, I'd like to leave your service as soon as it's possible to go . . . It's one thing to be accused of such murders as take place among your friends, sir, but to drag my wife's name into it, that I cannot allow.' He took up the dish again with shaking hands, and began his round of the table.

Gloria dabbed fish soufflé on to her plate, hitting the spoon against the china irritably to shake it loose. She said: 'Well, that's a great display of just indignation, but I don't see that Sparrow has *proved* anything.'

Sparrow made no attempt to respond, but his lips were set in a thin white line. Tiggy, hanging gaily to his coat tails as he bent forward to present the dish, announced sentimentally: 'Mrs Sparrow's got such a *dar*ling little baby. She found it under her bed at Taddlecombe Hospital.'

Sparrow glanced up and shook his head warningly at her.

'It's such a *darling* little baby,' insisted Tiggy, taking a pineapple from the dish on the sideboard and tenderly nursing it. 'It's got a teeny little nose and teeny little blue eyes when they're open, but they're shut all the time. And it's quite bald; but Sparrow says that's all you can expect from a fledgling.'

Sparrow gave her a sudden, sweet smile. Dickinson leaned back, tipping his chair on to its hind legs, and caught at the little man's arm with a kindly hand. 'When did your wife find the baby under the bed in the hospital, Sparrow?'

'That would be the day she was muckin' about on the cliffs with the two gentleman, I dare say, sir,' said Sparrow, directing a look of contempt at Gloria and Miss Pye, who sat with forks poised motionless above their fish. 'The child came a little bit· early, I believe. I went over home on the Tuesday night, sir—Mr Thoms will remember, he gave me leave—and she'd been to the hospital for her examination. And she didn't come back; the baby was born the next day, and I took Miss Tiggy to see it this afternoon. I didn't like to trouble anyone with my affairs, sir, while things was in such a mess.'

'Mrs Sparrow's going to call the baby Tommy,' said Tiggy, blissfully nursing the pineapple which had cost fifty shillings. 'After Thom-Thom, because he's always so kind to Sparrow. Isn't she, Sparrow?'

Mr Thoms put his head in his hands; and Evan got up and went round to the steward and gave him a little friendly pat on the shoulder. 'So there, you *see*, Pye, you were *absolutely* wrong as usual,' said Gloria; and went on with her fish.

And so Roy Silver was out. And Sparrow was out. And there

remained seven people of whom one had committed murder:
Mr Thoms, Evan Stone, Gloria Winson, Miss Pye, Jenny Sandells.
Truda Deane, Julian Messenger. Motives: passion, fear, concu-
piscence, greed? Opportunity—as far as the human eye could
see—none! And Mr Dickinson was pledged next day to reconstruct the crime, to tell them: Who; and How; and Why. And
so far he had not the faintest idea.

PART VI

Another day of sunshine: of blue sky and blue sea, of gulls
wheeling over the harbour, of little wavelets lapping the side of
the quay, of the sea-scented warmth of the air struck up from
sun-baked stone. But in the hearts of the seven victims being
driven before Mr Dickinson along the quay to where the launch
waited to take them out to the yacht, there was no sunshine.

Gloria was uneasy and frightened, trying desperately to keep
the balance between Mr Thoms and Evan Stone, till at last it
should be possible to announce to the world that the money-
bags had won. Thom-Thom, jealous and suspicious, doting and
anxious, tried by forced geniality to conceal from his secretary
that anything could be wrong; Evan felt wretchedly that he was
somehow disloyal to his employer in stealing the prize from
him, by reason of twenty years of devotion compared to Mr
Thoms' one.

Jenny walked droopingly with downcast eyes, Julian very
upright and handsome, but obviously ill at ease. Only Truda
forgot her personal troubles, overwhelming though those might
be, and gave her mind to the full significance of the horror that
overshadowed them all. One of them—one of *them*!—walked
even now in the terror of shameful death; one of them, before
this morning was out, would stand accused of murder.

Was one of them afraid, now; afraid in his heart, coldly,
desperately despairingly afraid of what was so soon to come?

Oh, Julian, my love, not you! Not you! She could not endure to see his brown eyes so clouded, to see the insouciant laughter wiped so bleakly from his troubled face. Julian, the gay, the smiling, the irresponsible, the clean of heart—with downcast eyes and grim, set mouth, and nervous hands . . . Oh, Julian—not you! She closed her thoughts against the bare whisper of it. Mystery there might be, and questions unanswered and an undercurrent of ugliness that she did not understand; but she walked along at his side in her cool, summer dress, and looked up into his face, and gave him all her trust. Let the mind whisper ugly doubts the heart knew best.

They sat silently in the launch as it scudded across the blue waters to the little white yacht nosing at her mooring out in the bay; or stood in the stern, the light breeze ruffling their hair, the light spray needling their faces with a million tiny tonic touches, barely perceptible.

When they boarded the *Cariad*, Mr Dickinson assembled them all in the well and faced them, leaning back against the wheel, Inspector Trickett standing stolidly beside him, silently looking on. 'I want to take you down afterwards to the cabin; the lunch will be laid out just as it was five days ago, when Mr Winson died. They're doing it now.'

Tiggy's little face, upraised to his in wonder and curiosity, was the face of a flower; for she had for the moment left off her spectacles. He said; 'Why don't you go and help them lay the table? You could have fun down there!'

As she scudded brightly off, clambering up ungracefully out of the well, he said, half-apologetically: 'I had to have her here, because of her part in the "reconstruction"; but she needn't listen to all the discussion, poor little soul!' As Tiggy scampered happily off he shifted his weight from one foot to the other, but could not shift the weight off his mind. This was the beginning of the scene through which he had impetuously and rashly announced he would reveal the murderer of Geoffrey Winson, and he had still no glimmer of how it could be done! In a slightly unsteady voice he plunged into his nerve-racking ordeal:

'One of you seven people killed Geoffrey Winson last Wednesday, here aboard this yacht, at the table down below. Cyanide is a quick-acting poison, and the dose must have been administered within two minutes of the time he died. *One of you administered it.* Mr Thoms, Mrs Winson, Evan Stone, Miss Deane, Mr Messenger, Miss Pye, Miss Sandells. *One of you administered it.* We are here, to find out Who. And How. And, if possible, Why?'

Seven pairs of eyes stared back at him, inimical, carefully blank. He went on:

'Each of you had a motive for wishing Geoffrey Winson out of the way. Some of the motives aren't very strong; but many murders have been committed for reasons which, to anyone but the murderer, wouldn't seem reasons at all, and this may be one of them. Each of you had *some* motive. And each of you knew of the existence of the poison in Mr Stone's pocket-book. Each of you may have had access to it during the night before the murder. We are here to run through what happened at lunchtime that day, and discover who had the opportunity to administer the poison. We are going to "reconstruct" that luncheon party. I'm afraid it'll be rather grim. I'm sorry.'

There was a little rustling as the tension relaxed for a moment. He passed a nervous hand through his shining hair and uttered a small prayer to whatever gods might be, to keep, for this brief hour, his mind clear, his perception quick, his resolution high.

'First, we must have a few words about the night before the murder, during which the poison was stolen. And immediately we come across a very curious discrepancy. Mr Messenger!'

'Me?' said Julian, jumping.

'Yes, you. You were out of your room that night. What were you doing?'

It had to come. Truda sat rooted to the wooden seat, staring at Julian with terrified eyes. Julian said, stammering: 'I—I was out of my room?'

'Yes. You were out of your room during the early hours of the morning. What were you doing?'

Julian's frank face was ashen. He said at last, stammering: 'I—I expect I was in my bathroom. There's a private bathroom to my room.'

'The bathroom door was open. You weren't in there,' they would wriggle, all of them; he must remember every detail of that night as it had been guilelessly recounted to him by Tiggy telling him of her search in the 'miggle of the night'.

Julian was silent.

'Perhaps, Miss Deane,' suggested Dickinson, looking at her rather miserably, 'you could give Mr Messenger an alibi?'

Truda remained with her eyes fixed upon Julian's face, terrified. ('You mustn't say a word to Dickinson about us, Truda. He mustn't know!' that had been Julian's tense voice speaking to her. She had said, bewildered, 'Why on earth not?' and he had repeated again, violently: 'He mustn't know!') She did not know what to say now, and at last temporized feebly: 'Are you suggesting that Julian was with me that night?'

Mr Dickinson was almost apologetic. 'Now I come to think of it, he couldn't have been; because you were out of your room, too—weren't you?'

'I was in my bathroom for a little while,' said Truda, after a moment. 'Round about midnight, I believe it was.' She gave him a nervous half-smile. 'And you can't say I wasn't because *my* bathroom door *was* closed.'

'Right. You were in your bathroom. But Mr Messenger wasn't there with you?'

She did not know what Julian wanted her to say. Again she played for time. 'What on earth would he have been doing in my bathroom?'

'So much depends on this,' said Mr Dickinson, standing,

swaying, looking around him with hands in his pockets. 'Whoever got possession of that poison killed Geoffrey Winson.' He changed his tone a little. 'Perhaps instead of trying to find out who could have gone to Mr Stone's room and taken it that night, it might be easier it we try to find out who couldn't.'

Miss Pye spoke up.

'Well, I couldn't for one,' she said. 'I was drugged.'

'So you were, Miss Pye.' Miss Pye had received the gin-and-tonic dosed for Jenny by Roy Silver. 'So you were asleep and snor—were asleep all night.'

'The same would go for me,' said Mr Thoms mildly.

'And that's right too, Mr Thoms. And I'll tell you another thing,' said Mr Dickinson, warming to his story. 'We've naturally been cross-examining Master Silver at the station, and he now says that on his way to Mr Thoms' room to get the impression of the key of his safe, he turned the lock of Mrs Winson's bedroom door. He had taken the opportunity during the day of just slipping his hand inside the door and transferring the key to the outside.'

'He locked me in?' said Gloria.

'He said—he said he didn't want to be disturbed by—er—by anyone coming to Mr Thoms' room while he was there. I'm only telling you,' said Mr Dickinson hastily, 'what Roy Silver says.'

Gloria went first scarlet and then very white. She kept her eyes lowered. 'It's a vile lying suggestion.' And it was true that, with all her dilly-dallying, she always contrived to steer clear of actually compromising herself.

'Well, anyway, the point is this, that Mrs Winson was locked in her room and couldn't have been prowling about after poison. Now, as for Miss Sandells, we know that she was out of her room—but we also know what she was doing.' He looked at her gently. 'She was keeping her—very innocent—assignment in Roy Silver's room. My—my informant heard her in there. So that cuts out Miss Pye, Mr Thoms, Miss Sandells, Mrs Winson; and—

if we accept the fact that Mr Stone didn't have to steal his own poison—leaves one person whose movements during that night we cannot ascertain—Mr Messenger.'

('*Promise* me that you won't tell Mr Dickinson about "us"!') Truda said at last: 'Yes. I suppose it does.'

Mr Dickinson ran through the alibis in his mind. They weren't watertight, of course. There was nothing to show that poison had been stolen early in the night and Gloria's door had been unlocked by Silver on his return from Mr Thoms' room.

Moreover, a sleeping-drug did not last for ever, and either Thoms or Miss Pye might have woken up in the early hours of the morning, and still had time to commit the theft. Stone might simply have kept the poison and used it himself. All the same, Messenger had been out of his room; and if he had been with Truda, surely to God she would admit it when his very life was at stake . . . Even if *he* would not give *her* away, surely she would refuse to let him be accused of murder.

But Truda, white and shaking, kept her silence, and into that deathly vacuum Dickinson played his trump card. 'Mr Messenger—how much money have you in the bank?'

Julian's nervous hands were suddenly still. He said at last: 'Not much.'

'Fifty pounds?'

'You seem very well informed! Yes—fifty pounds.'

'I *am* very well informed,' said Dickinson quietly. 'I know that two days before Winson's death you had three hundred pounds in your bank, and Winson had nothing in his. But that after he died he was found to have two hundred and fifty in his; and you had fifty in yours. It seems a coincidence.'

Julian began to grow angry and some of his colour came back. He said: 'Why the cat-and-mouse stuff? You must have seen my cheque passed through the Daunton bank.'

He shrugged hopelessly, and then continued:

'I drew out two hundred and fifty pounds in cash and gave

it to Winson on the Tuesday. He spoke to me at Lady Templeton's dance, and I agreed to—to lend it to him.' Having spoken, he straightened his shoulders with the air of a man who has picked up the burden and means to carry it on with him after all.

'If it were merely a loan, why didn't you just give him a cheque?'

Julian shrugged. 'He said he preferred it in cash. I don't know why.'

'I think *I* know why,' said Dickinson. 'Blackmailers don't like cheques.'

'Blackmail?' said Julian uncertainly.

'Yes, blackmail. Winson came to you at the dance and told you he had persuaded his stepdaughter to bring action against you for breach of promise. You paid him all you had, to stop his mouth.'

Truda sat with clenched hands, white and sick.

'If you think two hundred and fifty pounds would stop Winson's mouth, you must be a fool,' said Julian calmly to Dickinson. 'There was a great deal more to be made out of an action for breach of promise.'

'He knew he'd never succeed in such an action. It was all just a threat. But you'd pay the earth to keep Miss Deane's name out of such a mess.'

'Yes, I would,' said Julian. 'But I don't happen to have the earth.'

'No. Winson began to realize that. You had the reputation of being wealthy, Mr Messenger, but the money was a trust, left for your education, and it finished when you came down from the University. You told Winson that. He decided to take what he could get.'

Julian looked at him levelly. 'He could get a great deal more by going to Truda's grandmother. Now she *would* have paid the earth to keep the matter quiet; *and* she had it. You don't think I'd have handed over all that money without some sort of written undertaking from Winson that would prevent him going on with the action? And you can bet your boots he wouldn't have given it up for a mere paltry two hundred and fifty pounds.'

Mr Dickinson looked down at his rather particularly elegant 'boots' and decided that he would not risk them. Messenger was right. He wished they could have had this out before, but he had only just learned about the money paid to Winson. He hummed and hawed a little.

'So it was just a loan?'

'Just a loan,' said Julian steadily.

The danger had passed. Truda's taut hands relaxed, the light came back to her eyes. But Dickinson had not done. He said smoothly: 'Very well. Then there's nothing against you, Mr Messenger, except this: that on the night before the murder, at about the time that the poison must have been stolen—you were missing from your room. And you can give me no alibi.'

'No,' said Julian.

'And Miss Deane can't help you?'

('Whatever happens, Dickinson mustn't know . . .') 'No,' said Truda.

Gloria sat on the narrow bench which ran round the well, swinging one little foot, and suddenly she laughed.

'What does that mean?' said Truda, very cool and quiet.

'I mean that under all your airs and graces you are contemptible,' said Gloria, enjoying herself. 'You go along in your cool way, rich and safe and smug; no worries, no fears, no temptations; and people think you are "good" and "sweet". But as soon as trouble and temptation come you fold up, you're not good at all, you're just rotten like the rest of us . . .' She looked round triumphantly.

'Those two are in love; Julian was in Truda's room that night, and now, though he's in danger of his life because of it, though he's in danger of being accused of murder, she won't admit to it. She's so terrified of losing her precious reputation, so terrified of her grandmother hearing about it and doing her out of her precious fortune, that she won't admit to it. One word from her would give her lover an alibi for the whole night; she could save him from the slightest suspicion of murder, and she won't say that one word!'

Julian started to his feet. He said, staring at Gloria: 'My God!— so it would!' and suddenly swung round upon Truda, flinging his arms around her, holding her close. 'Oh, my love, my darling, what a silly, blind fool I've been! I *couldn't* have stolen the poison; so whatever sort of motive I've had, I couldn't have murdered Winson; and that's all there is to it!'

To Dickinson, he said; 'Gloria's quite right, I was with Trudie that night. I was with her all night, and I couldn't have stolen poison, and so I'm clear!' And he kissed his love and said; 'We here married last week!' and held her close to him again.

Gloria took one of her neat about-turns: 'So there, with my reproaches to Truda for seeming not to want to admit being— well, rather naughty!—I've revealed that Julian is free of all suspicion!' But nobody noticed her. They were all intent on Mr Dickinson. If Julian were free of suspicion, upon whom could it fall next? But apparently he had not quite finished with Julian. 'There's still the matter of that cheque to clear up,' he plodded on relentlessly.

'Winson came to me that night at the dance,' said Julian, one arm still held firmly about Truda's shoulders. 'He told me he had just arranged with Jenny to bring this action against me. I told him to bring it and be damned; that I was married to Truda now, and that was the end of it. The minute I'd spoken, I saw what a fool I'd been. He was on to it like a stoat . . .'

He glanced wryly at Gloria. but she was intent upon her white shoe. 'He said that that wasn't necessarily the end. He knew he couldn't get away with the action—he admitted it—but he said it would make an awful stink; and he suggested that Truda's grandmother would pay a good deal to keep it quiet.

'I made another mistake: I—well, I'm not used to—to coping with this kind of thing,' said poor Julian, wincing at the revelation of his ineptitude in dealing with crooks. 'I blurted out that he mustn't let my great-aunt know yet: that she hadn't been told. As a matter of fact, we'd come down here to tell her, only, as you know, we found she was in London. Winson changed his tone. He began to be quite chatty; he talked about a "loan" and things like that; but what it all boiled down to was that if I didn't oblige him, he'd ring her up straight away and tell her. Well, I couldn't have that. It would have been the most awful shock to her to have our marriage blurted out over the telephone by a perfect stranger: it would have broken her heart.'

'Of course the fact that her displeasure would deprive Truda of a large fortune had nothing to do with it?' suggested Gloria.

Julian looked down at her with a twist of his eyebrow, a little look of half-humorous contempt. Honestly, one couldn't keep up with ugly minds of such women as Gloria! He said: 'At that moment the only thing I thought about was not distressing her. I knew how much Truda loved her and wanted her not to be hurt. As for money—yes, that did have something to do with it, naturally. Truda's never gone without money, and I felt that it was up to me to try and keep it for her if I could. She didn't tell me, till after we were married, that my great-aunt had actually said that she would cut her off if she married me—our being cousins was what mattered.'

'Of *course* I wanted to persuade Aunt Edwina to let Trudie have her money, if I could. And there was a hurry, too, because we wanted her to know about our marriage before Trudie's twenty-fifth birthday next week.'

'Why?' asked Dickinson.

'Because after Trudie's twenty-fifth, the money is hers whatever she may do.'

'I still don't see the connection,' said Dickinson.

'I wanted granny to know before my birthday that I had married Julian so that she could do as she liked about the money,' Truda explained.

'You see,' cut in Julian, looking straight at Gloria, 'I did not marry Trudie for her money, but I didn't want her to lose it; through any fault or failure of mine.' He turned to Dickinson. 'Perhaps I should have come clean about our marriage to you . . .'

'But you thought I might insist on making it public before you could get to Lady Audian yourselves?' Dickinson saw and sympathized with their predicament.

'Exactly. It doesn't seem perhaps important to you, but it went on being important to me—even when by keeping our marriage dark I seemed to be heading straight for the dock as Winson's murderer.' Julian's apologetic, modest words disclaimed for himself all heroism.

'Your husband's motive was entirely chivalrous, Mrs Messenger,' Dickinson made Truda a courteous little bow, 'and he is completely free from suspicion.' Truda's answering smile was sweet and grateful as she proudly gathered Julian's hand in both of hers.

So that was that. Julian Messenger had an alibi, and a perfectly good alibi it was; for if he had not been with Truda, why should she have slipped into the bathroom and closed the door when Tiggy's little knuckle came knocking at her bedroom door that night? Julian Messenger and Truda were both out. And that left—five people. Mr Thoms, Gloria Winson, Evan Stone, Miss Pye, Jenny Sandells. Mr Dickinson left them all on deck under the care of Inspector Trickett, and went slowly down the little saloon.

Sparrow had finished laying the table, a vase of flowers and fern stood in the centre, and round it were grouped the food and drinks, the pie and the sandwiches, the salad, the iced coffee, the lemonade. It was very hot and most of the company had abandoned their coats and cardigans in the launch; the steward had brought them all down and hung them carefully on hooks behind the bunk-seats.

Dickinson sent him up on deck with Tiggy, and himself sat down alone at the head of the table; sat for a long time deep in thought, rolling grubby bread pellets between thumb and fore-finger and sticking them in an irregular pattern all round the edge of a plate. Mr Thoms, Mrs Winson, Evan Stone, Jenny Sandells, Miss Pye. Miss Pye . . . After a while he got up and went to the head of the companionway. 'I say—Miss Pye!'

Miss Pye scrambled up from the well where they were all still sitting. 'Yes, Mr Dickinson?' She came towards him:

'That day Mr Sandells died, Miss Pye: you were at the house?'

'I arrived ten minutes after he was found,' said Miss Pye carefully.

'I see. You couldn't—er—you couldn't somehow substantiate that, could you? Did anyone see you arrive?'

'Gloria knows it's true,' said Miss Pye, beginning to gabble slightly in her anxiety. 'Gloria can tell you it's true. I came in at the door and she said, Oh, *Pye*, where *have* you been?—John's dead,' she said. The nurse has just found him dead in his bed! I'm so upset,' she said, 'do ring up and try to get Evan Stone to come across and help me, and look after things.' So I rang up Mr Evan at the aerodrome, where he kept his aeroplane, you know; and he said he'd come at once.'

'Thank you,' said Dickinson. He got rid of her. 'Mr Stone— would you come here a minute, please?' Evan came forward. 'How far was your aerodrome from the Sandells' house on Haverstock Hill?'

Evan looked at him oddly. He said at last: 'Well, I told you the other day. It was twenty miles away; about that.'

'Oh,' said Mr Dickinson. After a moment he added: 'And it never occurred to you that that constituted a perfectly watertight alibi? That if you had killed Sandells, you couldn't possibly have been at your aerodrome by the time Miss Pye rang up? I've only just understood that it was there, that she rang you up.'

'Well, yes,' said Evan. 'I suppose it does let me out.'

'Didn't you realize, Mr Stone, that you were pretty seriously in need of a let-out?'

Stone laughed weakly. 'Well, what do you think?'

Mr Dickinson did not laugh. He looked him straight in the eye. 'I think, Mr Stone, that for a number of years you've been protecting somebody else at the cost of your own good name.'

He returned to the table. He knew now the Who. And the Why. For a little while he sat there silently, rolling bread pellets between his fingers and thumb, then he jumped up and walked round the little saloon, went carefully through the pockets of the coats, hanging on the pegs where Sparrow had put them. With haggard but no longer puzzled eyes, he summoned the party to the reconstruction lunch.

Tiggy greeted darling Mr Dickinson with rapture, and settled down on her stool (there was room for only a couple of chairs, besides the side-bunks, in the saloon), swinging excited legs and eyeing the feast before her, all unconscious of its significance. The rest of the party scrambled self-consciously into their places in an embarrassed silence. Dickinson stood in Geoffrey Winson's place, back to the companionway. Sparrow faced him, standing beside a flap-table, holding the drinks. Trickett looked uneasily at Dickinson and hoped he was not going to make a fool of himself.

There was a pretence at remembering the small talk that had been talked several days before. They helped themselves to coffee and sandwiches, pie and salad and cake, and what they could not eat or drink was set aside. 'I want to get things to exactly the same stage that they were in when Geoffrey Winson came down,' said Dickinson.

Tiggy was given her cue and started working her way round

the table with the plate of sandwiches. 'But you, Miss Pye,' said Dickinson, holding out a hand, 'didn't you pass Mr Winson something in the meantime?'

'Oh, yes, the serviette,' said Miss Pye, rather breathlessly. She picked one up from the table and gave it to him. 'And what about that sea-sick tablet?' asked Mr Dickinson coolly, still holding out his hand.

'Sea-sick tablet?' She stared at him, petrified.

'Wasn't that what you agreed upon at breakfast that day? He'd been talking to Sparrow about his fear of being sea-sick during the race? He went on talking to you about it; *didn't* he? Sparrow could only suggest his getting some stuff from the chemist; but you—you're a great one for patent medicines, Miss Pye—you had something to give him, hadn't you? He was to take a second with his meal, to settle his stomach. There was an exchange of looks, perhaps—you passed him the serviette, and with it a tiny pill . . .'

'No, no,' cried Miss Pye, paralysed with terror.

Dickinson shrugged. 'Very well; we'll leave it for the moment. Now, Tiggy, old girl . . .'

Tiggy gobbled up one egg sandwich; he took the other from the plate and ate it slowly.

'Then I asked Winson to have a drink,' said Thom-Thom from the other end of the table.

Sparrow began to open a bottle of sherry. Jenny drank the remains of the iced coffee in her glass, and handed it to Dickinson.

'I've taken great care not to drink from this side,' she explained politely.

Evan passed over the heavy vacuum jug, lifting it carefully in both hands. 'Winson helped himself and shoved it back across the table and I poured out some more into my own glass and drank it.' Evan waited until Dickinson had gulped down the coffee as Winson had done; and then went up on deck. The sherry was passed up the table after a ceremonious tasting by Mr Thoms; and Trickett, acting Roy Silver's part, handed him a piece of pie. 'I suppose I'd better try and eat it,' said Dickinson. There was a gleam in his eye.

Truda mixed a dressing and Jenny oiled the lettuce. Tiggy hung over his chair, the only person present not strung to a pitch of excitement almost unendurable; the only person present not acting a part. 'I *would* love some,' she said.

'I don't think we need go through that bit,' said Dickinson. He put down his knife and fork and leaned back in his chair.

'Oh, mummy, can't I finish it? Do let me finish it.'

'No, Tiggy, nonsense, don't be silly. You can't eat any more on top of all you've had.'

'Oh, *mummy!*'

'No, Tiggy,' said Gloria. '*No!* You'll be sick.'

'Daddy was sick,' acknowledged Tiggy thoughtfully. She turned hopefully to Mr Dickinson. '*You've* eaten some, haven't you? Are you going to be sick?'

For answer, Dickinson put his hand to his stomach, staring in front of him with glassy eyes, and toppled forward, suddenly, across his plate.

They sat round the table, paralysed with fear, staring at him. Dickinson gave a little, horrible, grunting groan and was still again. 'He's poisoned!' said one of the constables in a horrified whisper.

'An emetic!' said Trickett. 'Quick. give him an emetic!' He grabbed the mustard, and Sparrow in a daze passed him a jug of water. The constable, galvanized into action, lifted Dickinson and together they forced the mixture down his throat. 'I'll take him on deck, I'll get him out into the fresh air,' grunted Trickett. 'Here, Boot, you stay and watch this crowd down here.'

Trickett dragged the stumbling body up the short ladder and on to the deck. Stone met them there, starting forward, stammering out questions. Dickinson reeled to the edge and vomited violently. He gasped out: 'Trickett—go down to them!'

Below, in the saloon, Miss Pye began to scream. Constable Boot took the jug of water and slopped some over her face and she suddenly ceased. Gloria had kept her head sufficiently to cling to Thom-Thom. Julian and Truda stood helpless and appalled. Tiggy hung, howling, to Jenny's arm, and Miss Pye began to scream again. Sparrow stood with a bewildered air, stock still beside his table.

Out in the sunlight. Dickinson lay moaning on the deck. To Trickett, bending over him, he whispered: 'Go back. Look after things.'

'I'll stay with him,' said Stone, looking across the prostrate, writhing body. 'He seems to want you to go.'

'I'm done for, Trickett,' whispered Dickinson, feeling blindly for Trickett's hand and tugging at it. 'Cyanide. You can't do anything. Go down and see . . .'

Trickett stared helplessly across the stretch of water between themselves and the land. 'Is this . . . Is he going to *die*?'

'He says it's cyanide again . . .'

'Frightened . . . murdering me so he wouldn't be—found—out . . .' Dickinson slumped again on the deck and was still. Trickett turned suddenly and stumbled down below.

Stone crouched beside Dickinson on the dick. 'My God, this is frightful!' Dickinson was deathly white and beads of sweat glistened on his forehead. 'I—I can't bear to see you,' said Stone, turning away his head from the terrible face and writhing body.

Dickinson groped blindly about him. 'Trickett! Trickett! Where is he . . . ?' His voice was as feeble as a kitten's.

'You sent him below,' said Stone.

'No time . . . to call him . . . going now . . .' He made a great effort. 'Tell—Trickett—murderer—was . . . ?'

'Yes? Tell Trickett the murderer—tell him the murderer was . . . ?'

'Pye,' whispered Dickinson; and lay still.

Stone sat back on his heels. He repeated incredulously: 'The murderer was Pye? Miss *Pye*?'

Dickinson had, somehow, a stub of pencil in his hand. He raised himself painfully and began to print it in big sprawling letters on the pale silver of the deck. 'P–Y–E . . .'

For God's sake,' cried Stone. 'You—you can't do that! You can't write that . . .' He snatched the pencil out of the feeble fingers. 'I could never tell them . . . I could never explain to them . . .' He repeated: 'You mean you thought the murderer was Miss Pye?'

'Pye killed John Sandells,' whispered Dickinson, his hand groping for the pencil again. 'I—knew—when you told me she—rang you up that day . . . Now she's—killed—Winson . . .'

'Oh, God!' said Stone.

Down in the little saloon seven people sat round the table, staring like dummies at the companionway; they lifted their eyes as Evan Stone came down the steps with leaden feet and stood at the head of the table with Trickett a little behind him, watching him. Trembling, he passed his hand over his face where the sweat stood out in beads along the line of his hair. He said: 'Inspector, you'd better go up to Dickinson. I think he's dying. He's got it into his head that—that Miss Pye killed John Sandells and that now she's killed Winson; he wants to leave a message to tell you so. But it isn't true. Pye didn't kill Sandells.' He paused for a moment and then said, as though it were an effort for him to speak the words: 'Geoffrey Winson did.'

Trickett said softly: 'Yes?'

'He killed him,' repeated Evan quietly, looking beyond them all, as though far away and into the unendurable past. 'He crept up and murdered him while he lay there helpless in his bed. Sandells, who loved him, who was one of his dearest friends . . . Who was my dearest friend . . .'

'And so,' said Trickett, softly again: 'You killed Winson. Didn't you?'

'I executed him,' said Evan Stone.

There was a footfall on the companionway; and Mr Dickinson came briskly down the steps.

Trickett mumbled a formula; but Stone brushed him aside. He stood gazing at Dickinson as though he had been a ghost. 'I—I thought I had killed you . . .' And he asked, incredulous, thunderstruck: 'Do you mean to say you've been acting a part all this time?'

'Only up to the mustard and water,' said Dickinson, and wiped his palm across his face and shuddered. Over his shoulder he said to Trickett: 'Did you have to make the stuff so strong?'

They had risen to their feet at Dickinson's buoyant entry and now remained motionless, watching him, stricken into silence. Gloria, white-faced, shrank back against Mr Thoms's protecting arm; Tiggy hung trembling to Jenny's hand; Julian and Truda looked on with eyes of pity and terror; Miss Pye gaped stupidly. She stammered out at last: 'Mr Dickinson—you thought—you thought it was *me*?'

'Not really,' said Dickinson. 'Though you're lucky I didn't. Why didn't you own up to having given Winson a pill of sea-sick cure at lunch that day?'

'I thought—I knew that you'd say I was the only person who could have given him poison, if I'd admitted that I'd given him *any*thing. He asked me that morning at breakfast; he said not to tell anyone. He didn't like being thought a bad sailor. I—I passed him a tablet at lunch-time, but he gave me a sort of a wink and I think he just left it, it was such a calm day . . . I don't know what happened to it.'

Jenny had a flickering half-memory of a little white object rolling away when she had grabbed up the paper napkin to wipe Geoffrey Winson's dead face; but the recollection had come too late to be of service and she thrust it back in the subconscious where it had lain dormant all this time.

'I thought there might have been something of the sort,' said Dickinson. 'So I went and asked Stone about your movements on the day of John Sandells's death: the two murders were almost certainly connected. In confirming your alibi for you, he automatically gave himself a perfect one. I began to wonder why he hadn't used it before.'

'I knew then that you'd tumbled to it,' said Stone, still white and shaking, staring at Dickinson's face. 'I—I couldn't face failure after it had all gone so well, after I'd got away with so much. It's—it's ghastly, Dickinson, but I did—I tried to murder you! Winson's death was different: that was an execution—but . . . Well, I must have been mad, I had this ghastly impulse, and the trick had worked to well the first time . . .' He added incredulously: 'But there *was* some poison there: I saw you take it!'

'Bread pellet,' said Dickinson briefly.

'You—you substituted it?'

Dickinson jerked his head towards a constable: 'Go up and signal the launch. Tell them to come alongside at once; and to come on down again, quick.' To Stone he said: 'Yes, I substituted it. I went through your pocket-book and found the second dose of cyanide there. I'd guessed you had it, of course. We knew that your brother had some, too, and that he'd been killed in the last war. You were his only close relative, so naturally his belongings would have come to you. You kept it for yourself, I suppose, in case anything went wrong?'

'Yes,' said Evan. But he lifted his head; he spoke more strongly than before. 'I didn't intend anything to go wrong though. I had no intention of suffering for punishing Geoffrey Winson; the law had let him go, but *I* wasn't going to; but I had lots of time, I could plan it all out . . .'

'You could surround yourself with people who also had motives for killing him!'

'None of them had really adequate motives,' protested Evan quickly. 'I chose people who might be sufficiently implicated to diffuse the suspicion, but who could never be in real danger of being wrongly convicted. For the rest it was easy: I was in a position to invite people aboard Mr Thoms's ship or to his house . . . I had only to suggest Julian and Trudie coming . . .' He looked at them apologetically. 'And then I could see to it that everyone knew about the poison . . . I could arrange the "picnic" in the yacht . . . and if anything went wrong, I could hold off at the last minute; actually, I'd had it planned for several occasions before that day here in the *Cariad*; I'd waited six months . . .'

'How were you sure Winson murdered Sandells?' asked Dickinson.

'Geoffrey let it out to me one night when he was very tight and he would insist on talking about those old days . . . I'd thought, all that time . . .'

'You'd thought it was Mrs Winson who'd killed her first husband,' suggested Dickinson bluntly. 'She seemed to be strange, she seemed to be allowing you to take what suspicion there was; you thought she was guilty. That was why you tried to crash yourself: you couldn't bear thinking the woman you loved was a murderess.'

Evan looked for the first time directly at Gloria. 'Of course, when Winson let it out I realized how terribly I'd wronged you . . .' At the sight of her white face and the stillness of her little hands, he seemed for a moment to lose his calm, and cried: 'Gloria—*don't*! Don't mind so much! It isn't as bad as you think— I've faced death before, I know all about it. I shan't suffer . . . It's only you that I shall be thinking of . . .'

Somebody should tell Evan, thought Truda. Somebody should have the courage to speak now, to tell him that this at least might be spared to him—the thought that Gloria would be suffering for him, agonizing with him, identifying herself with his tragedy . . . Somebody should break to him now, before he entered upon the terrible solitude, the terrible loneliness of imprisonment and trial and conviction and—and death; somebody should tell him that Gloria was false and worthless and had been always so.

Truda glanced at Mr Thoms, but his fat face was white and beaded with sweat, sealed in self-gratification and blind obstinacy; at Gloria, but she was staring ahead with compressed lips and hard, bright eyes. Somebody should tell Evan that these two . . . She tried to speak, tried to force her lips to say the words— but could not.

Jenny spoke. She moved forward and put her hand on Evan's arm quietly; and in that moment she was born from childhood into womanhood. She faced Gloria. She said in quiet tones; 'I think before Evan goes you should tell him the truth.'

Gloria shrank back against Mr Thoms's heavy arm. Evan said: 'What truth? What does she mean?' But already in his eyes realization had begun to break.

Jenny waited a moment, and since nobody said anything, continued, quietly and pitifully: 'It's not you, Evan. It never has been. Last time it was Uncle Geoffrey; now it's Mr Thoms.'

Thom-Thom spoke at last. 'I'm sorry, Stone. But—but don't think that I've come between you; Gloria told me long ago, she told me before ever Winson died, that if it were not for him, she would have given her love to me . . .'

'I see,' said Evan. He lifted his head and looked into Gloria's eyes. 'She told me the same thing,' he said.

Into the agonizing silence intruded the phut-phut-phut of a motor approaching the yacht. Evan turned suddenly to Tiggy who hung, white and bewildered, to Jenny's arm. 'I do believe that's the launch, Tigs; what about you running up to see?' As she scampered off up the steps like a puppy released from its string he looked at Dickinson and, without a word, held out his hands. The gleaming steel rings clicked about the unresistant wrists; but Trickett was watching Dickinson's young face. He suggested: 'Perhaps it would be best if I took Mr Stone . . . ?'

'Thank you,' said Dickinson. 'Yes, I think that would be a good arrangement . . .' (Of course, it was only the effects of the mustard and water that were making him feel so sick!)

The launch coughed and sighed, nosing up against the *Cariad*'s hull. As Evan went to the foot of the companionway, Julian said suddenly: 'I'll do everything I possibly can for you, Stone. I'll get the right people and all that . . .'

Evan almost smiled, standing and looking back at them as they drew towards him. 'It's very good of you, but—don't bother. I want it all over as soon as possible. I shan't deny anything. Thank you, all the same.'

Gloria stood alone, outside the circle of their pity and their grief. With his foot on the companionway, Evan looked across their heads at her, and spoke his last, coldly bitter words before them all: 'You've killed two men, Gloria: John Sandells was murdered for your sake, and Geoffrey Winson was killed because of that; and I shall die because of him . . .' He paused, and then went on as though he were thinking aloud: 'Through a little window one can see a wide view; and I see now, Gloria, that you knew all the time . . . You knew that Geoffrey Winson had killed your husband. And knowing it, you married him; you tried to thrust the blame on to me. The happiest thing in the world for me will be to die and get this thought out of my mind.'

The phut-phut-phut of the launch died away into silence; up on deck they could hear Tiggy's cheerful voice screaming out her innocent farewells. Thom-Thom would look after Tiggy, thought Truda; whatever happened, Thom-Thom would see that Tiggy was safe. And Jenny was grown-up all of a sudden, and could look after herself until, one day soon, someone should come along and take over: Mr Dickinson, perhaps, or another nice, clean, smiling young man—it didn't really very much matter who. And Roy Silver, with his first prison record behind him, would pop in and out of jails for the rest of his life, impudent, reckless, rather shoddily debonair. And she and Julian would be rich or poor, according to Lady Audian's whim—but, rich or poor, would be together, and so all would be well.

As for Gloria, Truda had a sudden ugly vision of Gloria, of Gloria living on through the years with old Pye, two women disliking and despising one another, but banded together by the uneasy past; of Gloria existing on the bounty of Mr Thoms who gave because he was rich and generous and in the habit of giving—but who was no longer in love, of Gloria living on insecurely into old age, a little hard grasping woman, closing bright, frightened eyes to a future when Mr Thoms and his charity should be gone . . . But perhaps, after all, she would catch him in the end? Perhaps, after all, the one-sided smile and the scented white hands would win!

Tiggy appeared at the top of the companionway. 'It's lovely and sunny on deck. Aren't you all coming up?'

They turned and looked back for the last time at the little room that had been constructed only for pleasure, and yet had seen so much of tragedy, of horror and doubt and fear; at the table where Geoffrey Winson had fallen forward in a single terrible spasm of death, and so had paid the price of his cruelty. As the rest went on up the stairs, Julian stepped forward. He said: 'But how did Evan do it?'

'It was the bread pellets that gave me the idea,' said Mr Dickinson. 'I was sitting here thinking and thinking and I found that I'd rolled a whole lot of them and stuck them in a rather grubby pattern round the edge of a plate.' He crumbled a fragment of bread and rolled one more. 'Look—you're Geoffrey Winson, and I'm Stone, passing you the vacuum jug . . .' He lifted it, his right hand on its handle, his left forefinger and thumb holding the spout. As he put it down, drawing his thumb away, Julian saw that inside the dull metal of the open spout there stuck a grey-white, bruised pellet. He took the jug, holding it by the handle alone, and poured. When he put it down again, the pellet was gone, washed into his glass.

Outside, the seagulls swooped, white winged, against the sky; and the sun threw a shimmer of sequins on the rumpled blue silk of the sea. The two men made their way slowly up to the silver deck and, shutting the gate of the companionway behind them, closed in the gloom.

CHRISTIANNA BRAND

Mary Milne (1907–1988) was born in Malaya where her father was working as a tea planter. She lost her mother at an early age and was brought by her father to England, where she was schooled at a convent in Berkshire. At the age of seventeen she was effectively abandoned by her father and drifted in and out of various jobs before meeting a young surgeon called Roland Lewis, whom she would go on to marry, somewhat to his amazement. One of her many jobs around this time was a spell selling kitchen appliances, which brought the future prize-winning crime writer into contact with a woman so loathsome that she was memorialized as the victim in *Death in High Heels* (1941). This was the first of many mystery novels published by Mary Lewis as 'Christianna Brand', a soubriquet that combined her grandmother's 'catch-penny' surname with the first name of her beloved mother.

Writing came easily and as well as a series of very highly regarded detective mysteries—novels and short stories—'Christianna Brand' reviewed books and wrote plays, romantic fiction and a series of children's stories featuring the redoubtable Nurse Matilda, latterly known as Nanny McPhee in a pair of films written by and starring Dame Emma Thompson. She also published novels under several other pseudonyms. Although her career as a crime writer suffered a twenty-year hiatus for private reasons, 'Christianna Brand' made a welcome return in the late 1970s, but her health was poor and she died while working on 'Death on the Day', a final case for her best-known detective, Inspector 'Cockie' Cockrill.

Over thirty years after her death, 'Christianna Brand' is rightly recognized as one of the most significant figures in crime fiction in the 1940s, memorable for her ingenuity, light touch and macabre sense of humour, a woman loved not only by those who enjoy her books but also by her many friends in the Detection Club and Crime Writers' Association. Happily, a new collection of her short fiction, including some unpublished stories, is due soon from the American publisher, Crippen and Landru.

'Shadowed Sunlight' was first published as a six-part serial in *Woman*, the 'national home weekly', between 7 July and 11 August 1945.

THE CASE OF BELLA GARSINGTON

Gladys Mitchell

PROBLEM

CARTARET: Have you ever noticed what tremendous consequences hang upon seemingly trivial things? A chance
impulse—or an unexpected encounter—a postman decides
to have a drink at his village inn. Could anything be less
important? On the face of it, no; yet because he chooses
the evening and the time when a certain young woman
happens to be coming away from her father-in-law's house
he is the means of bringing a murderer to justice. You see,
if Bella Garsington hadn't met Sam Hughes the postman
that night, no one would have known of her visit to her
father-in-law and so no one would have suspected her of
his murder. A treacherous and brutal business. She had
married above her, as I believe the saying goes, and had
had the misfortune to lose her husband in a car smash on
the first day of their honeymoon; and, of course, this
excited a good deal of public sympathy at the inquest. I
can see her now: a short, plump, rather hard-faced young
woman, expensively dressed but in very poor taste, standing
in front of me giving her evidence . . .

BELLA: . . . It was quite a shock to me. I declare I never dreamed I'd get his money.

CARTARET: Would you say that the deceased had offered no objection to your marriage with his son?

BELLA: We never liked him much. Of course, he was always quite a gentleman. Still, I mean to say . . .

CARTARET: Quite. Now you say that, as you came up the drive, you could see that your father-in-law had a light on in his study?

BELLA: That's right. That's how I knew where he was. There was an opening in the curtains. Being it was such a dark night, it kind of glowed, if you know what I mean.

CARTARET: About what time was this when you walked up the drive?

BELLA: Oh, just nine o'clock. You see, not being invited, I didn't want to interrupt his dinner.

CARTARET: And when did he usually dine?

BELLA: Well I couldn't say for sure. But whenever he'd invited me, which he'd done about six times a year—to go over my money and that—it was always at seven o'clock.

CARTARET: I see. But you say you arrived at the house at nine o'clock. How are you so sure of the exact time? Can you substantiate it?

BELLA: Can I? Oh, swear to it, you mean? Well, as it happens, I can. There's a clock on the church down the village. It chimes. It struck nine as I came up the drive.

CARTARET: Did it? I believe the servants were all at a dance at the village hall that evening.

BELLA: That's right, they were.

CARTARET: Then how did you gain admission to the house?

BELLA: Me? I had a key.

CARTARET: Oh, really?

BELLA: Oh, yes. It had been my hubby's key, you see.

CARTARET: You're accustomed, then, on these occasional visits which you paid to your father-in-law, to let yourself into the house?

BELLA: 'Course I wasn't. What was his servants for? I used to ring the bell like anyone else. I tell you, he was most particular. His manners, his clothes, his little ways of doing things. Always the gentleman. Never nothing wrong nor out of place nor familiar nor nothing of that, if you know what I mean.

CARTARET: Yes, I think I do. Why did you arrange to visit him, I wonder, on a night when the servants would be out?

BELLA: Me? I just blew along to cheer him up, seeing he'd be alone 'til nearly midnight. He was over sixty, you know.

CARTARET: Did it not occur to you to ring the doorbell and have him let you in? If he was not expecting you, I should have thought . . .

BELLA: Oh, it's not me to stand on ceremony. Besides, I wouldn't trouble him. Goodness knows, I'm sorry enough now I didn't do as you say, but how did I know I was going to find him . . . (crying) To find him . . . (she breaks down)

CARTARET: Perhaps a drink of water?

BELLA: I'm all right. But to think of him, lying there on the floor, all stiff and cold.

CARTARET: Did you move the body at all?

BELLA: Me? Touch him—in the state he was in? Why, he was lying all out, with his nice black dinner jacket all creased up under him and his nice white hair all stained. And as for his tie—it was spotted and splashed with nasty red. I could see all that without going nowhere near him as soon as I come in the door. Me. Touch him? Not bloomin' likely! Not me.

CARTARET: We have heard medical evidence to the effect that the deceased must have died not later than seven. What time, I wonder, did the servants go to the dance?

BELLA: They can tell you better than I can. But I happen to

know they left the house, or should have done, at six. He wrote it me in a letter. He used to write every month to send me my money.

CARTARET: I understood you to say that your financial affairs were settled when you visited him.

BELLA: Yes, that's right. Only, you see, I'm kind of expensive. The best is good enough for me and sometimes I get a bit overdrawn at the bank. That's why we used to meet and settle. Though if you want to know what I think, I reckon he used to like a bit of company, for he used to say to me sometimes, 'I *only* put on my glad-rags for you, my dear.' It's a proper compliment to a lady.

CARTARET: His glad-rags?

BELLA: Oh, you know, full evening dress, black tail-coat, white tie and that. 'Til that evening I'd never seen him in anything else. He was always the gentleman in everything. He would always order up a good wine and a nice drop of port if he'd asked me to come. Although he said he never hardly took it when he was alone . . .

CARTARET: . . . Yes, Bella Garsington made it sound very convincing—except for one small point which gave the flaw to her evidence. One small point which betrayed her and showed us what she had done. I wonder if you noticed it?

SOLUTION

COMPÈRE: Well, 'The Case of Bella Garsington' seems to have puzzled everybody. Quite a number of you got very hot but only one person guessed exactly what Bella had done. That she had had dinner with her father-in-law, killed him and attempted to conceal the fact that she had been there by changing his tail-coat—his glad-rags, which he only wore for her—for his dinner-jacket. But she had forgotten to change the white tie as well. She could not have seen splashes of blood on a black tie. So the only prize of ten and sixpence this time goes to Lieutenant J. V. Palmer. And congratulations, Lieutenant Palmer, on solving what seems to have been a pretty tricky murder.

GLADYS MITCHELL

Gladys Maude Mitchell was born in 1901 in what was then the village of Cowley near Oxford. After her parents moved to Brentford in west London, she attended the Rothschild School and from 1913 to 1918 the Green House for Girls, where she had a free place (and, incidentally, was exempt from daily prayer). It was at the Green that she wrote her first novel which, as with other juvenilia, appears to be lost.

After leaving school, Mitchell completed a teacher training course at Goldsmiths College in London and took a history diploma at University College, London. Mitchell was what used to be termed a 'mannish woman' and at college was known as 'Mike'. On coming down, she embarked on what would be—other than one brief 'retirement'—a lifelong career in teaching. Her first engagement was at St Paul's, a small boys' school in Brentford, where she met Winifred Blazey, an older teacher whom 'Mike' would come to call 'Fred'.

In July 1925, Mitchell was appointed as an assistant teacher at St Mark's, a local boys' school where she had previously worked as a supply teacher. The following year, she moved to St Ann's, a girls' secondary school in nearby Hanwell. At St Ann's, as well as teaching, she ran the amateur dramatic society, for which she wrote plays such as *On Christmas Eve* (1929), as well as playing a leading role in the delightfully named Joy and Pleasure Club, whose games' evenings she coordinated. On New Year's Eve in 1926 at a 'carnival dance' held by a local church at the school she won a fancy dress competition dressed as Prince Charming; not entirely uncoincidentally, cross-dressing—that characteristic of English pantomime—would feature in one of her earliest crime novels.

Mitchell loved writing, albeit in longhand and not on a typewriter, because she loathed the sound made by the keys. There appeared to be a lively market for detective fiction and she decided to write a mystery; as she happened to be reading Sigmund Freud, she made her detective a psychoanalyst. *Speedy Death* was published in 1929 and, while some critics felt Mitchell had failed to conceal the identity of at least one of those with something to hide, her ingenuity was widely praised. Similar praise was heaped upon her second mystery, the exceptionally gory but 'unusually brilliant' *Mystery of a Butcher's Shop* (1929). Gladys Mitchell had arrived. Her detective, Beatrice Adele Lestrange Bradley, was soon recognized as one of the most extraordinary detectives in the genre and would become one of its most enduring, appearing in sixty novels over nearly sixty years.

After leaving St Ann's Mitchell moved to Brentford Secondary School, where she was appointed as a fourth form teacher alongside Freda Blazey. She experimented with new teaching methods, writing in 1950 for *History* magazine about how she and Freda taught the subject by bringing out the connections with geography, archaeology and engineering. Mitchell said she valued the discipline that went with a teaching career and, although she did retire briefly on turning fifty, she seized an unexpected opportunity to return and in 1953 joined the staff of the Matthew Arnold Secondary School for Girls, where she taught history and English and wrote plays on classical and traditional subjects for performance by the girls. She finally retired from teaching in 1961 when she felt the cultural distance between teacher and pupils had become too great. To mark her retirement the school's staff and pupils presented her with a five-month-old Boxer puppy called Robbie, and in 1962 the BBC gave her a half-hour radio programme, *The Plaid Bag*, in which she reflected on parallel careers as a teacher and novelist.

Defiantly unconventional and eccentric in every respect, Gladys Mitchell's detective, Mrs Bradley is, in the words of the critic Frank Pardoe, 'a true original'. She dresses like a cockatoo, smiles like a lizard and laughs like a hyena. But the eccentricities conceal genuine expertise. She is a trained psychoanalyst and is made a dame for her work with the police. She is a superb detective, adept not so much with physical evidence as with psychological clues. And like Mitchell, Mrs Bradley was a crack shot. In an interview with Barry Pike, the authority on Mitchell's contemporary Margery Allingham and on crime fiction generally, Gladys Mitchell explained that Mrs Bradley, later Dame Beatrice, was 'based on two delightful and most intelligent ladies' and that the character had been born in 1929 in her mid-fifties, the age at which she would remain—more or less— for the whole of her long career.

Mitchell's books, at times grimly comic, have a unique 'taste' and are often rooted in the folklore of the United Kingdom, with instances of witchcraft, druidic practice and satanic ritual. *Winking at the Brim* (1974) incorporates the legend of the monster of Loch Ness, while others have more prosaic settings such as the schools in *Faintly Speaking* (1954), following her return to teaching, and *Death at the Opera* (1934), which was inspired by the 'Summerhill' educational theories of Alexander Sutherland Neill. Some were influenced by the country's landscape and lore, featuring morris dancing, scarecrows and the like, while others had their origins in prehistoric sites such as the Nine Stones at Winterbourne, which she fictionalized in *The Dancing Druids* (1948).

As well as conforming—largely—with the 'very strict rules' established by the Detection Club, Mitchell had her own rules and would not criticize the church or the police. She was similarly respectful of the Scouts and the Guides, and in 1957 created an entire regatta to celebrate the centenary of the West Middlesex Guides.

In 1932, Mitchell was elected to the Detection Club, her sponsors being the Club's founder Anthony Berkeley and the Australian crime writer Helen Simpson, whose expert knowledge on witchcraft would inspire Mitchell's sixth mystery, *The Devil at Saxon Wall* (1935). At one time Mitchell was the Club's secretary and also acted as the librarian. She contributed to two collaborative crime novels: the immensely enjoyable *Ask a Policeman* (1933)—in which she and Helen Simpson wrote about each other's detectives—and the less successful all-female round-robin mystery *No Flowers by Request*. Mitchell was also a member of the Crime Writers Association which, on the publication of her fiftieth book, awarded her the Association's Silver Dagger.

As well as writing under her own name Mitchell wrote under two pseudonyms: as 'Malcolm Torrie', she wrote six detective novels featuring Timothy Herring, secretary of the Society for the Preservation of Historic Buildings, an organization not unlike the Ancient Monuments Society of which Mitchell was a member. While she would claim that Mrs Bradley's secretary, Laura Menzies, was an idealized version of herself, it is perhaps not too fanciful to suggest that there may also be much of Gladys Mitchell in Timothy Herring.

Mitchell's second pseudonym was 'Stephen Hockaby', as whom she wrote five vividly drawn historical novels, a novel for young adults entitled *Shallow Brown* (1939) and a play, *The Master of Dreams* (1934), set in ancient Egypt and performed at St Ann's. Although the Hockaby novels were reviewed well, the last was apparently rejected by the publisher—this might be *The Spears of Morning*, a novel referenced in her agent's records that has yet to come to light.

As well as fiction for adults, Mitchell also wrote half a dozen juvenile mysteries and a volume of poetry, *Winnowings*, which was published privately. Her agents' records suggest that in the 1940s and '50s she wrote for various women's magazines. She also wrote several radio plays for the BBC including *Full Fathom Five*, a Mrs

Bradley mystery of which the second half has been lost, as have the scripts of three other plays that were not accepted by the BBC: the tantalizingly titled *Le Jour de Gloire* (1941), *The Case of the Tidy Waiter* (1945) and *The Limping Hound* (1953).

After Freda Blazey's death, Mitchell moved to Dorset to be near her brothers. She died in 1983 at her home at Corfe Mullen.

The Case of Bella Garsington was first broadcast on 10 February 1944 on the BBC's General Forces Programme as one of a series of mystery plays entitled 'A Corner in Crime', a feature in the long-running feature *Here's Wishing You Well Again*. The solution was broadcast on 23 March. This is the play's first publication.

THE POST-CHAISE MURDER

Richard Keverne

It was a matter of business that took Sir Christopher Hazzard down the road that autumn night for a meeting with Mr Amble, the country attorney who dealt with the affairs of a small estate Sir Christopher owned in Hampshire.

Sir Christopher had put off the tiresome journey again and again. Then on the spur of the moment he had decided to get it over and had driven like fury from his chambers, in St James's, to catch the Portsmouth Post Telegraph coach at the Angel Inn, St Clement's, hoping to get his business done and to be back in London again the following evening.

Through a cold, wet night he dozed restlessly on top of the lumbering night stage, and he was weary and bored when, at length, the coach rattled over the cobbles of Ashmarket's narrow High Street, turned into the Square and pulled up sharply before the archway of the Bear Inn.

Sir Christopher swung himself stiffly to the ground and stamped his numb feet. Although it was not yet sunrise there was an unwonted air of bustle about the place. Men stood in knots, talking eagerly. Scraps of excited conversation came to Sir Christopher's ears.

'Shot him dead he did, not two mile outside the town—Sammy Chale, he caught 'un, him and Mr Bond from the "Wagon"— gentleman posting from Portsmouth, so it's said . . .'

Sir Christopher turned to the inn boots who was waiting to receive his baggage from the coach.

'Some trouble here?' he queried casually.

Boots was eager to talk.

'Aye, indeed, there have been, sir. One of our chaises stopped close by Squire Easton's lodge gate, not two mile outside the town, just after midnight. Gentleman shot dead, and Sammy Chale the post-boy lucky to be alive himself.'

'Indeed. And have they taken the rogue?'

'Red handed, as you might say, sir. Within ten minutes of his bloody murder. Sammy were too clever for 'un, he's sharp is Sammy Chale. Slipped off his horse when the robber stopped him and ran for help.' Sir Christopher smiled dryly. 'Come upon Mr Bond from the "Wagon" at Dean riding up the road and told him, and they goes back and finds the robber. Mr Bond claps a pistol to his head and takes him.'

'Ah well; he's not likely to molest honest travellers on the road again,' Sir Christopher commented casually.

'That he won't, sir. He'll swing. And good riddance to all such murdering scoundrels, say I.' Boots busied himself with the luggage, now deposited on the cobbles, and Sir Christopher took a pace or two towards a sly-eyed little fellow in a yellow-sleeved waistcoat who, surrounded by a curious knot of listeners, was shouting his story to the Coachman of the stage.

Sir Christopher regarded Sammy Chale with interest. The man was more than half-drunk and his story had already grown in oft telling to one or two, or maybe three, highway robbers whom he had bested; to shots fired that had missed him by a hair's breadth; to a mighty struggle that he had made in over-powering the villain.

The coachman laughed good humouredly and chaffed the little man.

'Reckon I'd better take you with me, Sammy, case they other rogues be waiting for me down the road,' he said.

The post-boy protested his story the louder and Sir Christopher, mildly amused, made his way to the inn door.

To Kit Hazzard all crime was interesting. He had made it his study for many years and his own curious methods of detection had met with amazing success. It was his sport, as he often said, to hunt the criminal as others hunted the fox. He pitted his own brains and observation against the cunning of the malefactor and beat him more often than not. But this seemed no case to exercise his ingenuity. A straightforward and all too common robbery with violence on the highway with but one unusual fact about it—that the robber had already been taken.

He put the incident from his mind and gave his attention to a change of attire and to breakfast, which he badly needed, and to the affairs that had brought him to Ashmarket. Nor might he have given it more than a further passing thought but for Mr Amble, the attorney.

Sir Christopher had sent a note to Mr Amble immediately upon his arrival, announcing his unexpected visit. The lawyer appeared in person while he still sat at breakfast. Sir Christopher greeted him with surprise.

'I had not meant to bring you out so early, Mr Amble,' he said courteously. 'I have dallied so long over my affairs already that they might well have waited another hour or so.'

Mr Amble raised a plump, deprecating hand.

'No, Sir Christopher, I cannot claim it's your affairs that bring me here so early,' he said. "Tis a far less agreeable matter that roused me from my bed two hours since.'

'Indeed?' Sir Christopher regarding the usually correct and dapper attorney realized that he had the air of one who had dressed hurriedly. His old-fashioned wig was awry and his cravat carelessly tied.

Mr Amble nodded.

'A most unwelcome and strange matter, Sir Christopher,' he continued. 'A matter of robbery and murder on the highway.'

'Oh? I heard some talk of a robbery and a man shot dead when I arrived,' Sir Christopher said. 'But I hear they've taken the rogue.'

'That is so, sir; but there are some curious points about the affair. For example, here is a robbery that, if I may so put it, was no robbery. Over two hundred guineas were found upon the unhappy victim, aye, and thirteen more in his purse. It was to place this considerable sum in my sole keeping, that my good client Mr Charles Easton aroused me from my sleep this morning. Mr Easton is a Justice, sir, before whom the rogue was taken and the outrage took place close by his own lodge gates at Dean Grange. Mr Easton came to me for a dual reason, the one I have stated and because, as perhaps you will recall, I have the honour to be His Majesty's coroner for this Liberty and upon me falls the duty of determining the facts of the unhappy man's death.'

Mr Amble spoke with conscious pride.

'I recall your important office, Mr Amble,' Sir Christopher responded with becoming gravity, though in fact he was not at all sure that he did. 'May I offer you some refreshment? A glass of wine—'

'No, I thank you, Sir Christopher. A cup of coffee perhaps, for in truth I have not yet breakfasted.'

'Then you shall join me, Mr Amble.' Sir Christopher rose to summon a waiter, adding as he resumed his seat: 'Tell me more of this affair. Who was the victim who travelled so well provided with guineas?'

'There, sir, is one of the curious facts of the case. You may take my information as accurate for I have it from Mr Easton's own lips. There is nothing on his body to say who he was, or what his business. No document, no scrap of paper, nothing.'

'Curious. Very curious. What of the rogue who shot him?'

'A notoriously bad character. A man named Jem Vaughan. A poaching, smuggling rogue who hails from a neighbouring village. A man who has often seen the inside of a jail.'

'Ah! I know the type. Yet in my experience one more given to petty robbery than to stopping a chaise on the highway.'

'I would not offer an opinion, sir,' Mr Amble said politely.

'Yet a poor robber, I think you'll concede, Mr Amble, to miss so rich a booty as two hundred guineas.' Sir Christopher said with a smile. 'How came that about? Was the fellow disturbed?'

Mr Amble frowned perplexedly.

'There, sir, is another most confusing point. Disturbed, yes, when he was taken; but no, in that he had, as the evidence holds, fully ten minutes in which to carry out his designs. Aye and more, sir, the body had been searched, the clothes were in disarray—'

'And was nothing found on this man Vaughan to show what he was seeking?' Sir Christopher asked with a suddenly aroused interest.

'Nothing. The mere trivial articles that one would look to find upon such a person. A few shillings, but, sir, a brace of pistols, both discharged, and powder flask and bullets.'

Sir Christopher sipped his coffee in silence for some moments.

'And yet he shot the man—that's curious. Was there any sign that the unhappy man had resisted?'

'None, sir, according to my information.'

'Tell me a little more about this, Mr Amble,' Sir Christopher said, pushing back his chair. 'As you know, an unusual crime has a deep interest for me, and this is both a curious and a stupid one on the face of it. Start from the beginning, Mr Amble, and give me your facts with a lawyer's precision.'

Mr Amble cleared his throat and began in a dry, expressionless voice, 'As I know the facts, Sir Christopher, they are these.'

Sir Christopher had taken a stout memoranda book from his pocket and prepared to make notes. He used the art of stenography or short writing as it was known, and wrote rapidly as the lawyer continued.

'Shortly before midnight last, this unfortunate traveller arrived at his inn in a chaise from the 'George' at Portsmouth. He was posting in haste to London. He is described as having the appearance of a seafaring man. Here he was to change chaises. He waited some quarter of an hour for refreshment, then proceeded on his way in a chaise from this house, Samuel Chale post-boy. Some quarter of an hour later, close by the lodge gates of Dean Grange my good client's house, some two miles on the road, the chaise was stopped, by, as Chale reports, an armed man who leapt from the darkness and seized the horses' heads.'

'And following the custom of post-boys, Chale ran away, I take it,' Sir Christopher put in.

Mr Amble smiled frostily.

'His story is that he slid from his horse and ran for help to the Wagon Inn, a humble place, some quarter of a mile distant.'

'Why didn't he go to Mr Easton's lodge?' Sir Christopher asked, as it seemed, of the air.

'A point to be determined,' Mr Amble conceded. 'But his story is that as he approached the 'Wagon' he met Silas Bond the landlord riding home from Ashmarket. He told Bond what had happened and together they returned to the chaise. There they surprised the man by the door. He took alarm. There was an exchange of shots but Bond hit his man and between them he and Chale secured him.'

'Eh? Shot him, did he?' Sir Christopher commented.

'A trivial wound I am assured. But sufficient to check the rogue.'

'I see. Pray continue, Mr Amble.'

The little lawyer proceeded deliberately.

'Now, sir: Chale states that he flung open the door of the chaise and found the passenger shot dead. Bond corroborates. Chale then went to the lodge and roused the keeper Fratton whom he sent for Giles Pedder the parish constable, returning to the chaise to assist Bond with his prisoner. When the constable arrived, he at once took Vaughan into custody, intending to secure him for the night and bring him before a Justice in the morning.'

'Yes. Yes,' Sir Christopher said, raising his eyes from his book.

'But, sir,' Mr Amble continued, 'Mr Easton, who is a Justice, had heard the shooting and had sent down to the lodge to inquire what was the cause. On learning from Fratton's wife what had occurred, he himself came down, arriving just after the constable came. So Vaughan was at once taken to the house, brought before him and committed to jail. Meanwhile, Mr Easton, a most humane and conscientious gentleman, had sent Fratton on one of the post horses for Mr Ives the Ashmarket surgeon, hoping that even then there might be some chance of saving the unfortunate victim's life. But alas! Mr Easton's hopes were unfounded. Mr Ives stated that the gentleman must have died almost at once.'

'A very proper action of Mr Easton's,' Sir Christopher said. 'Dead or alive, a surgeon should always be called in such circumstances. Believe me, Mr Amble, fewer rogues would go unpunished were that the law of the land.'

'I dare say, Sir Christopher,' Mr Amble replied without much conviction. 'But it was fortunate in this case, for in the course of his examination Mr Ives discovered the guineas in a belt round the dead man's waist and at Mr Easton's request made a search of the clothes in an endeavour to establish the identity of the victim. A search which, as I have told you, proved fruitless. Those, sir, are the facts as I know them.'

'Thank you, Mr Amble,' Sir Christopher added a note or two in his book. 'Now what of this fellow Vaughan? Protested his innocence, of course?'

'As you say, sir. And impudently. Professed some cock and bull story about walking along the road and seeing an abandoned chaise and going to find out what was amiss with it. Then as he says, Bond and Chale fell upon him and he fired in self-defence.'

'Well, why not?' Sir Christopher asked suddenly. 'It sounds a plausible story to me.'

'Plausible, sir!' Mr Amble seemed shocked. 'Plausible, maybe, had he not been found where he was found with his pistol discharged and a ball in a man's heart close by him. No, Sir Christopher, Vaughan killed that man, *but why?* is the question I ask myself. It is my belief that there were more than one in it. There's something behind it. Vaughan knows, but he'll not say: he'll not even give an account of his doings, nor can he offer a witness to say where he had been. It's a dark mystery and I doubt we shall ever know the solution.' Mr Amble's head shook dubiously.

A flash of mild amusement showed in Christopher Hazzard's puzzling grey eyes.

'Oh, come, Mr Amble; let's hope it's not as obscure as that,' he said. 'I am almost persuaded to look into the matter myself, so profound a mystery do you make of it.'

'I would not presume to ask that, sir, but I should be vastly grateful if you would,' Mr Amble responded, brightening.

'Yet maybe you'll regret it, Mr Amble.'

'Regret it, sir, how?'

'Ah, how?' Sir Christopher repeated cryptically. He rose. 'Let us see if I can answer that question for you. Now can you arrange for me to see this fellow Vaughan in jail?'

'At once, I'll—'

'No, not at once, Mr Amble. I must know more about the affair before I question him. First, I'd have a few words with Mr Easton, then I'd see the corpse. Where shall I find it?'

'The corpse?' Mr Amble shuddered slightly. 'Why, it remains at Dean Grange awaiting the inquest.'

'Then Mr Amble, let us proceed to Dean Grange,' Sir Christopher responded.

Mr Easton of Dean Grange appeared a bluff, red-faced, fox-hunting squire. He received Sir Christopher and Mr Amble in his library and instantly ordered a bottle of his oldest Madeira to be brought.

'Mr Amble has already told me of your art in ferreting out a mystery, Sir Christopher,' he said, 'though damme, such arts are beyond my understanding. I am a plain and simple country gentleman, sir, and I can but deal with plain and simple facts.'

'You can do no better, Mr Easton,' Sir Christopher responded with a bleak smile. 'It is for facts that I am come to you that we may endeavour to establish the truth of this unhappy affair.'

Mr Amble put in: 'Sir Christopher would have us believe that Vaughan's story is true, Mr Easton.'

'True!' Mr Easton exclaimed in surprise. 'Nay, you're jesting, Sir Christopher.'

Sir Christopher smiled indulgently.

'I only said that on what Mr Amble told me, I thought his story a plausible one. But doubtless you have more evidence.'

'I'll show you some evidence,' the squire said, rising. He crossed to a cupboard, unlocked a strong box and produced a brace of pistols.

'There, sir,' he went on. 'These were taken off the man and left in my charge by the constable. Two pistols, both discharged. The fellow admits he fired one at Bond; at whom did he fire the other?'

'Did you ask him?' Sir Christopher asked innocently.

'Eh? I'm not sure. I'll look.'

Sir Christopher examined the weapons with interest while Mr Easton searched a drawer in his escritoire.

'Here, I have it,' Mr Easton said after a few moments. 'Vaughan states that he was set upon in the darkness by two men, one of whom fired at him. He fired in return in self-defence.'

'Quite understandable,' Sir Christopher commented, still toying with the pistols. 'Mr Amble tells me that his powder flask and bullet bag were taken from Vaughan. Might I see them, Mr Easton? These are unusual weapons for a man of his kind to carry, as doubtless you've noticed. A very fine pair of pistols of the modern type.'

Mr Easton went again to his strong box.

'Here you are, Sir Christopher,' he said, returning with a leather bag and flask.

Sir Christopher inspected both at some length and Mr Amble was curious to know what he found in them to demand so keen an attention. He asked. But Sir Christopher evaded the question.

'I am merely noting my facts, Mr Amble,' he replied. 'It is surprising how significant even the smallest detail sometimes may prove. Now, sir,' he addressed Mr Easton, 'if I might ask you a few questions I should be vastly obliged.'

Sir Christopher produced his memoranda book and for some ten minutes he questioned Mr Easton shrewdly, recording his answers word for word. At length he closed his book.

'It was fortunate, Mr Easton, that you had not already retired,' he said.

'Yes. Indeed it was. For I am a man of early hours, save when I entertain.'

'And you heard the shots clearly?'

'Distinctly. Here in this room. First one, which roused me from my reading, and, I'll admit, caused me some apprehension. I summoned a servant instantly and sent him to the lodge to inquire the cause. And then two more.'

'A very natural apprehension, Mr Easton. I am grateful to you, sir, for your patience with my tiresome questioning. And now, I should like to see the unhappy victim's body. You will accompany me, Mr Amble?'

Mr Amble consented reluctantly and the three of them went out into the stable yard. Mr Easton unlocked a stable door. The dead man lay on a trestle table decently covered with a sheet.

'Let's see what this poor devil has to tell us,' Sir Christopher said as he drew it back and then for many minutes he appeared to be oblivious to the presence of his companions.

Mr Easton and the lawyer, standing a little aloof, watched him in fascination as he examined the body. It was not a pretty sight. The man had been shot in the throat and his attire was drenched in blood. But Sir Christopher was heedless of this. He turned the still form about, examined the clothing minutely, gazing for some time into the set face.

'Well,' Mr Amble queried, 'and what has he told you about himself?'

'Little, and much,' Sir Christopher said. 'An older man than he would seem and one in disguise'

'Disguise?' Mr Easton put in. 'Why do you say that?'

'Look for yourself.' Mr Amble followed the squire with obvious disinclination. Sir Christopher lifted the dead man's head. 'A man of dark complexion and hair you'd say—until you used your eyes. See, you observe by the roots of the hair, it's grey. The hair was dyed. And note the darkness of the face. Death has changed its hue hardly at all. A face tanned by sun and weather, you'd say? Observe.' He rolled back the bloodstained shirt. 'The effects of sun and weather cease strangely sudden.'

They looked, and it was plain even to them that the weather-tanned hue of the man's face was due to stain.

'He was no seafaring man,' Sir Christopher continued. 'Did you ever know a sailor with hands like this? Why, they're as soft and delicate as a woman's. They never hauled on a tarry rope.'

'Nor sailor's clothes, save the reef and the rough trousers. Unless seafaring men have taken to the wearing of cambric shirts of a fine quality as you will observe this one is. And of the French fashion I would risk a wager.'

'You think then the man is a Frenchman?' Mr Amble demanded.

'I would not say that yet, But I'd say Frenchman or English he is a man used to good living and luxury. Beyond that I'll go no further at the moment. He was shot at close range. You'll note there is much scorching of gunpowder about his attire. Yes, I would say from the position of the wound that he who shot him leaned through the window of the chaise, perhaps the near side window, and thrust his pistol close against the poor devil's body. Now the chaise, may I see that, Mr Easton?'

The squire led them to an adjoining coach house where Sir Christopher regarded the cumbrous vehicle with characteristic care. It was a heavy old-fashioned chaise, swung on sturdy springs, well suited to the rough, downland roads. The near side window was open, the other closed. After a while he flung open a door and entered.

An ugly, dark patch smeared the seat where the traveller had sat. Sir Christopher began to inspect the interior with immense patience.

Presently a hole in the leather back of the seat caught his keen eyes. It was not easily discernible, but he examined it at length, then with a penknife deliberately slit the leather and probed with long thin fingers in the horsehair stuffing. At last a soft ejaculation of satisfaction told that he had found that for which he was seeking. Carefully he withdrew a pistol ball.

'You have found something?' Mr Amble asked, peering into the chaise.

'I have made some few observations,' Sir Christopher answered, 'but of what moment I cannot yet say. Still, enough to start my simple sum.'

'Your sum, sir?' the squire queried in a mystified tone.

Sir Christopher climbed out.

'Merely to make two and two add to four, Mr Easton,' he said courteously, 'and if it makes four to find two more to add to six.'

Mr Easton seemed unconvinced.

'I cannot follow you,' he retorted. 'I can but hope your sum will add aright. What would you see now, sir?'

'There is some small further examination I would like to make of the corpse,' Sir Christopher answered. 'I'll not ask you to return with me, Mr Amble, it is not a pleasant task I have to perform.' Mr Amble looked relieved. 'And, sir,' he continued, addressing Mr Easton, 'if I might summon Mr Ives the surgeon, he would help me in my addition.'

'Certainly. I'll send a groom at once.'

'Perhaps it were better if I wrote him a note. I can explain what I need of him.'

Mr Easton nodded assent and they went to the house. But presently Sir Christopher returned to the stables alone and began a minute examination of the dead man's clothes.

Mr Ives arrived post haste in his gig in response to the letter Mr Easton's groom had brought him from Sir Christopher. Mr Ives was flattered by the summons, but for the life of him he could not imagine why he had been asked to bring certain instruments, for Sir Christopher had said that it was no case of illness.

Sir Christopher received him alone. Mr Ives was mildly agitated.

'Mr Ives,' Sir Christopher began. 'I am informed you are a man skilled in anatomy and possessing great discretion.'

'I have some small skill, sir,' Mr Ives agreed modestly. 'I have studied in the London schools, and it is the first essential of my calling to be discreet.'

'Indeed, you are right there. Now, Mr Ives. Mr Easton tells me you have seen the body of the unfortunate man who was killed in a chaise close by here last night.'

'I have, sir.'

'There were signs that the man's clothing had been searched, I understand.'

'Indeed there were, sir. The rogue had nigh stripped the body, yet curiously enough missed the prize. It is clear that he was disturbed just in time.'

'Very fortunate,' Sir Christopher said dryly. 'Now how did the man die, Mr Ives?'

'How, sir? He was shot.' Mr Ives spoke with surprise. 'It was plain to see.'

'But is it plain to prove?'

'Prove? Why, sir, you have seen the body yourself. The ball must have entered by the throat. It must have penetrated the trachea and reached the lung. There was considerable haemorrhage—'

'Yes, Mr Ives, and that ball is still in the body, I take it.'

'Without doubt, sir.'

'Then I'll ask you to extract it. It would, no doubt, be a delicate operation, and one for which skill should be adequately rewarded. You may name your own fee, Mr Ives.'

'You are indeed generous, Sir Christopher,' Mr Ives responded rubbing his hands.

'Then shall we proceed to the operation?'

Mr Ives was all excitement as he and Sir Christopher left the house.

'This is an operation I have never before performed,' he said. 'Many a ball have I probed and extracted from a wounded man. But from a corpse. Would you count it impertinent, Sir Christopher, were I to ask why you are so set on seeing the ball that killed the unfortunate man?'

'By no means, Mr Ives. I seek to discomfit Mr Easton and Mr Amble.'

Mr Ives glanced at him sharply, feeling that in some way the words carried reproof for his question, but Sir Christopher met his gaze with an engaging smile.

'Maybe there is another reason. You shall know that presently. But you speak of this task as a new one. Mr Ives, the time will come when no man shall die by violence, but a surgeon shall be the first to examine him.' And then for some minutes Sir Christopher held Mr Ives fascinated as he spoke earnestly of the observations that a skilled surgeon could make upon how and when a man had been killed and of their application to the detection of the murderer.

Mr Ives agreed eagerly.

'What you say, sir, is true. It had not occurred to me before. As you point out, from the position of the body, its condition and from the nature of the wound, one could tell much.'

'I trust you will help me to tell much today,' Sir Christopher put in as they reached the stable.

He left Mr Ives to his grisly task, bidding him follow when he had completed the operation. The squire and Mr Amble were awaiting him impatiently, but Sir Christopher damped their ardour.

'No, no, my task is not so easily accomplished,' he said in reply to their eager questions. 'I have not begun. But I'd thank you, Mr Easton, if I might see Vaughan's pistols once more and inspect your notes of evidence at some length.'

They left Sir Christopher to his research, Mr Amble to return to his office, where Sir Christopher promised to wait upon him later in the day.

When, presently, a servant brought Mr Ives to him, Sir Christopher was gazing reflectively from a window at a distant vista of rain-swept downland. He turned, an expectant expression on his lean face.

'Well, Mr Ives?' he queried.

The surgeon answered excitedly: 'I have it, sir. I have it. It was as I thought. The ball had penetrated the windpipe, passed downward, striking the collar bone and entering the lung. Death would have supervened very quickly. Here is the ball, misshapen as you will notice as a result of impact with the bone.' He extended a battered piece of lead which Sir Christopher seized avidly.

He eyed it for some moments, turning it this way and that in his fingers. Then from a pocket he produced the ball he had found in the upholstering of the chaise.

'One might surmise that your ball originally was similar to this one,' Sir Christopher said.

'That, sir, I doubt if anyone could say,' he responded.

'Then let us proceed to a small experiment, Mr Ives. You have your apothecaries' scales?'

'I have, sir.' Mr Ives undid his bag.

'Now, Mr Ives: I place in one pan of your scales the ball you extracted from the corpse. I place in the other this ball and—ah!' Sir Christopher exclaimed with satisfaction as he regarded the balance. 'You note that, Mr Ives. These balls weigh precisely the same. And since a pistol ball is spherical, I think we may assume they could have come from the same barrel.'

'They tally to half a grain, to less,' the surgeon agreed thoughtfully. 'You're right, sir. It's patent proof, and simple, now that you demonstrate it. Such an idea would never have occurred to me.'

Sir Christopher raised a deprecatory hand.

'Perhaps it would, Mr Ives, had you given the same study to the science of crime as you have to that of anatomy. I thank you for your help and maybe I shall ask more of it.'

'I'm always at your service, sir.' Mr Ives bowed.

'Then you may expect a call from me about noon, Mr Ives,' Sir Christopher said.

Sir Christopher walked back to Ashmarket later in the morning. On, his way he spent some time with Fratton, the lodge keeper, getting him to indicate exactly where the chaise had stood, and chatting in seemingly careless fashion.

When he reached Ashmarket he made for its bleak and cheerless jail and hammered on a great iron-studded door. To the turnkey who answered his summons, Sir Christopher presented an authority from Mr Easton and he was conducted to a dingy airless cell where Vaughan sat dejectedly on a plank bed.

The jailer yelled to the man to stand up and Vaughan obeyed defiantly. But Sir Christopher bade him be seated once they were alone and spoke to him with courtesy.

'Vaughan, I've come to talk with you about last night's bad business,' he began. 'Sit down now. Are you in pain?'

'What if I am?' Vaughan answered roughly. 'And what do you want of me?'

Sir Christopher eyed the man keenly before he answered. A dangerous fellow in a fright, Sir Christopher assessed him, and one who had known a rough and violent life, he did not doubt. He noticed the man's arm slipped from his sleeve and bound up crudely in a blood-stained bandage.

'My name is Christopher Hazzard and what I want of you is to hear exactly what happened last night,' he answered.

The man glared at him suspiciously.

'If you think you've come here to trick me with your soft speaking, you've made a mistake, guv'nor,' he said.

Sir Christopher smiled.

'On the contrary: I've come here to help you.'

'The gentry don't help the likes of me,' the man said. 'All I got to say is I didn't do it.'

'I know that, Vaughan. You didn't shoot that man,' Sir Christopher interrupted quietly.

'What?' Jem Vaughan gaped. 'Here, was you there, guv'nor?'

'No, unfortunately. But I want to know who did shoot him. Do you know?'

'No, sir, no. I take my oath I don't.'

'Then tell me what you do know.'

It took some little while to break down the man's suspicions, but Sir Christopher was patient. To Vaughan's first bald story, the same that he had told Mr Easton, he listened without comment. Then he asked:

'What were you doing on the road last night?'

'That's my business,' the fellow answered, returning to his early mood of defiance. Then, 'Beg pardon, sir. If you can help me I'll tell you the truth, though I wouldn't say to Squire Easton. I'd been up in Dean Woods after pheasants.'

'Ah! Now I understand something,' Sir Christopher put in. 'So that's why you had that neat pair of pistols. Shooting them off the trees at roost, I suppose.'

'That's right, sir. The pistols is handier than a fowling piece and don't make so much noise,'

'Yes, I can see that. But, Vaughan, you didn't have much luck, did you?'

'No, sir. Too dark. I only had one shot. Then I give up.'

'That's fortunate for you, though you mayn't know it. Now you say you were coming along the road when you happened on the chaise. Were the horses restive at all?'

'No, sir.'

'You stopped to see what was amiss?'

Vaughan nodded.

'Had you heard any shot?'

'No.'

'Tell me, how soon after you stopped did Bond and Chale set upon you, as you put it?'

'Why, they come at me almost at once. Sammy Chale calling out that I was a dirty murdering ruffian, and Silas Bond shooting—'

'Who shot first?'

'He did. Got my arm just as I fired.'

Sir Christopher sought to test Vaughan's story by subtle questioning, but the man held to it though Sir Christopher extracted the fact that he called out: 'What's amiss here,' when he had approached the chaise and found it apparently deserted and it was when he was about to open the door to see if anyone was inside that he was attacked.

But he was definite that he had heard no shot nor had seen nor heard anybody in the vicinity of the chaise.

'You'll hear from me again, Vaughan,' he said as he closed his memoranda book. 'Be of good heart, man. They shall not hang you for this crime, anyhow.'

'You're not lying to me?'

'I'm not lying to you. Now what of this damaged arm of yours?' Sir Christopher seized the arm as if to examine it and Jem Vaughan let out a groan of pain.

'Eh, what's this? Has this not been seen by a surgeon?' Sir Christopher asked in apparent surprise.

'They don't have surgeons for them as can't pay for 'em,' Vaughan stated.

Sir Christopher shook his head.

'And we call ourselves a Christian people,' he murmured. Then, 'I'll see what I can do about it,' he said, and summoned the turnkey.

To him he issued certain instructions before he left the jail, and gave the man a guinea for himself to see that they were carried out. An hour later, Mr Ives the surgeon arrived. But by then Sir Christopher Hazzard was already on the road for Portsmouth.

Sir Christopher dined at the 'George', bidding his post-boy to be ready for the return journey in an hour's time. Then he set out on foot through the driving rain for the 'Lugger', a waterside tavern near Portsmouth Point.

It was a shabby place, of unsavoury reputation. Rumour had it that the 'Lugger' was a rendezvous of French spies and highwaymen and rogues of every kind, and many a good burgess shook a disapproving head when the tavern's name was mentioned, and prophesied that Abel Carter, the landlord, would come to a bad end.

Yet Abel Carter did not. Though many a complaint was laid against him the law let him alone. Strong influences worked in his favour, for Abel Carter was counted one of the cleverest of the company of secret agents His Majesty's Office of Foreign Affairs employed. Much useful information about Bonaparte's plannings and schemings came up the road to Whitehall by messengers of Abel Carter's, riding express from the 'Lugger' at Portsmouth.

Sir Christopher Hazzard knew the ways of the 'Lugger' and the door at the back by which a man might enter the tavern unseen. To it he came that afternoon, his heavy travelling cloak drawn close about him, as much against chance recognition as against the weather.

His knock brought Abel himself to the door, and Sir Christopher entered after a few curt words of greeting and turned unbidden into a snug little parlour that was close by.

'Eh, but I wasn't expecting you, sir,' Abel said as he closed the door.

Sir Christopher smiled.

'I want some information and you can give it.'

'Something amiss, Sir Christopher?' Carter asked anxiously, poking the fire to a blaze.

Sir Christopher flung off his cloak and drew his memoranda book from his pocket.

'Have you had a traveller here lately, five foot nine in height, blue eyes, grey hair; a man going to fat with good living. A Frenchman, or come from France recently. In disguise of a seafaring man. Dressed in reefer coat and blue trousers, and shoes. Hair, face and neck dyed brown. Usually wore a ring on the third finger of the left hand. The scar of a sabre wound, I'd say, on the right arm. Age, maybe fifty, maybe a year or so older—?'

'Aye,' Carter interrupted. 'That 'ud be Mister Nicol. He's been here a week. Left last evening.'

'Who is Mr Nicol?' Sir Christopher demanded sharply.

'He's a Frenchy, sir, though you'd never guess it. One of his lordship's gentlemen.'

Carter was speaking of Lord Camber, the sinister, cunning old peer who, from his room in His Majesty's Office of Foreign Affairs in Whitehall, organized that amazingly efficient intelligence service that England maintained in France. Sir Christopher himself had undertaken delicate missions of investigation both in England and France at Lord Camber's urgent request.

'What was Monsieur Nicol doing here, Abel?'

'Waiting a letter from France. Job Harding brought it yesterday afternoon, and I fixed him a disguise so as he'd look like a seafaring man and not attract notice. He were a bit nervous for he'd had word that Boney's spies were looking for him this side as well as the other. When Job came, he set off at once for London.'

'The poor devil's made his last journey, Abel.'

'You don't mean they've got him, sir?'

'They have. Shot dead in a chaise two miles beyond Ashmarket soon after midnight.'

'Was it his money or his papers they were after?'

'His papers. And they got them; all but one. That I found hidden in the lining of his coat. It brought me here.'

'I warned him not to go by night, but he wouldn't wait,' Carter said. 'Who done it, sir? Do they suspect anyone?'

'Ah, that's what I want to establish.' Sir Christopher put away his book. 'Abel, what do you know of Sam Chale, post-boy at the "Bear" at Ashmarket?'

Abel Carter's brow furrowed.

'Nothing but that he's a loud-mouthed sort. I doubt he's the guts to do a job of that kind, if that's what you mean.'

'Do you know Silas Bond of the "Waggon" at Dean?'

Abel laughed curiously.

'Course I do, sir. And the "Waggon". There's some queer coves use the "Waggon"; almost as queer as some as uses my house, though 'tain't everyone as knows it.' He laughed again. 'There's always a quiet stable and no questions asked nor answered for certain gentlemen as arrives in a hurry at the "Waggon". If that's where your nose leads you you're on the right scent, I'd lay. Bond, he's careful, he's a downy cove. You won't never prove nothing against him, though if it was done from the "Waggon" he'd know; yes, Silas would know.'

'Haven't seen him about the town lately?'

'No, sir. But Sammy Chale's been about. Come in here once.'

Sir Christopher spoke thoughtfully. 'He's been here while Nicol was with you?'

'Yes, sir.'

'I wonder. Did Nicol post from London, do you know

'He did, sir. Thursday. Come in here just after dark.'

'All right, Abel; thank you.' Sir Christopher remained talking with Carter for some minutes before he slid out by that back door into the driving rain to return to the 'George'.

Mr Amble was growing impatient. The important hour of his dinner had arrived, yet Sir Christopher had not paid his promised call.

Darkness had fallen before a hammering at his front door proclaimed visitors. Mr Amble, left alone in his dining-room seeking consolation in a decanter of port wine, sighed with relief at the sound of Sir Christopher's voice. Mr Amble went himself to greet him.

With Sir Christopher were Mr Easton and Mr Ives, the surgeon. Sir Christopher was apologetic.

'You must pardon this intrusion, Mr Amble,' he said, 'but I find that I must return to London tonight and there are one or two points about this unhappy affair that I should like to make clear to you and Mr Easton before I go. So I have taken the liberty—'

'No liberty, Sir Christopher; a privilege, a privilege,' the lawyer interrupted politely. 'Have you solved the problem, sir?'

'That I must leave for you and Mr Easton to judge,' Sir Christopher responded.

Mr Amble led the way to his dining-room and offered wine.

'Well, gentlemen,' Sir Christopher began, 'I think you may count the man Vaughan cleared. I think I can convince you of that. But first, I'd have you take note of one or two matters. I may have that bag, Mr Easton?'

The squire produced a bag and from it Sir Christopher drew out the pistols, the powder flask and the bag of balls that had been taken from Vaughan.

'If you'll notice,' he continued, 'this powder flask. It's full, full to the top. That's significant.'

'How, sir?' Mr Amble put in.

'I submit, Mr Amble, that it is a proof that Vaughan did not reload his pistols.'

'Maybe, Sir Christopher,' Mr Easton said. 'But what need to reload them? The rogue fired two shots, one he admits at Bond and the other as we hold at the man he murdered.'

'I propose to prove to you that there were four shots, one only fired by Vaughan,' Sir Christopher said quietly. 'And I'll show you three of the balls that were fired.'

'How, sir?' Mr Amble demanded in puzzled tone. 'You say you can show us the actual balls that were fired?'

Sir Christopher smiled bleakly.

'Here is the ball that killed that ill-fated stranger,' he said. 'Mr Ives will swear to that, Mr Amble, for he extracted it himself from the corpse.'

Mr Amble winced. Mr Ives bowed in agreement. Mr Easton took the misshapen piece of lead and examined it with fascinated interest.

'You mean to tell us that that's what took the man's life?' he asked sceptically.

'Mr Ives will tell you that.'

Mr Easton looked up sharply while Mr Amble examined the ball, holding it gingerly by the tips of his fingers.

'And now,' Sir Christopher went on blandly, 'I'll show you another ball. This I'll swear to. I took it from the upholstery of the chaise cut a matter of nine inches to a foot from where the traveller was sitting. I contend, gentlemen, that this ball was fired first, missed the man, and a second shot killed him. For, as I will show you, both are of a size and could have come from the same pair of pistols.'

'I cannot follow you,' Mr Easton protested. 'How can any man say that?'

'By the simple device of adding two and two and making it come to four,' Sir Christopher smiled. 'Already I have demonstrated it to Mr Ives.'

Mr Ives produced his scales. Sir Christopher placed one ball in each of the pans.

'You see, gentlemen, they tally precisely.'

'As I said when Sir Christopher first demonstrated this to me, to a fraction of a grain or less.'

'But—but—' Mr Easton began in argumentative tone.

Sir Christopher lifted a thin hand. 'Maybe I can answer your objection, Mr Easton. You have seen they are of the same weight, but, you ask, how do we know they were of the same size?'

'Yes. Yes.' Mr Easton agreed.

'A pistol ball, sir, is solid and spherical. Could you then mould this,' Sir Christopher calmly picked up the misshapen lead that had come from the corpse, 'into any other size?'

'No, sir. No. By God, he's right, Mr Easton,' the lawyer said with conviction. ''Tis a proof that would not have occurred to me, but I accept it.'

'Yes, I see what he means.'

'Then, Mr Easton, let me add two more to my little sum. You will note this.' Sir Christopher took a ball from Vaughan's bag and tried it in the muzzle of first one and then the other of his pistols. 'This ball, you observe, fits exactly.'

'It undoubtedly does, sir,' the squire said, leaning forward.

'But we place it in the scales against the ball that killed the man and—'

'Damme! They're of a different weight!' Mr Easton exclaimed

as the scale dropped, showing the ball from Jem Vaughan's bag to be the lighter.

'This is most significant,' Mr Amble said. 'It is a conclusive proof.'

'And if you want further,' Sir Christopher said with a shrug, 'I draw your attention to this.' He picked up the undamaged ball he had found in the chaise and passed it with the pistols to Mr Easton, 'Now, sir. You ram that into the barrel if you can.'

Mr Easton tried, but it was patently impossible. The ball was too big.

'Well, I'll be damned,' said Mr Easton, shaking his head.

'Why, it's clear as daylight, Sir Christopher,' Mr Amble put in, 'Vaughan could not have shot the man with these pistols.'

'Vaughan did not shoot him.'

'Then who did? You spoke of three balls, sir?' Mr Amble demanded excitedly. 'You have cleared Vaughan beyond doubt. But can you convict another?'

Sir Christopher turned to the surgeon.

'You have the third ball, Mr Ives?'

'It is here, sir.'

'Will you weigh it against the others?'

Mr Ives obeyed. The squire and Mr Amble stared in fascination. The ball tallied precisely with the first two that Sir Christopher had produced.

'Yes. It is the same,' Mr Amble said, as if to himself. 'There is no doubting it.'

'Where did that come from?' Mr Easton demanded anxiously.

'I extracted it from Jem Vaughan's arm this morning,' Mr Ives replied.

'What?' Mr Amble cried. 'You can swear to that?'

'I can swear to it, sir.'

'You have in your notes of evidence a confession of the man who fired that ball, Mr Easton,' Sir Christopher said.

Mr Easton made no answer, but Mr Amble's eyes opened wide.

'Good God!' he exclaimed slowly. 'Bond. From his own lips. Bond killed the man. But why?'

'Ah, that is a matter,' Sir Christopher said, 'on which I'd not venture an opinion.'

Mr Amble went on, 'Bond! It's incredible. You know the man, Mr Easton; he is a tenant of yours.'

'I find it hard to credit,' the squire answered gruffly. 'A very civil, honest man, who pays his rent regularly. You must be mistaken, Sir Christopher.'

'I have but offered you the evidence,' Sir Christopher said, extending his hands.

'Then what of Chale?' the lawyer said in a bemused way. 'Was he in league with Bond?'

'So it would seem.'

'How do you come by this extraordinary conclusion?' Mr Easton demanded.

'It was quite simple, Mr Easton; I did but add two and two and make it come to four,' Sir Christopher said with an engaging smile, 'and I offer you the evidence. Now I must ask you to excuse me. for I have a chaise at the door and I have a tiresome journey before me. But I shall return tomorrow, Mr Amble, to be present at your inquest.'

Sir Christopher rose and bowed.

It was to the saturnine Lord Camber that Sir Christopher told the full story of his investigations some hours later; Lord Camber, dragged from the card-table at the Cocoa Tree Club in the early hours of the morning. In his talon-like fingers he held the document that had been found on Nicol's body. It bore a list of names of men and women, many of them well known in the great world, some even at court itself. Sir Christopher had guessed their significance. They were names of Bonaparte's chief agents in England, the advance guard of his long-dreamed-of army of occupation. Nicol's was the fourth life to be lost in securing those names, and Sir Christopher himself had investigated the secret activities of more than one of them, at Lord Camber's request.

He told his story briefly.

'As you will appreciate, my lord,' he said when he had finished the outline of the affair, 'it was obvious from the first that the fellow Vaughan was innocent and that there were half a dozen things to proclaim an unusual crime. Vaughan was not of the type to engage upon such a crime, he had robbed the man of nothing, yet the man was killed. Your highway robber does not kill unless he meets with resistance and it was clear that Nicol offered no resistance. The man's full powder flask confirmed my surmise. When I found the ball and realized at once that it could not have come from his pistols, it was proof.'

The old peer nodded. He was ever ready to listen when Kit Hazzard spoke of his methods of detection.

'But, my lord, certain other facts emerged, and—er—possibilities presented themselves in the course of my investigations. Doubtless you have noted some discrepancies.'

'Eh? What are you starting now?' Lord Camber said, leaning forward.

'It's obvious that Nicol's business was known. He was remembered. I discovered, at the "Bear" as a traveller who had passed that way before. It is not wise, my lord, for one engaged on secret missions to adopt regular habits.'

'You are right,' Lord Camber frowned.

'It is clear, too, that the man was watched. He delayed some time at the "Bear" for refreshment. I would surmise in that time Chale contrived to send word to Bond of his arrival. Were I investigating further I would seek to know where Bond had been that night. and maybe I should find that he had been no farther than some neighbouring Ashmarket tavern. I would surmise, too, that on getting word from Chale he rode on forthwith to a point close by Mr Easton's lodge gates, on reaching which point

Chale halted his chaise. Indeed there were hoof marks, such as would be made by a waiting restless horse, to be seen yesterday beneath a clump of beeches not a hundred yards from the lodge.'

'So it is not all surmise?'

'All is surmise until it be proved. Such as my surmise that when the chaise stopped, Bond came forward and committed his crime; that he began his search for Nicol's papers and was disturbed by the unexpected appearance of Vaughan; that he drew off for some moments to reload, then came at the man and shot him, intending to make him the scapegoat, But after that, my lord, I surmise something of greater significance.'

'Yes. Yes.'

'For the first time Fratton, the lodge keeper, is apprised of the affair, as Chale has stated. And yet Fratton, being questioned, tells me another tale. He had already gone to the scene of the crime, being aroused by two shots—two shots only, mark you—and on being told by Chale to hasten to the constable's saw his own master, Mr Easton, emerging from the lodge gates.'

Lord Camber's heavy eyebrows lifted.

'I thought it curious that. Mr Easton, a bucolic squire, should be up so late at night when he had entertained no company as I established from his own lips, more curious that he should have heard three shots within his house so far from the road on a boisterous windy night. For, in fact, four shots were fired, but he only knew of three—so he heard three.' Sir Christopher smiled dryly. 'And two of those four were fired within the chaise. Even Fratton heard but the exchange between Bond and Vaughan, and Vaughan heard neither of the first two shots at all.'

He paused for a moment, then continued:

'But it was more curious that Fratton should be sent for a surgeon to attend a man about whose death there could be no doubt, and'—again he paused—'that when the surgeon arrived, the chaise with the body should already have been driven to Mr Easton's stables, and as Mr Ives avows the body's attire in such

disarray as to surprise him. Indeed, my lord, I would surmise
that the search interrupted by Vaughan was continued in those
stables, and that the surgeon was summoned to justify the
searching of the body should the question be raised.'

'What? You suggest that your bucolic squire—'

'Was cognisant of the whole affair,' Sir Christopher broke in.
'Indeed I would add his name to that list you hold in your hand,
for, as I see it, though Bond's was the hand that fired the fatal
shot, Charles Easton's was the brain that instigated it.'

Lord Camber rose abruptly. There was a savage light in his
dark eyes.

'By God! I'll deal with the scoundrel,' he said hotly. 'Sir
Christopher, I call on your help.'

Sir Christopher too had risen.

'You will find me at the Bear Inn at Ashmarket,' he said. 'I
am returning there at once, for, in faith, I am concerned about
the fellow Vaughan. I took a strange liking to that rascal, yet if
I be not careful Mr Easton will get him hanged for all my proof.'

'But what of the man Bond?'

'I would surmise,' Sir Christopher answered, 'that Bond and
Chale will be found to have vanished when I reach Ashmarket
and that my bucolic squire will have propounded a theory that
they have been removed by confederates of Vaughan's to prevent
them giving evidence against him. The fellow's cunning as a fox.
Already he had planted the idea that Vaughan was but one of
many concerned in my good attorney's mind.'

'We must kill that fox,' the old peer said grimly.

'For once, my lord,' Sir Christopher responded, 'I shall be glad
to be in at the death.'

RICHARD KEVERNE

'Richard Keverne' was the pen name of Clifford James Wheeler Hosken (1882–1950), who was born in Norwich, Norfolk, where his father, James J. Hosken, was head of the Norwich branch of the Post Office.

In 1911, Hosken married an American woman, Emma Harris Foster, and on the outbreak of war, he and his elder brother enlisted in the Royal Flying Corps, with Hosken ending the war in a nursing home. While in the airforce, he had written and been published as a freelancer: for example, 'Stories of the Iron Duke' appeared in the *London Magazine* in 1915 and 'Blood-stained Thrones' was published in the *Penny Pictorial* in 1916.

On being demobbed, Clifford and Emma Hosken moved to London where he got a job with the *Daily Mirror*, a national news-paper for which—using his own name and the pen name of 'Richard Keverne'—he wrote lightly humorous and sometimes provocative editorials on all manner of subjects, such as golf, the joy of labour-saving devices, the weather, horticulture, the risks and benefits of a 'Channel Tunnel' between England and France, healthy eating, tobacco and 'the horrors of shaving', horse racing, war memorials, aviation and (something of an obsession for Hosken) oysters. One editorial—'Are Americans afraid of their wives?'—was published in 1920 just after the introduction of prohibition in the United States, and was the subject of much debate.

Outside work, Hosken was something of an amateur historian and he became involved with the restoration of Chelsea Old Church where, in 1922, he was responsible for the rediscovery of a fourteenth-century stained-glass window that had been hidden from view for nearly 300 years.

Around this time, Hosken began writing novels. As 'Richard Keverne', his stories were serialized in the *Daily Mirror*. The first, *The Secret of John Bastian* (1923), concerns a famous actor who stages his disappearance and his attempts to build a new life; *The Greater Sacrifice* (1924) is 'a vivid and unusual story of temptation, surrender and final triumph' and *The Forsaken House* (1925) is on similar lines. The novels published under his own name were serialized in the *Mirror*'s sister paper, the *Sunday Pictorial*: *The Treasure of Truce Haven* (1923) deals with a young doctor's mysterious legacy, *The Harrington Heiress* (1924) a young woman's battle to save her ancestral home and *My Lady Madcap* (1925) the escapades of 'a vital, warm-hearted and impulsive young girl whose innocence and disregard for convention land her in piquant situations'. All six books were written on predictable lines, but for his fourth 'Keverne' serial, Hosken put the emphasis on mystery. Promoted by the *Daily Mirror* as a story of 'smuggling, love, detection and mental patients', *Michael Carteret's Dilemma* (1925) was very well received and for the first time Hosken saw one of his novels published in hard covers, as *Carteret's Cure*.

Each of Hosken's next three serials was a 'novel of modern life'. Two appeared under his own name: *The Climber* (1926), 'a young man's fight to live down his early associations', and the self-explanatory *Cinderella* (1927). The third, a 'Keverne', was *The Gate to Fortune* (1927), touted by the *Mirror* as 'a breathless romance'.

As with the first six serials, none attracted much notice beyond the newspaper's readership, so with his next 'Keverne' novel he decided to write a thriller, the genre dominated at that time by Edgar Wallace. By this time, the couple was living in Suffolk, the eastern England county that provided the setting for *Michael*

Cartaret's Dilemma and many of his other novels. These include *The Havering Plot* (1927), in which a new design of military aircraft is under development on an island off the east Anglian coast; *William Cook, Antique Dealer* (1928), which deals with smuggling and fences; and *The Secret of the Tower* (1928), published as *The Sanfield Scandal* whose focus is the sinister Burgrave Castle, based on Suffolk's Orford keep, a tower whose restoration was managed by a board of trustees, one of whom was Hosken.

While he would continue to publish as 'Richard Keverne' for another thirteen years, Hosken published only three more novels under his own name: *The Shadow Syndicate* (1930), the Ruritanian *The Pretender* (1930) and the superb *Missing from His Home* (1932), about the search for a vanished spy. Among his many 'Keverne' titles, two are outstanding: *Behind the Shutters* (1931), later published as *He Laughed at Murder*, and *Open Verdict* (1940), in which a man is suspected of killing his uncle a few hours after meeting him for the first time.

There are several collections of short stories, as well as many uncollected ones, and Keverne also authored *Tales of Old Inns* (1939), a marvellously atmospheric tour of English hostelries, which was revised in 1946 by Hammond Innes to take account of the destruction wrought by the Second World War.

While writing fiction was Hosken's main focus, he took a close interest throughout his life in history and art, for example writing about glass-painting for the *Connoisseur* in 1924 and photography for *The Strand* in 1930. And, despite some success as a writer, he never abandoned journalism, contributing editorials to *Good Morning*, the daily newspaper of the Navy's submarine service, on issues like the need for leap years, dowsing, the Sutton Hoo hoard and the public houses of his beloved Suffolk.

In 1950, Clifford Hosken died at the age of sixty-seven, and Emma moved back to Florida.

'The Post-Chaise Murder' was published in *Britannia & Eve* on 1 December 1940.

BOOTS

Ngaio Marsh

In the first bedroom of the Trampers' Club Hut Mrs Marriott lay, half on her face which was turned to the wall. She was curled up in her bunk with one hand under her cheek and the other on the pillow. She always slept in that way: like a kitten.

She was not alone. Three men stood awkwardly watching her: her husband, his brother Kit and their friend Collington. A fourth man waited near the door. A fifth reached down and turned back the bedclothes.

The haft of a sheath knife stuck out freakishly from between her shoulder blades. Kit could hardly believe in it: it looked silly.

'There! You see!' her husband said. 'That's what I told you, Inspector. Do you want me to show you how I did it? Look.'

'I've already warned you, Marriott.'

'I know, I know, I know. But I *want* you to understand.'

'For God's sake, shut up!' said his brother violently. 'Shut up, Frank. *Frank!*'

'But I insist! Don't take me away yet, Inspector. I want these chaps to hear.' He turned on the second of his companions.

'Yes, you too, Collington. It's your doing as much as mine. You didn't think I knew, did you? You didn't think I'd been watching you all these weeks. What fools you were, the two of you! What bloody, complacent fools!' He looked at his brother.

'You knew, Kit! You knew—and anyway, you always hated her, didn't you? All right. Now get this, Inspector.'

He passed his hand over his mouth and went on in a level voice as if he repeated something he had memorized.

'We were all in the sitting-room. The others said they were going to turn in. I said I'd put my boots on and go for a walk. I went out on the verandah as if I was making for my room. Am I speaking too fast?' he said anxiously. The detective-sergeant looked up from his notebook and said: 'You're doing all right.'

'Good. Well, I didn't go to my room. I went into the passage and hid in that curtained-off cupboard near the door. It was as simple as that. I could see, all right. I saw you, Kit. You went into your room. It's the second one, Inspector. Next to this. And then she came in here. And then he came along. This fellow. Collington's the name. Into the end room beyond mine. Got it? My wife. Kit. Me. Collington. In that order. All right. So I wait. I wait a long time and at last it happens. Out he comes, this Collington, and opens her door and goes in. I'd got it all worked out. Only a matter of waiting. When he sneaked back, I went in and did it. She never knew a thing.' He turned as if to go out and came face to face with the sergeant. 'Got it? he said. 'God, what a relief.'

Collington said: 'He's lying. God knows why, but he's lying.'

'Yes?' said the Chief Inspector. 'Care to elaborate?'

'He *went* for his walk. He's done it every night since we've been here. Half-an-hour to the minute. He went.'

'How do you know?'

'Because of his boots.'

'His boots?' The detective glanced at Marriott's rubber-soled sneakers.

'That's right. We've had arguments. Every night he comes in from his walk and dumps his boots. Crashes on the floor against my wall.'

Marriott lifted his head and giggled.

'Not only that. He winds his alarm clock and lets it clatter and then winds it again. On purpose. To wake me up. It drives me crackers. He did it tonight. Took off his boots and dropped them. And then the alarm.'

'You were in your room?' asked the Chief Inspector.

'I certainly was. And had been. I don't say there weren't other occasions. There were. Not tonight, though. She was frightened.' He turned on Kit. 'She was frightened of you. You'd got at her. Go on: admit it!'

'I told her what I thought.'

'You keep quiet,' said his brother. 'You're out of this.'

'Is he out of it, though?' said Collington. '*Is he?*'

The Chief Inspector said to Kit Marriott: 'These partitions are very thin, aren't they? Single sheets of wallboard. You must have heard the boots and the alarm?'

There was a long silence. 'I sleep very heavily,' said Kit. 'I sleep through anything.' He was staring at Collington.

'Like to add to these statements?'

'Yes,' said Kit. 'I would. It was all over. Finished. She told Collington it was. She'd come to her senses. He took it badly.'

Collington swore at him.

The Chief Inspector said to Marriott: 'Mind if we look at your room?'

'No,' he said. 'Go ahead.'

His room was like all the others: untidy. Heaps of clothes on the floor; books, periodicals, wrapping paper and, near the wall under the lamp bracket, a pair of heavy, studded, lace-up boots. The Chief Inspector picked one up and dropped it. It made a great noise. The clock was on a shelf on the same wall.

'The alarm's set for ten,' he said. 'And run down. How do you account for that, Mr Marriott?'

'Easy. It's as it was last night.'

'Then you didn't set it for this morning?'

'Yes, he did,' said Collington. 'For seven. I heard it.'

'You're imagining things,' said Marriott.

Kit Marriott began to abuse Collington. 'You're lying. You're cooking an alibi for yourself. There wasn't any alarm, or any boots. You went into her room and when she told you it was all over you killed her.'

'So Frank puts his head in a noose for me, does he? That'll be the day! No, by God! Frank's looking after his hero-worshipping younger brother.'

The Chief Inspector had picked up a length of string. He displayed it. One end was glowing and a faint wisp of smoke rose from it.

'Know anything about this?' he asked Marriott.

'It was round a parcel of books. I opened them earlier in the evening. I'd lost my knife and I burnt the knot. Careless.'

'You'd lost it? And yet you used it to murder your wife.'

'Oh, my God!' said Marriott. And then, 'All right, I give up.' He jerked his head at Collington. 'You aren't worth it,' he said. 'But I tried.'

'There's a trace of ash on the floor. Under the lamp bracket. And on these boots. Would that be there if the boots were thrown down at ten o'clock? String burns slowly,' said the Chief Inspector. 'Suspend a couple of heavy boots from a lamp bracket with string and light it near the knot—sooner or later, it'll do the trick and down come the boots. As you say, you'd got it all worked out. Quite an idea. Accuse yourself. Confess. Make sure your statement's palpably false.'

Chief Detective-Inspector Alleyn pinched out the glowing end of the string. 'But it's playing with fire,' he said.

NGAIO MARSH

Edith Ngaio Marsh (1895–1982) is one of the so-called 'Big Four' women writers of the Golden Age of crime and detective fiction, the others being Agatha Christie, Dorothy L. Sayers and Margery Allingham. She is best known for creating Roderick Alleyn, an aristocratic professional detective who appears in thirty-three mysteries, including *Money in the Morgue* (2018), a posthumous collaboration with the writer Stella Duffy, who completed a book that Marsh had abandoned when the Second World War came to an end and rendered its plot irrelevant.

Marsh was born in 1895 in the Cashmere Hills, now a suburb of Christchurch, New Zealand. Her parents were keen actors and encouraged their daughter to share their passion for all things theatrical. When Marsh was only five, she was invited to attend a fancy dress party to mark Queen Victoria's eighty-first birthday; while other children went as nursery rhyme characters and the like, Marsh was dressed as Marion Delorme, an obscure French courtesan of the seventeenth century. Marsh was also encouraged to write. She produced several 'fairy plays' and sketches such as *An Imaginary Conversation between Queen Elizabeth and Queen Victoria* (1912). As well as appearing in her own pieces and in other plays, she acted outside school, appearing occasionally with her parents, including in a production of Sir Arthur Wing Pinero's *Preserving Mr Panmure* (1914).

Marsh's academic achievements were also impressive and at school she won multiple prizes for subjects as diverse as botany and divinity. In 1912, she won a national competition with an essay on 'The Influence of the Navy on the Growth of the British Empire during the last 150 years'. Two years later she won a competition for overseas writers run by the Countess of Jersey: Marsh's entry, 'Three Pages, Taken at Random from the Autobiography of a New Zealand Pioneer', deal with the bush, a sheep run and a murderous sheep-stealer.

Marsh was a talented artist and she attended Canterbury Art School between 1913 and 1919, winning among other prizes a competition to design a war medal. In 1919, she joined a touring repertory company and, when home, took part in charitable activities such as a production of A. A. Milne's play *Belinda* (1923), in which she appeared alongside her father.

Eventually, Marsh concluded that a stage career was not for her. Following an attempt to set up an interior decorating business in London, she tried writing a detective story. The result, *A Man Lay Dead* (1932), introduced Roderick Alleyn, a tall, good-looking policeman whose cases often feature unusual, sometimes bizarre, methods of murder. A more rounded and plausible 'great detective' than most, Alleyn takes a relatively realistic approach to the investigation of crime, interrogating each suspect in turn so that the professional police—and the reader—are literally on the same page. In his definitive *Companion to the Mystery Fiction of Ngaio Marsh* (2019), Dr Bruce Harding provides an overview of the character and that of Alleyn's wife Troy, in some ways an idealized version of Marsh herself.

In parallel with her career as a crime novelist, Marsh pursued her passion for theatre and the works of William Shakespeare, whose birth date she shared. For over twenty years she directed for Canterbury University College Drama Society, delivering acclaimed productions of *Hamlet* and *Othello* among others, and she also helped Doinal Dhu O'Connor to found the British Commonwealth Theatre Company, for which she directed several plays.

Marsh's dramatist's eye and understanding of theatre can be seen in the way she deftly realizes colourful and memorable characters and settings without labouring the detail. It is therefore surprising that, while she wrote several plays for children and an original Alleyn mystery for television, she wrote little for the stage. While she started but did not complete an adaptation of *Opening Night* (1951), her adaptation of *Singing in the Shrouds* (1959), entitled *Murder Sails at Midnight* (1972), was well received with the original London run starring Valentine Dyall (radio's 'Man in Black') as Superintendent Alleyn. Marsh also shared credits on three plays: *Exit Sir Derek* (1935) with Henry Jellett, based on their co-authored novel *The Nursing-Home Murder* (1935); *A Surfeit of Lampreys* (1950) with Owen B Howells; and *False Scent* (1961) with Eileen Mackay.

Ngaio Marsh died in 1982 in Christchurch, New Zealand, the city where she had been born almost ninety years earlier. As well as for her superb crime fiction, she is remembered as a leading figure in the New Zealand arts world and it was for this that in 1966 she was appointed a Dame Commander of the Order of the British Empire.

This is the first publication of 'Boots', written in the 1940s. The title was Marsh's second choice, the first being 'The Tramping Club Hut'.

FIGURES DON'T DIE

T. S. Stribling

From the telephone, I repeated to Poggioli that a Mrs Maria Owens wanted to know if her own life were in danger. I shrugged at the absurdity of such a question. Poggioli, however, with his amazing memory and powers of association, began thinking through the morning paper. He murmured aloud, 'Owens . . . Owens . . . her *own* life in danger . . . I see; she is probably the wife of Cyril Owens, a certified public accountant who was shot through his kitchen window at 2417 Orange Street, this morning at 1.15.'

I repeated this into the telephone, and asked if it were correct. It was. I couldn't restrain my own blank smile and shake of the head at this marvellous feat of memory and deduction which my friend had tossed off almost absent-mindedly.

'Tell her,' he said, 'we'll be over to make a personal investigation of her husband's case.'

'Why don't you let me telephone her that she's safe, and let her go?'

'She probably *is* safe; but if she remains a little frightened, she'll be more cooperative when we get there.'

'Why should we visit the scene of an accountant's murder? That strikes me as a sort of namby-pamby murder—if you know what I mean.'

'You feel that way because there is nothing definite about it.

But that's what makes it interesting. You see, accountants are seldom murdered; but they are continually dipping into the affairs of criminals, and men on the fringe of crime.'

'You mean they work on people's income taxes?'

'That, and a dozen other fields. You see, the curse of a big criminal organization is that books have to be kept. When a man employs thousands of accomplices, he can't possibly keep all the details in his head.'

I had never thought of it like that, but I could see the source of Poggioli's interest. I got ready, and went with him very willingly.

2417 Orange Street was a middle-class home, with two or three grapefruit trees in a tiny back yard, a layout every Northerner plans when he buys a home in Tiamara. It was behind one of these trees that someone had hidden, and pumped a stream of bullets through Cyril Owens, at 1.15 that morning.

Mrs Owens herself was a slender, sweet, oval-faced brunette; she wasn't blatantly beautiful, but of the sort that gives one an impression of Giotto's paintings of the Virgin—a quiet, exquisite kind of loveliness

Poggioli glanced over the kitchen—at the bullet-sawed window pane, and at the kitchen clock, smashed by a line of slugs that moved across the wall and stopped it at exactly 1.15. Naturally, since Poggioli approaches any crime from a purely psychological point of view, these material details did not interest him further than to fix the personality of the murderer.

'Hired job,' he diagnosed 'Did your husband have some very wealthy enemies, Mrs Owens . . . or some very wealthy clients?' I felt a touch of admiration for his adroitness in leading up to suspicions he had already formed.

But Mrs Owens was as innocent as her appearance. 'I don't think anybody was mad at Cyril; I never heard of it. The people he worked for must have been pretty rich. Cyril always had a lot of money—more than was good for him, I thought.'

Poggioli agreed gently with her moralizing. 'He probably had; a great many of us fail to use our money wisely. Now—your husband; do you happen to know his list at clients?'

'I don't know any at them, Dr Poggioli.'

'He never mentioned them to you?'

'No; he said he wanted to keep business away from me.'

'Do you know whether he ever talked his business to anyone or not?'

'I don't think so; I don't think he even talked about it to Mark.'

'Mark?'

'Yes—Mr Mark Sumner; he was an accountant, too. We saw a lot of Mark and Iris.' She spoke in a controlled grey monotone, in contrast to her physical colouring; but it just struck me that her grief would presently bring her lovely face, and profound black hair, to the same colour as her voice.

Poggioli continued his interrogation. 'Did your husband work out or in?'

'In, mainly. They brought his work to him . . .'

'Mrs Owens, just why did you leave your voice elevated at the end of your sentence? What was peculiar about their bringing his work to him?'

'They always came at night; he would work all night, and usually take it back to somebody about dawn.'

'You didn't approve of that?'

'No, I didn't. I often told him it would be better to work for people in the regular hours, and not make so much money. I told him it would be better for his health.'

'I know you told him that,' agreed Poggioli; 'but what you meant was that it would be more conventional.'

The widow of a few hours was surprised, 'I—I suppose I *did* mean that. It always bothered me, receiving bundles of notes at night, taking them back in the morning. M—other accountants didn't do like that.'

'You say he was paid so much money? Was it in cash or cheques?'

'Cash . . . bills.'

'Was there anything else peculiar about his salary?'

'No-o. He would give me as much as I would take. He had quite a number of bank accounts around in little banks. He had some of them in my name. Was that wrong, Dr Poggioli?'

'Mrs Owens, the lines between wrong and discretion, and right and rashness, are so delicate I never try to draw them. Now one more question: Do you know whether your husband had been summoned to appear before any court, or investigating committee, or anything like that?'

'He wouldn't have told me, but would that have depressed him . . . frightened him?'

'I rather think it would.'

'Well, he wasn't depressed. He was very gay . . . a great deal too gay, I thought, for the Lord marks our every idle word.'

Mrs Owens was too orthodox for the purposes of modern mystery stories, so I left her and Poggioli and began looking through the house to see if I could hit on some theory of Cyril Owens' death. I didn't quite believe Poggioli's drift that his employers killed him; it was possible, but it didn't sound probable.

The house, as I have said, was a typical middle-class tropical home. As I looked around, I discovered one difference between the Cyril Owens home and others of the same class. This residence had a closet filled not with feminine but with masculine wear. I have never seen such an array of men's style outside a haberdashery. He even had canes to match his ties and shoes and socks. His wife's holdings were a few simple frocks. I wondered why in the world she hadn't spent some of her money on clothes, and at least kept in sight of her husband.

But, with this thought, it suddenly dawned on me why Cyril Owens was shot down through his kitchen window. I turned, went back into the kitchen where Poggioli was comforting the widow. He assured her that her own life was not in danger and advised her to go into some benevolent work so that her days would be filled—if not with happiness, at least with good deeds. She replied sadly that her days had never been filled with happiness.

Here I took over the conversation, and went directly to the point I had in mind: 'Mrs Owens, your husband was a very carefully dressed man, was he not?'

She said he always had been. I continued, 'He went out a great deal and had a lot of friends, both men and women?'

She agreed to this very gravely. 'I imagine,' I went on, 'that Mr Owens went out on many occasions when you didn't go with him?'

'I didn't want to go,' she replied defensively.

'I know that. You are of a quiet, thoughtful temperament. I imagine the chatter of a party, cocktails and smoking didn't amuse you greatly?'

'The Bible warns all of us against vanity,' said the widow.

'Quite true. Your husband, I imagine, begged you to go with him at first; but you didn't do it. Finally, he stopped pressing you, and after a brief invitation went on without you. That's what happened, wasn't it?'

Mrs Owens became disturbed. 'What are you suggesting? What would that have to do with Cyril's . . . death?'

I put away my indirection. 'It's this. Mr Owens could have fallen in love with some woman who already had family connections, and the woman's husband could have resented it. Would you give Dr Poggioli and me the names of Mr Owens' intimate married friends? Couples he saw frequently at parties?'

The woman went a little paler. 'No, I wouldn't do that. If I were wrong I wouldn't want to direct suspicion against an innocent woman. And besides, it would be speaking unkindly of my dead husband. I couldn't do that.'

Such charity was very trying. 'Listen, Mrs Owens,' I said. 'Do you prefer to set aside the law of our land in favour of a barbarous, outdated custom?'

She asked what outdated custom.

I continued, 'The old Southern one of allowing a husband to attack and kill another man for some intimacy with his wife. That is no longer condoned, Mrs Owens—not even by custom.'

The woman looked at me and Poggioli for a moment, then began weeping. 'Did my . . . staying away from the vanities of . . . of this world c-cause my husband's death?'

'Don't look at it that way,' I begged; 'don't twist this into a self-accusation . . .'

'If . . . if he killed Cyril . . . but I know he didn't . . . I know it is impossible. But, if he did, God will punish him.'

'Did you ever hear of him threatening Cyril?' I asked, still using no names.

'Of course not! He wouldn't do such a thing! I always felt sorry for him . . . he was just as much against the . . . the frivolous life as I was.'

'You won't give us his name, and the name of his wife, as a mere start for investigation?'

'I will never willingly get anybody into trouble . . .'

Poggioli intervened. 'Mrs Owens, don't you think you ought to give me the names of your husband's friends to let me clear their names in this terrible affair?'

She was amazed. 'Clear their names?'

'Certainly. It is plain to me that you believe in their innocence, but you *did* have them in mind. Now your other friends—they'll think things. You know how people are; they hatch up all sorts of suspicions. So if I knew who they were, then I could go down and interview them, and prove their complete innocence. It would be doing them a great favour, and would be a very generous act on your part, Mrs Owens.'

The madonna-like woman interrupted him. 'I know they had

nothing to do with Cyril's death, and that it ruined my life. I forgive that: maybe it was meant to test my charity, and my faith,'

'You would certainly stand the test, Mrs Owens, if you furnished me the information to let me go and interview them and prove absolutely they had nothing to do with the murder.'

'Well—of course she wouldn't have.'

'Or him, either? I'll clear his reputation, too,'

Mrs Owens looked fixedly at the criminologist. 'How could you clear it?'

'Simply enough, Mrs Owens. Your husband was killed with a submachine gun. No jealous Southern husband ever used such a weapon in all history; that is used by professional gangsters and murderers for hire. Your husband's assailant, whoever he was, was simply a hired assassin. There was nothing personal in the murder, so far as he was concerned.'

Mrs Owens was overcome. She studied herself by the kitchen table. 'Could he . . . couldn't he . . . ?'

'No,' assured Poggioli, divining what she meant, 'it is impossible for a Southern husband to avenge his wife's honour by paying somebody to do it. It would have to be his own work . . . here in the South.'

'Dr Poggioli, I am so glad to hear you say that. Oh, that's such a burden off my heart . . . even to think for a moment that . . .one who had been your friend . . .' She hushed, and stood looking at the bullet holes and the smashed clock.

The criminologist changed the painful subject. 'How long have you devoted your life to spiritual things, Mrs Owens?'

'You mean—when did I begin to lead a blameless life?'

'That's what I mean.'

'I don't hardly know—maybe two, two and a half years. I had thought about taking the veil.'

'What gave you that impulse?'

'I . . . when I tell you this, you'll think it's silly.'

'No, go on, I won't think it silly. People seldom act silly. They

do things without understanding why; that goes on all the time—
sometimes for better, sometimes for worse. But it's never silly.'

'Well, one day I was standing right here, looking out that
window, thinking how untoward I was . . . when all of a sudden
a mockingbird began singing in that second grapefruit tree. Its
song seemed so pure and lovely, I began to cry. I asked God to
let my heart be like that . . . I shouldn't have told you that.'

'Indeed, you should. And you had been knowing these friends
of yours for about a year or a year and a half?'

'About that, I suppose.'

'Thank you, Mrs Owens, very much. And now will you write
down the address of your friends? You see, his wife won't be any
surer about your husband's death than you are, Mrs Owens. You
do see that, don't you?'

'Why, poor Iris . . . I had never thought of that. I suppose
she wouldn't be. I suppose she must be in a terrible torment . . .
If she can feel anything at all.'

I must admit to a little thrill of satisfaction when I heard Mrs
Owens use this last phrase—which proved to me that after all
she was not a complete saint. Poggioli then asked her to write
the address of her former friends on her husband's typewriter,
because he couldn't read handwriting very well. She left the
kitchen for her husband's office and presently returned with a
folded sheet of paper. The criminologist looked at it.

Mr and Mrs (Iris Hyde) Mark Sumner, C.P.A. 861 Hibiscus Ave S. E.

She had put all of her information, rather unconventionally,
into a single line. When we had thanked Mrs Owens once again,
and were outside, I asked Poggioli why he had her write the
address on the typewriter. I knew he could decipher any writing,
if it had any meaning at all. He passed it all, said it was just
routine.

I then said that if the Sumners had nothing to do with the

murder, as he seemed to think, that we were just wasting my time to go to their home. He asked why.

I said, 'Because according to your machine gun theory, Sumner didn't commit the murder; and American mystery story readers aren't particularly interested in light women. It is the great American bestseller-reading public that go for them.'

Poggioli retorted that we had no clue whatever to the murder except the strictly impersonal machine gun; that the Sumners might know something further about the matter, and that if we didn't visit them, we might as well get in a taxi and go home.

That certainly was true, so I went along with him to the Sumners.

Mrs Iris Sumner met us at the door with an air as if she had been expecting us; that, of course, was a faint hint of guilt within itself and I wondered if Poggioli had noticed it. Mrs Sumner was not a pretty woman. She had eyes underlined with cocktails, and relaxed lips. Nevertheless she was attractive; she met us understandingly—even sympathetically—and the first thing she asked was how Maria was standing it. I answered that Mrs Owens' faith bore her up.

'It would,' agreed Mrs Sumner earnestly. 'I admire Maria; even in the middle of our trouble I think she is a wonderful person. I'm awfully sorry for her . . . as well as myself.' The intonation of her last phrase admitted her relations with the dead man so frankly that I was shocked—not with condemnation, but with astonishment that anyone should be so forthright.

'You were expecting us to call, were you not, Mrs Sumner?' I asked shrewdly.

'Yes, I was. Expecting both you and Dr Poggioli

I hated to say my next sentence to so straightforward a woman; but it was true, and I wanted Poggioli to see that my own powers of criminological deduction were improving. So I said to her gravely, almost reluctantly: 'Do you realize, Mrs Sumner, that your expectation of us suggests—at least in a slight degree—that you and your husband might have some connection with the crime?'

The woman opened her eyes. 'I . . . think I do . . . that,' she said uncertainly; 'maybe I shouldn't talk so . . . so freely . . .'

'Talk just as you feel, Mrs Sumner,' reassured Poggioli, 'I understand the reason you expected us; it is quite simple. Mrs Owens telephoned you that we were on our way here.'

Both the woman and I were amazed—she, that Poggioli should know this; I, that Mrs Owens would telephone the woman who had taken her husband from her and warn her that we were coming.

Iris Sumner said, 'Dr Poggioli, how did you know Maria telephoned me?'

'Because you called both our names when we have never met you before. Somebody had to have told you; the only person who knew you, and knew we were coming, was Mrs Owens. Therefore, she must have telephoned you.'

Poggioli's simple deduction would have surprised even me more—even though I was accustomed to him—if I had not been so greatly astonished at Maria Owens' magnanimity. Imagine, telephoning and warning a woman who had stolen her husband, and whose own husband was under suspicion for his murder. I was forced mention such a marvel of generosity.

'Oh, that's Maria,' agreed Mrs Sumner earnestly. 'I've never known such a woman. I wish I were like her. I think I'm going over to see her pretty soon, and sympathize with her for . . . for both our losses.' Her last remark further admitted her relations with Cyril Owens.

Poggioli called her attention to this very gently. He asked her if she knew that what she had just said might throw suspicion of the murder on Mr Sumner. She didn't see how that could be.

'I'll explain it so . . . so you'll know,' said Poggioli. For some reason, both of us felt that we must protect Mrs Sumner from herself, so far as we could ethically. 'You see, when you admit an intimacy with Mr Owens, you have given a reason why your own husband should have assassinated him. Of course, perhaps your husband didn't; I hope he didn't. But you do see, don't you, that your confession lays the groundwork for such a suspicion?'

'I . . . I suppose it could be looked at that way.'

'It certainly could, and *would* be looked at that way; some persons would say further, that you were deliberately betraying him out of revenge—because he had killed your lover.'

'Oh, Dr Poggioli,' cried Mrs Sumner earnestly, 'Mark didn't kill Cyril; I have no reason to be angry at Mark on that score. He wouldn't have killed anybody.'

'Then you do have some "score" on which to be angry,' suggested Poggioli.

Mrs Sumner was a little disconcerted to be picked up like this. 'Well . . . yes, I do have . . .'

'What was it?'

'He . . . he had given me up . . . he had quit dating me.'

Even Poggioli was astonished at this. 'You put this in the past perfect tense, Mrs Sumner; your sentence means that he quit dating you before something else happened. I suppose that something else was your liaison with Mr Owens?'

'Yes it was . . . it was before that.'

I could see this gave a sharp turn to Poggioli's reflections. He stood pondering. Finally, he said, 'Even so, Mrs Sumner—even if your husband was cool towards you—when you formed an intimacy with another man, it would affect his pride, his feeling of honour . . . Men are very strange animals, Mrs Sumner. They have a physical and also a legal sense of sexual property; it just happens that legal sexual possession is more advertised, and more influential, in a man's social relations than his simple physical possession. He will murder over a wife he doesn't love more quickly than over a mistress he does.'

Mrs Sumner held up her hands negatively, 'Oh—no, Dr

Poggioli; none of the men in our set would do such a thing as that. Our set was on . . . well on a higher plane than most social groups here in Tiamara. We didn't play contract or canasta. 'We would discuss morals and peoples' right to love. We used our minds; we were all very free thinkers, so I know Mark would never really have killed anybody about me—especially when he didn't really want me. He was too sophisticated for that; all of us were.'

I grew sorrier and sorrier for Mrs Sumner. I hardly knew why, except that she was making such an earnest, pointless fight for something. I said, 'Did Maria Owens attend your parties, and feel the same way the rest of you felt?'

'No, Maria hardly ever went. We called on the Owens and they came to see us . . . at least we did before Cyril and I . . . found out that we loved each other. After that she didn't go out much anywhere, except to church. Really—it almost broke my heart, she was such a sweet, sweet woman. But, of course, her viewpoint was very simple . . . and primitive.'

I didn't know what to say. I felt that Mrs Sumner was very wrong—but she was so intricately wrong that I would never be able to straighten out her tangle. Besides, it was too late.

Poggioli had no interest in our casuistry. He asked Mrs Sumner, if she knew her husband was innocent, had she any idea of who might have attacked Cyril Owens. She had none. Did she know anything of Cyril's clients as a public accountant? Well, he had told her once or twice that he had some 'beauties'.

'Beauties,' repealed Poggioli. 'You took him to mean by that, questionable clients?'

'Something like that.'

'Did he mention some of these "beauties"?'

'Oh—no, of course not. When Mark and I used to see the Owens a lot, Cyril would sometimes let slip a remark to Mark. They were both C.P.A.s, you know. But that was usually after we had all had a Tom Collins—all except Maria.'

'Did your husband make any such remark about his clients as a C.P.A.?'

'No, he didn't. Mark is really a sobersides . . .' Mrs Sumner gave a little rueful laugh. 'It's the queerest thing. I had a dozen chances with easy-going boys like Cyril when I was a girl, then Mark came along, and he was so serious and so different—I got just utterly wrapped up in him. I wish I could tell you about our wedding—how I felt . . .' Her underlined eyes took on something of the light realism of her set. 'Of course it didn't last; it couldn't.'

Poggioli has no interest in human emotions; his preoccupation is crime. He broke off with an abruptness that embarrassed me 'Mrs Sumner, would you be kind enough to give me a sample of the typewriting of your husband's machine?'

Such a request in the middle of her description of the ecstasies of her vanished honeymoon took Mrs Sumner aback. 'You want something written on Mark's typewriter?'

'Yes.'

'Why, certainly; I don't mind . . .' She turned inside to get a sample of the script. When she came back with it after a few moments she said, in a changed voice, 'You don't believe what I told you, do you?'

'Oh, yes.'

'Then . . . why do you want a sample of Mark's typing if you know he didn't do it?'

'Because you don't know where Mark was on the night of the murder. You and Mark sleep in separate rooms; you have just said so. You never visit each other. He could have been gone all night at the time of the murder and you never have known it.' He took the paper, and was evidently about to say goodbye and go away.

Mrs Sumner caught her breath. 'Dr Poggioli, then . . . there is something else I will have to tell you.'

I turned back to her, realizing there was not the slightest telling what this painfully frank woman would have to say.

'I am listening , Mrs Sumner,' said Poggioli.

'Well, it's just this; on the night when . . . when Cyril died . . . I was with Mark.'

'You were?'

'Yes—all night long.'

'It was the first time for years?'

'Yes.'

'Did he suggest it?'

'I see what you mean; you think he suggested it to prove an alibi—that he really left me in the night, did this thing, then came back and came to bed again. In the morning, there we were together, and he would have an alibi. Is that what you mean?'

'Certainly, that's very clear; it's exactly what I mean.'

'Well, it wasn't like that. I suggested it.'

'Why?'

'Because I suddenly got sorry for him. He looked so wretched. I thought, here I am a free uninhibited woman, making Mark more miserable than he need be by our staying away from each other. I knew Cyril wouldn't really care because he was a broad thinker like all the test of us. I said, "Mark, I'm going to stay with you tonight." He said "Are you?" I said "Yes . . . if you don't mind—but if you mind, tell me and it'll be all right.' He said he would be glad if I came. So I went with him.'

'Mrs Sumner,' said Poggioli, 'I must tell you that everything you say draws the suspicion a little closer round your husband. You stayed with him the night of the murder?'

'Yes I did.'

'But don't you realize that to have you again made him feel more keenly his loss in the past, and stirred morc deeply his hatred of Cyril Owens? Also your occupancy of his bed gave him a complete alibi; so in the night after you were asleep, he might have crept out of bed . . .'

'No, he didn't do that.'

'How can you be sure? Did you stay awake? I know you didn't.'

'No. I didn't stay awake—but I woke up. I had the most terrible dream. I dreamed that Cyril had been shot and I woke up screaming "Cyril! Cyril!" Of course that waked Mark. He shook his head and asked what did I mean? I told him I had dreamed Cyril was shot. Then I realized I ought never to have said that; I should have made up something else and told him, but I never think to do these things in time.

'He was furious. He caught me by the arms, lifted me out of bed, told me to go to my own room and never come back to his so long as I lived. Of course I should never, never have mentioned Cyril, even if I dreamed about him. I went to my own room and turned on the light and sat down on my bed when my ormolu struck the quarter of an hour. It was fifteen minutes to one. That of course was when he was shot; I saw it in the paper next morning. It took me a long time to get from the table to my bed and lie down when I found out what I had seen in my dream was true. I have thought maybe Maria would have said it was a punishment on me for taking Mark back when I really loved Cyril; I'm sure I don't know what it meant.'

This seemed to be the ultimate of the sophisticate. We bade her goodbye as Poggioli folded the specimen of her husband's typewriting and put it in his pocket.

As we went away I asked Poggioli what he was going to do with the typing samples. He said he didn't know, that he picked them up as part of his routine.

I said, 'Do you suppose Mrs Sumner made up that entire tale as a positive alibi for her husband?'

'No, that was the truth, *prima facie*; she couldn't have invented such a story in a thousand years.'

'All right,' I agreed; 'then who under heaven could have killed Owens? The gangsters he was working for? Did he know too much?'

'There are more than one set of racketeers,' pointed out

Poggioli; 'they have wars between themselves. Owens might have been a casualty in one of their fights.'

I didn't like such a conclusion. It was a little too indefinite and impersonal for a marketable mystery. I suggested, 'How would it do to have Sumner hire a gangster to kill Owens? Then Sumner could have known the very night of Owens' murder and have asked Mrs Sumner to come to his room for an alibi . . .'

'Listen, Mrs Sumner invited Sumner; and a gang wouldn't kill their own accountant at the bidding of an outsider. Why don't you let the story go through as it is?'

'Do you mean to say that it is insoluble?' I was a little shocked at the idea; never before had Poggioli completely failed on a murder mystery.

'It isn't insoluble,' said my friend; 'but it is some phase of gang activity, and it lies beyond our venue. We will never reach the proper evidence out of that maze of interlocking crimes. The best thing I think we can do is to get another paper and start investigating another crime. We might as well give up this one.'

This was the most sardonic ending any of our joint researches had ever reached. We bought another paper, got into a taxi and started home to Acacia Street. I took half the paper, and he took the other half.

There were some very good things in the paper—a big scandal about a private sanitarium; a kidnapping; a swindler who impersonated the nobility; the usual woman found dead in a lonely palmetto hammock. I was so preoccupied and distressed about Mrs Owens and Mrs Sumner, that all this daily record of crime seemed like the accompaniment of a drum to a sad and disturbing melody.

When we got home, I had an impulse to ring Mrs Sumner up and see if she had learned anything new about her lover's death. But of course she hadn't. Then I really wanted to telephone Mrs Owens to try to say something to comfort her in the loss of her husband, but there was nothing to say. Then, too, Maria

Owens had a consolation in another realm of being which Iris Sumner would never know . . . and neither would I.

Happily, those feelings of sympathy which rise up suddenly for this person or that die away just as suddenly, and you are set free from the kindness of your heart. So, as the mornings passed, and new editions of the *Times* dropped on our stoop, I became interested in the sanitarium scandal which was just reaching its full swing. Gebhardt, a reporter I knew, was reporting it, and he made such a foul disgrace out of it that I enjoyed it very much along with everybody else.

On this particular morning, I read two columns on the sanitarium on the front page and then turned to page eight to get the rest. I finished his story, and was thinking of how well Gebhardt was doing when my eye fell on a small single paragraph headed *Woman Smoker Burns Self to Death with Cigarette in Bed.*

I almost didn't read it; it's the sort of thing that happens over and over. I am sure none of them think they will drop off to sleep when they light their cigarettes in bed, but apparently many of them do. I was about to glance away, in search of something more entertaining, when I saw the name Mrs Iris Sumner.

I had a feeling as if something had slid loose in my chest. The paragraph told that she had come in late from a cocktail party; she and her husband had gone to bed in separate rooms. Some time later, Mark Sumner, her husband, smelled smoke. He traced it to his wife's room and found her asphyxiated in a smouldering bed. Mrs Sumner left two sisters—Mrs Anna Wilkes of Los Angeles, California, and Miss Nellie Loughram of Canton, Ohio. Funeral services would be held at the Hibiscus Avenue Episcopal Church, the Rev. J. Des-Liger Smith officiating.

As I read this, my strange feeling of oppression and grief returned to me. I took the paper in, silently, and handed it to Poggioli, showing him the paragraph. Underneath my feeling for the woman herself, I had a vague hope that Poggioli would

be able, through Iris's death, to unravel the mystery of Cyril
Owens' murder, but he was not. This was clearly an accident—a
very unusual accident. It happens mainly in hotels, where people
are lonely; they lie and smoke in bed until they fall asleep, and
set fire to their covers.

After a day or two, this also passed out of my thoughts. It
was helped along by Gebhardt's story of a Dr Drummond, who
had turned up as the chief actor in the sanitarium scandal.
Poggioli and I finally became so interested in Dr Drummond
that we went down to the City Hall to see for ourselves exactly
what the Police Department had found out.

We were in the street-level lobby, waiting for our lift in the
elevator bank, when I heard a man ask Information on what
floor he would find the marriage-licence bureau.

I turned at the request, because—after all—anybody looks to
see who is to be the next man married. I didn't know him, of
course. He was a serious—almost taciturn-looking fellow. I
couldn't believe he would make any woman very happy—unless,
of course, she herself was a serious melancholy sort of woman.

The next moment, I saw the bride-to-be standing a little way
from the window. She took my breath; I had never seen such a
change come over any woman. Of course she was not happy; it
was impossible even to imagine Maria Owens as happy. But she
evidently was filled with a kind of solemn joy that was natural
to her madonna face and figure. It just struck me that this would
be the way the persecuted and harassed saints would look when
they first entered heaven. Just then, she saw us; she caught the
man's arm and drew him towards us.

'Mark,' she said, 'I've told you so often about this wonderful,
good man, Mr Poggioli. When my heart was at its lowest point
I telephoned him. He came to me and told me I was in no
danger; that everything would work out for my happiness: and
for me to just trust in providence and walk forwards in faith.
And Dr Poggioli, look at us now!'

She compressed her lips to restrain her own feelings. We, of course, were very happy in her happiness. Then her elevator came down and took her and Mr Sumner away.

When they were gone. I said to Poggioli, 'Did you tell her all that?' Poggioli said he didn't much think he did; it was probably an illusion . . .

He left off talking, in the middle of his sentence; as we got into our elevator, he suddenly reached his hand into his pocket and drew out two slips of paper. Instead of going up to the Police Department on the eleventh floor, we got off at the Internal Revenue offices on the third.

Naturally Poggioli was known here, for he had been a consultant in several revenue cases. He went to one of the cages and handed his two sheets of paper in to a Mr Bill Butlin. He asked Bill would he do him the favour to take these two typewriter samples and compare them with the letter of the man who sent in some information that broke the Anzetti Income Tax prosecution.

'How do you know anybody sent in any information?' asked Butlin.

'I don't, but someone easily could have. I want to know whether it came from the man who wrote this sample or this one.'

'You understand that the case is closed,' reminded Mr Butlin; 'you can't bring in new evidence . . .'

'This is for my own personal information.'

'O.K.' Butlin took the two sheets and went away.

I stood trying to fabricate some sort of explanation for what my friend was doing. I had a feeling that I was about to get a story, and in the same breath I had a fear that Mrs Maria Owens' heavenly happiness would pay for my solution. I was torn between my flair as an author, and my loyalty as I friend: it is a point of imbalance where writers often stand.

Mr Butlin reappeared at the window. 'It's this one,' he said, delivering a sample marked with a blue pencil, then he handed back the other. 'I spoke to the old man about this and told him who handed these in. He said to tell you that the case would be closed to anybody else; but if you had anything new it could be reviewed.'

'Thanks; I appreciate that very much, Mr Butlin.' And we walked back out to the elevator bank.

I had the most uncomfortable hot-cold sensations run over me. When we reached the street floor, and could talk in the crowd, Poggioli said, 'It was Mark Sumner's letter to the department.'

'Yes, I gathered that much. What did he write to the revenue men?'

'He gave them details of the Anzetti mob which he picked up at the Cyril Owens home . . . enough to identity Owens as the leak. When the F.B.I. closed in and showed their proof, they thought, of course, that Owens had squealed. So the rest of it happened.'

'Why did he deliberately get Owens into trouble? Was that after Owens' familiarity with Iris?'

'No, it was before; it was what led to his coldness towards Mrs Sumner, and her desertion of him later. And still later than that—after Cyril was assassinated—it led to his cremation of his wife in her bed while she was drunk.'

'What led to it? My Heavens, man . . .'

'Why, Mark Sumner's passion for Maria Owens, and Maria's love for him—which made a religious recluse of her . . .'

'Well, does she know . . . ?'

'Certainly, certainly not; she thinks a kindly providence marked her tears and relieved her of the great sin of not loving her husband, and of deeply loving a man who was not her husband.'

We were out of City Hall now, and Poggioli tore up his two typewriting samples and loosed their shreds in the windy street.

'But . . . Poggioli,' I objected. 'Are you going to let it rest at that? Sumner is morally guilty of one murder, even though the law could never touch him for the death of Owens. But there's no doubt about his guilt in Iris's case.'

Poggioli nodded. 'In our minds, perhaps. We have discovered this through psychological deduction, not through evidence that would stand up in court. Only a confession would make his conviction possible.'

I thought of what this situation would do to my story; how could I conclude it satisfactorily if a known murderer were permitted to escape Scot-free? 'Surely,' I mumbled, 'we could play upon his guilt in some way and bring out the evidence.'

There was a faint smile on Poggioli's face. 'Yes,' he agreed, 'that might be possible. You want to see justice done, my friend?'

'Why . . . yes,' I answered quickly.

'And, of course, once justice is complete, you will have a story . . . Well, I'm afraid you may have to wait awhile, but I promise you that you will see justice—unless Mark Sumner suffers a fatal accident, or illness, beforehand. I predict that he will come forward and confess within a year—and there will be enough substantiating evidence for a conviction.'

I pondered a moment, trying to puzzle out my friend's reasoning. 'You—you think Maria will find out and persuade him to confess?'

'She will persuade him, whether she knows or not. There are some men who could commit the "perfect" crime and never worry about it afterwards. Mark Sumner is not that kind of man—his is the psychological type that should avoid murder.'

I smiled at Poggioli's delightfully abstract reasoning; yet, it did make sense, if you wanted to look at homicide strictly on the basis of calculated risk. Then the smile left me as I thought of Sumner's new wife. 'Poor Maria,' I said; 'her happiness won't last long.'

'No . . . it will be short-lived, as any kind of happiness of this world. But she will be comforted in her own way, feeling sure that his soul has been saved through repentance and suffering. And she will still have the past . . .'

We stopped at a news-stand to pick up the latest editions of the papers. 'Do you think you will have your story, now?'

'I'll wait,' I replied.

And Poggioli was right; I marked the date on my calendar, and it was a little over ten months later when the papers were filled with stories of Mark Sumner's amazing confession, trial, and conviction.

T. S. STRIBLING

The American novelist known as T. S. Stribling (1881–1965) was born in Clifton, a small town on the bend of the state river in Wayne County, Tennessee. His mother, Amelia Annie Waits, was a teacher and keen equestrian, while his spectacularly named father, Christopher Columbus Stribling, edited the local newspaper and as a younger man had fought in the Northern Federal Army at the infamous battle of Shiloh. Tom Stribling's birth name was in fact Thomas Hughes Stribling, the name taken from one of his father's friends, a local dignitary, with whose daughter Tom would later 'walk out'. However, after an incident in which Tom threw rocks at her parents' home, Miss Hughes abandoned Tom, who chose in retaliation to adopt a new middle name, Sigismund, and consequently new initials.

Tom Stribling *always* wanted to be a writer, and his first published work, which came out when he was only twelve years old, was a ghost story entitled 'The House of Haunted Shadows'. As a child he spent summers with his aunt, Martha Waits, whose black servant, George, was to prove a strong influence on Stribling's literary life. Stribling attended State Normal School in Florence, his Alabaman mother's home town, from which he graduated in June 1903 with the additional honour of a medal for the best graduating essay, 'Climatic Influence on Southern Verse'. That same year he gained a teaching certificate, possibly intending to follow in his mother's footsteps, but he found teaching difficult and abandoned the profession after only a term.

He returned to study, and in 1904 graduated from the University of Alabama with a law degree. Stribling practised law in Florence and for a year in the office of Governor Emmet O'Neal, before abandoning the legal profession and moving to Nashville, where he secured a job as assistant to the editor of the *Taylor-Trotwood Magazine*, which also published some of his adventure stories, for example 'The Thrall of the Green' in July 1907. Other stories, like 'The Loot of the Dog Star' (1909) were published in newspapers. Stribling also produced many 'moral' stories for Sunday school magazines, characterized by more or less overt warnings about the evils of alcohol and cigarettes. Finally, frustrated by the limitations of the shorter format, he decided to expand one of his short stories into a novel and the result, *The Cruise of the Dry Dock* was published in 1917, the same year that he joined the staff of *The Chattanooga News*.

Stribling's first book, though jejune, was sufficiently well-received for him to consider writing a novel for adults and, in parallel with his newspaper work, he began work on one while turning out the odd poem and countless short stories. Stribling once claimed, jokingly, that by this stage of his career he had written more than 10,000. Many were rejected but others sold to journals like *Southern Women's Magazine*.

In 1921, *Birthright*, Stribling's first novel for adults, was published after serialization in *The Century Magazine*. The story concerns a young black graduate of Harvard who travels south with the aim of founding a school only to find prejudice and discrimination at every turn. Although the book was widely praised, others slated the author for suggesting that the post-bellum South was a less than perfect place, a criticism that would echo throughout Stribling's career. Astonishingly, some newspapers even sought to 'explain' the author's evident sympathies for the Southern poor by altering photographs to give him the appearance of African heritage.

Stribling's next two books were less controversial. *Fombombo* (1922) is an adventure story featuring an American arms dealer in Venezuela, a country that the author had visited and which also provided the setting for *Red Sand* (1923). Other novels followed and in 1930, by now a successful and nationally celebrated author, Stribling married Louella Kloss, an accomplished violinist and music teacher. During the 1920s he also wrote a series of short detective stories about Dr Henry Poggioli, a professor of psychology. These were collected in *Clues of the Caribbees* (1929) and more Poggioli stories appeared in the early 1930s but were not collected until *Doctor Poggioli: Criminologist* (2004).

1931 saw the publication of *The Forge*, the first volume of a trilogy centred on Colonel Miltiades Vaiden, a fortune-hunting blackmailer, rapist and member of the Ku Klux Klan. Stribling's intention, as Stribling later made clear, was to provide 'a survey, more or less, of the foibles and amusing social kinks of the whole South from Civil War times to the present', some of those 'foibles' being, as he well knew, utterly abhorrent. While many praised his vivid, if not florid, writing, he was condemned for setting his fictional novel in Florence, Alabama, and for incorporating some events from the town's history. But if *The Forge* aroused annoyance, the following year's second volume—*The Store*—would arouse fury. Stribling found himself the focus of sharp criticism, often deeply grounded in racism and prejudice against anyone daring to suggest that the South was built on shame. One reviewer criticized Stribling for suggesting that lynching had ever been used other than as a reasonable weapon of law enforcement, while one local man threatened to sue Stribling for libel, a suit that the author offered to support on condition that it was brought 'while the offending book is still on sale at the bookstores'; like many of the anecdotes told about Stribling, this might even be true. Parochial criticisms aside, and despite sales that were to a degree depressed by the state of the American economy, *The Store* was widely praised, winning the prestigious $1,000 Pulitzer Prize in 1933 for the year's best American novel. The title of the final volume in the trilogy gave Stribling some difficulty and he mused on 'The Study' and 'The Temple' before settling on *Unfinished Cathedral* (1933). This book was also set in Florence to which, with authorial licence, he transplanted from Scottsboro the trial—on a charge of rape—of nine black teen-agers, considered by many to be the most egregious miscarriage of justice in American history.

In 1934, Stribling wrote a radio series for Columbia about the rivalry in Tennessee between ships and railroads. He then went on to write two more novels, *The Sound Wagon* (1935) and *These Bars of Flesh* (1938), political satires that have some similarities with *Birthright* and which also draw on aspects of Stribling's life, including his time teaching at Columbia in New York in the 1930s. While Stribling published no more novels, he resurrected Dr Poggioli in the 1940s and '50s for a series of stories for *Ellery Queen's Mystery Magazine*. These were written during the winters the Striblings spent in Florida, and were collected as *The Best of Dr Poggioli* (1975). He also wrote his autobiography, revising and extending it over the next twenty-five years; edited by Randy K. Cross and John T. McMillan, it was eventually published in 1982.

In 1959, Tom and Louella Stribling returned to Clifton, but his health began to decline and he died in a retirement home in 1965, shortly after moving back to Florence. While his novels have to an extent not dated well, T. S. Stribling did perhaps more than any other writer to highlight the fundamental immorality of racism and the toxic legacy of the Civil War.

One of a handful of uncollected Dr Poggioli stories, 'Figures Don't Die' was published in *Famous Detective Stories* in February 1953.

PASSENGERS

Ethel Lina White

Just before the blow fell Edna felt unusually well and happy. Her holiday was over, her bill at the hotel was paid, and her suitcase lay on the station platform. For over an hour she had sat—the sun beating down on her uncovered head—feasting her eyes on the scenery.

Before her was a grass-green lake, sparkling with diamond reflections and backed with white spiked mountains.

She had just spent a glorious three weeks rambling the mountains in congenial Anglo-American society, and it seemed strangely civilized to be wearing a skirt and silk stockings again after shorts and nailed boots. The rest of the crowd had returned yesterday, but she had chosen to stay one day longer, alone.

She was sorry to be leaving, partly because she was not going home, but merely 'back'. At these times she felt she paid a heavy price for her freedom as an attractive orphan of twenty-two with no relatives, clumps of friends, and a private income.

Suddenly the sun struck her. Owing to the altitude, the air was cool and bracing so that she had not realized the fierceness of its rays. She felt a violent pain at the back of her neck, followed by a rush of sick dizziness. As the white-capped mountains darkened and rocked she had a ghastly moment of panic.

'I'm going to be ill—alone—amongst strangers.'

Then everything slipped away . . . When she opened her eyes

she was on the cool gloom of the primitive little waiting room, while a black-pinafored woman held a glass of raw spirit to her lips. People stared at her curiously and spoke to her, but she could not understand a word.

Luckily, she soon felt better and was able to reward her Good Samaritans. But, after they had left her, she had another bad minute when she wondered if she had been robbed while she was unconscious. Examination of her bag, however, proved that her tickets, passport, and money were untouched.

She was now in a fever of impatience to get away, for her experience had unnerved her. It had made her realize, for the first time in her life, the horror of helplessness far away from familiar things.

Suddenly the signal fell and a coil of smoke whirled around the bend of the rails. With a whistle and a roar the engine steamed into the little station.

The porter had difficulty in finding a place for Edna, for, although her seat was reserved, the carriage already held its quota of six. He appeared to be abjectly apologetic to a majestic lady in deep black, who plainly resented the newcomer.

The whistle shrilled and the engine began to throb slowly on its way back to England. Except the frontiers, there was only one stop—Milan—before Basle, where Edna changed into the Calais express.

A family party—two large parents and a daughter of about twelve—sat on the same side of the carriage as herself. Opposite was a fair and beautiful girl in black and white, who appeared to have modelled herself on a film star, a typical British spinster and the lady who had opposed her intrusions.

Veiled and draped in heavy black, she was an overwhelming and formidable personality—essentially of the ruling class—with an arrogant beaked nose and fierce proud eyes.

Presently the majestic lady received a visitor—a pallid man with dead eyes, a black spade beard and glasses. As they carried on a low conversation Edna was amused to notice that the British spinster was straining her ears to listen. She also remarked that the black-clad lady looked in her direction as though in annoyance and made a low observation to her companion.

Sensing their hostility, she closed her eyes and only knew when the man had left the compartment by the absence of guttural whispers. The motion rocked her to a light sleep.

Her torpid trance was broken by an official who poked his head through the door and shouted something to which the company, in general, was unresponsive. The British spinster, however, tapped Edna on the arm.

'You're English, aren't you? she asked in a crisp, pleasant voice. 'Tea is ready in the restaurant car. Coming?'

Edna's head was aching badly, so that she was glad to follow her guide into the corridor. As they passed the next compartment to theirs, they saw through the door a figure, covered with rugs, stretched out on the seat. Both head and forehead were bandaged, while a criss-cross of plaster strips concealed the features from brow to chin in a diagonal line.

The invalid was in charge of the pallid, black-bearded man, who had just visited their carriage, and a nursing sister, who was dressed like a nun. Her face was hard and repellent, with a brutal mouth, so that it was difficult to connect her with the profession of nursing.

'How ghastly to be ill on a journey,' shuddered Edna with a memory of her recent attack.

Her companion was able to tell her all about the invalid, for she was the type that collects information.

'Yes, a motor smash higher up the valley. Her face is terribly cut, poor thing, and there's head injury, so they're rushing her to Milan for an operation. The doctor was telling the baroness about it just now.'

She shouted the information over her shoulder as she led the way down the corridors, across the clanking connections, and into the crowded restaurant car. Wedging herself into a corner, she looked blissfully at the smutty tablecloth, the thin flakes of butter, and the cherry jam.

'Isn't this fun?' she cried.

The lady was nondescript—being middle-aged, dowdy, and vaguely oatmeal in colouring; yet there was a sparkle in her faded blue eyes which suggested youth.

Edna learned that her compatriot was a Miss Winifred Bird, who had been English governess to a titled family for two years and was now going home on her first holiday. To her surprise this adult lady actually possessed living parents.

'Mummy and Daddy say they can talk of nothing else but my return,' Miss Bird told her. 'They're excited as children and so is Ruff. He's an old English sheepdog, not pure, but an appealing dog, and so devoted to me. He understands I'm coming home, but not when, so he meets every train. Mummy says he always comes back with his tail down, the picture of depression. They're both imagining his frantic joy the night I do come, and that's tomorrow.'

Edna felt quite a lump in her throat at the thought of the reunion. It was the dog that really won her, for she got a clear picture of him—a shaggy mongrel, absurdly clownish, with amber eyes beaming under his wisps.

But she grew rather to like the old parents, too. Daddy was a parson-schoolmaster, who, when he retired at the age of sixty-five, began to learn Hebrew as a light holiday pastime.

'Are you going back after your holiday?' Edna asked.

'Yes, but not to my post.' Miss Bird looked around her and then lowered her voice. 'I'm coming back to give evidence in a murder trial. I'll mention no names, but I was governess to the very highest in the place. You've no idea of his power. What he says goes, and he hasn't got to speak, for a wink is enough. But, although he rules absolutely, there's a small communist element in the town and their leader—a young man—accused the—my employer—of corruption. I'm afraid it was true. There was an awful scene at the castle and the—my employer—shot the young man. I saw it all.'

'You've really seen a man killed?' gasped Edna. 'How terrible.'

'Terrible at the time, my dear, but afterwards it all turned to a thrilling adventure. Life's so interesting because things are always happening. Everyone wanted to hush it up and said it was suicide. But, of course, I had to insist on being heard for the sake of justice. You've no idea how unpopular I was. The children threw stones at me in the street and the shop people refused to serve me. Even the police were quite angry with me. And I'm sure the muddle about my seat was intentional.'

'What muddle?' asked Edna.

'I booked my seat second class, but when I got to the train they said my place was already taken. But the baroness was kind and said I was to travel "first" with her and she would make it right about my ticket. I felt awkward as she's related to the—my employer.'

Edna gathered that the autocratic lady in black was the baroness and that she had annexed her own reservation for Miss Bird. By this time, however, she was growing tired of Miss Bird's confidences. After they had blundered back to their compartment she felt she must make a bid for silence.

'Do you mind if I don't talk?' she asked. 'My head is nearly splitting. I've just had a touch of sunstroke.'

As she knew Miss Bird's curiosity had to be appeased she gave a brief account of her attack. While she did so she had the feeling that the baroness was listening to her story with concealed interest.

Miss Bird kindly supplied aspirin, which made Edna feel pleasantly drowsy.

Down, down. She drifted into sleep. Suddenly she gave a violent start and her heart began to leap as though she had just stepped into vacancy. Opening her eyes, she stared around her confusedly.

Miss Bird had disappeared.

She was astonished by her own pang of sudden loneliness. The baroness slept in her corner. As her nerves were still on edge, Edna had a nightmare impression that these people were not really human but a lot of dummies.

The family party read different sections of the same newspaper. The father was big, polished and clean shaven, even to his head. The mother had a straight fringe and her eyebrows appeared to be corked. The girl wore babyish socks, but her expression was adult.

As they remained dumb and motionless as waxworks, Edna glanced at the beautiful blonde, and she was reminded of a model in a shop window.

Common sense told Edna that Miss Bird had probably gone to wash and would soon be back. She looked at her watch to time her absence. In five minutes she would be surely back, with her warm humanity, her curiosity, and her stories about family and home.

Five minutes passed, then ten, then fifteen. Still Miss Bird did not come back. When, after twenty minutes had passed, Edna chanced to look up at the rack, she received a nasty shock.

Miss Bird's suitcase was not there.

She could restrain her uneasiness no longer. As the baroness still slept she appealed to the other passengers. She was probably the world's worst linguist, but she made a brave effort in three of the languages of civilization.

'Où est la dame?'

'Wo ist die Dame?'

'Where is the lady?'

She eked out her inquiries with pantomime, pointing to Miss Bird's empty place, while she raised her brows in exaggerated inquiry. But the passengers merely shrugged and shook their heads to show her that they did not understand.

Since no sign of intelligence gleamed on their blank faces, Edna decided to find out whether Miss Bird had changed her seat. But it seemed unlikely, in view of the fact that the train was so full., and she felt acutely worried as she worked her way down the shaking corridor—clinging to the rail, pushing past loiterers, and staring into every compartment.

Her quest reminded her of the hunt for the proverbial needle in the haystack. Although she visited every portion of the long train, including both restaurant cars—where men were smoking and drinking—she could find no trace of Miss Bird. With a leaden sense of apprehension she returned to her own compartment.

The baroness still slept. Suddenly desperate, Edna leaned forward and shook her awake. As she did so, she heard a smothered gasp from the other passengers, as though she had committed some act of sacrilege.

The baroness opened her proud eyes in a glare of outraged majesty. But Edna was too overwrought to apologize.

'Where is the English lady?' she cried.

'What English lady?' asked the baroness, speaking without a trace of accent.

'Miss Bird. The one who sat here.'

'I do not understand. That seat has not been occupied, ever.' Edna's head began to reel.

'Yes, yes,' she insisted. 'I talked to her. We had tea together.'

'No.' The baroness shook her head and spoke with slow emphasis. 'You make a strange mistake. There has been no English lady here except you, yourself.'

Feeling as though she was trapped in some bad dream, Edna sank weakly down in her seat, while the train rocked on its way, back to England. Slides of twilight scenery streamed past the window, but she saw only a rush of chaos.

Either they're all mad, or I'm mad, she thought. No Miss Bird?

Did I dream her? No, she was as real as me, with her old parents and Ruff . . . Oh, heavens! It's ghastly to be so helpless. I must think.

Presently she sprang to her feet in a burst of nervous futility.

'I must do something.'

Scarcely conscious of her actions, Edna began to make a second search through the train. But, this time, she was aware that she was an object of curiosity and amusement. In every carriage was a blur of faces.

As she entered the first-class restaurant car she thought she heard an Oxford accent. Unable to locate it, she made a general appeal.

'Please, is there anyone English here?'

The spectacle of a pretty girl in distress brought two men to their feet, although one of them appeared to regard chivalry merely as a duty. He was tall, thin, and of academic appearance, which, in his case, was not deceptive, since he was a university professor of modern languages.

The other was younger and rather untidy, with rough hair and audacious blue eyes.

'An English lady, Miss Bird, has disappeared on the train,' Edna declared, her voice shaking as she spoke. 'They say—but that's absurd. I'm frightened by it all. Something's wrong—and I can't speak their miserable language—and—'

As her voice failed, she was conscious of a tall grey man, bald as a vulture, who stared at her with piercing eyes as though she was something on a microscope slide.

'Could you pull yourself together and make a concise statement?' asked the professor.

The chill in his voice was tonic to her nerves, bracing her to compress the situation into a few words. To her overwhelming relief the professor was impressed, for he looked grave.

'This must certainly be investigated,' he said. 'Will you show me where your compartment is?'

The frivolous youth joined them and, somehow, managed to infect Edna with a sense of comradeship as they fought their way through the crowded corridor.

'My name's Carr,' he said. 'Much too long for you to remember. Better call me "John Michael Peter", like everyone else. I'm an engineer and speak the lingo, too. Look on me as a second string.'

Strong in the support of her compatriots, Edna felt certain of a happy issue as she entered her own compartment. The baroness was talking to the doctor, who was paying her another visit, but she listened, with gracious condescension, to the professor's statement.

He appeared to be in his element as he held his official inquiry and questioned the passengers in turn. She looked up at him with a smile and was unpleasantly surprised by his unresponsive face. Although she could not understand the language, it was easy to follow the proceedings by the negative shake of each person's head.

By degrees, her confidence began to cloud. The ticket collector was called into the carriage to add his contribution to the general confusion and noise. She glanced at Carr, but he only pulled down his mouth in a grimace.

Her heart sank and her head began to swim. It was inconceivable that all these people should lie—yet they appeared to be denying the existence of Miss Bird.

Presently the professor spoke to her coldly.

'You appear to have made a most extraordinary mistake. No one in this carriage—including the ticket collector—knows anything about the lady you say is missing.'

'Are you telling me I invented her?' asked Edna wildly. 'We had tea together.'

'Then, will you describe her so that I can interview the tea waiters?'

To her horror, Edna remembered that she had barely glanced

at Miss Bird. Most of the time she had kept her eyes closed because of her blinding headache.

'I'm afraid I can't tell you much,' she faltered. 'There was nothing about her to catch hold of. She's middle-aged, and ordinary, and rather colourless.'

'Surely you know if she is tall or short, dark or fair?'

'No. But I remember she had blue eyes.'

'What did she wear?' asked Carr with a flash of intuition.

'Tweed, I think. I didn't notice much because I've such a splitting headache.'

'Exactly.' The professor's tone was dry. 'Cause and effect. The doctor tells me you've just had sunstroke.'

Suddenly Edna saw her chance to convince him.

'How does the doctor know that?' she asked. 'I only told that to Miss Bird. How could I tell anyone else when I only speak English?'

The professor seemed impressed, for he took off his glasses to polish them. But as the doctor began to speak rapidly his expression hardened to its former fixity.

'It appears you were taken ill on the station platform. The baroness was there and she told the doctor.'

'It explains all,' said the doctor, speaking English with a grating accent. 'Your sunstroke has given you a delirium—a delusion. You went to sleep and you dreamed. Your Miss Bird is only your dream.'

The worst of it was they made her doubt herself. The mass of cumulative evidence against her story was too overwhelming. Even the friendly Carr did not believe in Miss Bird.

'I once had concussion, after footer,' he told Edna. 'The Bishop of London came into my room and did a music hall turn. He was as real as you. Suppose you play shut-eye for a bit. You'll wake up, right as rain.'

Edna wearily obeyed him. Once again she lay with closed eyes, listening to the clamour of the train. A long-drawn howl, as though a damned soul were lamenting, and a succession of rattles, like gunfire, told her that they were passing through a tunnel.

Suppose Miss Bird's body was, even then, being thrown out of the carriage in which it lay concealed. She was the victim of some treacherous plot in spite of all the evidence from the other side. As Edna's mind began to work again she remembered a story she had read in a magazine which, to her mind, surpassed in sheer horror the most lurid of crime stories.

Two ladies arrived by night at a continental hotel on their way back from an oriental tour. The daughter carefully noted the number of her mother's room before she went to her own. When she returned later she found no trace of her mother, while the room itself was transformed with different furniture and new wallpaper.

When she made inquiries the entire staff, from the manager downwards, assured her that she alone had come to the hotel. Her mother's name was not in the register. The cab driver and the porters at the railway terminus all supported the general conspiracy.

The mother had been blown out like a puff of smoke.

Of course, there was an explanation. In the daughter's absence the mother had died suddenly of plague contracted in the east. The merest rumour of this would have kept millions of visitors away from the exhibition about to be held in the city. With such important interests at stake a unit had to be sacrificed.

This story was declared authentic and Edna began to wonder whether Miss Bird's disappearance was not a parallel on a small scale. An unimportant foreigner dared to accuse a personage of murder. She would be chief witness at his trial. It followed that she must be suppressed—blown out, like the other lady, in a puff of smoke. In her case it would not involve a vast, complicated and fantastic conspiracy, merely the collusion of a few interested persons.

Edna felt her temperature rushing up as though she were in a furnace. Everyone considered her slightly mad and found her antics a funny spectacle. Mocking eyes followed her as she stormed the restaurant car.

The professor sat in interested conversation with the vulture-headed man while Carr listened. When he saw Edna he looked up with a slight frown.

'I must tell you something,' she cried. 'I've discovered that there's a conspiracy against Miss Bird. We've got to help her because she's English like ourselves. Do listen.'

The professor heard her story in stony silence and then he raised his brows interrogatively to the man with the piercing eyes. He nodded agreement when the other made some rapid explanation.

'Will you take some advice, offered in a friendly spirit?' asked the professor, speaking to Edna as though to a fractious child. 'This gentleman is a famous Russian alienist, and he is of the opinion that you may be, temporarily, very slightly deranged, as a result of your sunstroke.'

'D'you mean mad?' cried Edna in horror. 'Me?'

'Nothing to be frightened of, in the least,' the professor assured her. 'But he is not quite happy about your safety since you are alone. If you cannot keep quiet he may think it necessary to send you to a nursing home at Milan in your own interests until he can communicate with your friends.'

'He can't do that to me,' screamed Edna as England suddenly seemed very far away. 'I'm going home. I should resist.'

'Violence would be most unwise. Don't you understand? You have only to keep calm, and everything will be all right.'

The professor was not so inhuman so he appeared. He believed Edna to be a neurotic specimen who was telling lies from love of sensation.

He thought he was acting for the best and had no idea of the hell of fear into which he plunged her. White to her lips, she staggered into the adjoining restaurant car, where she shrank into the farthest corner.

She dared not go back to her own compartment, because she was afraid of everyone there. The whole world seemed roped into a league against her sanity. Lighting a cigarette with trembling fingers, she tried to realize her position.

Suspicious of everyone, she imagined the alienist might be in league with the baroness, and, if she persisted in her charges, he would send her to a home in Milan.

Any opposition on her part would only be used as evidence against her, and she might be kept imprisoned until she really crashed under the strain. It would be some time before she was missed, as her friends would imagine that she was still abroad.

She knew that Miss Bird existed, and that she had been tampered with; but her rescue presented a hopeless proposition. Utterly worn out and paralysed with fear, Edna slipped into the trough of lost hopes.

She closed her eyes wearily and let herself drift on the choppy current of the train's frantic rhythm.

She was recalled to reality by a friendly voice, and she looked up to see Carr smiling at her.

'I've been thinking over "The Strange Disappearance of Miss Bird"', he said. 'If you like, I'll tell you how it could be done. But first—when you came on the train, was there one nun next door to you, or two?'

'One.'

'And now there are two.'

'I know. But the other might have been somewhere else in the train. There's such a jam in the corridors.'

'Good,' declared Carr triumphantly. 'No one would be likely to notice them. Now, we'll assume your little lady has got up against the High Hat—and it's true about the feudal system being still in force in these remote places. So she's got to be bumped off. And what better way than on a railway journey?'

'Do you mean—they're thrown her on the rails in a tunnel?' asked Edna faintly.

'Lord, no. Her body would be found and awkward questions asked. What I meant was that a lot of valuable time will be wasted before it's proved she's missing. Her people will think she's lost a connection or is stopping for a few days in Paris. Even if they are influential and know the ropes, the trail will be cold by the time they get busy.'

'And they're old and helpless,' said Edna.

'Bad luck. In any case, when they make inquiries locally they'll find themselves up against a conspiracy of silence . . . This would be a natural matter of tradition and policy. But I believe the baroness, the doctor and the two nuns are the only people in the plot. All the other passengers are local folk who would back up the baroness as a matter of course. There's no doubt, though, there was dirty work at the crossroads over her reserved seat, so as to force her into the baroness's compartment, which is at the end of the train and next door to the doctor.'

'But what's happened to her?' asked Edna faintly.

'My theory is that she's lying in the next compartment to yours, covered up and disguised with bandages and trimmings. You were an unwelcome interloper, but when you obligingly went to sleep Miss Bird was asked to render some slight service to their invalid, and I'm sure she would go like a bird.'

'Yes,' nodded Edna. 'I'm positive she would.'

'There you are, then. Directly she entered she was gripped and gagged by two of them while a third gave her an injection. When she was unconscious they bandaged her up roughly and stuck plaster all over her face to disguise it. Then the false patient, who was already dressed in uniform, would only have to put a veil over her bandages, which would look like the proper bands, and peel off her own strip to look the perfect nun.'

'And—when they reach Milan?' asked Edna fearfully.

'I'm afraid the betting is she'll be taken in an ambulance to some lonely place near a river . . . But she'll know nothing of it. They'll keep her unconscious all the time.'

Edna sprang to her feet.

'We must do something at once,' she cried.

'Listen to me.' Carr pulled her back to her seat. 'All this is only my idea; because I was suspicious of the way the invalid is on view in order to show all is above board. If it was genuine illness I am sure they'd pull down the blind . . . But, remember, it is impossible to prove it.'

'But why? Why?'

'Because it may be a real patient. We can't insist on examining her bandages to see if they are wound on or in correct surgical manner, or rip off her plaster to spy her face. We might start the wound bleeding and she might pass out. We can't risk years in quod for manslaughter.'

Edna fought against his restraining arm, but he continued to hold her.

'Don't start anything mad,' he said. 'The truth is I can't forget your sunstroke. I just showed you how things might be done. But I'm like the old lady who saw a giraffe for the first time. I don't believe it.'

The passengers for the first dinner began to stream into the car. Feeling that food would choke her, Edna was driven out into the corridor. When Carr spoke to her she turned on him in a fury.

'Go away. I hate you.'

After an age-long struggle through two sections of the train where the connecting passages seemed clanking iron concertinas, in which she might be caught and pressed to death, she realized that she was near to her own compartment. The brainstorm, whose symptoms the alienist had detected, now swept over in full force, so that she lost her sense of identity and actually changed places with Miss Bird.

She thought she was bound, gagged, helpless—unable to cry

out or move a finger—surrounded with cruel enemies, awaiting a hideous end.

'I must find her,' murmured Edna confusedly.

Her fingers were touching the handle when the door opened and the doctor came into the corridor. His face looked like white wax above the blotch of his black heard, and his eyes, magnified by his glasses, were dark, muddy pools.

'Is madame better?' he asked.

At the sight of him Edna grew afraid. She nodded and looked out at the shrieking darkness rushing past the window. While the sinister doctor stood but a yard away she managed her own seat.

Very soon her mental and physical distress fused so that she lost all sense of time or space but seemed outside her own body, lying on the rails, while the engine drove remorselessly over her head. Clankety-clankety-clank. With every revolution of the wheels she felt a separate pang.

Her temperature rose until she was actually in a fever. Vivid pictures kept flickering before her eyes. Two old folk standing waiting in a lighted doorway. Ruff—blundering and eager eyed—waiting for the young mistress who would never come home.

They were getting near Milan. She could see scattered lights in the distance. In the conflicting reflections of the windows, walls and roofs appeared like quivering landscape and running water. She could hear movements in the next carriage. Luggage was lowered to the floor and voices called for service. The guard passed in the corridor, just as Carr came to the door.

'We're coming into Milan,' he said.

'Milan!' As though the word were an electric needle stabbing a raw nerve Edna sprang to her feet, inflamed by a dynamic impulse. She acted with the blind delirium of fever. Ducking under the guard's arm, she pushed into the next compartment, and—before anyone could guess her purpose—dug her fingers under the plaster, tearing it from the invalid's face.

The guard gave a gasp of horror which sharpened into whistle of surprise as the adhesive strip peeled off. Instead of raw gashed flesh he saw the skin of a middle-aged woman.

'Miss Bird,' screamed Edna.

There followed a panic of noise and confusion, in which Edna felt herself pushed roughly on one side. At the same moment she went to bits, utterly exhausted by her supreme effort. Staggering back to her own seat she collapsed.

Shouts and sudden flashes of light told her that they were entering a large station, and she felt the jerk of the train as it stopped. The tumult in the next compartment seemed to increase . . . Then it died down . . . Other passengers entered her carriage. She heard the whistle of the engine and the slow clank of wheels as it steamed slowly on its way to Basle.

Very soon someone spoke to her, and she looked up into the eyes of an old and intimate friend who did not know her name.

'I say, you,' said Carr. 'Everything's O.K., and I've had the time of my life. The guard was immense and knew just what to do. The doctor and his little lot went like lambs. They know they'll only have to stand for a charge of attempted abduction, and though the baroness sailed out—no connection—she'll work it for them somehow. Wheels within wheels, you know.'

Edna was indifferent to their fate, one way or the other.

'What happened to Miss Bird?' she asked.

'Responding to treatment, and all that. The alienist, who's a frightfully decent chap, is looking after her, and she'll soon be conscious. But she must stop at Basle and go on tomorrow. Will you break your journey to keep her company?'

'Will you be there, too? Then I will.'

Suddenly Edna felt wondrously happy. At the beginning of her journey she had been bored with life and her wasted youth, but the agony of Miss Bird's peril had wrought some change which seemed to be actually chemical. Her body felt composed of brand new cells—each tingling with the joy of life.

There was so much happiness in the world. Tomorrow would see the happiest of reunions. The carriage was crowded with fresh passengers, all shouting, smiling and gesticulating.

That night she slept like a log at Basle. When she entered the hotel restaurant the following morning, Miss Bird was taking café complet on the balcony which overhung the Rhine—green and sparkling in the sunlight. The little woman looked marvellously fresh, as though she had thriven on her experience.

'I'm just making up my story to tell them at home,' she said. 'Mummy will be thrilled.'

'Do you think it wise to tell her?' asked Edna. 'At her age it might be a shock.'

As Carr entered the restaurant and looked eagerly in their direction, Miss Bird gave Edna the conspiratorial look of one schoolgirl to another.

'I'm not going to tell her that,' she said. 'No fear. She might forbid me travelling—and more things might happen abroad. No, I'm going to tell her all about your romance.'

ETHEL LINA WHITE

Ethel Lina White (1876–1944) was born in Wales; or rather in what is now Wales, as until 1972 Abergavenny was in the English county of Monmouthshire. It seems likely that White inherited her creativity from her mother's side, as her father was a horticultural builder and general building contractor who made his fortune by inventing a radical new method of damp-proofing walls.

From childhood, White had written as a hobby, but it turned into a career after the family lost all its money during the First World War. After her mother died, White and her two sisters moved to London, where she eventually sold her first novel, *The Wishbone* (1927). The book owed something to *Jane Eyre* and her second, *'Twill Soon Be Dark* (1929), was similarly in debt to *Great Expectations*. However, her third, *The Eternal Journey* (1930), was completely original: part satire, part fantasy, it deals with reincarnation and redemption.

White's first attempt at crime fiction was *Put Out the Light* (1932) in which Anthea Vine, an unpleasant spinster, is murdered, possibly by one or all of her three young wards. In a prefatory note she explained that 'Most stories of crime begin with a murder and end with its solution. But as the victim is the dominant character in this novel, she has been retained as long as possible.' Pre-empting criticism that the murderer might be easy to identify, she went on: 'Readers, therefore, may decide who is going to kill her before the murder is actually committed. They will probably reach the goal before the detective, who is built to last and not for speed.' While it would be too much to say that White had a formula, she certainly had a particular style, similar to other writers of neogothic suspense and woman-in-peril stories like Mary Roberts Rinehart, although White's heroines are more likely to say 'Had-You-Believed-Me' than 'Had-I-But-Known'.

White's other novels include several that were expanded from a short story: the creepy *Wax* (1935), whose plot revolves around a run-down waxworks; and *The Man Who Loved Lions* (1943), an extraordinary story of murder at a wartime reunion of 'seven sullied souls' in a private zoo. Another is *The Wheel Spins* (1936), which has been filmed multiple times, most notably by Hitchcock as *The Lady Vanishes* (1938), and continues to provide inspiration for modern films like *Flightplan* (2005).

The short story 'Passengers', which provided the basis for *The Wheel Spins*, was first published in North Carolina's *Raleigh News & Observer* on 15 October 1933.

SIX MYSTERIES
IN SEARCH OF SIX AUTHORS

In the mid-1930s, many national newspapers in Britain published short detective stories and serial mysteries, sometimes offering huge cash prizes as with John Chancelleor's *The Mystery of Norman's Court* (1923) and Anthony Berkeley's *The Wintringham Mystery* (1926, reissued in 2021).

One of the most popular weekly newspapers was the *Sunday Dispatch* which, in 1938, commissioned two series of stories from the Crime Club, a publishing imprint created by the publishers William Collins. In his definitive and lavishly illustrated history of the Crime Club, *The Hooded Gunman* (2019), John Curran recounts how it evolved out of Collins' earlier initiative, the Detective Story Club, to become the best known and longest-lived brand in crime and mystery fiction. Between 1929 and 1994, a total of 2,012 Crime Club books were published, including titles by Agatha Christie, Ngaio Marsh and many of the biggest names of the genre.

The first series of six stories commissioned by the *Sunday Dispatch* was published in Volume 3 of *Bodies from the Library*, and included stories by Nicholas Blake, John Rhode and Ethel Lina White who, with the other three writers, were each asked to write a story on the basis of the same two-sentence plot.

For the second series, which appeared weekly between 17 April and 22 May 1938, six writers were challenged to write a short story around one of six curious drawings, which accompany the stories for their appearance in this volume. As a *Sunday Dispatch* journalist mused on introducing the stories, 'What will these authors make of the strange clues on which they have been asked to build a complete short story?'

AFTER YOU, LADY

Peter Cheyney

Will you guys take a look at Rudy Scansa? This baby is a one hundred per cent he-man with all the side dishes.

His square name is Rudolfo Antonio Scancinella an' he is a second-generation wop whose old man usta sell ice cream cones an' think he was doin' fine any time he got himself enough jack to eat two plates of spaghetti with cheese at one sittin'.

O.K. Well, Rudy is not all like that. He is tops in the big rackets an' he has got three roadsters, a penthouse on Lakeside Drive, an' dough stacked away in safe deposits in six different States.

Rudy is the boy all right. He has a lotta ambition an' gets steamed up very easy, which a lot of guys could tell you about, only these guys are not talkin' because they are all very nicely ironed out an' buried. So they do not have to worry any more.

Rudy is also one hundred per cent with dames. He has a line that blondes fall for like they was bein' hypnotized by an outsize in snakes. He has got black wavy hair, a long, handsome face, with sad eyes, an' a nice mouth that sorta smiles all the time.

Because I gotta tell you that Rudy has got a grand sense of comedy an' always sees the joke when the other guy gets bumped off.

It is ten-thirty one night an' the town is just wakin' up. Rudy is at the bar in the Club Carberry drinkin' highballs an' teachin' the parrot some new words.

He looks up when Tony Rhio—who is Rudy's collector for the North Side numbers swindle—eases in. Tony is not lookin' so good.

'Hey, hey, Tony,' says Rudy. 'How's it comin'? What's eatin' you?'

Tony sits down. He is sweatin'.

'Look, Rudy,' he says, 'things is not so hot. I just heard somethin'. I just heard they're springin' Jim Tullio tomorrow. They're lettin' that so-an-so outa Joliet Prison. The parole board . . .'

'Yeah!' says Rudy.

He gets up an' his mouth is like a thin red line. He stands there for a minute an' then he sorta smiles an' relaxes an' sits down again.

'So what?' he says. 'So they're springin' Tullio!'

He lights himself a cigarette an' sits there draggin' on it, sendin' the smoke outa his thin nostrils. Then he says:

'Where'd you get this stuff from, Tony?'

'Tullio's dame Mayola told me,' says Rhio. 'She don't know whether to take a run-out powder on Tullio before he gets out.

'She says she don't reckon he'll be outa the can for long because she says it's a cinch that when he gets out he's goin' to take a nasty poke at you to sorta even things out.'

He wipes his forehead.

'That guy is pure poison, Rudy,' he says. 'He'll get the lot of us. He'll . . .'

'Why don't you sew up that trap or yours an' relax?' says Rudy. 'Ain't you the scared guy? Always bellyachin' about somethin'.'

He starts grinnin' again.

'Maybe I can handle this,' he says. 'Say, where does this dame live?'

Mayola has got a swell apartment out near the Evanstown Highway. Just in case you don't know anythin' much about Mayola, here is the low-down.

When she is seventeen she takes a run-out powder on Pa and Ma, who are runnin' a small-time farm in Marinette. Mayola is as pretty as paint an' reckons that she wants to see her name in neon lights on Broadway.

You know the stuff—she thinks she can act. But her Ma is sorta strict and wants to bring her up to be the sorta dame that men look up to. Mayola don't want this. She wants to be the sorta dame they look round at.

So she puts her best hat on an' scrams to Chicago with 22 dollars an' a lotta ambition, to meet her big chance.

After three weeks she has got 15 cents, no ambition to speak of, an' the only thing she meets is Jim Tullio, who is pure poison where dames are concerned, an' very tough.

So that is that. She sticks around with Tullio until they pulled him in for a five-years rap, which was a sweet little set-up framed by Rudy Scansa, who don't like Tullio an' who proceeds to pinch his rackets.

So now you know.

Mayola was just goin' out when her dinge maid comes in an' says that Rudy Scansa is outside an' wants to see her. Mayola thinks for just one minute and then says tell him to come right in.

Rudy comes in. When he sees Mayola his eyes start poppln'. I'm tellin' you this dame is an eyeful. She is now twenty-five—a real blonde with a figure that would give you a crick in the neck—an' *very* easy on the eyes.

An' does she know how to wear clothes or does she?

She is wearin' a three hundred dollar plaln blue coat an' skirt cut by a guy who knew how to allow for curves, silver fox furs, an' a little tailored hat. She is carryin' a black suede handbag with her initials in diamonds an' a pair of white kid gauntlet gloves.

The perfume she is wearin' would make you sniff like a coupla bloodhounds. She looks a million dollars an' she knows it.

She throws Rudy a little smile.

'Well, *Mister* Scansa,' she says nice an' soft. 'What's on your mind?' She looks at him sorta wicked. 'It wouldn't be Jim Tullio, would it?' She says. 'Just park anywhere you like.'

Rudy sits down an' puts his hat on the floor. He can't take his eyes off this dame. He wonders what he has been doin' for the last live years.

He sits there lookin' at her smilin' nice an' polite, lookin' like the sorta guy who is kind to dumb animals an' always remembers Mothers Day—you know what I mean, that sorta polite 'After you, lady' stuff.

He says:

'Listen, Mayola, I don't know you very well an' maybe you don't know me much. But I reckon that we oughta have a little talk about Jim Tullio.

'I hear they are goin' to spring this guy tomorrow an' it's a cinch that he will be comln' back here to start a whole lotta trouble with me an' the boys which means a headache for all concerned. Now maybe you're stuck on Tullio an' maybe you ain't, but . . .'

'I am anythin' else but stuck on Tullio,' she says, sorta cold. 'I never was. I stuck around because if I hadn't he would have fixed me like he's fixed every dame who walked out on him.'

Rudy grins.

'Swell,' he says. 'Well, I'm tellin' you that I got all the rackets in this man's town sewn up an' in the bag. I'm taking a hundred grand a week in the numbers racket only. I'm takin' another fifty grand from the stock quotation lotteries.

'If Tullio comes back here an' starts tryin' to get back where he was there's goin' to be nothin' for nobody. You got me?'

She stands there in front of the fireplace lookin' at him.

'I got you,' she says.

She lights a cigarette.

'Jim Tullio ain't comin' back here for two weeks,' she says, 'an' when he does come back he's startin' plenty! I heard from him yesterday. He's told me to meet him at some hick place in the backwoods—near Peoria—where he was born.

'It's a small-time, one-eyed dump. I been down there with him before. He says he's goin' to do a little pistol shootin' practice before he comes to town to meet you!'

Rudy smiles.

'You don't say?' he says.

'Yeah,' she goes on. 'He's got a little road-house he owns own there, an' there's an old forge at the back where his old man useta work. Tullio's got the anvil stuck up on a mound in the forge an' he takes a half-dozen bottles of champagne down there, an' two-three dozen glasses. He takes a drink an' then he sticks the glass on the anvil an' starts in shooting.

'He's pretty good till he gets through the fourth bottle, after which he is liable to go a trifle wild on the trigger. I hadta duck once or twice. I don't think I like that guy—much,' says Mayola.

She stands there, lookin' at him, sorta smilin'.

Rudy gets up. He walks over to her. He stands lookin' down right into her eyes.

'Listen, honey-babe,' he said, an' his voice is like velvet. 'I reckon' that you an' me could get along swell. I'm an easy guy to string along with an' I'm worth plenty. You can have anything You want.'

She looks up at him.

'So what?' she says.

'Well . . . we gotta fix Tullio,' he goes on. 'You don't like him an' I don't like him. Now I gotta idea. You met him down there at his dump like he wants you to. You get him down at this forge on the pistol shootin' racket.

'Let him drlnk all he wants to an' then—well, there's an accident, see. He asks you to try a shot an' you ain't used to guns. You shoot him accidental . . . see?

'O.K. Well, everybody knows you're his girl an' that he's your meal ticket. They don't know about me. I'll fix you a swell lawyer who knows all the answers an' we'll have it all fixed in no time, after which you an' me can hit the high spots for plenty.'

He puts his arm around her shoulders an' looks at her like he can look at a dame when he wants to.

She thinks for a minute.

'Are you sure you can fix it for me?' she says. 'You're certain you can get me out of it on this 'accidental stuff?'

He laughs.

'Listen, baby,' he says. 'You *know* I can. It's a marvellous set-up. It's a cinch!'

She goes on thinkin'. Then, all of a sudden, she smiles up at him. He hauls off an' lights another cigarette. He reckons the job is O.K.

She starts pullin' her white kid gloves on. She works them down over her fingers carefully. Then:

'Listen, Rudy,' she says. 'Here's the way we play it. I'll go down there an' meet him tomorrow. O.K. Well, I reckon he'll want to shoot his mouth about his five years in the big house all day, so we'll leave the big act until the next day—the day after tomorrow.

'All right. Well, I'll get him down at the forge at twelve o'clock an' we'll do this pistol practice act. I'll wait until he gets good an' high an' then I'll give him the works. After which I'll bawl the place down about it bein' an accident like you said. O.K.

'Well, I reckon they'll take me over to Peoria an' hold me there for bail, so you be around there about one o'clock, sorta accidental, see? Don't let anybody know you're in the neighbourhood, be sorta passin' through an just heard about it.

'Then you can blow along an' get the lawyer an' fix bail.'

Rudy grins at her.

'Atta girl,' he says. 'I'll have you outa that jail by three o'clock an then, oh boy, will we go places.'

'O.K. Rudy,' she says. 'I'll do it because I got a lot on that guy Tullio. He's a plenty tough with me.'

She throws him an ace look, then she walks over to the sideboard an' takes out a bottle of champagne an' a glass. She opens the bottle and fills the glass.

She holds it up.

'Here's to me an' you, Rudy,' she says.

She takes a drink an' then she hands the glass to Rudy.

The State cops picked Rudy up in his roadster on the Galesburg-Peoria road just after one o'clock.

One of the coppers held a gun on him.

'I'm takin' you in for shootin' and killin' Jim Tullio this mornin' at New Rock,' he says.

Rudy laughs.

'Don't make me laugh,' he says. 'I been in this car drivin' around from New York early this mornin.'

The cop grins.

'Oh yeah,' he says. 'Anybody see you doin' it?'

'Nope,' says Rudy. 'But all the same this stuff about shootin' Tullio is just a lotta hooey. Why . . .'

'Save it,' says the cop. 'We got a call at five past twelve from a pay box in New Rock—from Tullio's girl Mayola. She said she saw you an' Tullio down at the forge. She was afraid there'd be trouble. We know how things were between you two.

'O.K. Well when we get down there we find him as dead as a cold hamburger. There was broken glasses all over the place an' the murder gun was lyin' on the ground. Some clever guy had wiped the fingerprints off of it.

'But you was the big mug after all, Scansa. Because stuck up on the anvil was a champagne glass an' it had your fingerprints all over it.'

'Come on, Rudy. We got a nice electric chair waitin' for you!'

PETER CHEYNEY

'Peter Cheyney' (1900–1951), born Reginald Evelyn Peter Southouse-Cheyney, was the author of a large number of often surprisingly violent thrillers, written in 'the American dialect in order to achieve the compressed atmospherics possible in that language'. Touted as 'the only crime writer in [Britain] who controls his own criminal investigation organization', many of Cheyney's books feature a tough private eye, Lemmy Caution—self-proclaimed as 'the greatest detective since Sherlock Holmes'—or the equally hard-drinking Slim Callaghan, whose sidekicks include his glamorous secretary Effie Thompson and Windemere 'Windy' Nikolls, a tiresomely verbose Canadian. Cheyney also wrote radio plays for the BBC and over 100 short stories, as well as reviewing crime fiction, with a particular focus on new writers. His journalism ranged from modern slavery and the drug trade to present-buying for men (cufflinks, socks and propelling pencils but never hats), the trial of the French serial killer Henri Petiot, and the contribution made to road casualty figures by the wanderings of 'unrestricted and unregulated' pedestrians.

With hobbies including fencing, pistol-shooting and gold, Cheyney was *very much* a man of his time and, while he was regarded by some contemporary commentators as among the crime and mystery genre's 'Grand Masters', it is sufficient to say that his style of writing is not as popular as it once was, not least because of his antediluvian attitude to women, reflected in the titles of some of his books, such as *Lady, Behave!* (1950) and *They Never Say When* (1944).

'After You, Lady' was published in *The Sunday Dispatch* on 17 April 1938.

TOO EASY

Herbert Adams

'What were you to John Howard?'

'I was his secretary.'

'Is that all?'

'I don't know what you mean.'

'I think, Miss Yates, you know perfectly well what I mean.'

For some moments, silence. The girl's dark eyes met the relentless gaze of her questioner. Twenty-four years of age, undoubtedly she was attractive; but she was afraid. Inspector Goff, burly but no bully, waited for her reply. Since none came, he spoke again.

'Two days ago John Howard was found dead in his flat. He had been poisoned. It is my duty to find out all I can about him. Had you been more to him than his secretary?'

'Don't tell him, Ann! He can't make you.'

Another girl spoke, fair-haired and pretty in a different way.

They sat in a large plainly furnished bed-sitting room in West Kensington, the joint home of the two girls who had been at supper when their unexpected visitors came, Inspector Goff and his assistant Sergeant Harrold. The supper things were still on the table.

'It might have appeared,' Goff disregarded the fair girl, 'perhaps it was meant to appear, that he had been alone. But someone had been with him. His office is in the City, but you had visited his flat.'

'Not for four months.'

'Four months ago you were living with him?'

'No. I—I went to his flat.'

'A service flat. The tenants work the lilt. There is a back entrance.'

'A girl can't lose her job,' said Gladys Fraser, the friend. 'Besides, Ann sends money to her mother, who is old and ill.'

'It wasn't that!' cried Ann quickly. 'Mr Howard was good to me. He was unhappy. And unwell. His wife had left him.'

'Your intimacy ended four months ago?'

'Yes.'

'Was that when you became engaged to Richard Parker?'

Ann's cheeks lost what colour they had. How did this man know about Dick? She nodded her reply.

'Did you tell Mr Howard of your proposed marriage?'

'No.'

'Did you tell Mr Parker of your—your friendship for Mr Howard?'

The colour flooded back. The answer was almost defiant. 'Yes, I did.'

'I see.' Goff sounded sceptical. 'Mr Parker was content for you to go on working for Mr Howard, in spite of what had happened; and Mr Howard was content with your services as secretary only?'

'Mr Howard was better. He knew I didn't love him.'

'When are you marrying Mr Parker?'

'At Christmas.'

'A long time to wait. You know you get £500 under Mr Howard's will?'

'Five hundred pounds!' echoed Gladys. 'What luck, Ann!'

Ann made no answer. Goff's next question was perhaps a trap. But she was not caught.

'Didn't he mention the will when you called on Wednesday night?'

'I did not call on Wednesday night.'

'That is strange,' said Goff. 'On his table there was a metal ashtray, and in this ashtray was a teaspoon. Peculiar, wasn't it?'

Again Ann was silent.

'Why peculiar?' inquired Gladys.

'The ashtray,' Goff went on slowly, 'showed that two people had been smoking.'

'Can you tell how many cigarettes one man smokes?' Demanded the fair girl.

'Are you another secretary?' asked Goff sharply.

Gladys tossed her head. 'No, thank you! No typing all day in the City for me! I am with Madame Vanesse, in Oxford Street.'

'You knew John Howard?'

'Never seen him in my life.'

'Then hold your tongue!' He turned again to Ann. 'That teaspoon, Miss Yates, bore your fingerprint.'

'No! No!' she cried. 'It is impossible!'

'How can he tell?' jeered Gladys. 'He hasn't taken your finger-prints yet.'

Goff glared at her. 'Oh, yes, he has. I was at Howard's office today after she left. There were plenty of fingerprints and they correspond with the print on the spoon.'

'It is impossible,' moaned Ann again.

'I told you not to talk,' muttered her friend. 'If he wants to ask questions he ought to warn you that all you say will be used against you.'

'Will you be quiet?' said Goff angrily.

Defiantly Gladys sat back in her chair and opened her case and lit a cigarette.

'You can smoke, too, if you like,' said Goff less gruffly to Ann. 'I won't hurry you.'

Ann shook her head, moistening her dry lips with the tip of her tongue.

'She doesn't smoke my sort,' said Gladys, 'or I'd have given her one.'

'Now, Miss Yates. I am not charging you—not yet. That spoon in Mr Howard's flat bears your fingerprint. It you were not there at nine o'clock on Wednesday night—*where were you?*'

'I—I was in Shaftesbury Avenue.'

'What were you doing there?'

'I was to meet Dick—Mr Parker.'

'Did you meet him?'

'No.'

'How was that?'

'He—he didn't come.'

'Oh, he didn't come! You waited for him I suppose. Where?'

'I—I didn't wait anywhere. He doesn't like me standing about. I always walk from Piccadilly Circus to Oxford Street, and he starts at Oxford Street the same side till we meet.'

'But you didn't meet. Did you speak to anyone?'

'No.'

'What did you do?'

'I went backwards and forwards for an hour. Then I came home.'

'Unfortunate no one saw you! When did you arrange to meet him?'

'That afternoon. He telephoned me.'

'Then why didn't he come?'

'I don't know. I wrote and asked him.'

'Why not 'phone?'

'I couldn't. He is a traveller. I didn't know where he would be.'

'Do you expect me to believe all this? You say you have not

been to the flat for four months, yet that spoon has your fingerprint, and you cannot show you were anywhere else at the time.'

At that moment there was a tap at the door. Gladys ran to it.

'Thank goodness you've come, Dick! These men are detectives.
Ann's boss has been killed. Poison in his coffee. They say she
did it!'

A well set-up young fellow entered the room. He had a clean,
straight look and it was evident the scene that met his eyes
astonished him. He went to Ann. who sat as though unable to
move, and put his hand on her shoulder.

'What does she mean?' he asked.

'Are you Richard Parker?' demanded Goff.

'I am.'

'Did you tell Miss Yates to meet you in Shaftesbury Avenue
last Wednesday evening?'

'No. I was away. You—'

'Dick!' cried the girl, in anguish.

'Sorry,' he muttered, 'but I was in Liverpool. I told you I was
going.'

'Her story,' said Goff, 'is that she could not have been in
Howard's flat because you had arranged to meet her. You say
you were in Liverpool.'

'I told her not to talk,' said Gladys. 'They found her fingerprints.'

'There must be a mistake.' Dick looked unutterably miserable,
but his hand tightened on Ann's arm.

'Have you anything more to say, Miss? You knew he went to
Liverpool. Why did you tell me he 'phoned you?'

'Someone 'phoned me.' Ann was persistent. though her tone
was hopeless.

'What did they say?'

'They said—he said—he was in a hurry, but he was back
sooner than he expected. Would I meet him at half-past eight
in Shaftesbury Avenue, as usual. He never came, so I wrote to
ask why—though I was sure I would hear in the morning.'

Dick looked puzzled. 'I've just got back. I found her letter, and came round to see what had happened.'

'You knew his voice?' Goff was sarcastic. 'You had no doubt who was speaking?'

'His voice was not very distinct,' said Ann, 'but no one else knows where we meet, and no one else'—she coloured a little—'no one else calls me Angel.'

'Dick generally speaks distinctly enough,' commented Gladys, tapping her cigarette-ash on a plate.

'I am sure he does,' said Goff. 'That is good enough. Take her along, Harrold.'

'Now, Miss Yates,' began the sergeant, lumbering to his feet.

'Not Miss Yates! The other one!'

'Me?' cried the fair girl, jumping up.

'Yes, you! I arrest you, Gladys Fraser, for the murder of John Howard, and I warn you anything you say may be used as evidence.'

'I didn't do it,' screamed the girl. 'Dick! Dick! Don't let them take me! It was Ann. Her fingerprint was on the spoon—not mine. I didn't know the man!'

'Best come quiet, Miss,' said Harrold. 'You can take anything you want.'

After a few painful minutes Goff was left alone with Ann and Dick.

'Sorry if I frightened you, Miss Yates. I had to ask the questions, but I never thought it was you.'

'But I don't understand,' she said. 'How can it have been Gladys? Why should she do it?'

'How did she know the poison was in his coffee? I never said so, and it hasn't appeared in the papers. But that is a small point. It was really the ashtray and the spoon that let you out.'

'But you said my fingerprint was on the spoon.'

'So it is. The ashtray contained two kinds of ash. I expect you have noticed that Turkish cigarettes are oval and Virginia round. Howard smoked Virginia; so do you. Gladys smokes Turkish.

The ash of a Turkish cigarette keeps its shape—look at that bit she knocked off just now. There was ash like that on the ashtray.'

'Lots of people smoke Turkish,' said Dick.

'Quite true. All her cigarette ends had been thrown into the fire. Everything had been left straight and there were *no finger-prints anywhere*—except on that spoon. And that was left in the ashtray. Almost too easy, wasn't it?'

'You mean you were intended to find it?' said Dick.

'It was planted where we couldn't miss it. And it was not one of Howard's spoons. It is a fellow to this.' He picked up one from the supper table.

'Who but Gladys Fraser could wrap up a spoon with your fingerprint and put it there? Who but Gladys Fraser could have faked that 'phone message—knowing his pet name for you and where you generally meet?'

They could not answer. But Ann found it hard to believe her friend could be so treacherous. 'Mr Howard did not know her. How could she go to him?'

Goff shrugged his big shoulders. 'To go to him was easy. Perhaps she had something to say about you. He would listen to that. She was nearly caught. He collapsed after ringing for help. The doctor says death must have been almost instantaneous, and when the attendant found him his cigarette was still smoul-dering on the ashtray.'

'But why should Gladys try to get Ann into such awful trouble?' persisted Dick.

'Perhaps you can answer that,' said the Inspector. 'You knew her before you knew Ann, didn't you?'

'About the same time. We all went together for a bit. Then I found it was Ann that I loved.'

'And Gladys loved you! She thought if she could get rid of Ann she would have you. A jealous girl can be the very devil. I don't know yet how she got the poison, but it won't be long before I do. Anyway, I wish you luck. You deserve it.'

HERBERT ADAMS

Herbert Adams (1874–1958), described in his day as 'the great thrill writer' by the *Daily Telegraph*, is regarded nowadays as one of the lesser lights of the Golden Age of crime and detective fiction. He was born in 1874 in Barnsbury, North London, the son of Clara and William Adams, a senior official with the London County Council whose father had been a famous manufacturer of redware. From 1890 to 1895 he attended City of London School, where he excelled in practical subjects. After leaving, he trained with the Surveyors' Institution (now the Royal Institution of Chartered Surveyors), qualifying in 1895, and moved into practice as an estate agent, auctioneer and surveyor.

In 1899, Adams published his first novel, *A Virtue of Necessity*, in which a young couple outwit a blackmailer. Its reception was mixed and, while a few short stories followed, he lacked the confidence that he could write on a full-time basis. In 1900, he married Jessie Louise Cooper, but funds were tight and the couple had to live initially with her mother in Paddington. Things were little better by 1911 as they were then living with her aunt in Hove.

Nonetheless, by the mid-1920s, at the age of fifty, Herbert Adams was confident enough to 'give up work' and become a full-time writer. Over the next thirty years he wrote more than fifty novel-length detective stories and thrillers—two under the pseudonym 'Jonathan Gray'—as well as several lightly criminous romances including *The Girl in Possession* (1935) and *The Lie She Lived* (1936), and at least one historical novel, *A Lady So Innocent* (1932), about King Charles II and Catarina de Bragança. He also wrote journalism and a handful of short stories for regional newspapers like the *Sheffield Weekly Telegraph* and its biannual specials, as well as annuals like *Summer Pie*.

Adams has two main series characters. The first is Jimmie Haswell, a London lawyer and amateur detective who appears in nine novels, including *The Golden Ape* (1931), where a corpse is found in Haswell's car, and *The Woman in Black* (1938), a superb mystery in which a man is accused of murdering his wife while he was disguised as a woman . . . only to be murdered himself the day after Haswell has secured his acquittal. Adams' better known detective is Roger Bennion, a member of Britain's Secret Service. Bennion appears in domestic mysteries like the bizarrely named *Exit the Skeleton* (1952), which finds him and his wife Ruth unravelling the truth behind the kidnapping of a child, as well as in wartime thrillers such as *Stab in the Back* (1941), featuring a double murder in a summer house, and *Black Death* (1939), wherein a professor's 'discovery to end all wars' ends in his murder.

After the death of Jessie Adams' aunt, the couple moved to Dorset, to Nairn Cottage in Canford Cliffs on the outskirts of Bournemouth, where Adams was something of a minor local celebrity, opening in 1935 a new library with two other crime writers, Vernon Loder and Gilbert Collins. He spent much of his free time playing golf at Parkstone Golf Course, a short drive away, and when the couple next moved it was to Wimborne Cottage, adjoining the links.

As he set out in his *Who's Who* entry, Adams had two hobbies— travel, which he enjoyed with Jessie, and golf. He played regularly throughout his life and in 1935 was elected club captain at Parkstone. Golf crept into his writing too—in fact his second novel, *The Secret of Bogey House* (1924), begins with the hunt for a lost ball and ends with the golfer bringing about the capture of a gang of smugglers.

Many of his later mysteries also have a golfing background, including *The Body in the Bunker* (1937), which is discovered through a badly sliced ball (and includes a debate about the ethics of the game), and *The Nineteenth Hole Mystery* (1939), which concerns murder in the clubhouse of a seaside golf links not unlike Parkstone. Adams also wrote *The Perfect Round* (1927), a very entertaining collection of amusing and sometimes ludicrous short stories about golf and golfers.

Herbert Adams died at Poole Road in Branksome, Dorset, on 24 February 1958. Jessie had died a few years earlier and he had been living alone in a Bournemouth hotel. He left over £25,000, equivalent to £600,000 or $800,000 today.

'Too Easy' was published in the *Sunday Dispatch* on 24 April 1938.

RIDDLE OF AN UMBRELLA

J. Jefferson Farjeon

This story may take you ten minutes to read, but it happened in five. In five of the most unpleasant minutes it has ever been my lot to endure.

I had missed the last train back to the sleepy village where I was trying to forget telephones and traffic, and from which I had wandered too far afield, and with a couple of miles still to go I came to a level crossing.

I was in the tired, dull mood, that pays no attention to surroundings, and my first intimation that I was anywhere near a railway was a bright red eye, high up on my left, staring unwinkingly at the pale moonlight.

'How do you keep your eye open at this time of night?' I asked the signal, as I passed through a little gate from the lane on to the faintly gleaming line. 'It's more than I can do!'

On the point of turning my head away, I saw something else. I often wonder what would have happened if I had not paused to make my idiotic remark to the unheeding red light.

What I saw looked something like an umbrella leaning at an angle against the base of the signal post.

This was not a usual place for an umbrella; so, bored to extinction, I walked a few yards along the track for the tiny interest of discovering what the object really was.

It was an umbrella.

'How on earth did you get there?' I inquired. Then followed a second thought. 'Do I leave you there?'

I have lost countless umbrellas in my day, but this was the first time I had ever found one! Could human nature resist the golden opportunity?

Do not judge me too quickly if I admit that the moment beat me.

I removed the umbrella from its unnatural setting, hooked it over my arm—I still recall the queer little sensation as the curved handle gripped my sleeve—and went back along the line trying not to feel guilty.

Teasing queries revolved through my mind as I crossed the track.

'Umbrella. Umbrella leaning against signal. How? Passing train? Fell out of passing train. Do umbrellas fall out of passing trains? Even if they do, do they land neatly on their ferrules? Not passing train.

'Wind? Blown by wind? The umbrella would have been open. This one's undone—untidy—but not open. And where's the wind? Not wind.

'Probably a pedestrian like myself just dropped it—and it bounced six yards—and pulled up at the signal with the self-control of an athlete—and its late owner never noticed anything! Why should he? It hasn't rained for a fortnight!'

But these were not the points that teased me most and that caused me to pause at the second little gate leading into the interrupted lane.

The most teasing point was the late owner himself, whoever he might be. (The untidiness of the umbrella and its size—it was a large one—were sufficient to define the owner's sex.)

I was walking off with his property, and I have a conscience of sorts. I do not even cheat over my income tax, though whether that is due to morality or fear of being found out I have never been able to determine.

Anyhow, I decided to replace the umbrella, and I turned back to do so.

As I turned, the red eye changed from its original colour to green.

You have probably seen signals change countless times. You may agree with me that there is a certain precision, a sense of inevitability, about the operation.

You would be surprised, for instance, if you noticed any hesitation or indecision or wavering. That is not to say that you would do anything about it.

I certainly imagined now that this signal had not quite behaved itself. I am not an expert on the subject, though I had recently had the system explained to me, yet I could have sworn that the red eye was not happy over its transformation and would have preferred to continue its ruby vigil.

The signal, as I stood with my back to the second gate, was slightly to my right.

Across the track, a short distance to my left, stood the signal box, dark below and illuminated above, like a little suspended chamber of uncertain light.

Well, of course, the signalman knew his job, so naturally I did nothing about it. My own job was to replace the confounded umbrella, and to get the silly business over as soon as possible.

Now that a train had been signalled, and the line was clear for it, I wanted to be off the track.

'I'm developing nerves,' I informed myself, as hurried towards the signal. 'This won't do!'

The green eye watched me while I replaced the property I had stolen. For some unexplainable reason, I wished it had still been the red one.

I say 'unexplainable' because I was not really worried about the train that was speeding towards me from some invisible source. There was as yet no sound or sign of it.

Hallo! What was that? A cat? My glance, travelling a little way along the faint streaks of track, had come to roost on a small dark object.

A little shadow that I expected to dart away as I moved towards it. But it did not dart away. Nothing tonight did what was expected of it. The cat turned out to be a cap.

I stared at it, my worry growing. Small, separate incidents seemed to be welding together with increased significance.

Umbrella against signal, cap on line. Let the signal itself go for the moment. Had the cap and the umbrella been lost by the same person? And where was the person?

The moon had slipped behind a heavy little cloud. Now it slipped out again. I looked farther along the line. And then I ran. There was no mistaking what I saw this time!

I came upon the man, face downwards, and stretched along six feet of steel, a few seconds later. Death can be deceptive, but I knew this man was dead. I knew too, when I touched him, that he had not been dead for long.

He was in his shirt-sleeves. (How did that fit with an umbrella? My distracted mind leaped from point to point without control.)

The shirt was still wet with blood. There was blood on his grey hair.

I paused for an instant and took a deep breath to steady myself. I had read about this kind of thing countless times. I enjoy good thrillers. But I had never come across it in reality. A very different matter.

The pause was only for an instant. Out of the corner of my eye I glimpsed the green light. The fact that it was still green seemed a surprising blow for normality. It should have gone back to red, or moved on to purple!

Since it remained green, however, it opened the way to the invisible train that would flatten a corpse out of recognition if I did not quickly do something about it.

I gazed back along the track. Still no sign or sound of anything. I stooped once more and began my unsavoury task. I couldn't lift the poor fellow. I am not particularly strong, and I was up against the origin of that expression 'dead weight'.

I shoved and rolled him clear. The last part of the operation gave me a fresh shock. For a moment, in fact, I just didn't believe it . . . Oh nonsense! . . .

But it was true. As I got the man clear of the line, I saw the length of steel he had been lying on. All of it was not bright and smooth and straight.

The man was gone, but something remained. A strip of iron, clamped to the steel rail in some devilish way.

And the signal was green.

I had raced to the man. Now I turned and raced in the other direction. I had to get back to the signal-box, and then yell to the signalman to turn the eye red again!

I started off at too great a pace, tripped and went flat. I rose with a bruise on my forehead. I also had another man's blood on my clothing.

If anybody were wanted for murder, I was transforming myself into a perfect subject for suspicion, but I did not think of this till afterwards.

All I thought of as I clambered to my feet was a throbbing that started me running faster still—if that were possible.

I visualized the engine of the train; and the driver in the cab,

unconcernedly continuing with his job; and the fireman shovel-
ling coal, his face illuminated by the glow, and perhaps cracking
a joke that would prove to be his last; and the revolving wheels
that responded to the throbbing . . .

The throbbing that turned out to be just the throbbing of my
heart.

I shouted as I ran. As the signal-box grew closer I expected
to see a face behind the glass. No face appeared, though I almost
broke my throat.

Now I had reached the silent signal-box and as I tottered
against the steep little stairs I endured a moment of violent
indignation.

A train was about to be wrecked. I had yelled myself speechless and run myself to a standstill. God, tomorrow's headlines.
What the hell! . . . I expect I was hardly sane.

And then I did hear the train.

I don't remember going up those steps. All I can say is that
obviously I must have done so.

The next recollection is at being in the little cabin, and feeling
violently sick.

The condition of that cabin—I cannot describe it. Even if I
could, I could never describe the effect of it upon a stranger
suddenly blundering into all the chaos.

Everything was in disorder. Everything seemed smashed.
Telephone, glass—the one whole window was the one that had
faced me as I ran—even a plate and a tea-cup.

The broken pieces lay on ground beside a thermos flask, a
piece of bread and butter, and an open book. Near them was a
knife—an ordinary knife—and a heavy iron implement.

But these were not the things my glassy eyes became glued
on. I found myself staring unbelievably at a second dead man.

A man in a thin, shabby coat, with long grey hair—yes, such
a man might have carried an old umbrella—and with one bent
arm against a lever.

And, now, memory again left me. I went out on a train whistle. But I must have worked that lever.

'That must have been the devil of a fight,' observed an old man, when I had recovered and told my story to the most attentive audience I have ever had.

'The signalman with the knife he had used for his bread and butter, and his assailant, rushing up to the cabin with the iron tool *he* had used for his dastardly deed.'

'Is that what you think happened?' I asked.

'That is what I am reasonably sure happened,' he answered, as his eyes travelled beyond the big black engine, snorting in stationary indignation, to a group of men busy along the line.

'The train-wrecker, returning from his completed work, came suddenly into the signalman's view. He saw he was spotted—eh? Knew the game was up unless he knocked the signalman out, and made a rush attack.'

'And each killed the other?'

'Yes, though neither died immediately. The dying signalman— cut off from the telephone, thinking his assailant dead, and with the signal set against the train—staggered out of the cabin somehow, reached the spot where the line had been tampered with, and died across it.

'Probably the poor fellow hardly knew what he was doing. Meanwhile, the train-wrecker recovered sufficiently to change the signal and open the track.'

'He must have had some tremendous motive for wanting to wreck the train,' I murmured.

'It was a tremendous motive,' nodded the old man. 'Twenty years ago, I sentenced him to penal servitude for life.'

While I stared at him in astonishment, he added, with a smile: 'Odd, how things happen. I wonder—I wonder whether we shall find that the umbrella which thwarted his intention was used to convey the strips of iron designed to carry it out?'

J. JEFFERSON FARJEON

Joseph Jefferson Farjeon (1883–1955) was born into an artistic family. He was named for his American grandfather—an actor famous for his portrayal of Rip Van Winkle—and his father Benjamin was a novelist. His three siblings were prodigiously talented, their creativity nurtured by Ben and their mother Margaret, a musician: Eleanor was an accomplished poet and librettist; Harry a composer and the youngest professor in the history of the Royal Academy of Music; and Herbert a critic and playwright.

In a forty-year career, J. Jefferson Farjeon wrote over a hundred books, dozens of short stories and non-fiction articles, as well as romantic comedies and thrilling mysteries for the stage and radio.

Joe Farjeon was born in 1883 in the North London suburb of Hampstead, where he and his siblings were home-schooled by his mother Maggie and played with the children of his parents' many theatrical friends, including Ethel Barrymore, who would grow up to become—in the words of the *New York Daily News*—'the First Lady of the American Stage'. Mindful of his grandfather's success on the stage, Farjeon tried acting as a career but soon realized that his true skill was in writing. In later years he would claim to have been published as a child, with a piece about canaries for which he was never paid. The story might be true, but with Farjeon one can never be sure, as exaggeration for humorous effect was one of his trademarks.

Around 1910, Farjeon met and married a Bostonian, Frances Antoinette Wood, and they settled down in Ditchling, Sussex. In 1913 they had a daughter, Joan, who would grow up to become an acclaimed set designer. At around the same time, Farjeon got a job with Amalgamated Press, working on the company's flagship, the *Daily Mirror*. He wrote regularly for the newspaper which, in 1924, would serialize his first novel, *The Golden Singer* (1935), a seaside romance about a Pierrot troupe. Farjeon's journalism included light-hearted looks at familiar subjects, 'interviews' with parlourmaids and ogres [*sic*], and on the side he also wrote sketches for magazines like *The Humorist* and *London Opinion*—where Anthony Berkeley cut his teeth—as well as turning out light short stories for *The Yellow Magazine*, *The Passing Show*, *Punch* and many others.

In the early 1920s, Farjeon decided to write a play. His first effort was a melodramatic comedy thriller called *Number Seventeen*. The central character was Ben, a tramp and former merchant navy sailor played by Leon M. Lion, a rumbustious actor manager who twenty years later would take the lead in two of John Dickson Carr's stage plays. *Number Seventeen* was a hit and even transferred to Broadway where it was presented as *Number Seven*, to avoid confusion with a play called *Seventeen*. A film version was released in 1928 and another in 1932, this time directed by Alfred Hitchcock. Never slow to exploit an opportunity, Farjeon novelized his play as *No. 17* (1926) and over the next twenty-five years published a total of eight novels about Ben—all of which have recently been reissued by Collins Crime Club.

Over the next thirty years, as well as the Ben the Tramp mysteries, Farjeon wrote dozens of standalone thrillers, in which sinister events are typically unravelled—eventually—often in an isolated location or an apparently empty building and usually by an unlikely hero or heroine who in the end gets the partner of her dreams: books like *Seven Dead* (1939), in which the septet of the title are discovered in the home of a man who ostensibly has just gone on holiday; or *The Z Murders* (1932), in which a hook-handed psychopath slaughters his way round Britain, forming a Z-shaped pattern with the bodies of his victims. Farjeon also wrote dozens of short crime and mystery stories, including a long-running series for *Pictorial Magazine* featuring a former criminal operating under the homophonous soubriquet of 'X Crook'. He also wrote three novels as 'Anthony Swift', including the very entertaining *Murder in a Police Station* (1943), which appeared in the United States under his own name. Perhaps his most extraordinary novel is *Death of a World* (1948), set in the aftermath of nuclear holocaust. As with many of the writers who had lived through two world wars, Farjeon's vision of the future was bleak; he also wrote a short story set in 2000, 'When the Roof Fell Down' (1934), in which every country in the world has succumbed to dictatorship.

Writing even on the day he died, Joe Farjeon died in a care home in Hove, Sussex, in 1955.

'Riddle of an Umbrella' was first published in the *Sunday Dispatch* on 1 May 1938.

TWO WHITE MICE UNDER A RIDING WHIP

E. C. R. Lorac

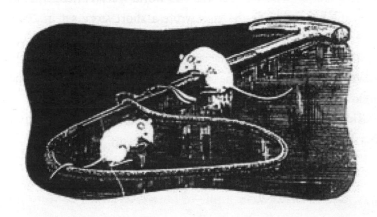

'As a drawing, it's a good drawing, old man. Reminds me of some of those early Chinese designs, because the mice are so delicately drawn—perfect, with that touch of pink about the noses. But if you ask me to interpret it for you, well, I'm beat. You're a psychologist. I'm not. Get on with it.'

Basil Remaine tossed the picture he had been studying back to the man who had first handed it to him.

Remaine was a barrister, a keen-eyed, long-jawed fellow of forty-five, who had a tremendous reputation for his skill at cyphers and cryptograms in addition to his reputation as counsel.

John Lathman, the psychologist who had proffered that quaint picture of the white mice, leant forward in his chair.

'You've got to take this seriously,' old chap,' said Lathman quietly. 'It means something, of that I'm convinced. Not something in my line. The mice don't represent an escape complex, nor does the riding whip signify fear.

'The picture was given to me by a woman who was making a desperate effort to get help and I want to help her.'

'The circumstances being—?'

'That I was summoned professionally to examine a case of hysteria or neurosis in a woman living at Wych Point, in Essex. She is a wealthy American, named Daphne Vancraig—'

'The woman whose small son was kidnapped on the train just after she landed at Southampton?' queried Remaine, his eyes alight with interest.

'That's the one—poor soul. In the opinion of her friends, the shock at losing her son has unbalanced her mind. She won't—or can't—speak. She won't—or can't—walk.

'I'm not going into the case in detail, but I want to impress this on you. She was sitting at a table, drawing vague, meaningless scribbles on odd bits of paper.

'Before I left her, she suddenly pulled this exquisite little drawing out from under a pile of others, and thrust it into my hand.'

Lathman's deep voice conveyed a pity which his prosaic words left unuttered, and he leaned forward again to Remaine with the picture in his hand.

'Despise telepathy if you will, but I could swear to this. That woman was appealing to me for help. She dared not utter her appeal in words, but her mind forced itself into contact with mine—and that picture represents the climax of her appeal.'

'And you're handing the baby to me—' Remaine picked up the picture again and studied it—the two white mice under the riding whip.

'Well, you'd better give me all the data you can. Mrs Daphne Vancraig, of Wych Point, in Essex. What was that kid of hers called? Derrick, wasn't he? Aged eight . . . I remember now.

'Is it Wych Point Grange she's staying at? Marvellous old house.'

'No, not the Grange. Mrs Vancraig's at Wych Point Manor—a much finer place than the Grange. She's being looked after by a couple of competent nurses, and the establishment is in the charge of a fellow named Bannion and his wife. Americans. Friends of Mrs Vancraig's, I take it.'

'You take it . . . Allow me to take it that you have an illogical and unfounded distrust of this Bannion and his wife. In short, you loathe them.'

Lathman laughed a little. 'Admitted. A psychologist can't always be logical. Mrs Vancraig wouldn't—or couldn't speak. Her silence wasn't a psychic paralysis or neurosis. It was an effort of will.'

'Proven?'

'No. My own diagnosis—not infallible.'

Again Remaine picked up the little picture and stared at it. He took a slip of paper and scribbled down a description of it. 'Two white mice under riding whip.' Then he looked up at Lathman.

'Leave me alone with this for a bit, old man. I'll see if I can make sense of it.'

It was an hour later that Lathman returned to his friend. Remaine was no longer studying the cryptic picture. He had pulled a road map out of one of the drawers in his desk and was poring over it.

'Wych Point . . . about forty miles isn't it? I used to go there when I was a kid. Grand shooting there. Old Mellor rented the Grange for some years.

'Game to come out there this evening and have a look-see, Lathman? It may be a wild goose chase, or it may be wilder than that, but if you like to trust a crazy hunch of mine, come and join the chase.'

'I'll come, of course—but won't you tell me what's our interpretation of the picture?'

'No. I won't. You've got the data before you, as I have it before me. Mrs Vancraig, whose son Derrick was kidnapped, has taken Wych Point Manor.

'She is now in a state of neurosis, or hysteria, or terror, which precludes her speaking, even to a psychological consultant.

'But she produced this amazing drawing and handed it to you, with a mute appeal for help.

'My own reading of the picture may be utterly wrong, but I'm backing my judgment, and I'm going to Wych Point.'

There was a tension underlying the deliberate speech, an excitement which communicated itself to Lathman's sensitive mind, so that he felt a tingle of anticipation thrill through his veins.

A little later, when he was sitting beside Remaine in the latter's big car, speeding north-eastward as they drew clear of London, Lathman cudgelled his brain for the message which had eluded him.

This expedition had a lunatic quality; a feverish, irrational business it was, in which the urgency was that of a nightmare—crazy, yet irresistible.

'Mice under riding whip . . .' Lathman repeated the words until he felt his brain spinning.

Out through the crowded suburbs on to the open road leading through Epping Forest the great car sped. Forty, fifty, fifty-five . . . the speedometer needle moved up, and Lathman's mind repeated the foolish words, faster, faster, as though the urgency of that dumb appeal was crying out to him ever more passionately.

'Lathman.' Remaine's quiet voice brought the psychologist back to reality. 'You've backed your judgment in backing me. You've got to follow my lead. Play up. You'll understand soon.'

'Understand? I'm in a fog—but I'll play up if you give me the lead. Where are we?'

The speed of the car was slackening: smoothly, with a silent change of gear they swung round a corner, off the main road.

Half a mile later another turn, and they were in a rough country road. The car slowed down, headlights were turned off, and they drew up.

A man appeared by the roadside, and Remaine opened the door of the car, signalling to Lathman to get out. To the man by the wayside the barrister spoke tersely.

'Keep your engine running after you've reversed her and be ready for the word "go". To Lathman he said, 'Follow close behind me, old chap, and play up!'

Still as in a dream, Lathman did as he was bid. A crescent moon gleamed between the heavy branches of oak and ash as they left the road, climbed a stile and set off across grassy park land.

After three minutes silent walking they came into an open space and Lathman saw the gables and chimney stacks of an ancient house, black against the star-set sky.

Close behind Remaine he drew near to the house and saw a small door, white and ghostly in the moonlight against the dark walls of the house.

An owl hooted, and then the silence was broken again by the shrill blast of a whistle, a sound which made Lathman's pulses leap with its unexpectedness.

Romaine was drumming on the door with the knob of his stick . . . rub-a-dub, rub-a-dub, softly, again and again.

The door was opened a crack: it was dark inside and Lathman could only see the dark line where the white door was held back. Remaine spoke, under his breath, his voice soft and sibilant.

'Bannion's sent me. Something's wrong. The cops are on to us. My God! They're at the front already.'

Again a whistle shrilled, a police whistle, Lathman knew it now. 'Give me the kid, quickly. It's the only chance, If he's found here, you're for it. Quickly.'

A voice spoke behind the door. 'We'd settled what to do if things went wrong. The well . . .'

'The well's in front of the house, you blasted fool. You can't do it now.'

Remaine flung himself at the door even as he was speaking, and Lathman remembered his orders. 'Play up!' The door suddenly released, swung back and Remaine staggered forward.

Lathman saw a dark figure, a hand holding something that gleamed. With all his strength behind his fist Lathman struck out, savagely aware of the violent contact with skin and bone as his blow reached the other man's chin. A thud, a stumble, and Remaine's cool voice said, 'The others will be busy with those fellows at the front. Grand things police whistles. Up the stairs, Lathman. There are two white doors on the top storey. You still know how to box, old chap.'

'Nightmare . . . it's mad . . . we're all mad . . . white mice under a riding whip.'

The words jumbled through Lathman's mind as he followed Remaine's torch light up the twisting stairs. 'Two white mice, two white doors. Do you believe in telepathy, old man? My God, here are the doors, just the same.'

Remaine opened one of those quaint white panelled doors. A voice, a very small voice, was singing a sad little tune in the big room beyond.

'Mummy, I'm lost. Come and fetch me, mummy.'

'It's all right, laddie. We've come to find you.' In a few strides Remaine was across the room and picked up the small figure from the narrow white bed. 'Derri Vancraig, aren't you, going back to mummy.'

It was Lathman who went downstairs first, thinking of the man at the foot of the stairs. There was a commotion in the front of the house but the man whom Lathman had struck still lay stretched out, silent, in the faint moonlight.

'In all humility, can I have the explanation, Remaine? *Was* it telepathy? Did you . . .?'

'Not a bit at it. Telepathy's not in my line. I read a message.'

The two men were back in Remaine's room and the barrister laughed, as a satisfied man may laugh.

'Mice under riding whip, Lathman. Turn the written words into phonetics: *Mi sun der ri*—My son Derry. Got that?'

'Good God, yes—and I repeated it by the hour!'

'My son Derry—but where? What was left in that message after *Mice un der ri* . . . ? The remains were the letters *ding whip*. Not easy. I took out the letter. *Hid in*.

'The message then read, "My son Derry hid in . . ." and w.p.g. for the remainder. I read it as Wych Point Grange.

'God knows how the poor soul discovered it, but she did. She dared not tell you in straightforward fashion.

'There was the well—and other possibilities like the deep well rivers, dene holes . . . God! What a horror. The real police can deal with those devils, not my man with the whistle, reliable fellow that he was.'

Lathman gasped. 'My son Derry', he repeated weakly.

Remaine laughed very gently.

'Did you notice what the kid was clutching in his hand when we got him into the car, Lathman? Two White mice. Little furry toys. Telepathy—or chance?'

Lathman shook his head. 'God knows,' he replied.

E. C. R. LORAC

'E. C. R. Lorac' was the pen name of Edith Caroline Rivett (1894–1958). She also wrote under her own name and as 'Carol Carnac', named for her Rivett-Carnac relatives. A third pseudonym, the London-inspired 'Mary Le Bourne', has recently come to light and the one novel she wrote using that name—*Two-Way Murder*—was published by the British Library in 2021, over sixty years after her death.

Carol Rivett was born and raised in London. She attended South Hampstead High School, which she loved and where she excelled in art and design, with a particular interest in pattern. It is no surprise, then, to find that, after studying at the Central School of Arts and Crafts, Rivett became a teacher. In parallel with her career, she also took on private commissions and used her skills, particularly in calligraphy, to support good causes, whether national ones like Westminster Abbey or local ones such as the Lancaster Art Group. She also found time to write, authoring more than seventy books, most of which are mysteries, as well as a single radio play and a handful of detective stories, including some written for younger readers such as 'Half-Term Hold-up'.

Regardless of the pseudonym under which they were published, Rivett's novels generally conform to the so-called rules of Golden Age detective fiction. However, her detectives sometimes play fast and loose with the law, including suppressing evidence in *Black*

Beadle (1934). Similarly, Rivett herself did not always play fair with the reader, for example in *The Greenwell Mystery* (1932), where a key fact is concealed until near the end of the novel. Nonetheless, her work remains very popular and first editions are much sought after, not least because many have superb jacket illustrations, in whose design it is not unreasonable to suspect that Rivett may have a hand.

Rivett's crime fiction is characterized by a strong sense of place, and many are set in areas of Britain where she had lived or visited. These include the London suburb of St John's Wood in *The Sixteenth Stair* (1942), the Sussex coast in *The Affair on Thor's Head* (1932) and, in *Still Waters* (1949), the Fell country of Lancashire. Rivett loved Lancashire and set several books there, especially in the Lune Valley, where after retiring she lived with her sister Gladys until her death in a nursing home in 1958.

'Two White Mice under a Riding Whip' was published in the *Sunday Dispatch* on 8 May 1938.

SIGNALS

Alice Campbell

Diamond rain shivered in the headlights. Through it and the darkness the motorist peered at the small inn. Closed, or should be, in this gone-to-bed village; but was it? Surprisingly, the door gaped and the drawn curtains glowed red.

The traveller frowned upward. Then his dubious survey fell, like a bolt, to the swinging sign just above. In scarred crimson and gold, a lion pranced over the appropriate legend; but it was what writhed from the corner which chained his attention.

Fluttering in the March gale—a pale cobweb of silk—a woman's silk stocking! He shut off his engine and stamped into the entrance.

Commotion met him—hell let loose—in the bar. Strident voices clamoured in unison, trouncing down an alien note of despair.

'It's not true!' shrilled in anguish. 'Oh, do let me go!'

Harsh yapping closed in; an angry pack at the kill.

'What's this?' blazed the man at the doorway.

Six mottled faces spun round. At the seventh he stared hard.

It was young, drained of all colour, and from it glared eyes possibly grey, but now black discs of fear. Below them, an open, blanched mouth; above, torn, dusky curls.

A leaf-green coat was huddled over fragile underwear which moulded small, straining breasts. One arm was gripped by a landlord with loose paunch and hastily donned trousers.

Its mate squirmed in the clutch of a virago whose head was a barbed entanglement of steel pins. By a pulsating stove loomed a constable, ready to take over. There were three fillers-in, non-descripts all.

'Stop! In God's name—'

Balefully the captive cut in.

'Need we have strangers in on this?' she muttered defiantly.

'Murderess!' The steel pins shook. 'And sneak-thief! Ruining of our 'ouse. Here, Alf Watterson, lock her up!'

The newcomer forced his gaze from the accused's. He came forward, flung down a card.

'I am a barrister,' he said crisply. 'Bletchley's my name. Now, then! What's the trouble?'

From the constable's throat issued something like 'Cor!' In slight awe came the question, 'Not *the* Mr Bletchley, sir? Guy Bletchley, is it?'

A curt nod. The landlord hitched furtively at his trousers. His wife took breath and tightened her hold. 'Picked him up, she did,' snarled she venomously. 'Oh, I seen her whispering to him in the coffee-room! Cos why? The big wad of notes he showed when he was settling for his supper.

'Proper gentleman he was, too. Missed his train, had to stop . . .'

'She bashed in his head,' explained the constable, 'when they was all gone up. Mister and missus heard the row ten minutes ago, first in her room, then on the landing above.'

'Just a minute,' said Bletchley. 'Is she staying here?'

'Yes, she took the room next to his.' The hostess sniffed with evil meaning. 'A-purpose to rob 'im—after 'anging about till she'd made sure wot he was good for.

'Well, we nabbed 'er leaning over his dead body, out 'ere at the foot of these stairs. She'd his wallet in her 'and—and she was just 'opping it for the street!'

'No!' wailed the girl. 'Oh, can't you see? The wallet had fallen . . .'

'So you just picked it up tor luck, eh?'

'I was trying to discover who he was.' She gave A piteous gulp. 'That is . . . his face seemed so familiar. I wondered if . . .'

'Save that for the jury!' muttered the landlord. 'Or think up a better one. Well, Alf . . .?'

'Quiet, please!' Bletchley held up his hand. Still curtly he said: 'Let the accused tell her version.'

She shrugged, running the tip of her tongue along dry lips. Then she spoke in low, terrified jerks.

'I was on my way to—to Cornwall. I lost my train connection. So, as it was raining hard, I had to come here for the night.

'This man—the one who's dead—was beastly—tried to talk to me. I got away, upstairs, locked myself in—never dreaming he was stopping here too, and had the room next to mine.

'I—I came out to find the bath. He was there, in the dark, lying in wait for me.' Her face twisted. 'He—he put his hand over my mouth. Pushed me back. I fought with him . . .'

'We heard!' sneered the landlady. 'But it was a good hour after the 'ouse was quiet. Afore that I'll bet there was whisperin' and canoodlin'—just them two, alone on that floor.

'When he was on to her tricks I dessay he did go for her . . .'

'It's a lie! I struck him, yes, with a candlestick. I'd have hit harder, only he was holding me, smothering me with his horrible fingers. If I have killed him, why should I care? He toppled back, down the steps.

'When I saw him at the bottom, lying so still, I—I had to run down to see . . .' Her sentence died in her throat.

Bletchley asked curtly: 'Where is the body?'

The constable led him out into the stuffy passage.

Across the lowest stair it sprawled—a powerful form, wrapped in a tailored dressing-gown of dark brocade.

Even for death the upturned face was arrestingly leaden. Good-looking once, it had lost its contour, and the bags under the blank eyes were tinged a sickly violet.

'That wound didn't kill him?'

With scorn Bletchley studied the cut on the temple from which oozed a sluggish trickle of scarlet

'Take a look at that pouched skin. You've sent for a doctor?'

'Just, sir. So you think it may have been . . .?'

'Heart. Fairly obvious, I'd say. Wait. Turn the lamp. Good God!' Bletchley uttered a low whistle.

He walked back to the bar. With ascerbity he announced:

'This man has died of a heart attack. Incidentally, I am not surprised the victim found his features familiar. Why, every paper in England has printed his picture! What was he calling himself?'

'James Banks,' wavered the landlord, 'of Maidenhead.'

'Oh? Well, five years ago I prosecuted him at the Old Bailey. He's Vaughan Marshall—just released from Parkhurst Prison!'

A stunned hush.

The constable murmured. 'Gor!' Then, uncertainly, 'fraudulent promoter, wasn't he?'

'And other things.' Bletchley spoke with revulsion. 'You've my word for it, he was a criminal of a singularly foul type. If it will save trouble, I'll remain to give formal identification.'

'Very good of you, sir,' began the constable, and stopped.

'Killing's killing, I say.' The landlady, releasing her charge, thrust forward and thumped a beer-stained table.

'Here,' she rasped, and lifted a weighty brass candlestick, 'is wot she done it with. And here'—pointing to a gold-rimmed pocket-book—'is wot she done it for. I've eyes, let me tell you. One wink, and she'd 'ave been off!'

Coolly the barrister took up the wallet—unmarked. He abstracted its roll of treasury notes, secured by a rubber band.

'Rubbish!' He tossed back the exhibit. 'What was to stop her helping herself to this money? As you see, she made not the slightest attempt. Officer, are you preferring any charge?'

'We'll have to detain her, sir,' said the constable awkwardly. 'Leastways, till the coroner's had his say.'

'Right!' Bletchley turned to the girl. 'You quite see the necessity, of course?'

'Y-yes . . . oh, certainly,' she agreed, but for the split second she faced him her eyes were glazed with stark tragedy . . .

'Anything that's—right. Only . . .' With an hysterical catch she hugged the green coat over her breast and knees. 'I'm—not presentable. And I'm cold . . . If I could just have a minute in my room?'

'More games!' spat the landlady. 'Clearing up traces, eh?'

Bletchley grated: 'That will do! You've had my opinion—an experienced one—as to why this lecherous brute died. As for your other vile notion, why, I'll drill a hole through it now.'

He leant over the table, compellingly, gathering eyes.

'What woman,' he demanded, 'prepares for a rendezvous with a man by greasing her face for the night? Yes,'—with heavy sarcasm—'*and by washing her stockings and hanging them out to dry?*'

Jaws dropped. With one accord curious gazes searched the

prisoner's cheeks—her naked, slight ankles. The landlady kept
her wits. Shrewdly she fired:

'And how'd *you* get this bit about washing out stockings?'

'That's perfectly simple! On your inn-sign outside there's a
wet stocking lodged. Evidently blown down from a window. Go,
see for yourselves.'

The long shot came off. When the inquisitives thronged
out, Bletchley swerved to the stove and threw wide the hot
shutter.

'Now,' said he, softly, and followed the crowd to the door.

The girl's hand darted to her coat-pocket. Paper crackled as
she flung the letters in the stove.

'I . . .' she faltered, but Bletchley did not turn. Barring the doorway
with his broad shoulders he mumbled: 'Don't spoil it . . .'

She collapsed on to a chair.

The inquest was over. As the coffee-room emptied, Bletchley
waited by his car outside, listening to the comments which
filtered past.

'Heart conked out on him. Well, and why not? Bloke like that,
wot had gone the pace, *and* done a stretch. Pop off like nothing,
he would—and a good job, too!'

'Deserved what he got—first crack out of jail getting his skin
full of drink and making passes at an 'elpless girl. Good-looker,
wasn't she? And young . . .

She slipped forth humbly, lugging her weekend case. Bletchley
bowed, hat in hand. He said:

'So that's cleared up. May I drop you at the station?'

Circled with stares, she hesitated.

'Thanks,' said she stiffly, and got into the front seat.

Upright, not speaking, they sat as the car edged down the
cramped street and out of the village. Well away nestled the
station. They whizzed past it at sixty. Green downland now—and
no eye to see.

Bletchley slowed, bent his head, and with deep tenderness kissed the strained face at his side.

'Tell me,' he bade.

'That message of his was a trick.' Her lips formed it brokenly. 'He guessed I would sneak off to be safe from him. So he let me think he'd be released tomorrow—in order to catch me unawares.

'I know now that at the very moment you and I were telephoning our plans he—he was hiding in my flat. So he heard all we were saying.'

'The swine!'

Swiftly he fitted it together—vindictive threats, follow by a surprise arrival; the released prisoner lying low, later to profit by the little private, silly signal which was to lead Bletchley to the obscure inn, where the fugitive would be sleeping, waiting to be picked up.

That had been her idea—a stocking left dangling outside a window. They had neither of them remembered the name of the inn.

'So he changed his scheme, after the bit of eavesdropping?'

'Naturally! It was better to catch us both—together.'

'To work a hold-up, you mean? Absurd. Marshall must have been mad to imagine anything he could drag up out of your poor little past could matter two hoots to me. Letters you wrote, at the age of nineteen, to an oily-tongued scoundrel.

'But there's one thing I don't understand—why did you pretend not to know me?' he asked.

She spoke slowly: 'I thought that they would not suspect you, as a stranger, of wanting to help me. And I needed help to burn those letters.'

'But did they matter, my dear?' said Bletchley. 'What could they have told me that I didn't already know? The past!—we live for the future now my decree is through.'

'But your decree was not through,' she answered, 'and if those letters had not been burned there would have been no decree—and no future for us.'

Bletchley knit his brow. 'How could your letters to Marshall have affected it?' he asked.

'No, my dear,' she said bleakly, '*your* letters to me; he stole them from my flat.'

ALICE CAMPBELL

Alice Dorothy Ormond—best known in America as Alice Ormond Campbell and in Britain as Alice Campbell—was born in 1887 in Atlanta, Georgia, a city that some of her ancestors had helped to found. The youngest of four children, hers was a precocious talent. Her first poem, 'The Story of Tallulah Falls', was published when she was only ten and her first short story, 'The Autobiography of a Very Old Doll', appeared two years later. Both were published in the *Atlanta Constitution*, a newspaper whose city editor was her elder brother, Samuel. However coincidental (or not)that might have been, it was not long before her poems started to be reprinted in other newspapers and by 1901, the fourteen year-old was reported to be writing a 'two volume novel'. If that was ever completed it did not find a publisher, but after graduating from Atlanta Girls' High School, short stories did appear from time to time, including 'White Nurse' in the prestigious *Ladies Homes Journal*, 'Roulade' in *Uncle Remus' Magazine* and 'The Silver Lamp' in the *Topeka State Journal*.

At the age of nineteen and accompanied by her widowed mother, Alice Ormond moved to New York to study music and foreign languages, and to continue writing. A year later she moved to Paris, where she renewed an acquaintance with a young Virginian whom she had first met in New York. James Lawrence Campbell was also a writer and he had ambitions to become a playwright. They were

Alice Campbell

married in 1913 and their first child, named Lawrence, was born
in 1914. As the First World War engulfed Europe, the couple moved
to 32 Albion Road in the central London suburb of St John's Wood
where they had two more children, Florence and Robert.

Although Alice Campbell was proud of her American roots—her
great grandmother had been murdered by Seminole natives—she
lived most of the rest of her life in London and is usually thought
of as a British writer. Her books often have European settings and
a mix of American and British protagonists, while there is always
a young woman confronted by danger and mystery. Her first,
Juggernaut (1928), was filmed in 1936 with Boris Karloff as the
central character, a doctor who is only too ready to take care of his
patients. Others include *The Murder of Caroline Bundy* (1933), a
mystery that includes a search for the Holy Grail, and *They Paid
the Price* (1937), which features the theft of a valuable Manet
painting from a Parisian gallery and was published as *Death Framed
in Silver* (1937). Particularly noteworthy are the superb wartime
thriller *The Chimney Crashed* (1937), published in book form as
Travelling Butcher (1944, in which an air raid leads to multiple
murder and an unusual treasure hunt, and *A Vicious Circle* (1934),
published the same year as *Desire to Kill* and succinctly summed
up by one critic as 'murder committed in a roomful of thirteen
guests at the height of a wild dope orgy'. As well as novels and short
fiction, she wrote poetry and a psychological drama, *Two Share a
Dwelling* (1935), which achieved moderate success on the London
stage.

'Signals' was published in the *Sunday Dispatch* on 15 May 1938.

A PRESENT FROM THE EMPIRE

G. D. H. & M. Cole

Lady Bowland leaned back in her chair with a suppressed sigh of relief as the entrée went round and parted her for a blessed few seconds from the man on her left.

Heavens, how *boring* he was! How boring Empire-builders were, especially Empire-builders from the great mandated territory of Malaria, and how unforgivable it was of Harold to have forced her to come to, and put on her best clothes for, this frightful annual dinner of Malarian Empire-builders.

Particularly as he ought to have known—though she had never actually told him—that the name of Malaria carried with it certain associations, certain memories of her early life, which she would have been very glad to forget, and, indeed, had almost succeeded in forgetting.

But there it was: she always, like a good wife, did everything she could to advance Harold's career, and as a result there she was, all in her best war-paint, prepared to receive that idiotic presentation of long, useless white gloves which the veterans of Malaria made annually to the ladies who did them the honour of dining with them—and condemned, meanwhile, to listen to the idiotic bleatings of that tiresome old prawn in the bulging shirt.

Thank heaven, he seemed to have taken the hint of the entrée, and was turning to the woman on his other side.

Lady Bowland prepared to be charming to the man on her right, of whom she had so far seen nothing except an evening coat excellently cut and the side of a smooth grey head.

Slightly to her annoyance, he was not ready for the change, but still engrossed in his own partner.

'Elaine.' The low-spoken word made her start for a moment. The man on her right had turned and was looking at her.

Rather deep-set eyes under grey brows in a lined and yellow-brown face—no, she didn't believe she knew him. But all Empire-builders looked like that in a few years.

'It *is* Elaine Horton, isn't it?' he persisted. And as she looked at him, searching in her memory vainly for the dim familiarity which she now began to feel, he pushed his card across to her. 'It's a very long time since we met, but—'

Lady Bowland glanced at the card and felt the colour flooding up beneath her make-up; it took all her twenty years' social training to repress a gasp.

For the name, HUGH LANGLEY, took her right back into her Malarian past, to the incidents which she had almost succeeded in forgetting.

Hugh Langley—she supposed now that it must be Hugh Langley, though she would never have known him without the reminder.

But there was something about the shape of the features, the forehead and the bridge of the nose, for example, which had not changed.

Hugh Langley had been David's greatest friend; and the last time she had seen Hugh Langley was a week after David's death, when he had burst into the room where she and Frank were sitting—and how worried Frank had been!—and said the most frightful things to her, practically accusing her of being responsible for David's death.

Which, of course, she wasn't; how should she have known that David, that earnest, heavy creature, really believed that she was going to marry him and spend her life in Malaria, without ever any chance of getting out or getting on?

A missionary's wife!—even if the missionary quoted poetry and played a ukulele and made love much better than you'd think to look at him.

Nobody could have expected it; only David and Hugh Langley apparently did, and David had died, and Hugh—well, that night she'd felt certain that Hugh would have killed her, if Frank hadn't been there.

At any rate, he had not sounded, to put it mildly, as though he wanted to meet her again.

Yet here he was, showing every sign of interest and bending upon her that smile which—she remembered now—she had found so charming even long ago, when her chief Interest was, of course, concentrated upon David.

'I must apologize for startling you,' he was saying. 'It wasn't quite fair, because I had the advantage. You didn't know I was to be here, but I knew that you were coming.

'In fact,' he smiled all over his face, 'I must confess that I pulled a good many strings in order to get myself put next to you—and on your right hand.'

'Why on my right?' Lady Rowland smiled back. She was recovering from the shock, and in fact, now that she came to study him, Hugh was very attractive in a weather-beaten way.

And his breast held a number of ribbons; he must be quite a big pot in his own line.

Possibly she ought to have known, but it was a long time since she had needed to remember who or what anybody was. Harold always knew.

'Oh, don't you know our ritual? . . . Of course, I forgot; you're not associated with Malaria now, are you?'

'No, my husband's always been in Kenya.' Really, he ought to have known that!

'Of course; stupid of me. So you didn't marry Frank Somers after all?'

'Oh, no.' Lady Bowland paused a moment. What was the best reason for not having married Frank Somers?

Really, she supposed, it was the fault of the man now talking to her; after that scene he had made, the thought of living with anybody who had heard it, even of living in Malaria at all—although Frank Somers, a brilliant young official, would certainly have got on and got out—had suddenly become distasteful.

So it had been a godsend to run across Harold on his Empire tour, and to realize that one's future was fixed.

But one couldn't very well tell Hugh that, at dinner; besides what business was it of his? So she sighed, repeated, 'Oh, *no*. We never really . . .' in a vague voice; and asked, 'But what about sitting on my right?'

'It's our old ritual,' the man answered, accepting the faint snub without a sign.

'You know, of course, that when the Malaria Association has ladies as guests it's our custom to present them with white gloves?

'Well, the actual presentation is the privilege not of the chairman, as in most societies, but of the man sitting on the right-hand of the guest.

'A sort of consolation prize, you understand, for not having the pleasure of taking the lady in to dinner.

'I have my privilege in my pocket now, and shall have the

pleasure of watching you put them on after dinner, when we go
to our teak-panelled room—you remember the Malarian
teak-forests, don't you?—and have our coffee.'

'I think your association might give one something more
useful than long white gloves which one's never going to wear,'
Lady Bowland interrupted with a small grimace.

She did not really mind about the long white gloves; but she
did not care to be reminded of the teak-forests, where David,
in the stage of romance in which the lover believes the loved
one passionately interested in anything which interests him, had
tried to teach her the surveying he had learnt before he threw
up architecture for the mission-field.

'You mustn't be unkind,' Hugh Langley said. 'It's our ancient
ritual and we're proud of it and consider it an honour. Like court
dress, you know. I'm sure Sir Harold doesn't consider his knee-
breeches a nuisance, even if he never wears them.

'And, after all, it *does* prevent our gifts being worn out and
thrown away—keeps the memory of Malaria green and all that,
you know.'

Lady Bowland frowned again a little. Why would he use such
inept phrases? She did not want Malaria's memory kept green,
not at all; she never wanted to hear of the place again.

'But never mind,' he went on, 'you won't be expected to keep
the gloves beyond tonight. And actually I've brought another
present for you which you may like better.

'I'll give it you before we leave'—he smiled as he saw her eyes
grow interested—'but we mustn't slow down the pace of dinner,
and I see the chairman looking at me.

'Tell me'—cutting himself a piece of turkey—'what have you
been doing with yourself all these years? I can't tell you how
excited I am to meet you again.'

And he looked it, and he certainly behaved like it. He listened,
and he entertained; he paid her compliments of exactly the right
measure of delicacy.

For the rest of the meal he all but ignored his own partner, and he even shifted himself almost imperceptibly in his chair until his knee was able to touch the smooth, close folds of her dress.

Undoubtedly, he had turned into a very attractive man, and a man, moreover, whom it was a feat to captivate so instantly and so obviously.

Lady Bowland was finding the evening far more entertaining than she had expected.

She drew closer to him; she returned his light pressure and dropped her voice as the conversation grew more intimate; and after the savoury she ventured to remind him that he had promised her another gift.

'Yes, I think it's about the time now,' waving away a dish of fruit. He felt in his pocket and produced an object which looked like a large, clumsy hunter. 'Do you know what this is?'

'No, I don't think so. It's a watch, isn't it?' Lady Rowland spoke lightly, but a chilly shiver went through her.

She was almost sure she *did* know it; why, again, why be so clumsy, just when he was being so charming?

'Oh, no. Don't pretend your memory's so short. Look—you must remember.'

He pressed a spring; the case came open and disclosed not a watch, but a compass needle hovering over a figured disc.

He fiddled with the case for a moment, and there stood up on either side two projections, one an eye-piece with a curious lump of glass behind it, the other a glass slide with a hair down its centre.

'Prismatic compass,' he said. 'Used in surveying; the mirror is in the lid . . . Ah, I see you remember. And I think you know whose it is, too, don't you?'

For Lady Bowland was staring at it blindly, almost too blind to see the initials D.R. scratched on the inside of the case.

Indeed, she had no need to look; the mere opening of the

thing brought it back to her all too vividly, the smell and the look of the swamps and David trying to teach her to take an elevation with the beastly thing.

'Yes,' she said faintly.

'David wanted you to have it,' her companion said in a low, earnest voice. 'I've never been able to give it you. I tried to give it to Frank Somers' wife, but she wasn't you.

'That's why I came here tonight really; it's yours now. Just try and see if you remember how to use it,' he said more loudly. 'Take a sight at the chairman.'

Slowly, her fingers trembling with shock and annoyance, Lady Bowland picked up the compass and tried to adjust it.

But immediately she gave a cry, for some sharp projection on the edge of the case had inflicted a long scratch on her little finger.

'Oh, I'm so sorry! Let me see.' He took her hand and bathed it in the finger-bowl, finally dabbing it gently with a tube he had taken from his pocket. 'There, that will stop it bleeding, and I don't think it's deep. But I'm so sorry; I'll take the compass away and have it properly seen to before you have it.

'Please forgive me,' as she still looked at him reproachfully. He took the wounded hand and raised it to his lips.

'May I kiss and make it well—or rather, put my glove on and make it well? For I see the chairman catching our eye.'

With some little difficulty, for she complained that the process hurt her finger, the long, white gloves were drawn over Lady Bowland's hands, and she and the other women went out into the panelled room while the men sat over their drinks.

After no more than a quarter of an hour, however, a waiter, obviously in a state of terrible agitation, came in and spoke to Sir Harold Bowland, who turned pale and sprang to his feet

After a few words from the chairman, the other men followed him into the panelled room whence Lady Bowland had been carried in what appeared to be a fit.

The long white gloves, which she had pulled off because they hurt her, still lay on the floor.

'It was the most mysterious death I ever heard in my life,' said the Chief Inspector, after the case had long been relegated to the category of the unsolved.

'There wasn't the shadow of a motive for murder or suicide, yet the woman died of cyanide poisoning.

'And the most mysterious thing was that she didn't take it through the mouth—which rules out all the food—it got in apparently through a newly made scratch on one of her fingers, and the only thing she touched, as far as we know, were the gloves which were given to all the women there.

'We've examined all those we could find, just as I matter of routine.

'But they were all new for the occasion, and, in any case, who puts cyanide into gloves? It is just a complete mystery.'

G. D. H. & M. COLE

Margaret Isabel Postgate was born in Cambridge in 1893. As a young child she enjoyed childish things, for example at the age of eight dressing up as 'Snowdrop' for the Mayor of Cambridge's Ball, but her classicist father had higher things in mind for his children. In October 1911, after an unhappy time at Roedean School, Margaret went up to Girton College, Cambridge, where she was awarded a first-class degree in, inevitably, classics. On coming down in 1914 she taught, equally inevitably, Latin at St Paul's Girls' School. In 1916, at the height of the First World War, she became active in the peace movement and worked for the next nine years in the Labour Research department. This brought her into contact with the Fabian Society, a socialist policy think tank, where she met the man she would marry.

Four years older than Margaret, George Douglas Howard Cole was raised in Ealing, where his father was the senior partner in an estate agency and auctioneer's business, and his mother Jessie Knowles was a dressmaker. He attended St Paul's Boys' School where he excelled, winning multiple school prizes including in 1906 the Milton Prize for Best English Poem, a work called 'Crete', and in 1908 the High Master's Prize for Latin Elegiacs and the Butterworth Prize for English Literature. He went up to Balliol College, Oxford, winning the Jenkyn prize of £100 a year for two years as 'the best man of the year' and graduating with a double first. He became a fellow of Magdalen College in 1912 and University College in 1925. His first book, *The World of Labour* (1913) provided an overview of the major socialist movements and promoted nationalization as the key to economic growth and a more egalitarian society. When he and Margaret Postage met, Douglas Cole was working on the campaign to end conscription. The two fell in love and as the European war raged, the Russian Revolution seemed to point to a brighter future . . .

In the year she and Douglas married, Margaret published her first book, *Margaret Postgate's Poems* (1918). This was followed, two years later, by a children's book, *A Story of Santa Claus* (1920). By this time the couple had moved to Oxford where they lived until moving to North London at the end of the decade. While living at Oxford, Douglas had written a novel—in a foreword, the publisher William Collins stated that 'G. D. H. Cole . . . has always loved detective fiction, and always wanted to try his hand at writing detective stories'. Sadly, *The Brooklyn Murders* (1923) was not well-received, with some critics suggesting that the choice of murderer too obviously reflected Douglas Cole's political prejudices. He returned to academia and, as a socio-political economist, went on to write fifty volumes variously dealing with the past, present and possible future of socialism—four with Margaret and one with her brother, Raymond. Douglas's publications include *The Intelligent Man's Guide Through World Chaos* (1933), *Practical Economics* (1937), *Great Britain in the Post-War World* (1942) and *A Short History of the British Working Class Movement, 1789–1947* (1947).

From 1925 to 1949, Margaret worked as a lecturer for University tutorial classes at London and Cambridge. In 1935 and until the outbreak of the Second World war she was the secretary of the New Fabian Research Bureau, joining the Fabian Society in 1939, the same year that Douglas served his first stint as its chairman—he later became its President. Margaret also wrote several books, including her husband's biography, and in newspapers like the

London Evening Standard and the *Daily Herald*, as well as in magazines such as *Highway*, *New Statesman*, *Fabian Quarterly* and *The Listener*. She was a champion of free speech and comprehensive education as a means to empower those less privileged than herself and to bring about a fairer, more egalitarian society. In 1941, she became a member and later chair of the Education Committee of London County Council, and she served as an alderman from 1952 until its abolition in 1965, when she took up a role with the new Inner London Education Authority.

In the early 1930s, to supplement their earnings the Coles had begun a second career that would run parallel with their political activities; they wrote detective stories. Over the years, 'G. D. H. & M. Cole' produced around thirty novels, several dozen shorter stories and two radio plays. However, the precise division of labour between the two has never been entirely clear. It has been asserted that they shared the writing of all of the novels, yet that is contradicted by contemporary newspaper interviews in which Margaret Cole claimed that, although they worked out the plots together and Douglas commented on drafts, the novels were written by her and her alone. The latter is plausible enough given Douglas Cole's prodigious output of often very lengthy and densely argued economic and political books. However, it is explicitly contradicted by their son, who suggested that authorship alternated between the two, and by Margaret Cole, who stated in her biography that, while they did work separately on some novels, they worked together on others.

Curtis Evans, the authority on Golden Age crime fiction, has carried out a stylometric and substantive analysis of all of the Coles' books and stories. Reporting this in 2012 in *Crime and Detective Stories*, the leading magazine for students and readers of crime fiction, Evans concluded that Douglas Cole 'should get credit for the books not credited by Margaret solely to herself', the latter being nine—or possibly eleven—of the 'G. D. H. & M. Cole' titles. Their most enjoyable novels include the gruesome *Death of a Star* (1932) and *Poison in a Garden Suburb* (1929); the latter was serialized in the *Daily Herald*, a newspaper for which Margaret occasionally reviewed crime fiction.

Douglas Cole died in 1959 after falling into a diabetic coma. Margaret Cole was made a Dame for her services to Local Government and education; she died in 1980. While both achieved much and had considerable influence in their lifetimes, they are little remembered today other than for their detective fiction.

'A Present from the Empire' was first published in the *Sunday Dispatch* on 22 May 1938. Unusually for *Bodies in the Library*, this story has been collected previously: it appeared in the Coles' collection *Wilson and Some Others* (1940) and is included in this volume to complete the 'six mysteries in search of six authors'.

ACKNOWLEDGEMENTS

'Child's Play' by Edmund Crispin copyright © Rights Ltd 2021.

'Thieves Fall In' by Anthony Gilbert reproduced with permission of Curtis Brown Ltd, London, on behalf of the Literary Estate of Lucy Malleson. Copyright © 1962 Lucy Beatrice Malleson.

'Rigor Mortis' by Leo Bruce reprinted by permission of Peters Fraser & Dunlop (www.petersfraserdunlop.com) on behalf of the Estate of Leo Bruce/Rupert Croft-Cooke.

The Only Husband by H. C. Bailey © the estate of H. C. Bailey 1941.

'The Police Are Baffled' by Alec Waugh reprinted by permission of Peters Fraser & Dunlop (www.petersfraserdunlop.com) on behalf of the Estate of Alec Waugh. Copyright © 1931 Alec Waugh.

'Shadowed Sunlight' by Christianna Brand copyright © Christianna Brand 1945. Reprinted by permission of A M Heath & Co. Ltd Authors' Agents.

The Case of Bella Garsington by Gladys Mitchell copyright © Gladys Mitchell 1944.

'Boots' by Ngaio Marsh copyright © Estate of Ngaio Marsh 2021.

'Figures Don't Die' by T. S. Stribling copyright © T. S. Stribling 1953.

'After You, Lady' by Peter Cheyney copyright © Peter Cheyney 1938.

'Too Easy' by Herbert Adams © Herbert Adams 1938.

'Riddle of an Umbrella' by J. Jefferson Farjeon © Estate of J. Jefferson Farjeon 1938.

'Two White Mice under a Riding Whip' by E. C. R. Lorac © 1938 The Estate of E. C. R. Lorac.

'Signals' by Alice Campbell copyright © Alice Campbell 1938.

'A Present from the Empire' by G. D. H. & M. Cole © 1938.

Every effort has been made to trace all owners of copyright. The editor and publishers apologise for any errors or omissions and would be grateful if notified of any corrections.